Intoxicated

Cynthia Dane
BARACHOU PRESS

Intoxicated

Copyright: Cynthia Dane
Published: 19ʰ August 2019
Publisher: Barachou Press

This is a work of fiction. Any and all similarities to any characters, settings, or situations are purely coincidental.

All rights reserved. No part of this publication may be reproduced, stored in retrieval system, copied in any form or by any means, electronic, mechanical, photocopying, recording or otherwise transmitted without written permission from the publisher. You must not circulate this book in any format.

CHAPTER 1

DREW

Tonight, I'm wearing Armani.

The woman I'm after appreciates a man with fine tastes. That's why I've raided my closet for the kind of clothes I usually only wear to weddings, funerals, and the charity galas in between. The kind of events my family "forces" me to go to, on pain of my mother's heart breaking. I'm more of a flannel and jeans. A real Oregonian *just give me a hoody and some decent boots* man. For the right person – the right *mark* – I'll don the Armani and pretend that I love being a high-rolling son of a bitch.

Not like I can't afford it.

I can afford a lot of things. Then again, most of the men in this ritzy lounge can afford a lot of *things,* some of them wealthier than me. That's why I usually avoid places like these. I've spent

Intoxicated

enough of my life parading around lounges, nightclubs, and uptown bars in search of validation and career prospects. I don't need that shit anymore. Don't believe whatever my family tells you. Drew Benton is a self-made man now.

Part of the career I've built for myself means meeting women of a certain... caliber.

Ooh, I can see the look in your eye now. That question lurking on your lips. You want to know if I'm a sugar boy? A hustler looking for his next mama? Or maybe I'm looking for a daddy. Hey, I may be straight, but I know what I'm worth. Most guys have a price. Mine is pretty steep, but I'm cheaper for a lovely lady who wants to ride this ol' stallion for a night.

Nah. That's not me, although I've dabbled in that before. Instead, my job usually sees me hired to sleep with *other* women. Well, I don't have to sleep with them – that's usually a side benefit, and often complements what I set out to do. You see, I offer a unique service here in the Pacific Northwest, a playground for the newly rich and old money fools alike. Tech bros and lumber dynasties are always getting their hearts broken by gold diggers and angry ex-wives. Some of these men are salty enough that they call me up to soothe their wounds.

No, not like *that*. My job is to locate and make her life hell.

That takes different forms, of course. I offer three tiers of services. Heartbreaker. Credit Destroyer. Self-Esteem Bludgeoner. There are dozens of women in this fine world who have had their twenties or fifties utterly ruined by yours truly. For the right price, I'll either be the sugar boy of their dreams – until I legally con them of all their money (which I usually donate,) wreck their embittered hearts, or cast them so low in self-worth that they cry themselves to sleep every night for years.

Hey! Don't look at me like that. Don't go crying over these poor, *poor* women, either. I'm discerning when it comes to taking on clients. I only toy with the truly deplorable. The dregs of feminine-kind. Women who have already ruined the men who are hiring me. My last mark was a first wife who abused her husband's loyalty by sleeping with every Tom, Dick, and Harry who would have her in the neighborhood Hilton. Her husband couldn't get proof, although their pre-nuptial agreement stipulated she got nothing in a divorce if it was proven she was unfaithful. Didn't take me long to sidle up to her and get the proof. Granted, that's my naked ass forever emblazoned on some investigator's phone, but I work out. My ass looks *fantastic.*

Tonight's mark is a real doozy. The reason I'm in a swanky, five-star lounge in the middle of Portland is because my research tells me my mark comes here once or twice a month to scout for new victims. You see, I'm up against one of the nastiest witches you've ever heard tales of, and that's saying a lot when you have my resume. I'm talking about a woman I've heard of before her latest victim called to ask about my services. That's how legendary she has become around the Pacific Northwest.

Being a professional sugar baby or trophy wife is one thing. Hell, I admire the people who recognize their skills and go for it. Two people consenting to that kind of arrangement doesn't faze me, and I've turned down my fair share of clients who wanted me to go after perfectly fine women because they were a little *bitter* about the breakup. Some guys are vindictive fucks. I get that, and take it into consideration when I judge whether or not a client is right for me.

Cher Lieberman, however, is in her own category of *holy shit what is wrong with you?*

She's also extremely beautiful. Which is why it's easy to find her in this half-crowded lounge on a sleepy Friday night.

A woman tries to gain my attention. A server, I believe. Yet I'm too awestruck by the bewitching beauty perched atop a barstool and swirling her tiny straw in a whiskey on the rocks to hear anything else but the sudden *thunk* of my heart.

Oh, be still, you bastard. Pump some blood to my cock if you must, but let's keep things in perspective. That raven-haired Aphrodite sitting alone at the bar, quietly scouting the room for her next rich boyfriend? She isn't to be won over for our own delightful gain. We're not here to seduce her into bed and show her who's a real man.

We're here to destroy her.

I sit at a nearby table, careful to stay out of her sight. My extensive background check into Cher Lieberman – who she is, what makes her tick, what her favorite brand of hot sauce is – can only tell me so much. I must observe the woman in her natural element. Before I make my move and expose myself to her willful wiles, I must become fluent in her body language and hear her voice say a few arsenic-laced words. Better if they're flung at an intended target.

Oh, see? I'm not the only one with a mark tonight. Cher may look like she's here enjoying a drink by herself after a long, *hard* week of being tragically beautiful, but I know her game. She's shopping for a new rich boyfriend. That's why her gaze is cast like a spindly net. It's why she slings one leg over the other, exposing the slit in her flowy black dress and drawing a man's lascivious eyes right to her thighs. It's also why she constantly repositions her silky black hair, so we all see the white of her throat and the cleavage that plunges down the generous bust of her dress. Bold, sultry makeup and a judicious amount of plain jewelry accentuate a woman who knows how to dress herself to make other women jealous and men hard in the pants. If her goal were to simply get laid, she'd have her pick of fine young men looking to get their precious rocks off. Looking for a husband? Turn on the charm and get a first date out of an elderly man for the hell of it. Except looking for a sugar daddy, a man who will fall in love with her without any reciprocation? It's not as easy as it looks.

And she makes it look easy.

A server asks me if I would care for a fresh Bacardi. I note the whiskey in Cher's hand and ask for a Sazerac. It might be my in later.

It's a good thing I'm willing to take my time, though. Hell, I might not talk to her tonight. Consider this reconnaissance, if we must. If Cher leaves before I'm ready to make my move, or she gets the attention of the man of her dreams? I might be leaving alone as well.

Or not. That server keeps making eyes at me from across the room, and she has a mighty fine look. Shit, it's no good that I'm swimming in a pool of beautiful women tonight. It's been five weeks since I last got laid, and I was too drunk to remember it. Merely looking at my intended target sends a rush of heat to my loins and tells my heart to go for it. My heart is a stupid bastard. Ask anyone in my family.

Fuck me, ask my grandmother!

Shit. Behold this poor sap over here. Some middle-management tech bro, old enough to be employed during Dot Com Boom but still young enough to garner sexual attention, waltzes up to the circular bar and sits a few stools away from Cher, who immediately glances in his direction. I see the same things as her. No wedding ring. Tucked-in shirt, but the top two buttons are unbuttoned because he's *relaxing*. (And wants to show off his fine collection of chest hairs to all the ladies in the room.) I can't smell his cologne, but I bet my bottom dollar that it's sandalwood. His hairline hasn't started receding yet, but he's got those worn lines on his face that suggest he's been around long enough to have some funds. A single guy making as much money as he does? Even with Portland rents the way they are right now, he could afford getaways and shopping sprees for a new girlfriend.

Let me guess, Cher. That's exactly what you want.

She pulls the lemon wedge off her old-fashioned glass and squeezes a little juice onto the tip of her tongue. The way her head rears back, spine curving and thighs pushing out of her skirt, has me glad that I'm not too buzzed. Trust me, if I had no idea who she was or what kind of woman she could be, I'd be shouldering Mr. Tech out of the way and seducing Ms. Lieberman into my Portland loft. She looks like the kind of woman who wants it hard every time.

Hm? How can I tell? Trust me, why don't you.

Trust me when I say I know these kinds of women well. You might call me a *Cunt Whisperer,* but that's not a name I've adopted for myself. That's what my secretary tells everyone he wants for my business. I prefer to not use such words, but you get the picture. I understand the personality. I also understand the body part.

Cher replaces her lemon wedge so precisely that you can't tell she's moved it. When she slides off her stool, it's with the intoxicating movements of a Muse. The Grecian kind. My God. I knew she was gorgeous from her photos, but in motion? Cher should be a model. Or an actress.

She should be in my bed. Ahem.

In due time, however. Tonight might be Mr. Tech's chance to bed and wed a woman of this seductive caliber. I've been getting sloppy seconds ever since I started this career. You think I mind it? For the right women, it's more of a point of pride than if they were totally available.

Seducing a woman who was just seeing someone else is as good as saying, *"I'm so desirable that such women can't say no to me. Sorry, bud. Grass was greener over here. Enjoy your ex, Palmela."*

The server brings me Sazerac. She lingers behind, asking if I need anything else. Her hand is on the back of my chair. Her hips cock in my direction. I give her what I want - a long, appreciative glance up her body. Yes, she would do as well. Would probably be enough fun to satisfy me for the weekend. She also looks the type who wants it a certain way.

What can I say? Certain women are drawn to me, because they sense that I deliver the goods.

We'll see how things go with Ms. Lieberman, who has made her move on the new guy. I take a sip of my drink. The absinthe is stronger than the cognac. Or perhaps that's my sweet tooth reacting to the sugar. Either way, my pursed lips are primed for kissing. Or sucking a girl to orgasm. Whether I'm supposed to destroy her afterward? Let's see how lucky this guy is and check back in later.

CHAPTER 2

CHER

Another Friday night spent looking pretty in someone's bar. The people in this place are lucky I'm not bloating, because I am *not* cute in this dress when I'm hormonal or have accidentally inhaled some take-out.

Don't look at me like that. I don't care what you think about it. If you're along for this ride – God knows why you've picked me out of every bitch in this sty of a city, but I digress – then we're going to lay down some ground rules. 1) Don't judge me. 2) Don't flirt with me. 3) Don't give me advice. Number three is the most important rule in this agreement. Suppose you can judge me all you want, if you do it silently and keep your poker face. Flirting? You can try, but it's never going to happen. All you'll do is greatly annoy me. I'm irked enough that you're following me around while I have mediocre sex. Just because I can't see you doesn't mean I don't know you're there. I'm talking to you right now, aren't I?

Got it? Good.

The last thing I need is advice. I've been doing this shit longer than you've been aware of my existence, and I don't care if you've been around since my Preston Bradley days. (Yeah, I know that you know about that. Thanks, Preston. Thanks to you and your buddy Julian, everyone knows about what a bitch I am. How lovely.) When you have a delicate existence like mine, you get *good* at it. This is what I excel at. This is who I am.

Actually, I'm this fucker's worst nightmare.

I've seen him around before. Oh, I don't know his name, but I know what company he works for and how much he might be worth. Enough to pique my interest, but I've been going through a consequential dry spell since winter ended. Sometimes I take purposeful breaks between relationships, but my funds are running low. I haven't had a proper job in so long that my entire income originates from men's pocketbooks and the few odd-jobs I do online. Pretty soon, I'll have to go back to camming. Do you know how demoralizing camming is? You put up with assholes wanting to see your pussy for free, all while they tell you what to do and how to do it. You ban more guys than you get tips from, and then where are you? Buying a coffee at Starbucks with your so-called tips?

I need some money. This guy has enough to keep me fed for a few months, if I play my cards right. Hopefully he won't ask me to marry him before I've completely milked him for all he's worth. Nothing ends a relationship early like some poor sod asking you to marry him.

Intoxicated

It's a tenuous game I play. These men must be in love with me to the point they throw their money at me. I'm good with money. I know how to spend it while squirreling away the rest for these dry spells, but they can't be *so* in love with me that they want to elope in Vegas next weekend. That's when shit gets really messy. I would only say "I do" for a man made out of a billion dollars and a foolish prenup. Beyond that? It's not worth it. I'm not wife material. I'm your fantasy girlfriend who has carved a niche out for herself in this region. Portland, Seattle... they're both the same. Tech bros and old-money snowflakes who want me to suck their dicks while paying me in food, lodging, and trips around the world. My closet is full of dresses I didn't have to pay for, and my feet are always covered in shoes that make other women seethe in jealousy. My expensive beauty regimen comes at the price of half my sanity, but when you reach the ripe old age of twenty-six and don't have many other skills, well... you do what you must to stay alive. Women like me have been doing it since the dawn of time.

How did I get into doing this? Hm... let me see where things go with this guy before I potentially tell you about that.

He's not too bad looking, I suppose. A bit pudgy in the middle and two years away from losing his hair, but I'll be out of his life before that happens. The most important thing is that he doesn't have a ring on his finger. Seducing married men is a *disaster* I should not like to do again. It's never worth it. Enough guys in this town are single, though. Commitment is a foreign word in Portlandese. Any guy with a collared shirt and enough money to rent a two-bedroom in the Pearl isn't looking for a serious girlfriend. He wants a toy. A hot girlfriend he can brag about to his buddies while chasing other tail on Tinder. I know my place.

I also know my worth. That's a big reason I don't let them marry me. I may be sad, but I'm not *pathetic* enough to go into a marriage I know will be rife with unfaithfulness. Give me *some* credit.

"Good evening," I say, turning on the silky-smooth tones that have seduced half the collared shirts in this city. "Couldn't help but notice you're alone. Are you waiting for anyone?" Say, a girlfriend? I'm not going to waste my time unless it's a first date or he's not serious about a girl he's casually seeing.

This guy almost drops his phone when he sees me in my full glory. That's right. For my perusal of the lounge tonight, I brought out my slinkiest black dress. I call it the Morticia Addams, although it's definitely more cocktail party than sexy funeral. Fantastic way to make guys think I'm a classy lady, though. They go nuts for the plunging neckline, the slits on the sides, and cinched waist. If I pair it with some stilettos or sheer pantyhose... well, I only bust out those guns if I've been scoping out a man with a known fetish for either.

"I'm Cher." I offer him my hand. He's taking it before saying a single word. "Like the singer." Thanks, Mom. Thanks, Dad.

"Brian," he croaks, as if I've found the opposite of a prince turned into a frog. "No, I'm not waiting for anyone." He welcomes the drink the bartender deposits before him. "Hanging out a bit before going home. Had a late night at the office."

"On a Friday?" I put on my best *oh, no!* face. Instantly play up my sympathy and hope he feels properly vindicated. "That's not fair. You should be out having a date or something."

Lord help this man, for he is daft. Here I am, playing the oldest tricks in the book – a trick I've played a hundred times over for other daft men – and he's falling for it. He thinks he's special.

Intoxicated

He thinks I'm attracted to him because I'm a lonely soul seeing another lonely sod. Or because he's handsome. Or has some innate charm that exudes from his whimsical soul. I'm not wrong about any of this, by the way. This is what he's thinking about himself right now. That's why I'm constantly adjusting my seduction style to cater to his reactions. The more he opens up - and he is, whether he knows it or not - the more I become his ideal girlfriend. His dream come true. His Manic Pixie Dream Bitch.

I will change his life. I will suck him dry.

"I don't have a lot of time to meet women," he says with a small, bashful smile. Aw. He's almost adorable. Two seconds ago he was a mildly confident manager of one of Portland's many software companies. Now he's succumbing to the sweetness I sweat from my covered pores. "Especially this month. I'm a software developer, and we've got a launch happening with one of our clients next week and, ah... oh, you don't want to hear this." He sips his drink. It must be to his tastes, for he gratefully nods to the bartender.

"I actually love hearing about that stuff." Cheekbones, get higher. Chin, tip up. Bust? Lean the hell forward and make sure he sees your gorgeous clavicle. You've got this. If this guy isn't asking you back to his place tonight, he's getting your number and texting you a picture of his dick as soon as he gets home. (Trust me, he's the type of dumbass to do that. Ask me how many unsolicited dick pics from guys are lurking on my phone, ready to be used to destroy a bastard's marriage. Assuming he pisses me off enough, anyway.) "I don't know a whole lot about computers and software, but I've always been curious to know more." Yes, Mr. Stranger! Tell little ol' uneducated me the same shit I've heard from the rest of your ilk over the years! *Totally* never met a software guy in Portland before!

I pluck the lemon from my Old Fashioned and run it down my tongue, acting as if this is a totally innocent move. Brian's eyes widen in confounded admiration. Oh, this lemon is absolutely sour as shit, but I pregamed this move a few minutes ago when I doused my tongue with lemon juice. I want him to think about my mouth on his cock. I'm not handing out the head candy tonight, but I want him *fantasizing*. Especially when I wipe a little smidge from the corner of my mouth and act like I hadn't done anything sexual at all.

"Besides," I say, my demeanor perkier than my breasts, "you're meeting someone right now, aren't you? You only had to step out of your comfort zone for a few minutes." I maintain my girl-next-door smile as I run my finger around the rim of my glass.

I look beyond stupid. Except... it works.

"Guess so, Cher." He likes my name. "What do you do?"

The glint in his eyes tells all. "*Please say stripper. Or escort. Or model. Cam girl? I bet you're a cam girl, honey.*" No, I'm not going to give him any of those. For one, I don't want him immediately treating this like I'm looking for a transaction. For another, I know his type. He wants the bubbly girl he grew up with. The one who was his first love at thirteen when he realized why his little dick always embarrassed him in history class. I'm the first girl he thinks about when he jacks off. I'm that unobtainable high.

He knows he can *buy* a girl like that whenever he wants, but I'll be the woman he's charmed into a genuine relationship. *That's* when the wallet comes out.

"I work remotely," is all I say. It tells him enough without piquing interest. Then again, he might still think I'm a cam girl.

Intoxicated

Besides, I want Brian to talk about himself. *All* about himself. I'm the dream girl right now. The one who never wants to talk about herself, because he's *soooooo* fascinating! Way more interesting than me! I'm only a boring girl who needs an exciting boyfriend in her life. One who will spoil her silly because she's never had anything like that in her life, and now he's the coolest guy on Earth. I'll play up inexperience in the bedroom if he'll fall for it. (I admit, that's one of my weak spots. You get used to playing the near-virgin so you know how to act like one, but when you've slept with enough guys, you forget what it's like to be a virgin. For real.)

The more Brian talks, the more buzzed on his cocktails he gets... the more I learn about him. Every word he says, every mannerism he picks up? I'm adding it to my little spot in my brain reserved for this tech guy named *Brian*. I shall use this information to model myself more into his perfect girlfriend. I will chameleon myself until I'm completely unrecognizable from the last girlfriend I pretended to be. He'll be so putty in my hands that I can ask him to pay my rent for the next three months and he won't think twice about it. He'll be grateful that I want to keep my own place instead of moving in with him right away. (Never move in with them, ladies. Don't give up your cute one-bedroom in Northwest Portland for any man.) If he has other women who aren't supposed to know about me, then we have a convenient crash pad. I will know about *them,* though. Either he'll tell me, or I'll figure out how many and how important they are to him in about three weeks. My next objective will be to decide if it's worth becoming his #1 focus or moving on to the next guy.

Remember, Brian. I'm not a woman who can be bought. Not the way you're thinking about it. I'm a woman you've *earned*.

You've been working so hard at your job, right? What has it gotten you? Mild respect? A few nice suits? Your favorite bars you and your buddies hit on a Saturday night when you're done with brunch at the trendy spots on Hawthorne? (Or are we doing Broadway hotspots now?) Your cozy little apartment you pay way too much for, but you're within walking distance of Powell's Books? You take the occasional trip, but your work hates it when you're gone for more than one day, so you stick close to Portland. Maybe Seattle for a business trip. You work so hard. You've got all this money. But you can't get the hot girl you know you deserve. Where is she, huh? Is it because Portland is full of hairy feminists who call themselves Queer before they'll call themselves your honey? Or is it because the hotter, richer guys in this town have plucked all the pretty girls for themselves? Oh, Brian. It must be so hard. Yet what if I told you it didn't have to be that way anymore? I can soothe some of those ails. I can suck your dick when you get home from work and dinner still cooks on the stove. I can wear cute little outfits as the weather heats up and you prance me around sushi restaurants and boutique ice cream shops. Want to help me try on new bikinis for our trip to Mexico? Ooh, I bet you do, Brian. I bet you want the girl of your dreams.

The one you *deserve*.

We exchange numbers before he insists on heading home to get some sleep. It's for the best. I want him to go to sleep thinking about how much he regrets not asking me out right there, but he'll ask tomorrow. We'll go out Sunday afternoon, kiss at sunset, and... well, if I'm in a good mood, I'll give him a preview of what he gets from me as his girlfriend. Depends how he handles himself, though. I may decide he's not worth it by then.

Intoxicated

Brian slinks away, his gaze over his shoulder as he gets one last look at me. I twiddle my fingers and continue to smile in his direction. As soon as he turns the corner, I drop my exhausting façade and blow some air out of my cheeks. So ladylike. So beautiful. That's me.

"What?" I ask the bartender, who is judging me with the full force of his face. "Can I get another one of these?" I shake my empty Old Fashioned. "I need it."

He moves out of the way to grab the bottle. I now have an unobstructed view of the man sitting along the wall on the other side of the room.

Hello.

I've never seen him before. Is that... Armani? A Blancpain watch? My goodness. That belt is made of real leather, isn't it? What a mighty fine five o'clock shadow this gentleman, currently staring at his iPhone as if he has nothing better to do, has. I do love a little scruff on a hot guy. He's quite... cut as well, isn't he?

Whoa. I definitely need that drink. Brian may have left me bored in the heart and loins, but one glance at this mysterious stranger has me thinking about all sorts of dirty things. That's rare anymore. When you've had sex with as many boring, mediocre fools as I have, it takes the fun out of a casual roll in the hay with a "normal" guy. Anymore, I wonder what the point is.

I'm thinking about the point as I look at this man over here.

He happens to look up from his phone and meet my gaze. Immediately, I look away, pretending to be sidetracked by the ice in my empty glass. The bartender brings me a fresh Old-Fashioned. I thank him. When I look back at the table, the man is already gone.

Musk envelops me. My favorite scent. The most masculine scent alive, if you ask me.

I look to my right. There's the hot guy, glass in his hand while the other props himself against the counter. Muscles ripple up his arms and disappear into the rolled-up cuffs of his sleeve. The fine craftsmanship of his watch momentarily distracts me from the delicious abs cut beneath his white Armani shirt. His trousers are tailored, but that only highlights the delightful package he's toting more.

Careful, Cher. We didn't come here to get laid. Although this guy speaks directly to the kind I'm usually after.

He's definitely... *rich*. Armani. Blancpain. Tailored clothes and spectacular grooming. A body he's taken good care of, as if he has no one to impress anymore but himself.

I could eat him for dessert tonight. Lick that hard stomach and gaze into those big blue eyes as I drive my cunt onto the length of his cock.

"I know it's not any of my business," a cool, nonchalant voice says, "but I couldn't help but notice the young man you were talking to." He lowers his lips to my ear. Shudders claim me as his breath touches my skin. "He'd be a giant waste of your time."

I'm listening...

CHAPTER 3

DREW

I'm far from the only man who's attempted my line of work. Ruining a woman's mascara because she's ruined a hundred men's lives is my specialty. Yet I'm one of the only guys who has survived this business for more than a few months.

You wanna know why?

Because I know genuine interest when I see it. I also know when a woman intends to play me like a fiddle.

Most women don't do it on purpose, of course. Only the ones who have perverted their morals to the point of no return. The ones who see every guy as either a mark, a threat, or completely inconsequential.

The light sparking behind Cher's devilishly brown eyes tells me I've ascended from inconsequential. That means I'm on her radar. It's time to play this as carefully as I play a game of chess against my assistant. The guy is a worthy opponent. He knows how to strike my king when I least expect it, always keeping me on my toes and teaching me how to think far, *far* ahead. Don't tell Brent this, but it's definitely the reason I've kept him on after a slew of call-outs at the expense of my business. (The guy had eloped with some jock he met in a nightclub. That same night. Don't ask me how they're still married four years later. Also, don't ask me how embarrassing their Christmas cards are.)

Now that I have Cher's attentions, however, I need to ensure I elevate to *mark*. Or, at least, she needs to think I'm a potential mark. Why do you think I dressed like this tonight? Everything I've researched about Cher suggests she's a woman with delicate, refined tastes. She goes after men with serious means. She's as likely to corner a freshly minted multimillionaire (easy pickings for someone as delicious as her, but they don't usually have money for long,) as she is to go after her billionaire boss with a death wish. I've got being hot on my side. I know how to dress myself in the brands that mean something to her. Never mind the fact I genuinely afford them. I come from both money *and* have my own successful business that caters to men either as rich or richer than my family. Everything I do around her is 100% natural.

I merely have an ulterior motive that's *not* sex, all right?

Well, maybe a little bit of my motive is sex. Like I said, this is a black widow on my hands. Women like Cher don't leave so much devastation in their wake without having both the looks *and* the skills to back up the résumé. The only reason I'm looking at her without pitching a tent in my pants is because I've read about her torrid history. I've seen the embarrassing video my client sent me, ensuring I got the full scope of her wretched nature. She's the kind of woman I'd hit and quit if the opportunity presented itself, but I don't want anything to do with her beyond that.

Except, you know, to make money off her misery.

"I know that guy," I say, splaying open my legs as I slump over in the stool I now occupy. My torso and arms say I'm keeping a respectful distance. My knee, which threatens to bump into her thigh every two seconds, says otherwise. Some part of me needs her thinking about sex the whole time I'm sitting here, laying on the charm and drawing her into a web so much like the ones she weaves every day. "You don't want to get involved with that guy."

Cher sits up, checking her posture and her appearance. It's a subtle move women make when I start to flirt with them. Cute, when it's an innocent lady who simply strikes my fancy. Absolutely unnerving when I have a jerk on my hands.

A jerk with fantastic side-boob, I might add. Is she using tape to keep them looking that perky? That's totally tape – but I bet they look as amazing without the tape.

"You know him, huh?" Cher has lost the girl-next-door air she adopted when talking to another man. She's sizing me up right now, isn't she? Debating what kind of woman I want for the night. Appearances aren't the only thing she has going for her. If she decides she wants my money, she'll have to play Perfect Girlfriend. I won't ever see the real her. I'll see a façade. A mirror reflecting my innermost fantasies back at me, until she decides it's time to move on. The only thing I haven't figured out about Cher Lieberman is why she's so keen to break up when her rich marks propose to her. Is it because they're not rich *enough* for her to go through with it? Does she have some insufferable code? Does she get cold feet once she faces a man hopelessly in love with her? In love enough that he flies to Berlin to get his grandmother's engagement ring to bring back to a woman who doesn't really deserve it? "Do you know what you coming up here to tell me that tells *me?*"

I'm slightly taken aback by her direct approach, but I attempt to not let it show. Curiosity is okay. I must look perpetually interested, after all. Yet Cher can't know that she's surprised me enough to sit back in mild wonder.

"What does that tell you?" I ask, smirk compensating for my brash response.

"Either you hate the man and can't stand the thought of him nailing a girl like me," she plucks a tiny plastic straw from a bin and stirs the ice in her glass. The remnants of whiskey swirl with ice water. "Or you find him appalling and think it's your duty to warn me."

Think fast, Drew. You may have to change course, but that doesn't mean you drop your lead. You *know* what she's doing. She's judging you as much as you judge her. You're playing each other, but that's your advantage, Drew. *You* know you're both playing each other. She doesn't.

So act like you've got this. Go with your gut, you suave bastard.

"I don't know anything about his ethics or what kind of lover he is." My legs open wider. Man-spread is on my side as I "absentmindedly" rub my knee against hers. She doesn't recoil from me. That's a good sign. "All I know is what I hear in my line of work. The guy likes to throw his money around. A little too much, if you know what I mean."

Intoxicated

Cher studies me, her mind working overtime to ascertain how much truth I tell her. Do I really know him? Is this so I can get under her skirt? How hot *would* I look on top of her, anyway? I dunno, Cher, you tell me. That's the look you've got in your eye before you shake it out, sigh, and say, "Good to know he's a total waste of time. You know, if I were a gold digger."

Subtle sarcasm. The real me likes it. The me working her over likes it more. Funny girls – the blacker the humor the better – are easy to seduce. "Didn't mean to imply that." I prop my chin up on my hand. Here's to my *fantastic* profile. Almost as good as her side-boob. "I don't like it when a lovely lady wastes her time on a man who can't keep funds in his account. Every woman deserves to be treated with financial respect."

Your average woman would roll her eyes. Yet Cher is far from *average*. Her fixation on money, money, money means she merely snorts and says, "Thanks for watching out for me, kind stranger. I'll keep that in mind when he inevitably calls me tomorrow."

"You'll tell him no, right?"

"Depends on what I'm doing this weekend. He seems like the kind of guy who wants to go on Sunday brunch."

"Oh, you'll be busy on Sunday."

"I will be, huh?"

She knows exactly what I'm going to say. I'm basically a pick-up cliché right now. Does it matter, though, if it's working? I exude so much confidence that *I* should be teaching those classes. Instead, I see ads for them all over Portland and Seattle. And the local guys wonder why women gasp in disdain when they put on their "smooth moves." Even Cher would be disgusted. Gentlemen, don't do what I'm about to do unless you've got the pedigree and confidence to back you up. Because it is *not* easy to pull off.

"You'll be busy with me. Because I'm about to ask you out, and you're going to say yes."

Cher is impressed by my bold statement, but that doesn't mean she's about to agree to everything I've said. Oh, no, now it's time for her to poke some holes into *my* façade. "Give me one good reason, Mr. I Don't You."

I extend my hand. "Drew Benton." It's important that I give her my real name. My marks don't *always* get my real name. Only the ones who need to be impressed by my background and family name. Trust me. Cher Lieberman knows *The Bentons*.

"Hmm?" Her fine eyebrows arch in surprise. "Benton, you say? I know that name."

Told you.

"Then you're a woman of solid tastes." I hail the bartender who, despite the professionalism he must entertain working in a place like this, can't help but gawk at Cher Lieberman getting *my* attention. "What are you drinking? I'll buy you another." I'll be shocked if she wants me to buy her anything, let alone more alcohol, but I have to offer. She expects it.

"Honestly would be happy with a ginger ale."

I don't verbally - or mentally, for that matter - judge her, although a ginger ale in a place like this costs as much as the whiskey on the rocks. Except it doesn't matter to me, right? I'm a Benton. Names and prestige may not mean as much on the west coast, but I still advertise my funds as I tell the good bartender to put her ginger ale on my tab. Oh, and put her unpaid tab on mine as well.

"You don't have to do that," she says.

"I insist. It's the least I could do for barging in on your evening like I have."

Intoxicated

"How nice of you to acknowledge it. Most men assume I'm graced with their presence."

"That, too. You seem like a woman who could use gracing."

"I believe you were asking me out on Sunday, Mr. Benton?"

Do you hear that? It's the sound of this little fishy biting my bait. Now, all I have to do is yank on my hard rod and drag her into my embrace. Whether she comes docilely or makes a big splash, one thing is for sure – it's going to be wet. "That reminds me. I didn't catch your name."

Have I caught *her* off guard this time? Because that might be a genuine smile of fragile disbelief on her face. "Do you make a habit of asking out women whose names you don't know?"

"You were ready to jump into that guy's second-hand Lamborghini before knowing his name." More like a secondhand BMW, but I'll give him a benefit of a doubt. "I thought my chances were pretty high."

"Are you saying I'm a slut?"

I had a glass of water halfway up to my mouth when she said that. Now, I'm spitting out a chunk of ice and hacking on the water burning in my throat. Cher primly sits in her seat, thanking the bartender for her ginger ale, while I am thrown *so far* off my game that I think she's scored the first touchdown of this match.

"No!" I gasp. There's no wit to respond with. Not when a woman is asking you *that!*

"Uh huh. You only imply that you think I am. Otherwise," she sips her ginger ale, "you wouldn't think I'm so easy that I'd go out with you without giving you my name first."

The bartender is on the other side of the circular bar, attempting to contain his laughter. Or, at least, I'm pretty sure that's what all the dramatic coughing is about.

"It's Cher, by the way." She tucks her silky black hair behind her ear while I attempt to rein in my embarrassment. God, if my client knew she had me by the balls like this... well, he could probably relate. Then fire me. "Cher Lieberman. Unfortunately, my name isn't as nice as yours. I'm not related to Senator Lieberman, as far as I know." She wistfully gazes into the distance, but I know that's no daydreaming lady inside of her. "I'm just a girl from Portland."

Now's my chance to gather my bearings and seal the deal. "A beautiful girl form Portland." Please, congratulate me on my ability to not choke out those words.

"Yes, and you're a handsome Benton boy who has asked me out in this nice bar."

"Would a handsome Benton boy *not* be in a bar like this?" It fits my family's image of being wealthy but acting like they're upper middle class. Or until my mother remembers most upper middle class people don't have personal drivers on their payroll. Moving out to Beaverton has really fucked with her head now that a dollar stretches a *little* bit farther. A whole ten cents farther, maybe, but that's thousands of dollars in Benton talk. Enough to hire a part-time driver to take her to appointments and out for brunch with her wealthy lady-friends. Last I heard, she's befriended someone whose husband owns one of the pro NW teams. My mother *can't* be seen driving herself around now. It's sooooo unbecoming!

"You sound like a playboy, Mr. Benton. I'm another hot girl to notch on your bedpost. If you bother keeping track now. You didn't care about my name, because you think I'm an easy slut, not that it matters to either you or me."

"Yet you keep bringing it up."

Intoxicated

"A woman is always concerned with her image around town."

Are you really sure about that, Cher? Because that line might work on a man who knows nothing about you, but I'm not such a man. It's taking as many reserves as the bartender has to not crack up laughing right now. You! Caring about your image! When you've made a lifestyle out of breaking men's hearts to the point one of them has hired me to break *yours!* Whew. I need a handkerchief. I've got tears in my eyes from laughing so hard.

"I could be a playboy," I say. "Or I could be a guy who dates around in the futile hope of meeting the right girl. You know, that fabled right one?"

"You might as well scream at me that you're a man-ho."

"If a slut and a man-ho enter a room at the same time, does it create a disturbance in the puritanical force?"

"Great," Cher glibly says. "He's making Star Wars jokes now."

"The fact you get it's a Star Wars reference makes you hotter, by the way."

This time she gives in to the eye roll. What a *dramatic* one it is, too! Every muscle in her face goes along with it, as if she's been waiting for this moment. This pivotal, crucial moment in which she finally lets me see a sliver of who she really is.

"I'm not asking you to go steady with me, *Cher.*" I stress her name to prove that I've remembered it. "I'm asking for one date. As much as I would love to keep chatting with you here, I'm afraid I have an early morning with my family. You know. The Bentons of Beaverton."

"I'm afraid I'll have to say no if all you're interested in is my body."

"I have no expectations, beyond some nice conversation. We could talk about Star Wars for a few hours."

She snaps her head around, that fragile disbelief now pure, uncut *Are you fucking kidding me?* "You're lucky you're rich and good looking," Cher snaps. "Because those are the only reasons I'm considering it."

"Hey, at least you're considering it."

"Give me one good reason to go out with you on Sunday."

I mull over my options. Do I continue to play the unlucky in love heir who stupidly keeps dating hot girls, thinking one will be his perfect bride? Or do I try to lay on a little romance? For a woman like Cher, who always has dollar signs in her eyes, I can think of only one thing to win her over. Me. A rich guy in a sea of available men who think they're hot shit and give her what she *really* wants.

"Because," I say, lowering my voice and leaning closer to her, "unlike every other guy in here, I can actually make you come."

If you're expecting her to slap me, you're about to be disappointed. Because Ms. Lieberman is the kind of woman who *wants* to hear that outlandish promise. This is a woman who has slept with so many mediocre men she's not even attracted to, that she's forgotten what it's like to have great, blow-your-top-off sex. She hasn't hidden her opinion that she thinks I'm attractive. We've got this chemistry sizzling between us, the one begging me to rip open her dress and dive right into that crazy-hot body. She's been glancing at my pants every five minutes since I sat down. You think I haven't noticed? Oh, she hasn't only been glancing at whatever bulge I may be packing. She's been daydreaming about fucking me since I sat down.

It may or may not be mutual.

Can you imagine us if we fooled around? We would make a pretty *good* looking couple. I bet she's a real tiger, too. The kind

Intoxicated

that acts like she can't be contained, and will go down clawing and biting until you turn those growls into howls. She's gone so long without caring about sex that she won't know how good it is for her until it's slamming her between the legs. Using my cock as its conduit, preferably. I wouldn't mind shoving my face in that cleavage, either. Would she like to keep the fashion tape holding those breasts up? I bet I can fuck her so hard it comes undone and, boom, say goodbye to your "natural" lift, Cher.

I won't care, either. There isn't anything we could do that wouldn't be as hot as the sun.

"That's a bold claim," Cher purrs. I shouldn't take that sound lightly. She's not looking to kitty-cat against my arm and beg for scritches. She's getting ready to arch her back and slash me across the face. She's that cat rolling onto her back, exposing her stomach, daring me to think we're close enough for me to touch her most prized spot. "Would be absolutely terrible if we put that to the test and you couldn't deliver."

"You make it sound like I couldn't." I grin. "Or that I would care I didn't. Getting you in my bed is reward enough for me."

"You're a cad."

"Yes, a cad you're going out with on Sunday." I pull a pen out of my back pocket and write my private number down on a napkin. "Text me when you decide you're ready to go out with a man who will actually take care of *your* needs for once." I slide the napkin over. She does not look at it, nor does she touch it. "I'm not promising you the moon, Cher. I'm promising a nice date that could lead to something you've been desperately searching for." I leave that open, assuming she's looking for good sex. Or, hey, maybe she's looking for love. That would be better. Would certainly make my job easier.

If she's only looking for sex, though? My job got *better*.

Trust me when I say I've stuck it in some batshit crazy before. Believe me when I tell you that my dick has plundered the depths of some truly reprehensible women. I knew they were when I fucked them. I wasn't always paid to bed them, either. It wasn't always about making them fall in love with me so I could absolutely wreck them. You want to know one of the reasons I got into this gig? Oh, you haven't realized it yet?

I've been doing this since before I realized I could turn it into a *service*.

I can't say no to pretty girls who aren't afraid to bite your dick while they blow you. Living on the edge with a volatile woman has its... advantages. Especially in the bedroom. Maybe a lot of guys fantasize about it, but few of the ones I talk to actually have the guts to get wrapped up with a chick they know is a huge piece of work. After a certain age, anyway. Teenagers and young studs in college tell themselves it's worth it 'cause she's hot. Maybe the sex is fantastic. (It usually is.) But the fallout that results in stalkers, used tampons sent in the mail, and your mother calling you up in the middle of the night saying your childhood home has been burgled quickly puts an end to those fantasies.

Unless you're me. Unless your name is Drew Benton, professional rake.

Cher no longer hides her interest in my cock. After giving it a critical look, she slips her hand between my legs.

She doesn't squeeze anything, though. She's content with staring ahead, boring a hole into the back of the bartender's skull and feeling how long my cock is. Naturally, it's happy to have her there.

"Jesus," she mutters, snatching her hand out like my thighs are about to detach it from her arm. "And that's soft, huh?"

"I'll be honest with you." I finish my drink. "It's only a *little* bigger when it's hard, but I damn well know how to use it. So, what do you say?" I nod to the napkin with my number on it. "Sunday?"

She slips off her stool, steely eyes never leaving my gaze. My napkin is left behind as she slowly walks away.

Oh, well. At least I get to watch that delectable ass sway in that slinky black dress.

"Nice try, buddy," the bartender says when he rounds the center island. "You're telling her that she's dodged a bullet? I could say the same thing to you. That woman's like a viper, man. She's always in here looking for some rich dick to plow her next."

I shrug. "Now I know."

As the bartender sagely shakes his head and turns around, a familiar face reappears.

It's Cher, and she's raced back to claim my phone number. The way she snatches it off the bar before scurrying away again tells me that it's going to be a *great* weekend.

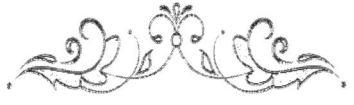

CHAPTER 4

CHER

Don't. Say. *Anything!*

It's bad enough I've got you breathing down my neck again. I don't need your thoughts, thank you. Remember the ground rule I laid when you insisted on tagging along whenever it struck your fancy?

No judgments. If you're a judgmental prick, you're outta here.

So what if I took Drew's number? You would have too, if you saw him! The guy is at *least* a nine on the scale. Maybe a nine and a half. It would be ridiculous to call him a ten, because my poor, feeble pussy would explode and I'd be worthless, both to myself and to anyone else who feels like using me. I thought he might be an eight when he first walked up to me. A very respectable eight. Then he had to go and say all the right things. *Then* I had to go and feel him up for myself. I wasn't being hyperbolic when I called upon our Lord and Savior after touching that thing. I've never been Catholic, but I felt the sign of the cross coming upon me when I realized Mr. Drew Benton had ascended to *nine and a half.*

I mulled over my options in my sleep, where I'm a much more logical entity, particularly when I have my essential oils diffusing and a sweet spring breeze blowing through my window. Except I spent more time having a sex dream - the infuriating kind where nothing actually goes anywhere, but you wake up horny as hell, anyway - than deciding whether or not I should accept Drew's offer for a date. I couldn't tell you if he was my intended in my dreamworld.

Actually, I can. I'm pretty sure it was him I desperately chased into a hotel room and begged to bone me like the slut I am.

Slut. Man-ho. What a pair we make.

Sure enough, Brian texted me Saturday afternoon and asked if I wanted to grab brunch on Sunday. I almost accepted his offer based on principles I had no idea I actually had.

Except I kept staring at that crumped up napkin, knowing that Drew was the better deal.

What's kept me from accepting his offer for a date? I'll tell you what. Chemical attraction. Desperation. A sinking feeling that he's bigger trouble than I usually want. Every rich guy is a certain level of trouble. Either he's got an addiction, he's an abusive dickhole, or his mommy issues are out of control. In the worst case scenario, you get a mixture of all three. (I've been there. I could write a book about Frank Griffin III. To this day, I'm grateful I never actually slept with him. He was one of the few obsessed with "purity," and although he was a multi-billionaire, I knew it would be over as soon as we got married and he finally defiled me. Goodbye, the only thing attracting him to me. Can you believe he thought I was a virgin?)

Benton, though. Do you know who the Bentons are? Of course you do. Even if you don't immediately recognize the name, you know what they do and who they hang with. All you have to do is hop a MAX train from Hillsboro to Gresham to see how much real estate they've developed, how many businesses they own, and how many financial institutions boast their investments. The Bentons go back four generations in the Portland area. Great-granddaddy Benton got his start in the fur trade, Granddaddy Benton got into banking, and Daddy Benton is a whiz at real estate development. Makes me wonder what Drew contributes to the family's coffers. Based on the semi-thorough Google search I did, he's one of the youngest of his generation, but he's a direct descendent. His older sister will be inheriting a bulk of the company. That doesn't mean a Benton of *any* caliber would be a bad prospect. Honestly, I should be salivating to sink my teeth into his money and his cock into my greedy, *greedy* cunt. He has CHER LIEBERMAN'S FUTURE HUSBAND written all over him. In calligraphy, no less. That's how fancy my flair is.

So why aren't I blowing up his phone? Am I playing a long game? A little hard to get? Not trying to look too eager? A little aloof? Like he's nothing to me.

Well, yes, but I'm also wary of any man I legitimately have the hots for, because it probably won't end well.

It's too easy to lose my head when I'm in lust. If my long term plan is to be an independently retired wealthy woman by forty, then I better *not* be falling in love with a handsome idiot. I don't need a divorce mucking things up, let alone the heartbreak that could come from a young, sexy, *rich* guy I might actually convince to put a ring on it. It's much easier to cut a man loose once I have what I need if, you know, I don't actually care about him. I learned my lessons early on in this rambunctious plan of mine. Remember Frank Griffin III? I didn't like him, but I almost married him. Now imagine what could happen to me if my feelings actually get involved?

Luckily, I've shut down most of those pesky bastards since then. My eyes are always on the prize. The monetary prize. I want to travel. I want a nice place in an expensive city. I want dinners out, new clothes, and the ability to sit in a teahouse at two on a weekday afternoon reading fine, aged literature. For that, I need more money. I need boyfriends paying my rent for me now so I can stash away his allowances and gifts in the bank.

I don't want to hear that I could accomplish this with "honest" work. The hell do you think I'm doing? Being a professional sugar baby and girlfriend *is* work! Maybe not the most honest work, but I'm not going to jail for it anytime soon. Not when I've got dirt on some of the biggest cats in Portland. And Seattle. And a few places in between and around.

Drew Benton. Yeah, I text him. I don't ask him out, though. I give him a time and a location. A trendy wine and tapas place not too far from my apartment in Northwest Portland. We'll see if he goes along with my requests. If he'll respect my neighborhood. If he'll actually show up.

Either way, I'm getting wine, cheese, and fruit. Three of my favorite things.

I don't dress up for him. I dress up for *me*. This flowy jumpsuit made of white silk and patterned with bold, purple flowers will keep me from tearing up a skirt and riding Mr.

Benton into the next week. Platform shoes that make me stumble every few steps ensure I'm not going anywhere with him, unless it's back to my place or in his car. I'm wearing my favorite sunglasses, which also happen to be so huge and "tacky" (don't you dare call them that) that so many assholes can't help but inform me that my face is much too small for them. My makeup is minimal and my jewelry refined. I could be browsing the stacks at Powell's or sipping coffee in whatever place people think is hip now. Maybe I'm making a bank run. Maybe I've off to meet my friends for tea. I could be leisurely shopping for better, more walkable shoes. You won't find me in Goodwill, but you *will* find me in every shop on 23rd, because that's where the suburban girls come into the city to shop.

I want Drew to know that I'm willing to push a cart in Fred Meyer wearing this ensemble. That's how little his presence means to me. Really, I'm *deigning* him with my winning personality and body. I'd assume I'd also be in the wine place without his ass sitting at the same table as me.

I make sure I arrive first. My reservation is honored by a dowdy young woman in a uniform. She doesn't look at me twice as she shows me to a corner table, where I consider the seasonal wine list and the tapas of the day. I think I'll pull out my tablet and peruse the last George Eliot novel I mulled over a few days ago. I told you, I love my wine. And my classics.

As the poignant words of *Middlemarch* entrance me, I'm slightly distracted by the black Chevrolet Camaro rolling up to parallel park right in front of my window. NW 23rd is a hot cruising spot for every middle-aged guy who has recently bought his first sports car. People will drive down from the hills *just* to show off. Tourists and locals alike frequent this place. Sure enough, everyone within a quarter mile radius stops to admire and take a picture of the black convertible turning off its motor.

Out steps Mr. Benton.

Wait, do you start the sign of the cross on your *left* side, or the right? I can never remember. I'm a Heathen. My appearance may be impeccable, but my religious references? Sloppy.

He's got the tightest pair of denim jeans clinging to his legs. A half-unbuttoned black linen shirt flutters in the breeze, his sunglasses adding an air of mystery to his otherwise young form. My Googling tells me he's recently turned thirty. The guy doesn't look a day over twenty-three. You know, that *I may have just graduated college, but I'm totally a mature adult,* look.

I stab a cube of cheese. My teeth pluck it right off the toothpick. I cross my legs and lower my sunglasses so I get a better view of that ass as Drew feeds the parking meter and smiles at a pair of young women in jumpers. I can hear their giggles from here.

There's only a one minute window between him disappearing from view and making it to my table. Now's my chance to gussy up. Freshen up my makeup. Ensure that every hair is in the proper place. Pull the wrinkles out of my silk jumpsuit and think about what I'll say to greet him.

I don't do any of those things.

"Afternoon." Drew doesn't remove his sunglasses until he's standing at my table. "I'm looking for a beautiful woman named Cher. Do you happen to know her?"

My elbow digs into the table. My hair slides down my shoulders as I cock my head up and say, "No."

"Pity." Drew helps himself to the table, anyway. His cologne is a respectable Calvin Klein, but I can understand why he went for that instead of the supreme quality they keep under lock and key in department stores. It's a fragrance that enhances him, all right. You know a man is familiar with his own scent and what it needs when he's always got you thinking about cuddling up to him.

Give it a few moments. The olfactory fatigue will settle in soon enough.

"Guess I'll sit with you, then. What should I call you?" He tucks his sunglasses into the only pocket on his shirt. "You look like an... Annalise."

Can you believe this guy? This is what he thinks is flirting. Then again, he's surprised me, hasn't he? I bet that's his only goal. Keep me guessing, or whatever. Those types tend to be exhausting. Maybe I don't want to guess. Maybe I want to know who you are up front, because God knows I'm keeping the real me from you.

"Not even close," I say.

"A... Margaret, but everyone calls you Maggie."

"Isn't that your grandmother's name?"

He laughs. Damn him and his dazzling white smile. "So you've been looking me up."

"I had to make sure you are who you say you are. Any guy can claim to be a Benton. How do I know you're not impersonating one to seduce women?"

"At least I look the part?" He stretches his arms above his head, shirt stretching across his broad chest. Yes, yes, those are lovely chest hairs poking out between his glass buttons. Whoop-dee-doo. "What do you think? Do I look and smell like I could pass for a Benton?"

"Yes." I pick up another cube of cheese. "The baby of the family."

His smile slightly falters. "You really dig in, don't you?"

Intoxicated

He doesn't mean the cheese plate. He means the information I mined about him. "Your family is easy to Google. When were you going to tell me that you're not inheriting the company? Although I'm sure your sister will do a fine job."

"That's what you care most about, yes?"

"I didn't say that. Yet you're acting like you're all that because you've got money."

"I don't *just* have money."

"Yes, yes, you've introduced me to your trouser snake."

Some guys are put off by my flippancy. Drew, however, digs right in, like he's about to tear apart the tapas plate he's ordered to go with a glass of Chardonnay. Not the drink I'd peg him to like, but I'm not surprised, either. He's always trying to circumvent expectations. Yet he's still a guy driving a Camaro and wearing Calvin Klein cologne.

I don't hate the conversation, although it takes me a little while to loosen up. The wine helps, although I've picked one I know doesn't turn me into a giggly mess of bad decisions quickly. I politely inquire about his field of work - naturally, he does things here and there for his family, but deep in his heart he's an *artist* - and he asks me about my family. When I tell him I'm a native Portlander but that my parents have moved to Arizona for an early retirement and a cheaper condo, he expresses surprise, as if I'm not the type to hang around Portland for too long.

"What, do you think I moved here from California?"

"No," he says.

"No?"

Drew appreciates the aroma of his wine before explaining. "I was thinking Seattle. You're very Pacific Northwest, but a bit more cosmopolitan than what I associate with Portland."

"Is that so? You know Seattle pretty well, do you?"

"I actually live there full time." He puts his glass down. How that manages to make a muscle in his arm ripple, I have no idea, but I'm not going to deny a free show. "It's true that my family has their roots in Portland, but we have properties all over the west coast. I've always preferred Seattle to Portland. Which is ironic, because I've also always fancied myself a country boy at heart."

I snort. "A country boy."

"I may not look it, but I'm a handy guy. Spent last weekend building a bookshelf for..."

"The poor?" I suggest.

"My grandmother." He doesn't miss a beat. "She lives in Eastern Washington. I visit her quite often, really. She has a little piece of paradise up there."

Eastern Washington. Really. That hell-hole? I'd rather drive through rural Oregon than get stuck in Eastern Washington. You want to know where west coast rednecks originated? Somewhere east of Centralia.

The Bentons and Eastern Washington do not compute. That's one of many things I'll have to investigate before I take things any further with Drew.

"I don't really get along with my family, honestly." He says that with a sigh. "I've always preferred to be a self-made man. I help out where I can, but I'd rather strike out on my own."

"Using your family's capital, of course."

"Never said I didn't have my own."

Is that supposed to be impressive? I expect most men to have their own capital, including the trust fund losers. Nothing worse than a thirty-five year old man still living on his family's money.

Intoxicated

He should at least be working for some of that money. I don't care if he's sucking the family's corporate teat or running his own business into the ground. At least show some initiative, you know? Otherwise, a guy risks needing a mommy more than a girlfriend. I play an excellent fake girlfriend. I'm an *atrocious* surrogate mother.

"So you spend most of your time in Seattle... what are you doing in Portland right now?"

"I pop in a couple of times a month to check in with my family. My mother especially hates to travel outside after her hip surgery. Can you believe it? Barely in her sixties and already having hip surgery."

"It's not that uncommon."

"You would know about hip surgeries, huh?"

I shrug. Noncommittal. That's how I like it.

He attempts to impress me with his knowledge of the wine we're drinking, but I've heard it all before. Every other guy I date is a connoisseur, you know. I have a sizable collection made of gifts from previous suitors and boyfriends. They make great party favors. When I have enough friends to invite over for a party. That doesn't happen very often since college.

I've burned a lot of bridges.

"So, tell me." Drew rubs his upper lip, as if anticipating my answer before he's asked the question. (As if I don't know what he's about to ask.) "What keeps you in a city like Portland? I know you said you were born here, but most people I know are fleeing as quickly as they came here. Even the natives."

That wasn't what I expected. (Yes, that happens sometimes. I can't anticipate *everything* a guy is going to say. Although I like it when I do. Makes it a lot easier to keep up with my games.) I thought he was going to ask me about why I'm still single. That's what men like him *love* to ask, because it's their way of filtering my crazy. Or if I'm cheating. Half the time, they don't care if I'm cheating. Goes to show the level of ethics around this town.

Ethics that I absolutely contribute to, of course.

"What can I say?" My smile is a mile wide, which he should know is me about to lie out of my ass. He doesn't know that yet. Because he has yet to become acquainted with my tics. Let me tell you about the smiles I've accumulated in my life. The *business* smile. The *socializing* smile. The *my boyfriend is fucking nuts* smile. Right now, Mr. Drew Benton is getting a mix of socializing and crazy boyfriend. If he starts talking money, though, I might slip into business. "I really love this town."

"Do you live in this neighborhood?"

"Yes." He might as well know. Even if he wanted to stalk me, there are so many houses and apartment buildings in this area he'd have to work a little. Too much effort.

"That's why you still love this town. Let me guess. You're young enough that this area was already being gentrified when you were a kid."

I was about to pick up my wineglass when he says that. Now what should I do? Sip my wine as I mull over my words? Choke on the fumes that suddenly gross me out? Or should I simply look around this wine tasting bar, located in a converted Victorian house? Like most of Northwest Portland, this used to be a predominately residential district, full of gorgeous painted ladies and parks on the outskirts of town. Now we're practically a part of the downtown area. Tourists flock up here because of how trendy it's been for most of my life. Drew isn't too wrong about a few things.

Intoxicated

"I'm not from this area, actually," I say. "I grew up in North Portland. Over by Arbor Lodge, although I spent a lot of time in St. John's."

"Did you go to Roosevelt?"

"Did you go to Beaverton High?" I shoot back, knowing damn well that he went to one of the many private schools for the rich. Could be Catholic. Could as easily be Jesuit or agnostic.

"Touché." Drew sits back in his seat, teeth dragging across his bottom lip. Is this the part where I tell you that I wish those lips were dragging across my body right now? I wonder what he looks like without his shirt on. He keeps teasing me with those chest hairs, but is that all they are? A chesty tease? Or is he basically a giant hairy bear? I've been with both. I can deal with either. I definitely have my preference, though. Even if I decide to drag this man into my flurry of games, I would definitely give him some bonus points for being my exact type. "So you're from North Portland. Yeah, I used to hang out around there a lot, too. Some of my buddies and I used to hang out in Cathedral Park after school. We'd cruise down Lombard."

"You. Cathedral Park." I can hardly imagine it. Especially when this guy would've been in high school. Cathedral Park is a nice place, especially if you live in the area. (Although you're hard pressed to find a Portland park that isn't filled with used needles and piles upon piles of garbage.) But it's so far away from Beaverton, let alone far from the kind of place a young heir would hang out that I'm struggling to imagine a younger version of this man "cruising" down Lombard and drinking with his buddies in *Cathedral Park*.

"Maybe I saw you around there," he says with a generous sip of his wine. "We brought a *lot* of girls through there."

Is that supposed to impress me? I don't want to hear about what a man-ho he is. I can see that for myself. Isn't it so unbecoming for men to brag about how many girls they bagged as teenagers?

I'm not jealous. Why would I be jealous? Because so many women around here know what it's like to be on the other end of his thrusts and I don't? Yet.

Yet! I'm still thinking about it. Even if this doesn't go anywhere, I might take him for a spin. Do you know how long it's been since I had sex with a guy I'm actually into? I'm simply speaking physically. Let's talk about true relationship compatibility.

"I think I would remember." The cheese is almost gone. I had no idea I made such short work of it. God help me, am I eating without thinking? I only do that when I'm either so distracted that I need to put the chip bag down... or I'm off my game. And I mean *off my game* to the point I'm going home with a guy who has one over me. "I've heard of you, but before Friday night, we have never met."

"You're right. I would remember you, too."

His wink is disgustingly diabolical. I might throw up. Then kiss him.

Usually, I know where I'm going with a potential mark halfway through our first real date. The end of our little meetup is where I either promise to call him again (and don't) or I lay on the flirtations *extra* thick, with the hopes of inspiring the man to whisk me away to a tropical island the next weekend. Or so he'll attempt to promise me. Some of them only want to meet up at a hotel, or make a big showing of taking me up to Seattle. Classy guys suggest the opera for a second date, and that tells me they're willing to spend some money on me – and I better make sure I'm worth spending money on, all right? New money men who come from lower class backgrounds love their lounges, pool halls, and *hiking trips*. Gag me with a spoon if I ever have to go on another hike on a second date. The guy has to be extraordinary for me to agree to that now. I can only hike through Multnomah Falls or Forest Park so many times before I'm bored to tears. And the weather! It can do anything!

Yet Drew is still a bit of a mystery. I don't like that. I don't *like* men I can't read so easily I might as well be sifting through a slush pile. One minute this guy is trying to impress me with his money, and the next? Regaling me with tales of hanging out in Cathedral Park with his "buddies," drinking cheap booze and hanging out with lower-class girls, like he's one of them. I don't doubt the veracity of his identity. I made sure of that before I came here, but guys who grew up like Drew either follow the Proper Trails blazed by their old money parents, or they rebel to the point of getting kicked out of the family. You don't find many in between. Not around here. Your average rich upper-middle-classer often doesn't understand they're middle-class in Portland. Not when property values are so high that your two million dollars buys you a five-bedroom house in a "nice" neighborhood and not much else. The Bentons are worth a billion dollars, though. Maybe more, since God knows they're not advertising the off-shore accounts and money pumped into whatever investment is lasting the longest these days. I don't know how much of that Drew will have one day, but he's both acting like he's entitled to it... and that he never expects to get it.

Right now, my only motive for dating him is purely personal. He's hot. He has a nice car. He knows how to blend into my kind of scenery. He's *apparently* got a big dick. All things I can take advantage of. Yet will it do me good to have a "real" boyfriend if I can't play him like the violin I pretend isn't a fiddle?

It's time for a test.

"Excuse me," I say, picking up my purse. "I need to use the restroom." It's partially true. I haven't "gone" in about two hours, and I've been drinking wine. A little tinkle is on the docket.

It's also the perfect excuse to see how he reacts to a few things.

Let's start with how I get up and sashay - yes, *sashay* - toward the ladies' room. These heels do amazing things for my legs. Behold as my ass hypnotically swishes my baggy pant legs. This jumper may not show off my thighs, but Drew is getting an eyeful of promises, promises, *promises*. I toss my hair behind my shoulder, exposing the white of my throat as I pretend to be checking my phone. I catch a glance of his face before I turn the corner. Sure enough, he's watching after me, lust attracting the attention of every other woman in this room.

Oh, good. We've established that he still wants to fuck me. Now, let's wait a *good* ten minutes to see how he feels when I come back out fixing my bra and smelling like my floral hand lotion.

Either he'll be so famished for my presence that he chokes on his own spit to see me reemerge, or his boredom will be as plain as day because I've made him wait so long. At least then I'll have an idea toward whether I should go for a second date. I don't have time for men who mess with my head and are bored with me. If I decide to pursue Drew Benton because he tickles my fancy - instead of my wallet - then I better feel like it's worth it. I could be giving up other prospects to spend some time with him.

Although I'm sure that time would be... well, you get the idea. We would be busy.

Intoxicated

He's writing something in a palm-size notebook when I reemerge from the women's restroom. I smell like flowers and walk like I've dispatched a giant weight. (He's not disgusted by a woman's natural body functions, is he? Let's find out.) When I sit down, he kindly looks up and puts the notebook and pen away. I'm greeted with a friendly smile. He's put out that I took so long, but he doesn't say anything. Nor does he act like he's been setting up a date with another woman.

"I'm sorry I took so long," I say. "There was an important phone call while I was in the other room, and..."

"No worries."

No worries, hm? Who was worrying? Him? Me? The poor server who keeps looking at him like she'd want to eat him for dinner? Or that obviously gay guy on the other side of the room who is *also* looking at Drew like he'd eat him for dinner? Don't think I don't know I could be the one with the honors tonight. I bet if I performed a trick with a cube of cheese he'd be begging me to go home with him. Think I'll keep him waiting. Make him think about the *potential* of Cher, the perfect girlfriend. That will give me more time to figure out who his perfect girlfriend is.

Does he want a girlfriend who "isn't like the others?" One who has a blowjob ready for him every day? One who happens to hate being eaten out, whoopie for him? How about a girlfriend who works for her own money, or one that wants to be babied all day? A cultured woman he can take anywhere without fear of her embarrassing him around the locals? Or a girl who will act like Montreal is the most foreign place on Earth? Maybe he wants a woman who reads Chaucer and Psychology Today. We'll discuss the latest research into global warming over Thai at the corner restaurant. Or I'll let him be the smartest man in the room. One who can lecture me about whatever strikes his fancy. Whatever he wants to talk about, I'll be completely ignorant toward. That's the beauty of being a chameleon who is only in it for the benefits and not for love. I can be anyone. I can be any*thing*. I'll be his personal blowup doll if it means a million dollars to my name by the end of the year. Why, yes, Drew, you *can* stick your big dick in my ass on the first date! I really don't know why other girls say no. Come on my face? Choke me a little? Handcuff me, though I barely know you? Oh, those other girls are *so prudish,* aren't they? I would love to play out your porn fantasies! Because I'm a cool girl. I get that your addiction and misconceptions about real sex are a silly thing to think about. We can have all the threesomes with other girls that you want. Why, I would *love* to finger another girl if that gets your wallet out.

What, are you sickened? Appalled? Do you think I'm "nothing but a slut" now? You haven't been paying good attention if you're only now starting to get it.

Because I get it.

Drew Benton wants a *cool* girlfriend. One who turns her nose up to other women who totally aren't like her. Because I understand his love of beer, video games, cars, and porn. All his jokes are hilarious, and all the ones I make are at the expense of my womanhood and intelligence. I'll play his game of "dibs" whenever we're surrounded by other women. "*Oh, Drew, I woul*d *love to claim that one, if you don't mind."* I'm bisexual when it comes to threesomes and super straight when it comes to his dick. I *get* it, don't you see?

Hmph. No. Neither do I. Guys looking for a "cool" girlfriend are often the most disingenuous and sometimes the most dangerous to get into bed with, but I know how to play it well.

Intoxicated

One might say it's my most natural inclination. Geez, says a lot about my own dating history and how I ended up here today.

"I'd really love to continue our conversation and drink a little more wine," I make sure to say this with a seductive smile that keeps him reassured that I'm still *very* interested in him and not about to ghost. In fact, maybe I'll rub my fingertip against his knuckle. I'll bite my red lip and tuck my hair behind my ear, as if to say, "*I really wanted to suck your dick, Drew, but I'm afraid I must dash. My grandmother is on her death bed. See? A good excuse.*" "But I have an obligation this evening I must get ready for. Shall we meet again soon, or...?"

The ball's in your court, buddy.

He cocks an assured smile. He does not pull his hand out from beneath mine. "So happens I have other plans this evening as well. You've done me a favor by breaking that ice. Was spending that whole time you were in the bathroom wondering how I'd tell you I can't take you home with me tonight."

Uh huh. Sure. "Then again, since you live in Seattle, it might be a while before we can meet again." Should he invite me up to Seattle? He really should. I'm a pro at Amtrak.

"I have a place here as well. I think I told you that." Drew's teeth are so white that he really *should* give me the number to his dentist. "It's a lot smaller and not as impressive as my Seattle abode, no, but it's cozy."

"I'm sure it is. I should like to see it next time." I stand again, this time with the finality that screams I'm heading home. "You have my number. Let me know what works for you, and... well, maybe we'll see where it goes from there, shall we?"

I don't give him time to answer. I do, however, give him ample time to gaze after me as I saunter out of the building. If

I'm not giving himself something to fantasize about when he touches himself later, then all of this was for naught.

Since, well... have you seen him? I know what I'm thinking about later. Let this be a mutual exchange of the sexually perverted minds.

I have a lot of other things to think about, however. Drew Benton remains an unknown-enough quantity that I must seriously consider what I'm getting myself into. He could be a fun fling or my worst nightmare. I don't hold out for love. Not with a guy like that. *Definitely* not a man like Drew.

One of the key decisions I must make is solidified when I get a text from Drew later in the evening. I'm fresh from the bath, patting dry some of my hair as I lounge across my bed and pick up my phone. I'm treated to an address that Google Maps *really* wants me to open. I don't bother. The cue that he lives on the riverfront is right there in what street he calls his. I've had plenty of lovers who live down on the South Waterfront. Drew probably lives in the same building as one of my exes.

Gee, hope I don't bump into any!

"*Wednesday evening. Let me cook dinner for you. My place. You tell me the time.*"

It's timestamped twenty minutes ago. Do you know what I was doing in the bathtub twenty minutes ago? I know you weren't there, but I'll tell you, anyway.

Oh, shoot. You've guessed it, haven't you? Suppose I'll save us both the embarrassment of confessing I was giving myself a nice, easy orgasm to thoughts of Drew's stubble and those little hairs poking out of his shirt.

Shit. This really is dangerous. Being so attracted to a guy means I might lose focus of what's most important. That's it. I'm calling in the big guns to help me figure out, once and for all, what it is I'll want from Drew Benton.

Instead of texting, I call one of my many contacts who is worth every dollar she charges.

"*You've reached Moore Investigations,*" says the recorded voice message. "*We're not in the office right now, but please leave your name and number so we can return your call the next time we're in. Thank you.*"

I wait for the beep.

"Hello, Stella." My purr isn't only effective on men. It works on women, too, and Stella is the kind of bubbly professional who responds to a hot woman purring in her direction. I may not be her butchy girlfriend, but I'm *sultry*. I can play those cards on almost anyone with a pulse. "It's Cher. I've got someone I really need you to look into for me. I need results by Wednesday. I'll pay the rush fee."

I'll wait for her to call me back before giving her the name. Hell, I might pop into her office tomorrow morning. It's up in Slabtown. At this time of year, it's a lovely walk, and I really *do* love my walks.

Not as much as I love thinking about Drew right now, though. To the point that I'm lying on my back and running my hand down my torso again, imagining how hard a guy like that can give it to a girl.

My imagination is so active that my eyes glaze over and I'm fishing for the first vibrator I can find in my nightstand.

I'd like some privacy now, thank you!

CHAPTER 5

DREW

With my target on lock, there's no reason for me to travel all the way back up to Seattle before next weekend. I call my assistant Brent to ask how things are going in our office. I have no new messages, not even from my current client. Then again, I prefer to keep a loose line to them until the job is done and I receive the rest of my payment. Better if I can provide evidence of ruined lives and broken hearts in the form of newspaper reports. Before you ask, *yes,* I have gotten lucky more than once. It's really handy when a woman you're working ends up in the news for starting a drunken fight because someone looked at her wrong.

But this all means I'm stuck in Portland. It means holing myself up in my apartment, where the walls are made of glass and my "excellent views" are constant reminders of how much this

Intoxicated

town has changed since I was a kid. Every time I gaze upon the eastside, I get this knot in my stomach. I can remember when it was all single-family homes, low-income apartments, and industrial neighborhoods. Now it's one high-rise after another. Progress is one thing. The entire decimation of a city and its culture is quite another.

Oh, and keep your opinions about how my family has contributed to yourself. I'm well aware of what my family has wrought. Especially the real estate side of my family. The whole reason I have this apartment is because my mother practically gave it to me.

Ah, yes, my mother! The third thing I have to face when I'm in Portland for more than a few days!

I don't take the Camaro to my family's house in Beaverton. Ha! That thing stays locked up tight in my personal garage. So does the Armani and Valentino. If my parents think I'm showing up in anything less than my *real* clothes and my beat-up truck that still gets amazing gas mileage, they don't know me very well.

Actually, I kinda wish they didn't.

"What *is* that wretched thing?" My mother already has the vapors as I pull up to her favorite sunning spot on the expansive property we Bentons calls "home." I may have grown up here, but it has never, *ever* felt like home. That's always abundantly clear when I park next to my sister's Maserati and everyone turns their noses at a perfectly good truck I bought off an old friend ten years ago.

Before you go turning up *your* nose, I invite you to take a quick look around. See? It's clean. No weird, funky man-smells. I have an air-freshener to go with my brand-new stereo and repaired upholstery. Sure, the truck itself is banged up and scuffed, but what good truck isn't? Who cares about some rust on the bumper or a giant scratch on the side? It still works! It still gets me from place to place!

Trust me, nobody is in a hurry to steal this thing. The Camaro? I'm always on the verge of a heart attack when I park it anywhere. That thing has *steal me!* written all over it. I only own a fucking Camaro because it makes seducing women easy. Women like Cher. Who live and breathe their precious name brands and are convinced they're what make a man.

"This is the same truck I've had for a decade," I say to my mother a few yards away from my truck. She's lying back on the settee wearing nothing but a sapphire blue one-piece swimsuit, a wide-brimmed hat flopped over and jewelry hanging from every limb. She's nursing a drink. Looks like orange juice, but I bet my Camaro it's got at least *some* alcohol in it. My mom likes to get the day drinking started early. Say, eleven in the morning early.

Mimosa? Probably a mimosa.

"I'm not talking about that truck," my mother spits. "I mean that thing on your head! I could see it from the driveway!"

I yank my ballcap off my head. Thought I had grabbed a brand-new Blazers cap before leaving my South Waterfront apartment earlier this morning, but it looks like I grabbed another one. Whoops. Instead, I have one of Brent's caps. Probably one he left in the cab of my truck the last time I gave him a ride somewhere. The guy has a cap collection to rival my own, you know. This one's a washed-out green with faded white text advertising some fishing tour based out of coastal Washington. Huh. Fishing sounds pretty fun right now.

The band is worn out and there are a few frayed threads sticking out on top of the hat. My mother looks like she wants to puke. I bet she's worn that hat on her head all of two times, and that's one time too many for her, usually.

"Why must you always dress yourself like a dirty lumberjack?" Her wrinkled hand picks up a small, black device from the end of her settee. A thumb jams into a button. Probably summoning Opal, the family housekeeper who has been around since I've been alive. (Yet somehow she barely looks a day over forty-five. Let me tell you about what young, pubescent Drew dreamed about when Opal used to run around in a short-skirted uniform that only changed when my mother realized both her husband and son enjoyed it a little too much.) Ah, there's Opal now! Alacritous as always. My father once quipped that Opal was the kind of woman who responded *very* well to orders, if I knew what I meant.

Yeah, I did. Which is why I thought it a swell idea to sleep with her when I was twenty. Turns out I can't give her the kind of orders she really likes, though. I daresay I disappointed her. I was pretty disappointed in my younger self, too.

Opal gives me a cursory greeting before standing at my mother's side. She's either really good at never once betraying who in this family she's slept with, or she really doesn't give a shit about me. I can take either explanation, honestly. "What would you like, Mrs. Benton?" she softly asks my mother.

"Bring me some Advil, please." My mother pushes herself up, mimosa sloshing in its glass. "My son is here, and once again he's dressed like a hobo." She inhales that drink. I mean, *really* inhales it. I'm half-expecting orange liquid to shoot out of her nose. At least a very unladylike belch. Not that my mother ever would.

Opal barely offers me a glance before she shuffles back into the main house. My mother searches for an adequate pose for sitting on the settee. Me? I remove my offensive hat.

"If you're looking for your father," my mother begins, "he's out golfing with some basketball player. Could be Phil Knight for all I know."

"Phil Knight isn't a..."

"I know that! You know what I meant." My mother finally looks up at me. Do I look more to her liking without the hat? Hm. Maybe I'll put it back on. I really hate making eye contact with my mother. It's like staring into a vacuous black hole. "So, what brings you back home, my wayward son? Do you need money? Your father and sister pull most of the purse strings around here. All I have is a few hundred in cash. You can't have it. I need it for my spa trip later today."

"I'm fine with money, Mother." She has a hard time accepting the fact I have my own successful business. Really grinds her gears that it has nothing to do with our family. Oh, and I won't tell her what it is I really do. Nobody with the last name of Benton knows, and I intend to keep it that way. All they know is that I run a "consulting firm" up in Seattle. My mother loses interest after that. My sister furrows her brows and demands to know *who* and *what* I'm consulting. My father merely slaps me on the back and starts bragging about his friends. "Thought I'd drop by and make an appearance. You're always badgering me to visit when I'm in town. Well, here I am. Will be here at least a week for work."

"Oh, how benevolent of you to come see your old hag of a mother! The one who *nags* you to visit her when you're in town for more than five days. So sorry we haven't moved to Seattle. Not that I believe you'd come visit me there, either."

Yes, Mother, it's about you. Everything I say and do is an affront. We're out to get you.

Intoxicated

"Whatever. I'd much rather you come crawling back here because you feel some twisted obligation to the woman who had an episiotomy when she birthed you, and not because you're announcing your marriage to some tawdry hooker who's having your bastard baby."

I yawn. Same shit, different day.

"I'm sorry. Am I boring you?" Mother flops back into her seat and motions for me to go inside. "Are you staying for lunch? Dinner? Be sure to let Opal know." She picks up a magazine left open on the ground. After licking her fingers and flipping the glossy pages, she announces that she's having some "me time." That's my cue to get out of her face before she loses her cool and I'm out a really nice hat.

I drag my ungrateful feet into the house where I grew up. My room is still mostly the same from my college days, although I elected to move into a campus apartment instead of commuting from here to Lewis & Clark College in Southwest Portland. Staying with guys I went to class with, threw footballs with, and attending parts with was way more important than keeping my family happy, let alone saving them the thousands of dollars it cost to room and board me across town. Do I regret it? Hell, no. I had two of my favorite girlfriends that were only possible because I lived on campus! Let me tell you, though, I had great fun sneaking them into my family's house for Sunday night dinner. It was the only way to drive it into my mother's head that I wasn't gay – because, for some really weird reason, she told herself that was why I wanted to live with a bunch of guys. (The 24/7 booze and girls wasn't it, huh?)

"Guess I'm staying for dinner," I say to Opal, who is scrubbing down the counters in the house's giant chef's kitchen.

She's not much of a cook, but my mom enjoys Opal's takes on Eastern European and Indian cuisines. Honestly, you get way better if you head east a ways and hit up the local neighborhood eateries, but whatever. My mom's never gonna do *that*. "Otherwise, her highness might have a conniption." I don't mention my father or sister, two people I rarely talk to if I can help it. My mother is enough drama. I don't need my father's golf stories or my sister haranguing me for not getting involved with the family business. She's got more balls than me for it.

Opal flips her wet towel over before giving me a sly look "Only for dinner, Mr. Benton?"

I tell you, she doesn't look a day over the thirty-seven she was when I made the grievous mistake of sleeping with the help. She has to be almost fifty by now. It's rare for Opal to openly flirt with me, but I suppose with everyone but me out of the house, she feels freer to do so.

Not sure how I feel about that, honestly.

"Yes, and it's only me. Afraid my girlfriend couldn't make it tonight."

Opal isn't the only one I lie to about having a steady love life. My parents are convinced I'm dating some Seattle socialite or working class girl at any moment. (As you probably noticed, my mother is *really* convinced I'm paying women to be my girlfriends. Which could not be further from the truth. While I may indulge in the occasional lap dance at the neighborhood strip club, I don't have the patience for shopping for temporary girlfriends around here.) It's better than them thinking I'm single, though. Otherwise, my mother would shove her best friends' daughters in my face, and my father would join my mother in questioning my sexuality. I may be the youngest, but my parents have always been more concerned about my genetic longevity than my sister's. It's honestly gotten worse since she took up the mantle of heir and I've struck out on my own. Granted, everyone in my family knows I like to date around - and they've faced the ire of some of my marks - but I'm half convinced that I'll wake up one day to a priest and a young, virginal bride hovering over me.

Telling Opal I have a girlfriend keeps her from flirting. She merely shrugs, makes note of my comments on the calendar she uses to keep track of family meals, and goes back to cleaning the kitchen. I don't linger.

I don't linger anywhere, really.

The house is a cocoon of memories, every single one wrapped in a fragile shell that could tear at any moment. The gardens are so expansive and immaculate that it feels like a waste to have all this space and no one around to enjoy it. Photographs and paintings on the walls remind me of people I don't like. Extended family who are more concerned with money and status and the soil they tread upon. Animals that are only worth what prestige they bring to the family - pets are not permitted unless they're prized racehorses or show dogs and cats. My father fancied himself a falconer when he had a platonic affair with eccentric, adventuring billionaire Mr. Bradley. (That didn't last long. My father wasn't willing to pack up and hike up Kilimanjaro whenever Bradley felt like it.) You can still see a few remnants of my family's meddling with animals all over the property.

Everything is disposable to them. I suppose I probably am as well.

That's the conclusion I always come to whenever I stroll the property and reflect upon my life. To the sounds of my mother summoning Opal for something or other, I sit beneath a tree and attempt to inhale the sweet spring air. June is around the corner. In a perfect world, I *would* be out there picking up chicks and showing them the summer of their lives.

Instead, I'm professionally breaking hearts. Because why not.

It's a winding path that led me to this point in my life. On one hand, I'm proud of myself for starting my own business with little input from my family. On the other, I'm now in my thirties and spending my time hunting down women like Cher Lieberman and trying to get them to fall in love with me - all so I can hurt them where it matters most.

Why? What has she done to me? I can read reports about her sucking the money and vitality of half the rich men around her, but come on, I know these men. Some of them deserve a little shakeup. They're so complacent with their young girlfriends that they take as much advantage of them as those young ladies do of them. The symbiotic - perhaps parasitic - nature of dating while rich is like that. You never know what women want from you. Men, too, I guess.

I bump my head against the tree and close my eyes. I focus on only one thing, and that's clearing my head.

Unfortunately, the more I try to empty my head of outside thoughts, the more it's invaded with the sly smile of the woman I'm supposed to be destroying with my wallet, words, and cock.

Somewhere in the distance of my broken head is the curdling laughter of Cher Lieberman, the frisky beauty who prophetically bats her eyelashes and draws her finger across her lips. Everything she hurls at me is meant to seduce me, deflect from her shortcomings, and make me give her everything she wants.

I get it, honestly. I get why so many men throw themselves at her the moment she crosses their paths. She probably fell into her

Intoxicated

role as naturally as she grew into her unforgiving figure and learned to flirt from an early age. She's as effortless as a black widow slinking across her web and going for her life-sustaining kill. She's never had to know anything else. I may be on to her – hell, so many of her exes probably saw the warning signs early on and chose to ignore them – but that doesn't stop her from putting a hand on my shoulder and whispering promises of everything I could ever want into my ear.

If you took away the belittling nature and ill-intentions, you would still have a knock-out, gorgeous woman who carefully wields her powers like a sorceress viewing the world from the tip top of her tower. Some women are like that, you know. They're unfathomably beautiful without trying. Angelic beings blessed by good genes. They're hit on by pervs from an early age and either get so knocked down by the system or they prevail enough to become the next queen bee of the social sphere.

Cher Lieberman could have any man she wants. She's *had* any man she wants. She's found them all so wanting that she's made a life out of breaking hearts and getting paid.

I suppose we're not so different. That may be why I find her so fascinating – while acknowledging the danger lurking within her calculating eyes.

You know, if I can look away from her cleavage for two seconds. That's the hard part.

Okay.

Not the only hard part.

You *know what I mean!*

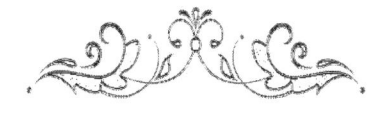

CHAPTER 6

CHER

If there's one thing I hate, it's when a man gets under my skin.

While attempting to get under my skirt, no less.

It's early Tuesday afternoon as I sit in one of my favorite nooks of Northwest Portland. We don't hurt for coffee shops, cafés, and teatime around here. We're a freakin' cornucopia of coffee, for fuck's sake. Pick up a rock and throw it. Bam. You've broken the front window of the corner coffee shop. Probably got someone right in the face, too. Someone either working on their MacBook or doodling in their artbook.

Students? Oh, them, too. Although at this time of year, places are devoid of the O-Chem kids and wannabe computer programmers. It's nice, really. You've got a few locals who come here to chill, and tourists who are tickled pink to see "real Portland." (While you whisper to yourself that this place was on the front lines of city-wide gentrification.) I don't mind either, honestly. When you lead the kind of life I do, it's important to have your sacred spaces. Those corners of the city where you can take a book, your Spotify playlist, or a notepad full of ideas you'll never fulfill. When the weather is a perfect eighty degrees with little to no humidity, you'll find me at the far corner of the patio, where I nurse my favorite bubble tea of the moment and munch on cookies I've smuggled in from the Trader Joe's two blocks away.

Or sometimes I don't bother to smuggle them. I'll brazenly pack my stack back to the patio while the baristas shrug, because I tip and they're not paid enough to care, anyway.

A breeze tickles my cotton blouse that threatens to flutter in the wind. I have it tucked into my knee-length skirt, however. Nothing – and I mean nothing – will cool down my midsection if I can help it.

Fingers thread my hair as I peruse my playlist and think about that blasted Drew Benton. You know, the guy I've been touching myself to almost every night since I first met him? The guy I'm supposed to be having dinner with tomorrow? His address is written down in my phone, so I don't forget. He's texted to ask me what kind of food I like. I don't believe for two minutes he's actually going to cook for me. He's going to order in, and I won't mind as long as he doesn't lie about it.

I also hope he doesn't lie about his intentions. It's obvious he wants to bang me into next week. Based on how much I keep thinking about it, odds are heavy I'll loosen myself up with a little alcohol and go for it. After all, it's been a good, *long* while since I last rode cock for the sake of it and not because it was part of the master plan. Do I remember how to do it? Come naturally, that is. Shit, I don't remember what I sound like when I orgasm during sex with another person. I think I've blocked that obnoxious whine more than one ex-boyfriend complained about from my mind. It's not like I get to hear it much dating the kinds of guys I do. I have, however, perfected my porn star moan. Men love that. Makes the act end quicker, too.

My fingers lower from my hair and drum upon the table. The soft hum of cars driving up and down the street lulls me into a half doze. My imagination instantly wanders to sitting next to Drew on his balcony overlooking the Willamette River, where we'll sip wine and he'll ask me to suck his cock.

Trust me, he will.

Ah, this is what blows about dating, isn't it? Even when I approach it from a genuine mindset, I'm still spoiled by the realities of men. Specifically, men like Drew, who are dashingly handsome and grew up so privileged that they walk into a room and expect women to flock to them. I don't consider myself lucky that he's taken interest in me. Of course he did. I'm exactly the type of woman they go for, and I use it to my advantage. Not to mention, I really played it up when he came to my attention, didn't I?

This is why I take precautions. This is why I call in backup.

Oh, you think I have friends. That's quaint. Even if I did have the kind of friends I could call up and bounce some ideas off, I still wouldn't trust them to give it to me straight about Drew Benton. They would be heavily biased. They'd want me to date him so they can live vicariously through me and hear the salacious stories about his body and how often he wants to do it.

They'd want me to plunder his wallet and take them out for lunch at the trendiest place in town. I would do it, too, because I can be a pushover if I'm in the mood for attention.

Including negative attention.

The door to the patio flies open. Out strolls my contact, a woman who looks as equally glamorous as me when she puts her mind to it. Today, she has. It's probably the sun that has Stella Moore marching in loud leggings, black pumps, and a flowy blouse that announces her to the entire room. Her big sunglasses almost detract from the healthy head of blond hair she currently has pulled back into a ponytail. The giant cloth bag hanging from her shoulder is full of her traveling private investigation business, something I throw money at now and again when I need her to dig into the men I'm dating.

The look on her face is damning, but she's too busy catching herself before she falls on her stiletto pumps. When she finally regains her balance, she sits down at my table with me and begins pulling out her iPad and Moleskin notebooks.

"Afternoon," she says, lifting up her sunglasses. "Absolutely lovely day, isn't it?"

I lean back in my seat, arms and legs crossed. "What did you dig up about Benton?"

"Getting right down to it, huh?" Normally, the good-natured Stella would chide me about my attitude, not that I pay her to do it. Her demeanor suggests that the news in her bag isn't good. I'm *assuming* she has news, anyway. That's what I pay her for. What good is she to me if she does her digging and hacking and comes up empty? I still have to pay her for the time, but what skill is there to speak of? It doesn't count unless I get dirty facts, like his diaper fetish or the ex-wife he's been hiding from me!

Oh, the ex-wife one is my favorite. Right up there with secret baby mamas. Rather hilarious how many of these guys try to hide them from me, thinking I'll be disgusted, but I prefer for Stella or another investigator to tell me long before my boyfriends come confessing halfway through our relationships. That way I can bequeath them a kind smile, a hand to the cheek, and the words, *"I don't care about that, baby,"* on my lips. I come across as an absolute angel because I wasn't shocked into tears or screams of disbelief.

Not that I would be, anyway, but I don't like it when these men catch me off guard. Tell me your dirty laundry up front. Tell me what I'm getting into!

"Let's start with the basics." Stella pulls out a stack of papers, both publicly searchable and the kind only she, a former FBI agent, can access. I really do love looking at my boyfriends' college transcripts. I want to find out who took Gender Studies for the "easy A" but got a fucking C in it. I also want to know who padded their schedule with remedial math and science. Looking at you, millionaire plastic surgeon I dated for two months! "Drew Benton is the youngest child of Cindy and Alexander Benton, of Benton, Enterprises, based out of Beaverton. They've got their hands in every industry you can imagine. Collectively, they're worth a few billion dollars, although your boy will probably only get a few hundred million."

Oh, no, whatever shall I do if I ever become the next Mrs. Benton? Ha! Sure.

"His sister is the one about to take over the company, though." A barista pops out with Stella's to-go order. She thanks him and returns to her files. "After he graduated from Lewis & Clark, Drew struck out on his own. Had a few startups that didn't go anywhere, until he finally landed into something big. Really big. You, uh, should probably know about it."

I raise a concerned eyebrow. "Tell me, is this the one who could check 'drug lord' off my bingo sheet?"

"Nothing like that. Well, nothing illegal. Morally reprehensible? Hmm."

She definitely has my attention now. "Excuse me?"

"Have you ever heard of Benton Leveraging?"

"No, I can't say I have."

"I didn't think so. It's an LLC based out of Seattle. They're commercially classified as 'relationship consultants.'"

There's no way to tell where this is going, and I do *not* like it. "What does this mean? Relationship consulting? Don't tell me Drew is a couples' therapist or something." That would definitely be new. And unexpected. "Or is he living the Hitch life?"

"One of those is *a lot* closer than you may anticipate."

Both of my eyebrows are up now. "I was joking about the Hitch thing." Awful movie. Awful premise. Awful everything.

"Drew is not a Hitch. He's like... an anti-Hitch."

"He's *what?*"

I'm presented with print-outs of a website. "Benton Leveraging" requires a paid membership to gain access to the juicy details of the site. When I look closely at the "Our Services" printout, I nearly gag.

"He's a professional heartbreaker, Cher." Stella spreads out more pages. Some of them are emails of her posing as a Vancouver-based millionaire having problems with his needy ex-girlfriend. Some guy named Brent goes over the same information available on the website while also saying, "*Our guy knows how to get the job done. He has a 96% approval rating from past clients. I'm sure he can help you with your little ex-girlfriend problem."* "Men hire him to fuck up their exes or other women they want 'rid of.' We're talking some really nasty shit." What she brings up on her tablet is from a private forum of women discussing Benton Leveraging. Some are talking about a group lawsuit to sue for emotional damages. "To put it briefly, Drew Benton is a guy creepy exes hire to pump and dump the women they want taken down a peg. Drew has an amazing track record of getting women to fall in love with him and then dumping them in humiliating ways."

"So I see." My hands are shaking. Why? So Drew has an abhorrent business. It's not like I'm in love with the guy. I was merely fantasizing about riding his face for a few days. Now I know he's not someone I'm going to see anymore.

So why am I *really* fucking angry?

"One of his marks from earlier this year was left at an altar in Vegas."

"I *see*." I'm imagining a lost woman standing in front of an Elvis impersonator as she looks around the Vegas chapel, wondering where the man she drunkenly agreed to marry has gone. I'm guessing Drew either returned to Seattle or here. Was this before or after someone hired him to...

Hired him to...

"Who did it?" My hands grip the edge of the table. My knuckles turn white. "Which one of my bastard exes hired Drew Benton to fuck with me?"

Stella shuffles through more papers. The fact she hasn't cracked a single joke, when she usually can't help herself, must mean that she agrees with me about one thing: Drew Benton is beyond an asshole. He's a dangerous slip in society, and he was *this* close to getting his claws in me. If I had been anyone else, someone less cautious than the devilish beauty you see before you, I would be in a world of fucking hurt. I may be continuing to fall for Drew's charms, like so many women before me have fallen for him. Women who were left standing at altars. Women who probably had their bank accounts cleared out. Women, I later discover, led to believe they were pregnant with Drew's baby because that was one of their nightmares come true. The cherry on the shit sundae is the woman who was put on a train to Amarillo, Texas, without any money or a change of clothes. The police report Stella dug up says that the woman was too intoxicated to know what she had been doing, but I know now.

Drew got her nice and fucked up, dumped her, and sent her on her way.

"Jason Rothchild," Stella finally says. "According to what I can find in his website's database, that was the last so-called client to be in contact with him. Well, one who has any connection to you, anyway. I remember doing a search on him for you last summer."

"Jason," I hiss. "That rat *bastard!*"

My voice carries from the patio into the streets below. A small fleet of tourists looks up at us as if we have single-handedly corrupted their young children's minds. Oh, the things I could tell them about the men of this world!

"I can't 100% confirm that it was him, of course, but if it makes sense to you..."

"It does. Jason took our breakup particularly rough." It's been months, though! Months since he sprung a last-minute marriage proposal on me at his family's Christmas party! I can still feel the horror bubbling up inside of me when I think back on that awful moment. Jason had been a lot of things, but impulsive wasn't one of them. This was a man who read every Yelp! review before taking me to dinner somewhere. He also refused to buy me clothes from department stores when he had a "qualified tailor" to make me whatever I wanted. When we went on a weekend trip somewhere, he planned it down to the last second, including where we would stop for me to pee.

So imagine my shock when we were having a semi-nice time at his family's house and he springs *that* on me! Got down on one fucking knee and showed me his grandmother's engagement ring from Germany. His whole family fell into a hush of premature thrills. They really thought I was going to say yes.

Jason thought I would say yes.

In what world would I say yes when put on the spot like that!

That night was our breakup. He took it about as well as you would expect. While I hadn't been planning on breaking up with him *yet,* I thought I had at least a few months left of playing his young girlfriend who put up with his weird pottery hobby and read his awful, *awful* poems. The man seriously thought he was Yeats. More like a fifth grader starting to come into their pubescent emo phase.

Jason ruined a good thing when he asked me to marry him. I could've continued to be that girl who sat in his lap when he watched the news and pretended his aftershave was the greatest shit in the world. I would've eaten his atrocious cooking he tried to pass as edible. I would've pranced around in his favorite color, forest green. A color that is so totally not me, but it always made him happy. When Jason was happy, he upped my allowance and paid my bills months in advance. Shit, he had paid for the first three months of 2019 by the time we broke up. The free ride was the least he could do after embarrassing me in front of his family.

Intoxicated

The thought of him hiring a professional heartbreaker – or, let's be honest, a Pro-Pumper-and-Dumper – to get back at me is both hilarious and mind-numbing. If I'm reading Drew's "menu" correctly, he charges *thousands* of dollars for different levels of services. If he's meant to completely wreck me, it's set Jason back a college education at a half-decent university. You can't tell me Drew, the child of billionaires, needs that kind of money. So why the hell is he doing it?

Besides, you know, being a terrible person?

"Sorry I had to break this to you." Stella sips her tea and hands me my copy of the files. I've already paid her half up front for her to do the work. Now she's going to slip me the remainder of my invoice. "I *really* thought you should know about this. The stuff I unearthed about Benton Leveraging is... woof. It's not illegal, but it should be. I wouldn't be surprised if he posts revenge porn on the internet or is responsible for a woman getting seriously hurt. I know you don't ask me my advice in these things but... stay away from him, girl. He's bad news."

My hands are white from clutching everything like it's about to strangle me. My eyes are wide and wild, searching the street for any sign of Drew so I can punch his fucking lights out. Every inch of my body craves to launch into the stratosphere and scream as if I am more wronged now than I ever have been in my life.

And there you are, daring to think you can judge me!

What I do is *nothing* like what Drew does! According to these papers, that guy sets out to *hurt* women. Whether by breaking their hearts, destroying them financially, separating them from what they love... Jesus, did he really cause one of his ex-marks to lose her dog grooming business because she was too depressed to pay her bills? The only reason this guy hasn't been taken to court is because he has his family's Teflon all over him.

I may not be the shiniest example of women, but I don't set out to *hurt* men. Most of them are angry when I break up with them. Few lash out at the world and hurt themselves. Shit, Jason is the first one I've heard of going to these extremes. Ask me what happened to most of my exes, and within a year they have totally moved on with a new love on arms. Even the guy I thought I hurt the most, a former boss named Preston Bradley, is now going strong with a new woman he's utterly smitten with. To the point that every time I see them around, either in real life or in the social blogs, I want to gag from how lovey-dovey they are.

I am nothing like Drew Benton.

I am also most definitely not going to see him again. Our date tomorrow is *off*, and he can consider himself refunding Jason's precious money.

After thanking Stella for her outstanding work, she takes her leave. I'm left sitting at my table, but instead of perusing embarrassing college transcripts or stupid letters to the editor, I'm beholding the nastiest guy I have ever almost slept with.

Blocking his number should be enough for me, but it isn't. The need to give him a piece of my fucking mind is heavy on my shoulders. Trust me, *I know* that I shouldn't do things when I'm angrier than a cat whose territory has been treaded upon, but I don't think you understand. You've never been in a position like this before. You don't know what it's like to be at this level of mind games and manipulation.

This guy thought he was going to play my fucking game! Only I stand to lose *way* more than he ever would had I played him like I play all the other men in my life!

I chuck the rest of my tea into the garbage and bring up the Lyft app on my phone. I pity the driver about to drive me down to the South Waterfront. He's about to feel my rays of *rage* beaming from my eyes the whole ride down there.

Because while I may have blocked Drew's number, I still have his address stored in my notes. He never, *ever* should have played his hand so soon.

Eat your heart out, Jason Rothchild. You thought I was cruel to you? Wait until you hear about what happened to the man you hired to ruin me.

CHAPTER 7

DREW

"Depends on how serious this guy is," I say into my Bluetooth as I survey my South Waterfront apartment. "I'm not coming back up to Seattle for a meeting until I'm well underway with the current mark." That's right, I don't say their names over the phone. A man never knows who might be listening. "If you hear from the guy in Vancouver again, tell him I could do a teleconference to go over any questions he may have, but I may be a bit delayed in getting back to Seattle. I also have a feeling this current job will take me until the end of June to complete." That's being generous. I'll get into Cher's panties right quick, but don't expect her to fall in love with me. Let alone get her heart broken by me. Yet.

I said *yet!*

Intoxicated

Brent shuffles some papers in the background. No doubt he's currently in our high rise office at Benton Leveraging, where from 10-3 he's answering emails, cleaning the office, and flirting with God knows who on his personal cell. When I'm accepting new clients or in need of backup, Brent is the man who dives deep into research. The man used to be a reporter, for fuck's sake. He knows where to scoop up information like a guy working at an ice cream parlor. "I haven't heard from him since yesterday. You know how these guys are."

"Yes, I do." For every twenty inquiries I get, maybe one guy actually follows through. That's the nature of the game. If it's not the money that freaks them out, it's knowing that I'm about to seduce their ex - whom they probably still love... *probably* – and fuck her up with my cock and attitude. Then out of the men who actually go for it, there's that one weird guy who I'm pretty sure gets off on it. As long as he doesn't send me pictures... well, Brent intercepts those things for me, anyway. "Like I said, keep me in the loop. Depending on how long this one takes me, it may be a while before I head up there."

"How's it going with her?"

I have a second date with her tomorrow. Here in my apartment, no less."

"Sly dog," Brent says with an audible grin. "Not a record, but dang fast."

No, my record is a woman whom I convinced to marry me by the end of our first weekend together. We drove to Vegas, I left her at the altar, and had a very happy client on my hands. He didn't care that his vengeful ex got over it within a couple of months and probably considers herself lucky for dodging a bullet now. He only cares that she got played by a professional player.

"Breaking her heart will take a miracle, honestly. She's more closed than the North Korean border."

"You always say you love a challenge. Especially a hot one, bro."

"Yes. She's definitely hot."

"I *know!* I've seen her pics!"

I shake my head. "Are you about to head home? Let me know if Mr. Vancouver gets back to you. You know I don't like leaving potential clients hanging." Even if it goes nowhere, I'll be damned if they go around badmouthing me for delayed communications.

"Heading home in T-minus ten minutes. I'll tell Rick that you said hi, though you never do."

"You're not lying if I'm saying it in my heart, bro." I lean against my kitchen counter, hand slapping against my chest. "Tell your husband I'm sorry I couldn't make it to his wine tasting fundraiser. Busy with work, as you know." I'm not entirely sure Rick knows what I do. Does his husband share everything with him? Like how I'm the master of bedding women and making them regret it?

Hm. There's something to put on my dating CV.

I hang up and consider my planner, currently spread open on the island counter. My Tuesday - today - is largely free. Tomorrow, I have in big, red letters *CL.* I think we both know what that stands for.

The current plan is to wine and dine her with some of my delectable cooking, not that I've decided what to make yet. Second? Start putting on the smooth moves while coming off as non-threatening as possible. I assume she'll be doing much of the same. I have to look like I'm putting in effort, though. This is a woman who wants to play me. Suck me dry. Make me regret the day I ever heard her blasted, '90s throwback name. Don't ever fall for her façade, though. Cher is no main character of a popular Shakespearean rewrite. She's not inane enough to think "poor people just need more money," although she probably would date her older stepbrother if he had enough money to beguile her.

I wonder how she looks in plaid...

Allow me to confess something to you: I don't really *enjoy* my career. It's something I'm good at. I feel like I have some moral obligation to follow through, and since I don't need the money, most of it goes into breaking even on overhead and ensuring Brent gets to keep his high maintenance house-spouse. The rest goes into charities, some of them I've started in the Portland and Seattle areas. Homelessness, job corps, food banks and the like... if there's one thing I've witnessed in these two cities growing up and striking out on my own, it's that rising real estate costs mean more people in trouble. Good people, I suppose, although I don't ask the people who benefit from my money to pass any bench tests. I occasionally have the urge to buy up otherwise empty apartment buildings and drop the rents on them so people can scramble for a place to live, but every time I start making a move, I'm reminded of how much I hate real estate.

Look at my family. Half of them are running around with dozens of properties beneath their belts, and they're always complaining about it.

You know who else is always complaining, I bet?

The woman who never has enough money or victims beneath her belt.

So, no, I don't *enjoy* what I do. Although it means I sleep with a lot of beautiful women. Half of them are flat-out crazy and I seriously risk my life with my neck sticking out around them. In a natural setup, I would not touch half of them. I might admire them from across the room, but it takes a rare mark for me to almost risk my own heart in the deal. That's only happened once before. The only woman who truly did not deserve what I did to her. Of course, I didn't discover her actual innocence until after the deed was done.

I often wonder what happened to her.

Cher intrigued me from the moment I saw her. It's not hard to understand why she's so good at what she unfortunately does. Even me, *me,* a guy cynical about love and aware of a woman's soul-sucking machinations, looked at her and instantly fell into lust. It helps that she's amazing at playing the vixen of your dreams. Within five minutes of meeting me, she had switched from girl-next-door chic to sexy, up-for-anything cool girl. That's what she sensed I wanted. To be fair, I find it highly amusing.

And damn sexy. Like her.

Cher Lieberman intrigues me unlike any of my other marks. She's whip-smart and can make up shit on the fly. One minute she's an innocent waif in need of a savior, and the next? Ready to rip off my dick and dine on my balls for dinner.

Guess which one appeals to me more?

She's a woman who has never been tamed, not that I believe women can be *tamed*. But let's assume we're living in a fantasy world where everyone is a romance trope and sexual desires always occur in a sweet, safe vacuum. In *that* world, Cher is a rabid, feral she-beast prowling the streets searching for her next victim. She does it to survive, you know. She can't help it. She's like a prodding panther who prowls the night. A succubus, if you will. One who, for some unknown reason, has had to earn her living sucking it out of men.

Intoxicated

What does that make me in this silly scenario? A beast hunter? A supernatural detective? A dog catcher? (Leave the bitch jokes at home, please.) The pussy police?

Nah. I'm only a guy who happens to cross her path and strikes her fancy.

Yet we know how this ends in a romance novel. I catch her, claim her, and tame her with my ridiculously huge and powerful cock. My dick is the balm that soothes her crazed soul and makes her end her terrible streak of vampiric tendencies. We'll settle down in a little Portland bungalow. I'll pump ten babies into her and she'll water the garden while all ten fat little lumps tug on her skirt and gnaw off their own feet. The dogs will prance in jovial domesticity, and I'll bestow my growing family with all of my family's riches.

We'll have so much sex, of course. Because that's what you do in a romance novel. IN, OUT. IN, OUT. COCK, PUSSY. COCK-A-DOODLE-MEOW. Bam. Marriage and babies.

What a beautiful life. One that sounds *really* stupid.

This isn't a romance novel. (Don't tell me otherwise. I have enough strange dreams as it is, and if I smoke the wrong stuff, I'm convinced that This Is A Simulation. Let's not feed into the reefer-induced-paranoias.) This is life. A really fucked up life of mine, but Cher has a really fucked up life for herself. If you think about it, we're almost perfect for each other. If I weren't out to destroy her, and her out to kill my soul, we could have an almost-romance-novel-like relationship.

We would definitely have a lot of sex. Also, if this really *were* a romance novel, it would be the kind where my cock does all the taming and she's never been more sated with her lot in life.

Think we should hold off on the babies. Maybe a dog?

I glance back down at the calendar I've abandoned to my thoughts. Unfortunately, I also catch sight of the tent pitching in my pants. Great. Thinking about Cher - and the fact we'll probably have really hot sex tomorrow, because what I need right now is a mark I want to bang into the horizon - has me hot and bothered. I've already taken care of things once today. Oh, oh, guess who I was thinking about in the shower! Guess whose pouty lips, pretty fingernails, and scintillating cleavage was in my mind? My brain is convinced she's as tight as a vise and loves to throw herself on some dick. She probably growls and power bottoms while she's at it. Ah, yes, power bottoming. My favorite. And a phrase I've learned from Brent and Rick and I'm *sure* I'm using incorrectly by applying it to my heterosexual life.

Geez, it is Wednesday yet?

My phone rings and brings with it a much-needed cold shower. That's my grandmother's number flashing on the screen.

"Hey, Gram," I greet. "How's the chickens?"

I saunter to my fridge to get some ice water. My grandmother, Irene Benton, immediately jumps into conversation. "Don't get me started on the chickens. Dolly has been on my shit list ever since she broke into the house and made a mess of my fine linoleum."

When I say I get a cold shower, I mean I get a frigid blast of icy proportions. In the best way. Because my grandma Irene is the only person in my whole family I like. She's not my blood grandmother, though she raised me like I was. My grandfather went through three or four wives before dying a bachelor. Irene was his wife when I was a little kid, and instead of hiring on nannies to raise me like my sister had been, my parents agreed to let my step-grandmother do most of the rearing. Her divorcing my grandfather when I was a teenager did nothing to stop me from following her to Eastern Washington, where she bought a farmstead and set out to accomplish her dream of being a self-sufficient woman. Not a bad way to use her alimony, if you ask me.

Nobody else in my family acknowledges her anymore, but I consider her to be the coolest person I know. I still spend half my down time at her house. I help with the maintenance, such as building the chicken coop that's *supposed* to keep dolts like Dolly inside where it's safe. There are coyotes and mountain lions all over the Pacific Northwest, and they love snacking on chicken as much as the next meat eater.

"When are you getting your ass back up here?" My grandmother's no-nonsense personality is one of my favorite things. I wish more people were like her in my family. "I need help with the fence again. Damn deer keep knocking it over trying to get to my vegetable garden. Do you think you could help me reinforce it?"

"Absolutely, Gram. With any luck, I'll be able to spare a day or two in the coming week. If you pay me in pot roast."

"I'll pay you in cherry pie, too, if that's what you really want."

"Hell, yes."

"Don't go knocking on Hell's door if you have any plans to get to Heaven."

"Depends who's there, Gram." We've had this conversation a few times before, and it always plays the same way. "If you end up in Hell, let me know so I can meet you there."

Some boys' grandmothers would scold them to the mountains and back for saying something like that. Mine hollers like it's the funniest thing she's ever heard. Let's say my grandma isn't a real church-going type. She wouldn't marry my grandfather in the family church. My dad would later say that the first sign the marriage was doomed was when my grandmother said, "*If I step into that church wearing white, I'll combust into unholy ash.*"

I still think it's funny, although nobody else did.

I'm closing the curtains to prepare for a night out enjoying my down time in a restaurant or bar – maybe catch a movie if I'm really frisky – when someone bangs on my door.

"What was that?" my grandma asks on the other end. "You got the cops at your house?"

A bad feeling creeps into my gut. As much as I hate to say it with my grandma on the phone, a *good* feeling creeps into my cock. Because before I peer through the peephole of my front door, I have a pretty good idea I know who it is.

"Sorry, Gram." I behold the burning visage of a woman known as Cher Lieberman. She's staring right back at me. Is she doing it on purpose? Because she knows I'm meeting her gaze through my peephole? Ooh. Fiery. I'm definitely into this. "Looks like someone's come for a social call. I'll get back to you later about when I can visit."

"Don't tell me it's a girl..." That's the last thing I hear before I hang up on my own grandmother. I toss my phone onto the chair a few feet away. I don't want *any* distractions when I open this door.

To my credit, I pretend to be shocked that Cher is on my doorstep. Let alone a Cher who looks angrier than the wasp who crawled through your open window and never figured how to fly back out again. The apple red of her cheeks is a lovely complement to the red swirling in her black skirt. A baggy black blouse is sheer enough for me to catch the outline of her pushup bra. Why, yes, I'm looking right at her rack instead of her eyes of swirling agony. Can I help it? This woman is only more gorgeous with rage radiating from her. She's playing right into my romance novel fantasies, and I can't wait to break out the whips and collars to tame the mighty beast.

"My, my." I coolly lean against my doorframe, my whole body blocking her from entering. "To what do I owe this pleasure? I didn't think our date was until tomorrow. I would've dressed up if I knew you were coming over."

Ah, she has caught me off guard. Fashion wise, that is. You see, I'm in my complete element. Fitted T-shirt. Old jeans. A belt buckle that is more country boy than city slicker. My mom thought I was a dire sight with that borrowed trucker hat? She should see me now! Because poor Cher is in for a real treat with my faded, ratty, yet oh-so-comfortable hat I bought the last time I drove through Oklahoma. Hey, those Okies make some *nice* hats.

It's the perfect outfit for treating myself to dinner and a movie in a town that doesn't give a shit about how you dress. (Lots has changed in Portland, but that hasn't.) Not so much for wowing a woman who likes her men finely dressed and smelling like a sandalwood supermarket.

Hey, at least we've established that I bathed today...

"Don't fucking play dumb with me." Ooooh, boy. That tone is a new one. Is this the real Cher? Or has she been possessed by a demon? Maybe that fantasy about her prowling through the streets at night isn't too far off. She's got the fangs for it. "You fucking piece of *shit*."

Uh. What did I do?

No, seriously. What is with the 180? This woman was ready to help herself to my wallet the other day. Hell, we were practically boning on the wine bar. Now she's out for my blood? I'm on the verge of death? I'm not entirely sure why I'm speaking in all questions right now?

Oh, fuck, I know why. I'm full of all questions and no answers!

"Is there something we need to clear up?" I ask, feigning innocence. "Hey, if you've got a friend who says I screwed her over or something, I honestly don't..."

There are only two things that can shut me up when I'm enacting damage control. Either she's kissed me...

Oooooor she's slapped me.

I reel against the doorframe the moment I feel the impact of her hand on my cheek. The growl of impertinence that erupts from her lily-white throat has me both excited and scared out of my mind. What the *fuck,* Cher?

Ow! That stings! Did she put some of those claws into it?

"I know who you are, Drew Benton. Or should I say I know about your *company,* Benton Leveraging?"

Ooooh shit.

Ooooh shit.

Look, this is not something I anticipate. Ever. My company may have my name in it, but unless you do some *serious* digging you 1) have no idea it's actually my company, because Benton could be anybody, let alone in *my* family, and 2) you're not going to find out what it's about unless you have a key to my online kingdom. I function entirely off word of mouth. I don't go by my real name to most of my marks. I'm as likely to be Harry Potter as I am Ron Jeremy, depending on who you ask. So it's not like a bunch of my ex-marks are blabbering to each other, as far as I know.

Intoxicated

Even if they were, how could Cher find out so quickly? Unless she's got friends in really high places. Which, if she's been playing this game long enough... she probably does.

"Who hired you, huh?" she snaps, ready to smack me again. "Was it Jason? Jason Rothchild? I bet it was Jason Rothchild."

I'm fucked. I've been made. All the way down to who the sack of shit who hired me was.

"So, uh..." Think fast, dude. She's got you by the balls, and it's *not* to blow them. Although, she's pretty enough for me to keep thinking about her crawling on her hands and knees to get to my cock, her body so famished for mine that I'm as hard as the rod always erecting tents in my pants. Seriously, can you imagine this modelesque beauty in her baggy-in-all-the-right-places clothes? Coming for me? Like that?

I caaaaaan. Heaven help us both.

"I think I better explain," I say.

Something falls on Cher's face. Was it the last of her disbelief? Was she holding out the tiniest bit of hope that she had it all wrong? That she had slapped me for no reason?

Oh, there is always a reason for a woman slapping you, my friend.

"You..." Trembling in righteous indignation, Cher looks like she's about to explode into a million meaty pieces. "You horrid bastard."

Is there any point denying it anymore? I've been made. She knows the truth. To deny it will only make it worse. Besides, if she's made me, then that completely botches my operation. Hey, Grandma, guess who is about to have some time to come visit you and fix your fence? Mr. Vancouver is about to get a personal phone call from me, because I need some work to occupy my time. Rothchild is going to be pissed as hell when I refund his deposit because "mission impossible, dude," but hey, at least I'll have my hands washed of these bared white teeth and two agile hands curling into powerful fists.

I'm fucked!

"I don't know what you've been hearing," I say, touching the stinging spot on my cheek, "but I assure you that I had the purest of intentions when I said hello the other night."

Her eyes widen to unnatural proportions. The breaths hitching in her chest only make me stare at her beautiful breastbone. "You're a piece of shit," she says with punctured breaths.

"What does that make you?" My hands tighten around my crossed arms. Not once do her eyes deflect from mine. "Because if I'm a bastard out to do what you're about to claim I do, then that must make you the insufferable, ruthless bitch of an ex."

"You know nothing about me," she hisses. Shit. Words like that only make me want to kiss her more. Yeah, I have a problem. It's called *wanting to fuck high-intensity women.* I may not be a kinky bastard who plays with whips and chains, but I live to absorb a woman's energy and fling it right back at her. She wants to go soft and slow? I'll be the gentle Casanova of her wet dreams. She wants to feel like a used Fleshlight by the end of the night? Hey, I've done dirtier because the gal was literally begging me to use her until I was too spent to care.

Right now I'm getting some fierce vibes from Cher. If we had sex right now, it would be an explosion of angry, *fuck you* sex.

It's been a long time since I did something as crazy as that. I think I was in Budapest when the girl I two-timed finally got her cunt on me.

Intoxicated

"I know enough about you." Best to be blunt, isn't it? "You're a woman who has for *some* reason dedicated her life to being the worst sugar baby in Portland. You use men for their status and money, and as soon as you're done with them, you black widow their souls. Guess what. You finally pissed off the wrong sugar daddy."

"Rothchild," Cher whispers, before finally turning her head in thought. "Is this because I turned down his proposal?"

"I don't ask those kinds of questions."

"No, I suppose not." Her words are meant for me again, and every one is like electricity to my tender flesh. "You just take the money and ruin lives."

"Are you trying to tell me that *you* haven't ruined some lives?"

"You know nothing about me!" Cher reasserts, as if I'm going to believe her for two seconds. "So stay the fuck out of my life. I never want to see your face or hear your name again."

"Considering the whole operation is compromised, I doubt you'll be seeing me around much. God knows I'm not interested in looking you up more than I already have."

"Trust me, I get it! You only hit on me because you were going to what? Pump and dump me? Did you *actually* think I'd fall in love with you or something?"

"There are other ways to... wait, *pump and dump?*" Gross. "You think that's all I can do, huh? I may have had other plans for you, Cher. If I can't get you to fall in love with me, I'm going for another angle. Maybe I'll suck you dry of all the money you've conned out of a hundred other men. Maybe I'll turn your family against you. See, that's the fun part. You never know what you're going to get from me. Well, except a venereal disease. I keep my shit clean."

You should see her face when I say the words *venereal* and *disease* in front of her. I think she's going to wring my neck.

"You're a spineless cretin," she spits, spine straight, shoulders squared, and head held high. Because she totally has the moral high-ground here. "That's what you are, Drew Benton. A spineless piece of shit who will never amount to anything more than the bum piss on the bottom of my shoe."

"Hey, leave the bums out of this. Most have done less than you in their lifetimes."

She moves to slap me again. This time, I catch her wrist as it flies through the air.

"Cool it," I growl. "Hit me one more time, and I'm calling the cops."

Her useless hand curls and shakes as if she'll never be vindicated again. I have to admit that it's rather concerning how *pissed* she is. I mean, I get it. I'd be pissed, too. But this can't be healthy. There must be something else lurking beneath the surface. I don't know *what,* but...

"Spineless," she spits again. The heat of her skin pummels my palm. Somebody save me. I'm really so pathetic that I keep thinking about throwing her over my shoulder and hauling her to my bed for a well-deserved hate fuck. One I'll probably regret the moment I come, but hey, sounds hot now! "Your balls must be shriveled up into your rectum."

"At least you know I'm good on my word about the thing you ladies *really* care about." Don't think I've forgotten about her feeling me up in the lounge. I had to seal the deal somehow. My name and money weren't apparently enough for her greedy ass. Had to throw in a sizeable dick to make it work.

Intoxicated

Is she flustered? For the apple red of anger has transformed into cherry blossom pink blush. Cher yanks her hand out of mine. Her bottom lip quivers. Is she going to cry?

Oh, God, please don't cry. I can take screaming and smacking, but once my marks start to cry, I lose my will.

Yet this is Cher Lieberman we're talking about. She only cries to get what she wants. She's playing me as we speak. She won't march off until she's had some form of a last word.

"You're so pathetic that I bet you wouldn't keep it up if we did it. I bet tomorrow would have been *really* embarrassing for you."

Wow. That's it, huh? That's her hard-hitting ouchie? Her slaps pack more punch. Hell, her terrible gaze levels me more than a crack at my dick. "You wanna bet?" Yeah, I like to play with fire. Stick my whole hand in the burning flames if I'll get a thrill for two seconds.

"Yeah." Cher is still a shell of fiery rage, but her demeanor has changed. Gone is the *I will fuck you up if you so much as think about touching me*. It has been replaced with *Come at me, bro*. "I bet you don't have the fucking balls to still try to get in my cunt."

My God. Is this my fantasy coming true?

Has the prowling panther come to my door and dared me to tame her?

Or is that another crazy chick meeting my lips as we both dive in at the same time?

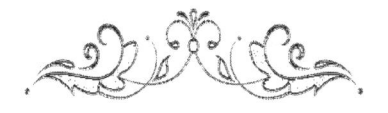

CHAPTER 8

CHER

In my twister of disgusting rage, I've single-mindedly decided that there's only one thing left to do with this giant shitstain.

Fuck him, of course.

The trail of thought that has brought me here has nothing to do with what's *right* and *sane*. More like my stupid pussy screaming at me to take the chance while it's still standing in front of me. In a trucker hat and enough stubble to make my legs cross before I let that shit come anywhere near my waxed nether regions.

But he's also in a pair of tight jeans that look like they've been worn long enough to contour to his powerful lower body. And a shirt that screams he put it on to entice me into his bed.

What can I say? I'm human. I'm a red-blooded woman who, even when she's subjecting herself to mediocre lovers, craves a hard cock now and then. Great if I'm pretty sure it's attached to a guy who can pound for hours. From the way Drew Benton kisses, every piece of him is a cannon ball ready to fire.

I hold onto his biceps and put up an admirable fight against his ruthless kiss. His tongue does not go easy on my mouth. When we're not gasping for air, we're grasping at body parts and simulating the kind of movements we should be doing in bed. Drew thinks he's gonna win by knocking me down with his tongue? I don't think so. I can lick and bite as hard as he can!

This is war, you see? Although he's a piece of shit and I'm a mess of my own, we still have this crazy chemistry between us. The kind of chemistry I haven't experienced in years. Not since I used to date because it was what I *wanted* to do, not what I thought I had to do. Not since I turned this ruse into a career of sorts.

Much like his career probably doesn't allow him much time to bone because it's what he wants to do.

This isn't a pleasure call, though. This is me asserting myself as the dominant force in this town. In the battle of our sexes, I'm coming out on top. I'll Billie Jean King him from here to Hillsboro. Hand me a racket. I'm about to jam it up his ass and turn him into my dancing puppet.

Ooh, I bet he'd like that.

"Get the fuck in here." His growl commands me to stumble into his apartment, where he finally shuts the front door and shoves me up against the wall. I don't think twice about swinging my arms around his shoulders and kissing him with every drop of strength in my crazed body. My legs aren't wrapped around his waist and I'm already simulating the exact motion that will draw his cock into me. For right now, though, I get his hand on my ass and his other grabbing chunks of my blouse.

I think he's going to pull it off. Instead, he grabs my breast and swallows my gasp. I'm rewarded with a hard squeeze that gets me writhing against the wall.

"Fuck you," I mutter onto his lips. Lips I can't stop mauling with my own. He tastes like pity and shame. Pity and shame for me. I guess that's my aphrodisiac today. "I bet you're not any good in bed. You would've been a total waste of my time."

He pins both of my wrists to the wall. One of my knees had begun its ascent up his leg, but I lower my foot to the ground again. "Say that again," Drew goads me. His hand hovers above my waist. I can't tell if he's about to yank up my blouse or pull down my skirt.

Wish he'd pull off my panties and drill me right here.

"I said I bet you're a *shitty* fuck."

His greedy eyes remain locked on mine as he unzips his jeans and lowers his boxers. The front-row seat I get of his hard cock popping out is enough to make me turn into a miserable mess of wanton needs. Really, my mouth should be all over that thing. Not rewarding it with my presence. Oh, no. We don't do *that*. We make that cock grateful to have *me* using every skill I've amassed over the years. I'll hum on that cock until he loses all control and makes me swallow his load. Then I'll get up, take off my clothes, and get him hard again in two minutes.

Yeah, *that* thing doesn't look like it tastes like pity and shame.

"Does this look like it can't give you a good fucking time?" Drew asks, both palms sprawled on the wall behind me. He has me completely cornered. I'm surrounded by his natural musk and that lustful look in his eyes. "You know what really pisses me off, *Cher?*" The way he says my name, as if it's an affront to his senses, turns me on enough to lower my hands from the wall and run them down his chest. My whole body calls to his in ways I can't describe. It's like the core of my being is shaking, shaking, *shaking*, and the only thing that can stop the shudders is *him*. "I was going to fuck you so damn good tomorrow. Was gonna take my time to pleasure every inch of your ungrateful body. I've spent every moment since I first laid eyes on you thinking about how I'm going to fuck you. Now you've thrown all that out the window. Now I have no choice but to fuck you like the succubus you are."

There were a million choice words he could have called me, each one more offensive. Don't get me wrong. *Succubus* and its meanings are pretty dirty, but I'm not offended. If anything, I admire his word choice when all the blood is currently in his cock. I definitely know what he's thinking about if nothing else.

"Don't you know a succubus *wants* you to fuck her?" My nails dig into his throat. My lips are only an inch away from his ear. "You'd only be giving me what I want."

"A woman gets it good and hard," he counters, "but a she-demon gets hunted down."

"Let me guess. Your cock is a weapon?" I don't touch it, but I definitely look at it. If I scoff, will that piss him off? I've honestly seen bigger. Definitely fucked a few bigger than this. But bigger isn't always better. There's a lovely medium between size and skill. He can have one, but I bet he doesn't have both. "How original. You gonna fuck the bitch out of me."

"I wouldn't dream of having such exponential skill."

"You don't have the means to try."

He growls again, and God knows I encourage it by lifting my skirt and giving him a glimpse of my underwear. I don't have to wonder if I'm wet. I'm probably soaked through. He could ram it in right now, and I'd be ready.

Don't tell him that, though. I'm not in the business of inflating his ego.

"If you keep talking like that," he says, a warning in his voice, "I'm not going to give you an out. You'd be begging me for mercy while I split you wide open without a care about it."

Tell me again how much you don't care, Drew. Go on. Convince me you're not ready to roar at the thought of you eight inches deep and exploding like an animal. You might as well fuck me like you think I'm the biggest trash disaster in the world. You clearly think I am! I think we've established that I'm unworthy of any genuine affection or tenderness. Treat me like your nasty sex doll already!

"I double-dare you."

I'm not a prophet. I'm not even clairvoyant. How am I supposed to know what he's about to do? He could pin me against the wall with nothing but his cock and words of clever condemnation. He could throw me on the floor and take me like the bitch he knows I am. Rip off my panties for all I care. Come on my face, if you dare. Make me choke on your cock or choke me with your grip like they do in the skin flicks these days. Be a depraved piece of shit alongside me, Drew Benton. You know it's what you want.

Clearly, you look at me and see a woman made for your pent-up rage and desire. If you're in this kind of disgusting business, you have issues with women. Go ahead and get them out with me. I make an excellent punching bag. Ask any of my exes.

Yes, including the nice ones. Go ahead. Ask them what I deserve.

You know, I was half-kidding when I said he might throw me over my shoulder and pack me off to his bed. Not only did I not think he was *that* strong, but I didn't think he wanted me so badly he'd put in that amount of effort.

I don't let him hear or feel the slightest bit of surprise as I end up over his shoulder, arms dangling down his back and hair clouding my vision. Drew turns around so quickly that I momentarily lose my ability to know where I am. He's knocked my lust all around my body. No longer do only my loins beg for attention. My breasts tingle for him to pinch and taste them. My thighs ache to have him between me, driving himself into the oblivion that is the cunt he knows he shouldn't want so badly. My hands grasp uselessly at the air. Give me something to touch. Give me shoulders to claw and an ass to smack. I'm as feral as Drew is now. There is no love, no sweet desire in what we're about to do. It's raw and emotional, all right, but I wouldn't call it passion. Just two people acting like fucked up children.

He slams his bedroom door shut behind us. When I land on his bed, I realize the curtains are drawn back, the whole of Portland's industrial eastside peering into the window and loving every moment of my debasement. And his. Because don't think for two seconds that I'm the only one lowering myself in this moment.

Drew has fallen hard enough to fuck me, after all. That says a lot about his character.

He doesn't say a word as he tosses his hat across the room and lifts his shirt over his head. Yes, yes, he has chiseled abs and the right amount of chest hair I've fantasized about! There! You happy? He's fucking perfect. A regular ol' Adonis. He's got the fucking V running into his pants, which he has completely unbuckled and pushed down his thighs. In case I didn't get a great look at his cock earlier. Well, there it is. Bigger and harder than ever. I half expect him to command me to suck it like his little golden whore.

Instead, he flips his shirt on top of my head. While I'm struggling to get his sweat-stained clothes off my face, he pulls my hips to the end of the bed and slides his hand between my legs. The movement is so sudden, and I'm so preoccupied with his shirt, that I yelp to feel his finger already pulling my underwear aside and dipping inside of me.

That's it, though. That's the only bit of vulnerability he's gonna get out of *me*.

Bastard.

"Do I have to say it?" His words are methodical, even in their grit. They also sound right in my ear, because his face is that close. So is his finger, in case I've forgotten what I smell or taste like. "You're wet."

"Did you expect anything less?" I snap back.

"Oh ho *ho*. I knew you wanted me, but you're wet enough for me to ram you in the ass."

I'd like to see him try, but that's the one thing I won't goad him to do. Not on a first fuck.

Ha! Like there would ever be another. Maybe I should let him fuck me in the ass right now so I can say we did it. Although I can think of *way* better places for him to shove that cock. Like... maybe two inches farther south?

"Fuck." Because he can't be bothered to actually do it, Drew has to say it. Right when he has his hands on my ass and is ready to drive his cock home. (Lest you think I'm not in the correct frame of mind for this, let me assure you that my thighs are spread and my pussy is flashing a neon sign that says STICK IT HERE.) "Condom."

Intoxicated

Two words that bring me so close to disaster.

I push myself up and round on him before he has the chance to walk to the nightstand. "What's wrong?" I ask, my pettiness dripping from my lips. My fingers travel down the length of his happy trail and grab his cock. Holy hell. It's like holding my favorite sex toy in my hand. Always hard. Always lubed. Always ready to roll me into pound town. "Don't have the guts to go for it? You must be the only guy in town who concerns himself with prophylactics." I have horror stories. For another time.

"All the more reason to go get one, right?" I've got one hand on his cock, and he's got one hand on the back of my neck. His thick thumb rubs the tender spot of my throat. My eyes flutter closed as my head rolls back. His teeth graze my flesh. My thighs are so wet that I'm about to start humping his leg. "I don't know where you've been."

"Yet you can't stop thinking about it." I slowly release him from my grip. "Fucking me raw and senseless."

Both of his hands are on the back of my head now, bringing my face closer to his. The force of his movements has me dropping my bottom lip and preparing for his tongue to make its grand reappearance in my mouth. "That's what you want, huh?" he asks.

My skirt moves to the side with one generous flick of my hand. "I think it's what we both want." When Drew doesn't move to kiss me, I lower my mouth down the length of his torso, never once breaking eye contact as my lips meet the tip of his hard cock.

If I've got one power, it's making men give me *whatever* I want.

It doesn't matter what common sense dictates. Doesn't matter what everything I've learned in health class says. A part of me feels like I deserve it. Enticing this man to fuck me the way we both *really* want is as thrilling as being touched for the first time. I'm usually so cautious about it. Even when I'm lying to a guy and telling him I'm not on birth control because he has an impregnation fetish, you bet your ass I'm keeping a close eye on my IUD. It's not going to save me from the other shit, though, and this is a town full of risks, if you know what I mean. My boyfriends don't get special treatment until they prove to me that it's safe. I know nothing about Drew Benton. For all I know, he goes barebacking through the Park blocks every Saturday night.

We've already established that I think I deserve the risk. That I'm getting off on the idea of his cock filling me up and fucking me until I scream. I put those thoughts in his head as I suck his length into my mouth and revel in the natural taste that makes him a man.

He's still a bastard of a man, but that's only turning me on more right now.

I taunt him with my tongue and goad him with my purrs. My legs spread open on his bed, allowing me to bend deeper and to slowly rub my thighs against the plush comforter beneath my knees. Drew stands at the end of his bed, absolutely mesmerized by my hard-earned skills. He doesn't get to have the upper hand even if this ends with him piled on top of me and roaring into my ear, I'm still the winner.

Or maybe he'll pop in my mouth and prove he wasn't all that, after all. Either way, I win the war.

"Fuuuuck," he moans, and I'm half expecting him to start humping my mouth. But Drew stands stark-still as I have my oral way with his cock. My eyelashes bat at his face as I stick my ass up in the air, skirt falling down my back and enticing him to rip apart my underwear. He doesn't. He's as stiff as statue, even when he grabs a chunk of my hair.

He's deliberating. He's planning. What should he do? Should he give into his animalistic temptations and punish me with his cock?

"*I'd like to see you try,*" I hint with nothing but a bat of my eyelashes. I hope he looks down at me sucking his cock and thinks of nothing but giving me what I *deserve*.

It all happens so quickly.

One second I'm working his whole rigid shaft, and the next I'm yanked off his cock with a handful of hair in his hand. I gasp, both for air and from the sudden jolt of exciting pain rocking through my scalp. When I fall backward, it's not with him on top of me.

He pulls me to the end of the bed again. Before I know it, my underwear is ripped to the side, the tearing of fabric sending shudders down my spine shortly before my pussy's deep, cavernous ache is finally satisfied.

The first slam of his cock is almost agonizing. I thought I was ready, but my position gives me an unnatural resistance, forcing his cock to bury inside me in ways I can barely fathom. When he pulls out, readying to go at me again, I grab the bed covers and prepare for battle.

Because that's what it is. A battle of fucking wills.

I don't anticipate how hard he'll slam into me. I fly forward, a scream of *something* falling from my lips - and directly into his hand, which quickly finds my mouth.

He can try to silence my moans all he wants. I know how to make sure he acknowledges how much I love everything he throws at me.

It's a gamut, all right. Drew's relentless thrusts crash deep inside of me, with only his other hand to hold my hips in place so he can *take me,* damnit. The rising release of lust tearing apart his chest gives me all the strength I need to fuck him back, my ass slamming against his hips in a noble effort to make him come completely undone. One of his fingers slips between my teeth and rests atop my tongue. As the sound of our bodies slapping together fills the air, I wrap my tongue around his finger and practically rip his comforter apart.

I don't give Drew the satisfaction of praising his cock or making him think I hate this. Both are too extreme, and *not* what a bastard like him deserves. No, what he's going to get is my unending drive to claim his cock. He doesn't have to rub my clit or pinch my nipples to make me come. Not that I'll give him the satisfaction of coming!

You see, that's the game. I may have a filthy rich and damn handsome man fucking me like we're in the middle of the woods, but *I'm* the one with the cards here. He's going to give me what *I* want, which is his ultimate demise in the bedroom. He's going to come. I don't care where. Drew will spill his seed and forever know that I did that to him. Me, the woman he was hired to seduce and destroy, as if I never had the power to wreck his ego.

Meanwhile, I shall commit the powerful way he fucks to my memory, because this is one of those once in a decade bangs. The kind that will leave me sore for the next few days, because once Drew has you where he wants you, best believe that your ass will be hitting his stomach until he's done.

God. It feels so fucking good.

I don't completely lose it, though. His cock grows thicker inside of my tightening walls, but I refuse to come. The bed hits the wall. Our bodies create the cacophonic sounds of sex. I don't doubt that we're a seriously hot sight as I brace myself against his bed and tongue his fingers. When his hand moves from my hip to my hair, however, I steel myself for the inevitable purging of his need to fuck me.

"Shit." That's angry defeat in his voice, but it has nothing to do with exploding within me. Oh, no. Instead, Drew pulls out, leaving the gaping, dripping hole that is my pussy behind. I catch exactly one breath before he rolls me over and looms over me.

He's much more intimidating like this, I have to give him that...

"Had enough yet?" he asks through a sadistic grin.

I can throw that right back at him. "Never."

My blouse flies up my torso, wrapping behind my head but still holding my arms together. Drew tears down my bra, hard cock pressing against my aching slit as I moan and reach my pelvis for his. His jeans are on the floor. The last of my dignity is about to join it.

"You look fucking good with your cunt full of cock." Drew yanks on my blouse pulling up my head and torso. The movement is only matched by his thrust into me. Instantly, my eyes roll back in my head. Fucking missionary position. I'm a sucker for it with the right man. Namely, a man with a big dick who knows how to use it. "Especially my cock. Spreads wide open for me, you know that, Cher?"

I prove his point by stretching my legs wider. He sinks a little deeper, not that it's easy to tell through the steady rhythm of his thrusts. I can seriously feel it now - orgasm, creeping closer and closer to my mind. It's rare for me to come from *only* penetration, but Drew's determined strokes and my brain convincing me that this is the hottest sex I've ever had are making me want to suck him dry. Oh, we *know* this isn't over until he comes so hard that he can't go anymore.

"You like it, huh?" My voice only betrays the slightest bit of a moan when I speak. "How does it feel? Like the best pussy you've ever fucking had? Will the bitch who figured out who you are be the one who..."

Drew pushes me back down, pinning my shoulders as he tortures me with long, languid movements of his cock. I refuse to cry out in pleasure. I'll get wet for him. I'll suck his fucking cock. I'll tempt him until he's driven to fuck me raw. I won't confirm what he already knows I'm feeling.

"Be the one to what?" he teases me. "To take my cum?"

"Oh, you'd *love* that, wouldn't you? Not that you have the fucking balls to do it."

I can feel his balls slapping against me right now, thank you very much. They're heavy enough to shake my ass with every impact. Delightful enough for me to rest my feet against his shoulders. He doesn't look twice at them.

"You're going to come for me, Cher." Drew picks up the thrusts, each one driving a little farther into the pits of my blackened soul. "When you do, you'll have no choice but to take every fucking drop."

"You don't have the guts," I continue to chide. "You don't dare to come inside me."

Of course, that damage is already done, thanks to precum and the like. I'm sure enough of it already drips inside of me, making way for the mighty orgasm about to bring Drew on top of me. Oh, I would die to feel it, too. The ripples of his cock as it bursts into the core of my being would be like ascending to a blissful plain. It's not something I regularly indulge in. Drew? The man who was going to do this anyway under the guise of loving me? He can go to Hell, and he can take me with him.

"If you don't want me to..." Drew kisses me, and I'm so happy about it that I fall back on my elbows and invite him down to nip my breasts. "Then don't come. As simple as that."

"You really want me to suffer."

"You saying you don't deserve it?"

I say nothing, actually. All I have to say is expressed through my trembling legs and the sound of my pussy getting punished.

Drew's not going to rest, though. Like an idiot, I let him shove me down and lean over me like he's about to rip out of my throat.

No, he's silencing me with his hand while going hard at my cunt.

If there's one thing that *will* make me come during sex, it's a man who knows how to take total charge while still thinking of my pleasure. Drew pounds me like he'll never have the fortuitous chance again, but he does so with the finesse of a man who is used to pleasuring women with his cock. He makes consistent eye contact that only inspires me to look back at him, daring him to play his hand. My toes curl over the edge of the bed. My lips beseech his. When he kisses me one last time, it's with his hand wrapping around my neck, a bold move that simultaneously gets me off and makes me understand whose bed this is.

Drew's cock is so thick with cum that it beelines straight for my fucking G-spot.

That's it. I'm a goner. Say goodbye to that small shred of dignity. My eyes have completely rolled back, and I'm gagging on my own breaths to get across how much I live for this. The man.

The sex. The wave of triumph I indulge in when Drew gently rubs my clit and makes me come so hard that I'm screaming incoherent sounds into his hand.

I'm convinced he's going to come. Yet after two hard waves of orgasm, I'm flat on my back and so wet that Drew almost struggles to stay inside of me. Lest I think him inexperienced, he tugs on my hips again, hands on my breasts as he's given unprecedented access to my pussy.

My orgasm subsides. He's still fucking me.

I suddenly realize what the *fuck* I'm doing.

You know how they say men have instant regrets once they come? We women aren't so different! I've come hard enough to knock myself unconscious, and now I'm staring into the triumphant grin of a man I detest about to fill me up and do God knows what else.

I let the tiniest shred of doubt creep onto my face. It doesn't matter I'm quickly getting fucked into another climax. I know what Drew is about to do, and my twisting toes and humping hips betray what I really think about it.

"That's right." His smug grin eats right through my soul. I want to protest. I want to tell him to stop, to get off me, to stop fucking me so damn good. Yet between the newer, harder orgasm about to hit me, and the realization that this is what I probably deserve, I stay silent outside of a few pitiful squeaks. My lip is beneath my teeth. My helpless hands grab at the air. I must look so pathetic, with my skirt up around my waist and my blouse looped behind my head. My tits are bouncing like we're riding cowgirl, but no. Drew is piledriving into me, and he's so damn hot doing it that I think I'll close my eyes and silently scream. "You fucking came," he continues, "so now I get my reward."

Intoxicated

It all comes undone. My brave face. My determination to win the war. I realize he's the winner. Any number of my exes could be watching us and laughing into their piles of money that a bitch like me is completely at the mercy of Drew Benton's cock.

He draws it out as much as he can. Every other word out of his mouth is about reminding me of what's about to happen. I get one hand loosely around my throat while the other pins down my hip so he can come to a still, back arching and cock so engorged that I'm completely entranced by his sweaty visage ready to thunder its triumph.

Drew's got me right where he wanted me all along. On my back, on his bed, legs spread and pussy drinking his cum.

The first wave shocks me to the point you'd think I had never done this before. My nails hopelessly claw at his chest as I let out my pitiful wails of defeat. I'm so seduced by the sensations that come in the rolling waves of a long, happy climax that I beg him to keep fucking me after he's emptied himself. His victorious gaze never leaves me as he swirls his hips between my legs and slides his tongue into my mouth. A satisfied sigh falls down my throat.

"Tell me how much you love it," Drew says.

I shudder. "I fucking love it." I don't recognize that whiny voice. It's definitely not mine.

Slowly, he pulls out, admiring his handiwork. I completely give in to the bed beneath me. Every drop of shame within me is only matched by the seed gushing out of me.

To add glorious insult to injury, Drew gives his cock one tug and shoves it back in. The mighty growl launching into the air matches the unnatural way his seed continues to spill out of me.

He's not going to let me go. Not until he's good and sure that I know what a slut I am.

CHAPTER 9

DREW

I pound this stake into the earth like I pounded my dick into that woman three days ago.

BAM BAM BAM. Witness me hammer a piece of freshly cut wood. The dirt splits open, bits of leaves and soil flying everywhere as the stake goes in a little bit deeper each time. Watch as I keep thinking about sex. *BAM BAM BAM.* That's about to be my thumb between hammer and stake.

A whistle flies out of me once I realize I'm about to kill my left thumb. Stepping back and wiping my hand on my jeans, I bend over and attempt to reclaim my breath. The fresh country air is heaven to my lungs, but it's not clearing my head the way I want. I'll be a lucky bastard if I can stop thinking about Cher for

Intoxicated

two seconds. The whole reason I'm out here in the middle of Nowhere, Washington, is so I can get away from *her*.

And to help my lovely grandmother, who has lost another chicken since this portion of her fence went down last week. She doesn't rely on the eggs to live, but I have a soft spot for animals, especially those that meet untimely ends because my jerk ass couldn't get here faster to fix a damn fence.

The real reason I'm near Onalaska, though, is so I can get the hell away from Cher. I haven't seen her since Tuesday afternoon, when she showed up and dared me to fuck her, but she's been haunting my dreams and appearing on the back of my eyelids every time I close my eyes. I want to blame it on the mind-blowing hate sex we had. Anyone else, and that's what I would say changed my perception of sex for a whole week.

Cher is not "anyone else," though. She's on a whole 'nother level of mindfucking existence. She's not merely a succubus out to suck me dry of my vitality. She's out to *destroy me,* like I was out to ruin her. Except there's no pay day in it for her. She flew by my apartment to chew me out, rip me open a new asshole, and to sink her teeth into my jugular the moment I came deep inside of her *holy shit fucking hot pussy like God damn.*

The hammer plops to the ground. I slowly stand up, crack my back, and shake my head. Sweat beads down my forehead. The old trucker hat - this one black and red, or at least I think it was always meant to be *red* and not some other color - clings to my hair. I sit back in the dirt. Arms wrap around my knees as I let out a sigh between my thighs.

Guess who's hard! Again!

A man can't touch himself in his grandmother's house. It isn't done, though this will be my second night camping out in my grandma's guest room. I can jack off all day in my childhood home, though. Shit, that's where I learned to do it! But in my grandma's little farmhouse, with her CPAP machine whining two doors down from me? I'd rather die, thanks.

Maybe I came here to suffer, not to get over Cher. Plague my imagination with memories of her tight cunt and the feisty snarl painted across her face. The way she demanded I fuck her though we clearly detest one another on a spiritual level was so hot it's a miracle I didn't come sooner than I did. I give credit to the round I had with myself in the shower before she came to my door. It's great for stamina.

"Is the fence done yet?" my grandmother's voice booms from the porch. Birds clear from the trees around us. A bee buzzes away. The screen door slams behind my grandmother's petite but hardy body. She wipes her hands on her apron and gives me her best scowl. "Why are you sleeping in my yard? That fence isn't fixed!"

No, Gram, it sure isn't!

"Had to take a break!" I lift my head to shout back. "Almost hammered my thumb!"

"You've got balls for brains or something?" She throws her hands up toward the clear blue sky. "Meanwhile, Henrietta is over here wondering where her best friend Lucrecia went. You know what happened to Lucrecia? *SNAP!* Right into the jowls of a coyote!"

"I know! Taking a break, that's all!"

My grandmother grunts something at my expense before going back inside. I roll onto my side and stare at the expansive woods growing on the hillside behind my grandmother's house. A few wisps of smoke announce that neighbors are burning

Intoxicated

something or other. The scent of pollen makes me grateful for my allergy medication.

This should be the perfect combination for clearing my head. I get to express myself in building my grandmother a new fence! You know me. I like to get crafty. And handsy. And be outdoors as much as possible, especially if I'm outside the cities.

Why isn't it helping today?

Lord help me, I know why. Her name is Cher Lieberman, and she hasn't left my thoughts for three whole days.

When the regret settled in after our hookup, she stole into my bathroom while I pounded my head against my pillow and chastised myself for being an absolute *idiot*. Nice and dumb of me to fuck her raw. Then I had to go and come inside her? I don't care if it sounded really hot at the time. That's *not* how I usually roll. Don't get me wrong. Like most men, I love a world of condomless sex. Only if that condomless sex comes with trust and sexual safety, though. I've been around the block enough times to know what's out there. Seen more than one of my idiot friends get infected with God knows what because they convinced their girlfriends to leave the condoms in the nightstand. I should have insisted, instead of letting my happy dick do the damn talking. What does he know! His motives are completely against mine. I learned that the hard way when I slept with my family's maid. One twenty years older than me, which I thought was tragically hot at the time. Now I'm embarrassed.

Like I'm embarrassed about Cher.

When she came out of my bathroom, it was with downcast eyes and tail tucked between her legs. We didn't say a word as she grabbed her bag, checked its contents, and hauled ass out of my apartment. I haven't seen or heard from her since.

But she's been in my dreams. I wonder if I'm in hers?

Why would I care?

Don't ask me why she haunts me like this. I think we can agree that she's a toxic lay, and that's being *nice*. Cher must not think much of either. I can't believe I was made. Not only does she know who I am, but she might tell other women about me. Whatever she did to find out about my company? Props to her. Usually, most women chalk up my dirtbaggery to me being the privileged asshole that I am deep inside.

Privilege my grandmother loves to smack out of me.

"You want this nice, cold ice water?" I hear my grandmother's voice before I feel the freezing cold water on top of my head. I leap up, hooting like a man who has pressed his hand against a hot stove. Instead of fire, however, I've got ice cubes going down the back of my shirt and drenched bangs pressed against my forehead. My hat is so soaking wet that I rip it off and toss it onto the sundrenched porch. My grandmother chuckles before turning her back on me. "Then get back to work!"

There's always something to be said for a cold shower.

I finish the fence shortly before dinner. Grandma serves up chicken fried steak, potatoes, and steamed corn that quickly finds its way into the depths of my potatoes. She's generous with the gravy, and loves to call me her "growing boy" although I'm an age where I should be watching what I eat instead of chowing down like I'm fifteen again. Irene Benton has the best home cooking this side of the Canadian border, though. She often fought with my grandfather's cooks to get more control in the kitchen. Sunday dinners were always cooked by her. That was how I came to appreciate *real* food made of grit and sweat. My parents prefer their personal chefs to be Italian superheroes, and while I love me

Intoxicated

a mean lasagna, I'm not as big of a fan of oysters cluttering up the pasta sauce or "freshly picked oregano" getting stuck between my teeth. I'd rather have a big pot of simple spaghetti and meatballs. I don't care if the meat is beef, pork, or turkey, nor do I care if someone named Mrs. Dash helped season it.

"I've got that cherry pie I promised you for dessert." Grandma is all smiles as we eat dinner. She lives for me chowing down like that boy she helped raise. Meanwhile, I'll forever remember her pouring ice water on top of my head. To be fair, Henrietta was appreciative of me fixing the fence so she doesn't have to worry about imminent death. When I fed the chickens shortly before dinner, she came right up to me and clucked against my leg.

Chickens are adorable. I'd take one home with me if I thought my mother wouldn't have a cow, instead.

"Not sure I'll have room for pie after I finish one of your amazing dinners, Gram." Props to me for saying that with a full mouth *and* not choking. Water washes down whatever I can't immediately swallow. "This is really good."

She's never minded the fact I'll speak with my mouth full. The only one in my family. People wonder why I love her so much.

"Growing boys need food. You'll find the room, son. Besides," my grandmother takes a small bite of her own cooking, "you've clearly got something on your mind. You usually finish your work in record time. I tell you, in another life, you would be a helluva contractor."

I've thought about it. I'm much happier building things than tearing people down.

"Work's been a bit nuts lately," I admit. "My most recent client has sent me on an impossible mission. I've gotta figure out a way to let him down and refund his money."

My grandmother doesn't know what I do. She only knows what the rest of my family does, which is that I have a "consultation" business in Seattle. Grandma never had much to do with her ex-husband's businesses, so I can get away with vague statements and using business jargon to make her eyes glaze over and the questions stop. That doesn't mean I don't occasionally have a rant about what I put up with. Especially if that something includes an impossible woman named after an old pop star.

"What makes it so impossible? Thought you said there wasn't anything you couldn't 'conquer.' Your word, by the way."

Thanks for the reminder, Grandma. "Sometimes you get so good at your job that they throw you a crazy curveball." Ah. Yes. Crazy curveball. Excellent way to refer to Cher. "Anyway, it's not going to work with the current client. I have to figure out how to let him know. I rarely fail, you know. So it's hard on my ego."

"At least you can admit it. Unlike your grandfather, who saw his failures as the perfect opportunity to invest more money into hair-brained schemes. Did I ever tell you that he took my inheritance and squandered it on a horse at the racetrack?"

"Yes, Gram."

"Still haven't forgiven him for that, and he's dead now." Her cackle startles me mid-swallow. You wouldn't guess that my grandmother is twenty years younger than my grandfather, but then again, you wouldn't guess that my mother is in her sixties. Has nothing to do with plastic surgery in my grandmother's case, though. She simply has the best genetics you've seen. The woman is well into her seventies and not about to quit the farming, country life. "So if you can admit that you've failed and it's time to step back and move on... well, maybe there's hope for you yet. By the way, I take credit for that."

"I definitely think you play a part in it, Gram."

"So, you've got a decent girl yet?" Boy, does she know how to jump right to the next topic sure to neuter my mood! "Last time I asked, you were seeing some blondie who could barely string a sentence together. One of these days you're going to want to settle down and realize you're surrounded by idiots, because that's all you've attracted in your life."

I chuckle. Naturally, my thoughts turn to Cher, who is somewhere in Portland right now picking her next mark. It's Friday night, after all. She's got my dick out of her system and is ready to shine her deadly star onto some poor sod who won't see her meteorite coming. "I saw someone real briefly. Lasted about a week. Last week, actually."

"She must be special if you have the balls to tell me about your most recent hookup."

I want to rebut that she was *not* a hookup, but I would be lying. I'm not sure if I would call what happened with Cher a *hookup*, per se, but we definitely had sex. That was definitely my dick pummeling her against my bed, and that was definitely her humping her hips against mine and her voice daring me to do the nasty.

I shovel more food into my mouth before my grandmother can see me blush.

"She was definitely beautiful," I mutter. That's the second thing that will haunt me about Cher for the rest of my life. That raven-black hair was as silky as I imagined it. Her figure was both impossibly perfect and carrying enough realism that I could tell she never had anything done. Those tits! Jesus! Have a pair ever bounced from the force of my hips like that before? *No!* I can't decide what was hotter. Cher unable to hold back her orgasm, or that defiant face she gave me every time I suggested we might be enjoying it. "Even for my standards."

"You dating beautiful women isn't new. I keep telling you it will get harder when you're older, but by then those lovely ladies will only be dating you for your money. Right now you've got good looks and that smarmy charm going for you. It'll be slimmer pickings and more obvious floozies flipping through your pocketbook soon enough. Trust me, once you hit thirty, the rest of your life starts coming at you like you've never believed. I'm still convinced that I was thirty-eight only last November."

"I wasn't born yet when you were thirty-eight..."

"Uh huh."

That's all she says before she goes back to her meal. I'm inclined to join her, although I've swallowed so much water I need to get up and refill the pitcher. Grandma barks at me to make sure the faucet filter is turned on. I wave that I was about to do that.

When my waist hits the counter, I remember what it was like to bend that brat over my bed and fuck the fight out of her.

I also remember what's so embarrassing about it now.

"You've got a look on your face that says you're a big ol' idiot, and you know it." My grandma points her fork in my face before shoving it back into her potatoes. "What did you do? It was that girl you were telling me about, wasn't it?"

"Something like that." I keep my nose pointed to my food.

"Didn't knock her up, did you?"

"I sure hope not, Gram."

"I wouldn't put it past you. You boys are more careless today than you were back in my day. You have all these birth controls and STD tests at your disposal, but do you do anything to protect yourself? Noooo. You keep leaving it on the women, and God knows half of them are too stupid to know the way to the nearest clinic these days. At least my generation can take the flak for some of that. You should've seen what your mother was telling your sister back when you were teenagers. Did you know that her big safe sex talk amounted to '*Don't do it, you hussy!*' Worked really well for your sister when she was dating three boys at once. That's why she came to me when she thought she might be pregnant and didn't know who the daddy was."

Wow. I learned a lot more than I ever wanted to know about my sister. Gross, Gram.

"You wrapping up your Johnson, boy?"

My fork clatters to my plate. "Come on, Grandma! We're eating dinner."

"I'm not going to your funeral in ten years because you contracted some incurable disease. I don't care how much money you've got. You're an idiot if you think you can inject your Benjamins into your bloodstream and fight off viruses like that."

"Sometimes I can't believe the things you say..."

"Sometimes I can't believe I raised such a stupid boy."

"Did not realize that was an admission of guilt," I almost snap at my grandmother.

"You wouldn't be handing your grandma so much snark on a platter if you didn't have something to hide. Jesus. Did I not raise you better than your father could? I know that dolt was telling you to keep your willy to 'good girls' but I had half a brain to give you the condoms I knew you weren't carrying in your empty wallet. Come on! If you're not out there knocking up some girl and getting your life in a tizzy, you're ending up in a coffin because the syphilis rotted out your useless brain!"

"I don't have syphilis!"

"You know that for a fact? Because I know what syphilis does to a person. I've seen it for myself. Ask me what I was doing in 1973. Go on. Ask."

I'm not going to ask her what she was doing in 1973. I'll probably get a long, drawn out, dramatic story about living in some Californian city full of STDs like syphilis, gonorrhea, and the clap. You know, wholesome stuff. My grandma has a little history in nursing, so I bet it was at a clinic where she got these first-hand accounts of syphilis and the like.

Good gravy. Did I really think about the word *syphilis* that much in so little time? That's a great way to kill the hard-on that keeps popping up every time I think about Cher.

"Wrap it up," my grandma says with finality. "Think of it as giving your lucky lady a very special gift she *might* get to unwrap one day. For the both of you."

Whatever food I was about to put into my mouth now ends up on my plate. We're lucky the stuff in my stomach doesn't chase it.

CHAPTER 10

CHER

There is nothing shameful about what I've done. That's what I tell myself – *and you* – as I hold my head up high, don my sunglasses, and stroll into the clinic on the corner of Walk and Shame.

Wait. I said that there was nothing shameful about it. Huh. Not my fault if these streets intersect and that's where the sexual health clinic is. I didn't lay down the grid that makes up Portland. Nor did I name them. If I had, I would've renamed half the Alphabet District. We're living in an age where Stark Street has become Harvey Milk Street. Anything is possible.

Like me committing a huge sexual snafu and now needing the expert advice and testing of some of Portland's most competent physicians.

Look, we all know I screwed up. Fucking Drew wasn't bad enough. Oh, no. I had to go and get off on the Bareback Extravaganza complete with Bonus Creampie for dessert because I don't love myself, probably. You know, the kind of thing you fantasize about late at night, alone in your bed, where you press a vibe against your clit and moan into your pillow?

Ah. Okay. Tough audience. I see that I am literally the *only woman who has ever done that.* Uh huh. Sure.

I hope you enjoyed your voyeuristic journey into the dumbest sex I've ever had. What turned you on more? Watching me get pounded into submission while a jerk like Drew Benton fills me up like he's getting ready to decorate a cake? Or was it those rippling ab muscles that flexed every time he slightly moved to the left or right? Let me guess. The hot part was watching me realize what a mistake I had made.

Well. We're moving on from that. After nearly a whole week of beating myself up and deciding what to do next, I've concluded that the best way to move on is to get a clear conscience before I jump back into dating. Most of my really rich boyfriends require an STD test up front - depending on how worldly they are, anyway - but I don't know when the next jackass will be. So. Here we are, putting my insurance to work.

It's the kind of clinic that goes out of its way to make everyone feel *safe* and *comfortable.* Pillow cushions are strapped to the chairs. Tasteful pamphlets are organized by color in a large display beneath the TV playing *Friends* reruns. While Phoebe prances about in yet another example of exquisite '90s fashion, two women fill out their forms, one of them biting their nails while the other looks like she's about to get the worst pap smear of her life. I'm not due for one, and I tell the receptionist as much as she hands me my forms and I give her my insurance card.

Every time I turn around I'm met with the picture of a baby. Either the super pink, wrinkly newborn kind, or the happy, fluffy, three-month olds that smile because they have so much shit in them they're about to gleefully explode in streams of baby diarrhea. At least the demographics of these babies has improved over the years. Whether they're white, black, or Asian though, they're all exhibiting the same big, round eyes, puffy cheeks, and happy demeanors that are meant to make sure all feel safe and warm.

Gag me with a spoon. Or, better yet, gag me with the clinic pen I'm about to ram down my throat as I prepare to construct an extensive list of my family's health maladies.

Father's side: strokes, testicular cancer, and dementia. Mother's side: narcissism. What do you mean that doesn't count? Fine. High blood pressure. Are you happy now, doctor?

I finally lift my sunglasses up my head so I can read the small print. Of course, now that I'm answering questions about my period - due in three days, hooray, me - past sexual experiences, and concerns I have about my health, I'm thinking about everything that could possibly go wrong. What if Drew Benton is such a man-ho he's infected me with God knows what? What if I'm - *gasp* - pregnant? Doesn't matter, because I have an IUD. We'll leave it at that.

Still, even if I can rationalize that I'm fine and this is simply for eternal peace of mind, I chew my nail like the woman next to me and pray to God that I'm not being punished for sexual idiocy. I have to ask myself if that fuck was worth it, you know. Say I've got chlamydia. Would the treatments, side effects, and sheer embarrassment I carry around be worth that lay? Will I look my doctor in the eye and say, "*Yeah, totally worth it!*"

We both know I want to say no, but dignity tells me I should say yes. It's the principle of the thing. I was wound up. Drew is - was - hot as hell, especially when he whipped out his beautiful cock. My anger manifests into horniness when I'm ovulating, which I'm pretty sure I was doing, or at least finishing when I marched over there. I'm a real riot after reading the political news. As soon as I calm down, I'm liable to hop on a guy's lap and scream how good it feels to get the rage fucked out of me.

We'll go with that.

I'm still trying to understand my thought process last week. When I got home, doggedly defying what had happened, I went straight for the shower and had a good, long soak. Instead of distracting myself, however, I kept replaying those fifteen minutes in my head. From the moment I kissed him until I felt the rush of his heat inside of me. *Boom. Boom. Boom.* One instance after another, each one hotter than the last. I don't know how a woman can be both sexually satisfied for a whole week *and* absolutely abhorring herself, but that's been me. I'm sure it's some kind of punishment that I deserve for being a whore.

The buzzer on the door alerts us that the receptionists have let someone in. I continue to mind my forms before I'm called back with them half-finished. With any luck, I'll be swabbing a Q-tip in my vagina within twenty minutes.

I'm slightly surprised to hear a male voice murmur to the receptionist. Riiiight. Some men are bright enough to come to these places. I hear they do great deals on cock-checks. What are they called again? That thing where they stick a finger up your ass and check the ol' prostate? There's nothing like a guy who will give you a tour of his prostate. Then again, depends on how the guy wants you to do it. I had an older boyfriend a couple of years ago who only got off on pegging. Luckily, I make a decent Domme, although I would never charge for it. When a guy wants me to scream at him and call him *sissy* so he can come, I'm inclined to indulge.

Honestly, if I were to become a dominatrix, it would definitely be the financial kind. That may be something I look into as I age out of being good sugar baby material.

The form asks me for my insurance number. Again. I *just* put my card away, so that means slamming the clipboard into the empty seat next to mine and digging through my purse.

I happen to catch the eye of the guy who has sat across from me.

Jesus. He looks a lot like Drew.

I shake my head, convinced that I've lost every marble rolling around in there. After I grab my insurance card, I heave a mighty sigh and pick up my clipboard. *1469...*

I look up again.

Drew looks back at me, clipboard in hand.

There are moments in life that are too ridiculous to believe, aren't there? Was it *really* not bold enough of the universe to throw this asshole in my direction in the first place? Now he's at the same STD clinic as me? On the *same fucking day?* It's Monday. It's literally been a week (well, minus a day) since I told him how much I loved the feeling of his dick inside of me. Bursting with cum, no less.

We maintain relentless eye contact. I pull my Starbucks drink out of my purse and give it a hearty sip. We'll pretend he's not thinking about me blowing him again.

"Cher?" A woman in scrubs steps out from the back room and looks at every feminine face before her.

I can't leap up from this chair quickly enough. I don't even fuck with Drew's head by sauntering past him, ensuring that my skirt swishes. Get me the fuck away from him.

I'm still not convinced he's an apparition. Then again, maybe he is, and that pot cloud I walked through to get here really fucked up my perception of the world. That was another scruffy Portland guy in flannel and a trucker hat. *God damnit I slept with a guy wearing a trucker hat.* Sorry. Had to get that out of my system. You know how it is. One moment you're following a logical train of thought, and the next? You've derailed into Ohshitsville.

I'm weighed. I swab. I pee. I answer invasive questions that ask me about who I'm seeing, who I've slept with, and whether or not I think I'm in any danger. Yes. Danger. Does, "*My pussy is out to get me by making me fuck the wrong dick*" count? Because that's all I can think about as the nurse takes my blood pressure and gives me a gown to change into.

We'll tell ourselves that it wasn't really Drew sitting out there. Only my brain playing tricks on me. We'll keep our anxiety down so our blood pressure doesn't crash through the roof. Things will go smoother that way.

"Not hearing from us is good news," the doctor says as I finish my check-up. "We'll let you know if there's reason to come back for a follow-up."

Nothing I've never heard before. Yet I get the usual, "*I'm going to fucking die, aren't I?*" thoughts as I pick up my purse, thank the doctor, and head out to the reception to finalize my insurance. I glance into the waiting room and don't see any men, let alone Drew Benton. It's a new crew of patients awaiting their fates.

Intoxicated

Friends continues to play on the TV, but by the time I walk out there, I barely recognize anyone.

Thank God.

"Come here often?"

I stop at the top of the stairs leading down to the parking lot. I have a bus to catch if I want to make it back home within the hour. My alternative is calling a Lyft, but after what I went through, I'm not in the mood to get into cars with strangers.

Slowly, I turn. Sure enough, that's the biggest douchebag I know standing like a creeper next to the clinic entrance.

Countdown until when he's asked to *leave*. I'll have my phone ready to take video and submit it to Reddit.

"What are you doing here?" I level my gaze at him. Although I'd rather look at the dirt on the bottom of my shoe, I refuse to let him think he's bested me. I will not submit to Drew Benton. Nor will I give him the satisfaction of looking at my ass when I'm turned around. "Are you stalking me?"

"Hardly," he says with a snort. "What do you think I'm doing here? Getting checked out, like you. We don't know where the other person has been."

I lower my sunglasses. I'll be damned if he can read any part of my soul. "You're right. Good to see you're taking good care of yourself, though. I'd hate to hear that either of us contracted something unsavory after... well, I'm sure you remember."

He grins at me. "Only if you do."

Typical. Men always want to gloat about the Conquests of Cunts. I'll be sure to carry cigarettes so he can have a celebratory smoke the next time we meet.

"Still not convinced you're not stalking me. Of all the clinics in Portland..."

"This one has the shortest wait times. Same reason you came all the way to this side of town instead of sticking to your woods. Did you make a donation? I left a sizable one. Should pay for some young lady's birth control for the next eighty years."

"Why are you gloating?" I ask.

"Why are you still here, if you detest me so much?"

"Why are you acting like you *don't* know why I would detest you?"

Drew drops his arms. "Oh, I know why." He motions for me to walk with him down the stairs. No wonder. There's a couple coming up them, and they're already looking at us like we shouldn't be hanging around the door. I go on ahead. Drew is obnoxiously right behind me. "It's because you can't get enough of me, yet you despise everything I do and stand for."

"Why wouldn't I?" I round the corner and go down the final few steps leading to the parking lot. "My ex paid you to do God knows what. You could still be doing it right now."

"I could be, but I'm not." Like a chivalrous ass in a trucker hat, Drew opens the door for me. I glare at him as I step out into the warm spring sunlight. "That job was compromised when you made me. Nice work, by the way. Nobody's ever done that before."

"How many dumb women are out there, exactly? Because it seems common sense to do the slightest bit of Googling into someone you intend to date these days. What, do you think I go home with any ol' Tinder date, fuck him bareback, and let out a *el oh el whoops!* when I'm fucked over?"

"I don't know about what you do with your pussy exactly, which is why I'm here..." Drew lets the glass door swing shut behind him. Now's my chance to high-tail it for the bus stop, but

Intoxicated

I'm inexplicably attracted to the knob standing beneath the green awning. He looks like a common Portlander who takes semi-care of himself. Nice jeans, tight T-shirt, fairly groomed with brown peach fuzz, and his hat doesn't look like it was picked up out of the gutter. Still not my type, but I don't feel like I want to throw water on him. Too bad I know who he really is. It *really* makes me want to throw water on him. "You might be surprised how hard it is to find that information about me. I have many layers of protection for my privacy. Did you hire a detective? Because one with loose morals may be able to find that all out in one weekend."

I snort. "What do you think?"

He says something I am not expecting. Let alone with such a soft, understanding voice. "I think you're a guarded woman who doesn't take chances. You've got enough money from your past relationships to hire a good PI to look into me. In retrospect, I should've anticipated it and acted accordingly. Instead, I let my dick do the talking, and now I'm out a few grand."

Wish I could say this should be the end of it, but if Jason were mad enough to hire this fuckboy to break my heart – and my loins, probably – I can only imagine who he would go to next. He's probably on the Deep Web right now hiring infected bug chasers to seduce me and give me God knows what. The kind of "God knows what" a condom will never protect me against, since we both know I've learned my lesson now.

Or he'll straight up hire a hitman. One never knows these crazy days.

"You want a medal or something?"

"No."

'You think you're gonna apologize to me?"

"Why would I apologize? I was doing my job. I've never apologized to the women I was hired to get back at."

I shake my head. "You're disgusting. What kind of creep goes into your line of work? I learned a few things about you." My accusatory finger comes right for his chest. I don't dare touch it, though. His chest is so nice I'll probably hop up and hump it if I'm not careful. "Some of the women you fucked with have serious issues now. Did you know one tried to kill herself?"

"There's no correlation between me and that."

"So you know?"

"Of course I know," Drew all but snaps. "What? You want me to feel bad? Like I said, there's no direct correlation between..."

"Shut up. You're a scumbag, you know that?"

He dares to take one step forward. Here we are, standing in the parking lot of a sexual health clinic, about to have the kind of altercation that would get the cops called on us. He's definitely about to get banned from the premises. If I'm lucky, I won't be caught up in his storm.

The closer he gets, the more I shudder. Don't tell me it has anything to do with how he makes me feel - sexually, that is. Because this guy doesn't deserve that kind of response from me. He deserves a slap to the cheek and a kick to the balls.

"Do you really think you're that much better than me?" he growls right into my ear. Okay. *Okay.* So I've got a few extra shudders from that, but I shall contain them. I won't give him the satisfaction of turning me on again. "Besides, if I'm such a scumbag, what does it mean that you come storming into my apartment and fuck me dry?"

"That was..." I sputter, my throat as dry as his balls had been when I was finished with him. "That was *different.*"

Intoxicated

"I mean, I get that we have this undeniable chemistry." Although Drew doesn't touch me, I feel his skin against mine. That's how close he is. That's how tactile my memory is. "But I would think if you found me so abhorrent, you'd run away from me instead of always coming soooo much closer."

"What?" I snap back. "You think I want to still fuck you? You're delusional. I'd rather be celibate for the rest of my life than hop on your dick again."

"Who says you'd be hopping on it? I was thinking piledriver. You're *gorgeous* on the other end of a piledriver." His fuzz grazes my chin. I can smell his breath. Every drop of heat within me rushes straight to my pussy.

I hate him.

"Cupping your tits while I use your cunt all night long. I'll let you scream all you want, too. I like it when you let me know how much you like it."

My hand pushes his face away. I had meant to slap him. Instead, he gets a forceful nudge. Either way, there's no way in hell he gets to see the color touching my cheeks. I won't give him that satisfaction. I won't.

"I'm not a conquest," I hiss, fire burning inside my belly. I swear it's not lust. It's anger. Seething, reeling anger that wants to burn him alive. I feel like I did when I went to his place last Tuesday. Ready to kill him. Instead, I fucked him. I dared him to fuck me. I dared him to come inside me. In my defense, he didn't exactly say no to either. He wanted it as badly as I did. "You don't get to fantasize about all the sick shit you want to do to me. I don't care if you're the second coming of a sex god. You don't get to do that with me."

"So what do we call it when I *do* get to fuck you?"

"First of all!" I raise my voice. "You don't get to do it again! Second, we can agree that it was something we should not have done and move on. Just... leave me alone, okay? I don't need your shit. You clearly don't want my shit. Go back to your job of driving women to severe depression because you're a sick fuck who gets off on it. God knows you don't need the money."

"How do you know that?" he asks. "You don't know anything about my personal financial situation."

"I have a pretty good idea."

"And I have a pretty good idea about yours, too. You're not doing too badly for yourself, right? Sounds like you gleam a lot of money from your marks before you break their hearts and move on to the next one. Someone has to pay for your apartment in Northwest, right? You don't have a day job, yet I see you in the trendiest, most expensive places around town. I hope you're investing your money well, though. You're only going to get older, and then what? It's so much harder to get old men with money to give a fuck about your pussy when it's not so..."

My heel meets his toes.

"Shut the fuck up!" Those words echo across the half-empty parking lot. Birds take flight from a nearby tree. Someone walking their dog looks in our direction. Cars slow down. Before anyone thinks to call 911, I take a large step back and hoist my purse up my shoulder. "Shut up and leave me *alone*."

"So..." Drew grits his teeth, as if he can't feel what I did to his toes. "Want to get a drink at a place up the street from here? They have great margaritas. After what they did to us in that clinic, I think we deserve a little alcohol. Hm?"

Intoxicated

I fix my hair and grumble that I would rather suck Satan's dick. When I speak louder, fully intending to verbally castrate him, I say, "Sure. Why the fuck not. I need a drink."

Somebody please, please save me from myself.

CHAPTER 11

DREW

Yes, I knew I was good, but I didn't know I was *this* good. Cher clearly detests the ground I walk on. She would rather take a shit on my grave than say a nice thing about me. I mean, it's not exactly like I'm smitten with her, either. She's an asshole. A hypocritical one, based on how she thinks she has any room to talk about making former lovers depressed enough to take drastic measures. At least I admit what a piece of shit I can be. Watching her bend over backward to claim any moral high ground? Priceless.

Maybe that's why I ask her out for a drink. I'm not out to get between her legs again, although the way she keeps huffing and puffing and biting her words at me makes me fondly remember how good it was to nail her against my bed. I suck in my cheeks

Intoxicated

as I walk beside her. It's my foolproof way of keeping a hard-on from springing in my jeans.

We don't need that. I definitely don't need that, although I know what I'm thinking about later when I'm in the shower.

Again.

We don't say much as we walk. Granted, it's a short one since we're literally going two blocks from the clinic, but conversation would be normal between two people, yes? Funny. Normally I'd be Mr. Talkative. Cher just makes me... *think.*

About the kind of woman she is.

About the kind of man *I* am.

About why I keep coming back to her, although it's clear we're too toxic for one another.

Besides, what would be the point? We can't have a real relationship. A friends with benefits situation would be too volatile. Our mutual attraction is fueled by our dislike for one another. I mean, sure, before she knew what a "scumbag" I was, she may have genuinely thought she was attracted to me. But I have a theory, and that says Cher is incapable of actual love and a decent relationship. She doesn't know how to do anything but use and manipulate people. Even when we were having sex, she was telling me what to do by making it sound like I didn't have the gall. We both knew I did, but she had to make it sound like it happened because of *her* will.

If she's not the narcissist... there's definitely one in her family. That's shit you either discover within yourself, or learn it from someone almost as toxic.

We sit at the bar overlooking the sidewalk. Mariachi music blares from the speakers, but this isn't a Mexican place. Never underestimate a Portlander's love for tacos and margaritas, though. That's one that hasn't changed from my childhood, God love it.

I order us a large plate of chips and salsa to share as we drink our watered-down margaritas. Cher props herself up on a stool and shivers as the air conditioner blasts against her bare shoulders. One must wonder what drives a woman to wear an off-the-shoulder color-block dress to the STD clinic. Is this the most casual thing she has in her wardrobe? Was she off somewhere fancier after her vaginal swabbing? Or is this how she must dress every single day, regardless of the weather?

How does Cher Lieberman dress in the winter, I wonder?

I mean, she's gorgeous. She's always so well put together and postures herself like a woman who knows her worth. It's attractive. And intimidating. I'm drawn to women who intimidate the balls off my body. It's not that I *want* to change them to be more submissive and demure. Some of that kinda happens naturally? Bringing that out of a woman, that is. Except that's only possible if that woman is capable of such sensations. Others merely want to use their teeth when they blow you. They gotta make sure you know who has all the power, duh.

(And, yes, that is mad hot.)

"So..." Cher stirs the ice in her margarita. She plucks the olive and touches it to her lips. She doesn't eat it, though. "You think we're infected. If so, who gave whom what? Besides your dirty dick giving it to me, that is."

I chuckle. "You ask the important questions, of course."

"Don't play coy."

"How do I know you're not out there poking holes in condoms and making men's dreams come true by saying you don't need them?" I can play this game. I *love* playing this game.

Intoxicated

Even better if I make her cringe on her stool. "I swear to God, if they call me up and tell me to come in to get antibiotics, I'm gonna be pissed."

"How nice of you to assume that I have a disease-ridden..." She snorts. "You know what? I'm surprised you're not worried about me being pregnant."

"Why? If you – yes, you, specifically – are gonna be paranoid about one thing, it's pregnancy. You're definitely on birth control. I'd be shocked if you said you weren't, and I would assume you're trying to trap men into..." I stop. "Fuck."

Her chuckles nearly wreck me. Not because I'm suddenly embarrassed, but because that *could* be her game, and I'd be fucked.

"Yes, what if I'm coming to terms with my old, *old* age of twenty-five and realizing that I need a better long-term plan than letting my tits hang out and spreading my legs for every millionaire who walks by me? Yes, let's trap some fuckers with a baby. Child support for the rest of my life. I'll be rolling in the dough." She narrows her eyes at me. "You assumed I was on birth control. Well, I assumed you've had a vasectomy."

I remain silent.

"Aw, did I freak you out by being right?"

This margarita is pretty good. Maybe they kicked it up a notch with a little more vodka than usual. God knows I need it. "You would only freak me out if you knew the doctor who did."

"Dr. Redding."

Alcohol shoots out of my nostrils. It burns so *badly* that I hunker over the bar, pinching the bridge of my nose as my eyes water and I gasp for air. Cher swings one leg over the other and continues to chuckle as she sips her margarita.

"How the hell do you know that?" I demand.

"It was a lucky guess. Figured I had a 50/50 shot." She puts her glass back down and tosses her hair behind her shoulder. How sad is it that I'm instantly alleviated of my burning woes? I look at her sleek lines, the lovely hue of her complexion, the silky hair... and I want to kiss her. I want to put my mouth all over her. Give her a hundred hickies that will mark her as mine for at least a week. Slip my tongue right into her ear and make her squirm so hard she's spreading her legs and begging me to fuck her, right here, right now. I'm gonna fondly remember the perfection of her pussy for the rest of my life. If nothing else, I understand *that* drawing in her victims. She's the kind of woman who can treat you like absolute shit and you're begging for more if it means fucking those depths.

That smarmy smile has my knees buckling.

"He's the guy most of my exes in Seattle went to. He has a wonderful reputation, or so I hear. Very discrete and makes it as painless as possible. I'm told he's the one to go to if you want a quick recovery time. So, since you live in Seattle now, I figured he's the one you're going to for a snip. I'm not a mind-reader. I'm simply observant."

"What else do you know about me?" I ask.

"I know you went to Lewis & Clark."

"I told you that."

"Yes, but you didn't tell me you almost had enough credits to minor in gender studies."

I snort. That was one thorough PI she must have hired. "Call me curious about the world of gender equality. It's kind of amazing how much history hides from us about the accomplishments of women. Did you know that we have your sex to thank for beer? Rock on."

Intoxicated

"I *did* know that, actually." Her grin is dazzling enough to make me kiss her, but I don't dare fall into her toxic trap. For all I know, she's still playing me to get to my money. Or my dick. Hm. I might not mind one of those.

But when a woman looks at me like this, it's hard for me to hold back from throwing a little money at her. Spoiling her, we'll call it. I buy all the meals. I get her that dress she's always wanted. Bedeck her in jewelry of her favorite color. Get her car fixed or buy her a new one. Damnit. This is why we're marks. At least I'm on to her!

It's rather weird how easily we settle into conversation filled with light – but not fake – banter. We play a game of *Did you know?* that results in, yes, we could actually guess that about the other person. We're both professional players, after all. We're good at reading people, let alone the opposite sex. She calls me out for sleeping with my family's older housekeeper long before I offer the information. I accurately pinpoint that one of her parents is a narcissist. (I'm still not unconvinced that she's not one too, though.) Together, we're a giant psych evaluation that we could package and pitch to pick-up artists.

"Was Rothchild your last boyfriend?" I ask her.

She leans her elbow against the table and wistfully gazes into the street. A flock of bicycles ride by. Beat-up cars and Mercedes share parking spaces. For every old, decrepit building full of character, there's a Soviet-esque "luxury" apartment currently in progress. It's what this part of Portland now looks like. A fury of old and new constantly fighting for a presence. Sometimes I barely recognize it anymore. These are my old stomping grounds, but I couldn't point out the place where I had my first kiss or almost crashed my car because I cruised a little too quickly through a certain intersection. All my old friends have moved away because this place has either priced them out or depresses them too much. Guess I'm not much better. Which begs many questions about why Cher still hangs out around here.

"He was my last 'real' one, I guess you could say." She shrugs. "I liked him well enough, honestly. His sin was moving the relationship way too quickly. If he had waited another year, I might've said yes to his proposal."

"So why didn't you tell him that instead of bailing on him in front of his whole family?"

"Because it was a giant red flag. Once men push you to get more serious out of the blue, there's usually an ulterior motive. Like suddenly wanting babies or finding out they might have cancer or dementia. Now they need someone to take care of them. That's not me."

"Maybe you should stop dating men who are so much older than you."

"Excuse me, they're the ones with money and mid-life crises. Sooo much easier to seduce than someone your age. For the long-haul, anyway."

Something she's said has piqued my interest. "Do you actually love them? Or are they marks?"

"You ever love the women you're paid to fuck over?"

"Not really, but I'm also told upfront about every dirty and cruel thing they've ever done. Kinda hard to fall for a woman you know once cuckolded her husband. Without permission."

"Ouch."

"Or threatened to kill a guy's dog. Or actually did."

Cher winces. Good to know she has *some* empathy. We're on a roll here. "The men I date aren't much better. They're either raging sociopaths looking for a young, tight hole to fuck or are so blinded by their privilege they don't realize how badly they're razing the neighborhood around them. It gets tiring. Some of them are decent deep down. Some of them made me laugh. Some were good lovers. Some would've been great dads, or already were to the children they had. Except there's always something, you know? At some point, it's time to bail."

The more I study her, the more the picture of *Cher Lieberman* comes together. "You don't want that at all, do you?"

She slightly turns her head in my direction. "What do you mean?"

"Marriage, family... a steady, long-term monogamous relationship with a guy who lives on the other side of town you see three times a week. That's not your style. You're too independent. All of your dreams of your future include you and only you. There's no room for another person. Maybe not even a pet. You like your independence. You prefer to be alone."

The cock of her head does wonders for my imagination. What is that look in her eye? Is she seeing a new side of me that she didn't consider before? Am I alluring her with my insight? Or is she about to tell me how wrong I am? I finish my margarita and await her response.

"Yes, I don't very much care for the thought of getting married right now. I don't mind relationships so much, but I have very high standards for the people I spend more than a few weeks with. It's not always about the money. I simply don't want to be tied down to anyone for a long while. Maybe not ever. It's hard to make men who are used to throwing their money at people and getting unbridled access understand that point of view."

"Especially if you're selling them a different image of yourself, I bet."

She coyly smiles, as if I've dug too deep and must learn to mind my manners. "You play a game long enough, you start to forget what your real personality is like. I've been doing it for so long that maybe that *is* my personality. I love seduction and watching a man completely give himself over to me. The first time we have sex is supposed to be one of the greatest moments of his life. Never mind everything else that comes before or after." She narrows her eyes, but that smile does not fade. "So?" she asks. "What about it? Was that sex some of the best of your life?"

I can't tell if this is part of her game, or if she's asking in earnest. How should I respond? Making her think it really was would simply be playing into her hand. Refuting it would either get me called a liar, or she'll be so offended our conversation will come to a premature end.

Suppose I can only answer honestly.

"It was definitely memorable," I say with a grin. "Top tier. Maybe not *the* best, but most men are gonna be all about the hot woman who storms into their apartment and begs to get hit hard. Between the legs, that is." I set aside my glass, allowing me to lean in a little closer while still maintaining some personal space. "Now, you tell me. How was it for you? Thinking about round two right now?" Hey, a guy has to try when he has nothing else going on in his life.

Cher pulls in her bottom lip and bats her eyes. "You'd love for me to say yes. Because you've spent the past twenty minutes thinking about how you're gonna ask me back to your place so you can fuck me again."

Intoxicated

"Maybe not *right away*," I confess. "We could put off the sex. Maybe watch some movies. Order in dinner. You know, that stuff we were supposed to do on our date we never had?"

She sighs. "I don't think that's a good idea."

"No, I suppose not."

"Doesn't mean it's not hot to think about, though."

"So you liked it?"

"You're trying to tell me you think I *didn't* like it?"

"Now you're playing mind games with me. I much prefer it when a woman I want to ask out for real doesn't do that. I'm not your mark. You're not my mark. We can be mature adults and have a casual fling, even if we think the other person is the scum of the universe."

"Isn't that a kind of self-flagellation? Fucking someone who makes you barf outside of the bedroom?"

"I make you *barf?*"

"Some of the things I read about your exes..."

"Could say the same about you, Cher." It's only now that I realize her name sounds like *share*. Sharing. Rhymes with caring. Wonder if she was absent that day in kindergarten when they taught "sharing is caring."

"There are a lot of things you could say about me," she sighs.

"Is one of those things an implication that you'll come over to my place now? I've got my car in the clinic parking lot. Could get us there in twenty minutes."

"That's generous, considering it's almost rush hour."

"You still haven't said no," I say.

"I'm thinking about it."

"If you have to think about it, that means you want to do it. Come on, Cher, go with your instincts. I am."

She turns her whole body to me, giving me a grand view of her little sliver of cleavage and the cinch of her waist.

It's that look in her eye that tells me I'm about to have my face in those tits.

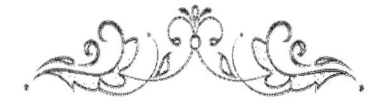

CHAPTER 12

CHER

Do you think I don't know what I'm doing or something? Of course going home with Drew can only result in one thing. We're talking about a man I can barely stop thinking about. Particularly in a certain *way*. He won't shut up about what happened last Tuesday, so I'm assuming he's obsessed with it, too. Short of my period coming three days early, I can almost guarantee that I'm getting into bed with him tonight.

If I stay the night will be another matter.

What? How many times do I have to tell you that I'm not interested in your judgments? I don't care if you're breathing down my neck, ready to wring it out in utter frustration. Or maybe you think I deserve it. We both know what kind of man Drew Benton is by now. He's really no better than me. Hell, is it possible for him to be worse than me? I won't push my luck that far. You'll think I'm crazy, if you already don't.

Besides, it's fate, isn't it? Okay. So I don't believe in *fate*. I believe in fathomable coincidences. Granted, it's pretty unfathomable that I would end up in the same clinic at the *same time* as Drew. I'm also not convinced he actually got checked out since he was in and out while I was seeing a different doctor. He claims "it goes faster for guys," but I'm not sure I believe it. What if he really is stalking me? What if he really is still trying to manipulate me?

Then again, can you manipulate someone who knows exactly what you're doing? What's the point? This guy and I have given up the game. We're probably gonna have one last bang and get each other officially out of our systems. Or, at least, I hope he'll be.

I really don't need a boyfriend. Let alone one who makes his living wrecking other women. Even if he's not sleeping with them, those women think they'll get to touch his cock, and I'm pretty damn possessive when I decide I like a guy.

He's a bastard. I'm a bitch. What a pair we make.

But when you're not trying to impress a guy - let alone asking him to dump half his riches on you - you don't worry about silly things like your clothes and your perfume. You don't care that you had watered-down margaritas at a dive bar right after walking out of an STD clinic. When he asks you what you should order in for dinner, you don't hesitate to suggest the best Chinese place you know. The one that's sure to make you smell like a winner in a few hours.

"I haven't eaten at this place since they last sold it." Drew munches on a spring roll as we sit on his couch, the TV blaring nonsense from Netflix. I keep my legs crossed and away from him as I stab chow mein and shove broccoli into my mouth. When I drop a large chunk of onion into my cleavage, I shove my dirty chopsticks down there and root it out. Into my mouth it goes.

Oh! What a lovely little burp. By little, I mean loud enough to make Drew jerk in his seat.

"That was you, huh?" he asks, one eyebrow raised as if he can't believe I'm capable of such volume. "Impressive. Here I had been holding them in."

I pull my legs up onto the couch, bare feet pressed against his leg. My chopsticks stab what's left of my dinner. Someone on TV tells a baking contestant that they'll have a better shot at finger-painting a grand masterpiece than achieving their dreams in cake decorating. I have to agree. It really is atrocious what appears on Drew's giant TV. "Why? Are you attempting to keep me from running off? I don't see the point. I already know how nasty you are. Why shouldn't you know how nasty *I* am?"

"Indeed, why shouldn't I?" He tosses his empty take-out box onto the coffee table and slumps down in his seat. The moment his jeans come undone, I know we're not talking sexy. He's pulling the old, "*I ate too much and now I have a food baby,*" move. Aw. Look. It must be at least five months along. "You already know how hairy it gets down there."

"That reminds me. My crotch really itches because I haven't touched it up since we last hooked up."

"Aw, don't tell me you waxed your little lady for me."

"I don't do it for anyone but myself, thank you."

"That's what you ladies tell yourselves."

I shove another piece of broccoli into my mouth. Speaking of bloating... oof. I may be wearing a dress, but the cinched waist is going to kill me if I don't adjust it. Got a food baby of my own cooking. I blame the fact that I'm eating chow mein *and* fried rice. When he asked me what I wanted from the take-out menu, I told him to fuck me up. I hear we have dumplings for dessert.

"Being a woman is complicated," I say with a sigh. "You like the feel of smooth, hairless skin on your body, but there's no denying that the ones in society who benefit from it the most are the men selling us the products."

"Whoa. Feminism and anti-capitalism during *my* Chinese take-out dinner?" Drew laughs. "You really are from around here."

"Just because I take men to the cleaners every few months doesn't mean I haven't read any books. I also went to college and took some gender studies courses, juuuust like you."

"Wow," he whispers. "This whole time the perfect woman for me has been in Portland. Who knew?"

"How many blue armpits and ear gauges did you wade through to find me?"

"How many manbuns and socks with sandals did you wade through to find *me?*"

I chuckle. "Too many. Turns out I had to look to rural Oregon to find a guy in a trucker hat and old jeans." He took off the hat after we arrived to his place. I saw the closet he stuffed it in, though. The back of the door boasted a series of hooks that hung a wide, *wide* variety of hats he must have collected through his life. He's like a woman with shoes and purses! "What's up with that, anyway?"

"You work outside enough, you learn to wear a hat to keep your face and scalp from burning."

This time I'm the one raising my eyebrows. "You work outside, huh?" Damn. I can almost see it. Imagine his shirt soaked in sweat and his brow glistening like a diamond as he chops wood in the sun. Ooh, those are some seriously rippling muscles. Muscles I know can move like a demon sent straight from Hell to punish me for my sins.

Hot! (Just like Hell.)

"I'm fairly handy. Spent a lot of time as a kid hanging out with the landscapers and handymen that came around our property. One of my best friends as a teen had a dad who owned a small construction company. Kind that builds custom cabinets, sheds, stuff like that. He taught me a few things. Combine that with shop and metal class in school... eh, I'm not going to change the world, but I can repair and build things for my grandma."

This isn't the first time he's mentioned his grandmother. That's not something I'm used to with this type of guy. The only ones who go out of their way to mention their grandmas to me are those playing up her diamond ring collection (thanks, Jason) or pretending that she thoroughly changed their lives before she died. "Could you build me a doghouse?" I ask.

"Sure. Why? You have a dog?"

He's surprised enough that I can tell such a fact would break his profile of me. Well, I don't have a dog. Or a cat, for that matter. So he can rest assured that his profile is up to date.

"No," I say, placing my trash next to his. "Thinking about moving, that's all."

He cocks his head, urging me to explain.

"I hear I'm a big bitch."

It takes him a few seconds, but when he finally gets my stupid joke, Drew is hunched over laughing. I can smell his breath from here. Very, *very* Chinese food-y. I'm sure mine smells as pristine as an untapped water source, too.

"That's right. Yuck it up." I snort into the back of my hand as I lean against the end of his couch. "I'm only saying what you've been thinking."

"Oh, I'm not entirely sure you know what I'm thinking."

I don't know where the serious tone came from, but he has my attention. Drew reaches into the take-out bag and removes two fortune cookies. I say nothing as I bite the plastic open and crack the spun sugar into two.

"*You'll make a painful decision you might not regret.*"

Drew is looking over my shoulder. I crumple the fortune and maintain my nonplussed demeanor as I toss the trash back into the bag. He doesn't hide his fortune from me.

"*You'll go on a trip soon.*"

"Who do you think writes these things?" Drew's mouth is full when he speaks, flecks of fortune cookie spewing across the floor and coffee table. I follow his lead, but keep my mouth closed, thank you. "Everywhere you go, they say the same freakin' stuff. Do you know how many trips I've gone on because of fortune cookies?"

"What do you want them to say?" I ask. "They'll never be accurate. You need tarot cards for that."

I almost had him again. "They could at least *try*. Tell me I'm going to make a thousand unexpected bucks. Tell me I'm specifically going to Mexico." He grins at me. Doesn't take clairvoyant gifts to know what he's about to say. "Tell me I'm gonna stick it in some dank pussy by the end of the night."

All right. I knew the gist of what he was about to say. Just not... *that*.

"Dank, huh?" I slowly turn my head, foot rolling in the air as I voice my disappointment with his words. "Dank. Pussy."

Intoxicated

He snorts up some snot, arms bent behind his head and food baby poking out of his pants. Drew is lucky he still has a sizable bulge in those jeans. Otherwise, I'd be outta here. "Yup."

"*Dank* pussy."

"That's the word you're hung up on, huh, Princess?"

My palm meets my forehead. As my hand drags down my face, I groan. And burp. Couldn't avoid that one. "My pussy is not dank," I assert.

"Do you not know what *slang* means? Maybe you're getting old and behind the times. Pretty sad for however old you are. What? Thirty-five? Woof. Older than me."

"You know damn well how old I am."

"Do you know how old *I* am?"

"Old enough to not be saying *dank pussy* to me."

"I had no idea that a woman who dares me to do dirty things to her would have a problem with my vocabulary choices. Aren't you the one getting turned on by me calling it your cunt last week?"

I push my hair out of my face and shrug. "Different context. I'm not about to start talking about your dank dick. Makes it sound like it's old, cold, and musty."

"If anything, I'm comparing your vagina to the sweetest weed on the market. That's a compliment! I'd love it if you compared my dick to dank weed!"

"Stop saying *dank,* oh, my God."

"Did I discover one of your squicky words, Ms. Lieberman?"

"Yes! Happy now?"

"Oh, ecstatic."

Don't know what I expect when I steal a look in his direction. His cocky attitude on full display? His lips moving across his teeth and his eyebrows waggling? His food baby now nine months along and ready to pop?

He smirks at me, but it's not a full-blown grin. Not the kind I anticipate. Drew would rather size me up and trace my reactions. He has to work harder than some bad jokes.

"What?" he asks, as innocent as a little cherub about to bite off your tit. "I'm not going to say it again if you really hate it."

"Uh huh."

"I'm a man of my word." Drew sits up. Before I dare imagine him coming in my direction, he gets a whiff of himself and declares that he needs to brush his teeth. And might take a shower while he's at it.

"If you think I'm joining you," I say as he cleans up the garbage and takes it to the trash can in the kitchen, "you're nuts. I prefer to marinate in my post-dinner perfume."

"You really are one of the guys, huh?"

"In my skirts, heels, and big, generous cleavage."

Drew cocks his head on his way to the bathroom, his fly still down and his shirt crawling up his torso. "Was way bigger the other day. You're not wearing a pushup bra today."

"Does that disappoint you?"

He mimics *a little* with his thumb and forefinger. Typical.

"I fully expect you to still be here when I get back!" he calls from the bathroom. Water sprays. A T-shirt lands outside the door. Before I get a full view of the goods, Drew slowly closes the door. I'd presume that he locked it, but considering the kind of relationship we have so far...

This is my chance to run, isn't it? Pick up my bag, mentally thank him for the free drink and Chinese food, and head home to sleep in my doghouse.

Intoxicated

That's what I should do. Drew's a jerk and doesn't deserve my dank pussy.

I think I'll wait until my dinner settles a little more, though. Don't want to get sick on my streetcar ride home, right?

Right.

CHAPTER 13

CHER

There exists a 50/50 chance that she's still out there. Either she's rooting through my things, or she's stolen some of my money and I'll never see her again.

When I say 50/50, I don't mean *she's either there or she's not.* I mean there's an equal chance she'll decide to stay. Or go. There's no overwhelming feeling one way or another. Why would there be? We both know that she wants to ride me like cowgirl, but she also greatly dislikes me, so let's not discount her growing a conscience. It really could go either way.

The question remains, as I put my hand on my door...

Is Cher still here? Or has she left?

If she's here, I know where this is going. I'm not going to wait anymore. I'm going to pack her off to my bedroom *caveman style* again. Ooh, yeah. That sounds pretty sweet, don't it? Rile her up a bit, maybe get my face all up in those wet lips, and then manically torture her with how much she loves my cock.

Because as cute as it was to share a drink and a meal with her, there's no denying that, well... there's nothing here. Nothing but sex. We're not boyfriend-girlfriend material. Even if I could overlook her history of fucking over rich men, I doubt she'd look over my, you know, job.

I'm not exactly thrilled to call her my girlfriend, either. She's the kind of woman everyone gets me wanting to fuck, but would warn me away as soon as they recognize her name. "*Ain't that the Black Widow?*" I can imagine someone saying. "*Man, what are you doing? Besides getting killed like a fool?*"

I open the door.

At first, I don't see her anywhere. She's not on the couch. She's not in the kitchen. She's not grabbing her bag and heading out the door. Naturally, I assume Cher is already gone. She's taken my hospitality and left after I gave her one last opportunity to leave. She must know what kind of lover I am after last time. She knows I respond to her hedonistic calls for rough love. Few women draw that out of me, and it's not because she's a terrible shitlord who needs a few lessons coming her way. (All right, maybe a tad.)

There's something about her, okay? Does it have to be more complicated than that?

I'm disappointed to find her gone. Good thing I didn't bother getting hard in the shower. If anything, I repressed it as much as possible. Thought about baseball, the most boring sport on Earth. Instead of, you know, those beautiful breasts in that delicious dress she's wearing. Or that ass. Or those legs. God, those legs!

I don't have to tell you why I keep thinking back to how good it was a week ago. Could it happen again? No point wondering now! She's...

She's in my windowsill.

Cher pretends to not notice my presence as she enjoys the view of the river and the old warehouses across the way. The sun is setting on the other side of the building, so all she sees is the twilight creeping across the land.

Innocent isn't the word I'd use to describe her. There isn't a drop of innocence exuding from this woman, and I don't think those who never heard of her would get that impression, either. You know how worldly she is from one look. It's in the way she gazes out at the world. The curve of her posture as she assuredly dangles one foot off the ledge and tilts her head as if absorbing what everything has to say. Her clothing drapes with purpose. Her hair wraps around her finger and flutters toward her waist as if it has nothing better to do. The only thing *innocent* about her is that blank expression on her face. She's not putting on a show. She's not playing a character. She's simply existing without reservation.

If you want to see the real Cher Lieberman, you don't simply feed her Chinese food. You load her up with greasy goodies and then abandon her to take a shower. That way you can come back to what she looks like when she thinks you're gone.

This must be what she looks like at home. Alone.

Goodness gracious, as my grandmother would say, she's absolutely beautiful.

Only now do I make my presence known, and that's done with a simple approach to her heavenly form.

I keep respectful distance. I kinda have to. You see, the only clothing bedecking my form is a pair of light gray sweatpants I happened to have in my bathroom. If I get any closer to her, I'll spring up like the first sunflower of the season.

There's a joke about seeds in there...

"Have a nice shower?" she asks, head still pointed toward the window. "Don't mind me. Making myself at home in your lovely apartment. Who pays for it, by the way?" Finally, her eyelashes bat in my direction. "Your daddy, or your business of heartbreak?"

With hands on my hips, I shift my weight to one foot. "You're ridiculous," I say. "Of course. With hard-earned cash."

"Uh huh. Hard earned." She glances at my abs, then my crotch, then out the window again. "Very hard."

I better not be showing. Or growing, for that matter.

"If you'd like to use my shower, go ahead," I say.

"I'm fine. I've got a shower in my own apartment."

"Uh huh."

"What?" Her head snaps around, hands linked around her knees. "You want me naked in your apartment? Come on, I thought we were done playing. Come out with what you want."

I half-expect her to snap the waistband of my sweatpants. Instead, she keeps her soft hands to herself. Hands I could be pinning above her head right now.

Twitch. *Twitch*. That's my cock, by the way. Wondering why the ol' Dirk Diggler isn't playing an arousing game of Dig-Dug with her pussy.

"Oh, gee, what *do* I want? Or am I supposed to pretend to want what you want?"

"I haven't told you what I want."

"I know what you want. Some things aren't so different between men, after all." She sniffs. "You want me to suck your cock. Or to fuck me. Guess you could take your pick."

"Honestly, either order would be wonderful. I wouldn't say no to you sucking my cock right here until I haul you off to bed for some of the other stuff."

"Uh huh." Cher stretches one arm above her head. "What if I told you I'd much rather see you flex your skills in other ways?" That hand lowers. There it is! Her fingers in my waistband! She takes a cursory glance at my hardening cock and pretends to be unimpressed. Except I saw that little glint in her eyes. She's as hungry to gobble me up as I am to get reacquainted with her delicious depths. "We'll start with that foul mouth of yours."

Let's not beat around the bush. Or shall we, since she said that's what she wants?

This time when I pick her up, it's not to throw her down and fuck her brains out. Oh, no, we must have more finesse today. She's not wet with wild anticipation already. Somebody needs a little foreplay. The more I can play with her, the better, apparently.

All right. Play, we shall.

***

If there's one thing Cher loves to do, it's pretend she doesn't really want it.

She's the kind of lover that makes you need a safe word. Otherwise you're constantly interrupting your fun because you feel like a jackass who doesn't know how to respect a woman's boundaries. *Then* she asks you, *"Why the hell did you stop?"* Gee, honey, maybe it's because you asked me to stop? I can be a giant asshole, but an actual monster? Not as big of one as she might think.

Intoxicated

If anything, I like to think I'm pretty fluffy for a monster!

Take this sweetness for example: imagine our intrepid princess with her skirt hitched up around her waist, her legs bent and spread around my happy head. Every other word out of her mouth is nothing but gibberish, because that's how good I am with my tongue as it slides up and down her wet slit.

Her taste is one I can't describe. Sounds like such a cop-out, I know, but there you are. I could compare her to other women I've tasted, but I'm told that's not appealing. Yet how else do I describe it? She's the sweetness of a young girl's heart before it's ever been broken. She's the bitter bite of a woman scorned. The natural salt of her skin blends into the myriad of desires pouring forth from her body. I can't take all the credit for arousing her, of course. My tongue may dance upon her clit and flick against her anxious hole, but her soul has completely gone somewhere else. Trust me. My eyes have been fixated on her face this whole time. Not because she graces me with eye contact. Oh, *nooo*. Cher is too busy squeezing her eyes shut and flinging her arm over her face. Is this because she's ashamed to know who's eating her out? Or maybe she's fantasizing about someone other than me. Ouch. I can take that, I guess. She could be fantasizing about whatever heartthrob stole her heart when she was seventeen, but *I'm* the one working my magic on the only thing that matters in this room.

Surprised? While I wish it shocked me how many men out there refuse to bestow attention upon the very thing we tend to crave most, I'm not. I mean, I know the kind of guys I hung out with as a kid and now as an adult. One of the easiest, fastest ways to a woman's heart is to at least *offer* to rub your face all over her pussy. Bonus points if you're not a punk who can't slam your tongue in there. Like, bros, *really* get in there. This is your chance to kiss every part of a woman's body! I don't care if she's that asshole who stole your Camaro and flipped you the bird on her way to the chop shop. You get pussy in your face? You make some fucking love to that pussy.

Even with your mouth.

Say it with me now.

Even. With. Your. Mouth.

I mean, it's fun! Especially if you've got a girl totally into it. Cher is on my bed gently humping my face as she rubs her nipples and whispers how much she fucking loves it. I don't care if she thinks she's a master string-puller getting exactly what she wants. I'm one happy dude when I've got a face full of you-know-what. Sure, there is the occasional lady who doesn't like it as much as, say, *Cher,* but they're always so tickled that you offered. Come on, men, step the fuck up and get laid! Don't you want your ladies to be happy?

Don't answer that.

Ah, yes, I'm busy, anyway. Busy with this orgasm about to clock Cher right in the body. I can taste it long before she begins to shudder, buck, and cry out that I'm a sex God. (All right. I'm not a sex God, apparently, but she's not holding back on the sounds of pleasure. Isn't that sweet music to one's ears?) There's that sudden twist. A zest, if you'll call it, when you get into a solid groove, your hands on a lady's hips to both keep them pinned down and so you can feel those sweet undulations of her passion, here comes the first wave of climax that nearly drowns a man.

Good thing I know how to swim. I'm actually a pretty strong swimmer.

"Fuck!" Her whole body stiffens. Everything but her hands, which twitch through the air, attempting to find anything to grab.

Intoxicated

I enjoy every second of it as I keep my eyes locked on her face. You know what's my favorite part of a girl's O-face? How it's so *her*. She can be prim, proper, made up and perfect with her makeup, but if you really make her come, she either has no neck or a giraffe neck. Her cheeks are puffed and her mouth twisted. Eyes squeezed shut and brows flying off her face. It's the most natural you will ever see her.

I intend to play with her a little. Get her to come down from that high, but not without a few teases that have her taking off again. My finger slips beneath her ass and taunts her slit. I get a hearty nod from my salacious princess. Perfect. Time to head for Puckerville, not that I intend to give her the full treat tonight.

Maybe next time.

"Oh, shit, you..." Cher sits up, pulling her pussy away from my face. She grabs the top of my head and lifts it for a kiss. Her mouth inhales mine. It's not our first kiss today, but it's the first famished one that leaves me knocked out. Almost like she really loves her own taste. Or maybe she only loves it on my tongue.

"That's right," I mutter on her mouth. "Me."

Cher is loosened up in more ways than one. The endorphins of her orgasm turn her into a palatable princess who wants to get frisky and help me on my own road to orgasm. When she grabs my cock, though, it's not to get me off. She's testing my rigidity. When she finds it to her standards, I get a lovely grin made only better by the flush in her cheeks and the fall of her tousled hair.

"You gonna fuck me now?" she taunts, hand slipping up and down my shaft. "You gonna take this super dank pussy?"

I'd say I regret saying that earlier, but no. Hearing her say that, with a dirty grunt to her voice, only makes me smile. "Gonna take it and utterly destroy it," I say.

"Don't make promises you can't keep."

She means it, doesn't she? I know she likes it rough, but after that kind of attentive oral titillation you'd think she'd want something... more tender. But I know that greedy look in her eye. Every inch of her burns to have me use her. Use *it*. She wants to be my little toy I do with as I will.

A flicker of regret hits me for the first time in a long while. Not regret for being with her. Regret for how I've treated some women in the past. Especially my former marks. Especially how I would have treated Cher had she not made me. Sometimes, the easiest thing to do when you have to stick it in some crazy to get to your ends, is simply treat them as "just another girl." No personality. No privileges. If they scream for some anal, by all means, fuck 'em in the ass, but it's not something you hunger for like it's two hours until Christmas dinner. You flip them over and lube up.

I think Cher knows that about me. Why wouldn't she? She knows everything else. Like I know almost everything about her.

Well, everything but what makes her... *her*.

Why would she want me to do that to her, exactly? Does she really get off on it? Does she fantasize about it when she's with other men, or when she's touching herself in bed? Is that what she wants? To be used and fucked into oblivion? It's one thing for a woman to declare how much she loves being stuffed by cock. It's quite another for her to ask you to completely disregard her personal boundaries. On the surface, anyway.

Maybe she's a thrill seeker. That would also explain how she entered her life of depravity.

"I could do that." I yank her dress over her head. As if its worth means nothing to me, I toss her designer threads over the

Intoxicated

edge of my bed, a literal pile of forgotten memories. As her body emerges, all I can think about is fucking her. Why not? It's what she wants. It's what I want. Memories of what happened a week ago flood my head and fill my cock. It's ready to ram into whatever I send its way. Sweet skies above, there are a hundred different things I could do right now. I could make her suck it. Ride it. Get on her knees like I did the first time we did it, her ass hitting my hilt and almost making me come right away. Cher isn't merely a beautiful woman. She's the nymph you can't say no to, because you're so under her spell you're willing to give her your soul. "Or I could torture you with tenderness. Make really slow and conscientious love to you." My lips linger against hers, our bodies falling to the bed together. Her hand wraps around the back of my neck. Nails dig into my skin.

"You won't do that," she tells me.

"Oh?"

"Hell, no. You're going to give into temptation and give us both what we deserve."

I don't quite yet get her meaning. I also don't care. I'm too busy hitching her hips to mine and seeking out her heat with the hungry tip of my cock.

It finds her so easily. Like she puts her arms above her head and jiggles her tits for me so easily. With her legs bent beneath my hands and her hips reaching up to meet mine, I take her with one long stroke of my cock.

She doesn't close her eyes. Nor do they roll into the back of her head. As I reel from the sensation of her soft, wet cunt grabbing onto my cock, I notice she's not giving me a single sign of expression.

If anything, that's triumph in her eyes.

What do I do with this? Hell, do I care? Not really. I'm already fucking her, and that's what we both want.

It's what *I* sure as hell want.

I want to drive my cock into her, hitting her so hard that she never forgets what it feels like. I want to watch her body shudder and jiggle with every impact I make. I want to pinch her nipples and listen to her squeal in appreciation. Fuck it, I want to slam myself into her, over and over, completely losing control as I attempt to find her deepest, hottest recesses. I want to come so deep inside of her that she lets out that gasp of recognition that I've claimed her once again.

I only want a reaction out of her. I want her to signify that I'm so fucking good in bed that she's going to think about me for the rest of her life. I want her to squeeze my cock and milk me dry. I want her to elicit such an animalistic response from me that I roar like a beast and fuck her until she breaks.

The harder I thrust, the deeper I go. I pull her hips up, her hair around her head as she braces her hands against her breasts. She doesn't give me the satisfaction of closing her eyes in happiness. She's still looking into me, daring me to do more.

"Fuck me, Drew."

Those are the last words she utters as I piledrive her like I've wanted since we first met. There's no escape for her. She's my little caught vixen, the nymph I've cornered in the wilds of the universe. She's going to take my cock. She's a prisoner of my onslaught. She's my spoils of war. The Princess offered up to me on my warlord's platter. She may not be a virgin, but I'll make sure she's so stretched that no man will want her after me.

I'll always want her. I'll look at her and think *that's the one. The one I fuck.*

Intoxicated

A little purr rumbles through her and she bites her upper lip as I'm compelled to come. Down, down, down my cock goes, swimming in its own cum as it fills her up. She finally growls like the nymph she is, her legs spreading a little wider so I can take her some more.

It's only when I start to come down from orgasm that I get what she meant when she said, *"give us both what we deserve."*

Yes. I get it now.

You know what we both deserve.

No emotion. No love. No shred of humanity.

I fuck her and come inside her, marking her like a caveman would mark his mate, yet that's all we are. Two reasonless cavepeople who have yet to unlock such complex emotions in our brains.

We're two broken souls who don't deserve love.

As if railing against that premise, I keep fucking her. I'll prove to myself it's not true.

It's not true.

CHAPTER 14

CHER

It's not Drew's snoring, twitching, or night sweats that wake me up around eight in the morning. Nor does the sunlight streaming through the window affect my ability to stay asleep.

No, what wakes me up from my exhausted slumber is something much more sinister.

My stomach.

Cramps, to be exact.

You *know* what I'm talking about. Maybe you think that Chinese food you devoured the night before is coming back to haunt you. *Maybe.* But when you're about three days away from your scheduled visit from Aunt Flo, you *know what it is.*

I jerk upright, half-awake. Right away, I feel the tell-tale sign of my uterus having a big laugh at my expense.

Intoxicated

It's all right. It's okay. I only spent half the night rough-fucking the asshole snoozing next to me. I may have taken a long shower before collapsing into his bed around eleven, and he may have loaned me a T-shirt to wear so I didn't have to sleep naked, but I'm not going to regret any of it.

Although you and I both know that a good, hard fuck sometimes encourages that asshole in your uterus to come roaring out like it's entering the Thunder Dome.

I'm not wearing underwear.

That reminder becomes painfully obvious as I roll over and attempt to creep out of bed. My underwear from the day before is somewhere on the floor, and I have a tampon in my bag. This should be okay. Get to the bathroom before...

Before...

Oh. No.

Oh, no no no no no no *no!*

I'm barely out of Drew's bed before I realize that the most horrifying thing that could ever happen to a girl has happened... to me.

Behold. Dark red splotches all over Drew's white sheets.

My thighs are covered in blood. I literally look like some serial killer has climbed through the window and stabbed my abdomen until I bled to death. Well, I may be ghostly pale, but it's not because I'm dead. It's because I'm utterly mortified to the point that I don't think to quickly grab my shit and *run.*

That's what I should do. Grab my clothes, throw something on, and get the hell out of here! *Never talk to this scrub again!*

I won't be able to look him in the eye, that's for sure. Not without turning the same hue as the shit that sloughed off my uterine lining.

"Morning."

My head whips around without my permission. There, standing in the open bedroom doorway, is Drew. His tousled hair goes swimmingly with the stubble all over his face and the generous happy trail descending into his gray sweatpants. The same ones he had been wearing when he hauled me to this bed and fucked me for half the night.

Words I intended to say come out in pitiful whimpers.

His smile falls off his face. Is it too late for me to run into the bathroom and lock the door behind me? It's not going to save me any face, but I'll feel better for two whole seconds! At least my fright has shut off the downstairs pipes for two extra seconds. A girl can only stand here with bloody thighs for so long.

"Uh oh." Drew, who had been holding a plate of toast in his hand, stands up straight and looks *right at the stained sheets.* "What the hell happened? Are you..." We make terrifying eye contact. He's about two seconds away from asking, "*Do you need to go to the hospital?*" and I'm about two seconds from running out of his apartment butt-naked. "Oh. *Oh.*"

There are a million things I want to say. Each one wavers between standing my ground and being a bold, confident woman... and a startled thirteen-year-old who still can't believe this shit happens every single month. I was definitely that girl who both boasted about getting her period to her female friends while simultaneously pretending it didn't exist around her boyfriends. What can I say? Some things are so ingrained into your little, young psyche that you grow up to be that woman who would rather die than ever admit you get a period.

Guess what comes out of my mouth. Go on. Guess.

Have you guessed? Are you ready?

Intoxicated

Ahem.

"I didn't... it wasn't... it wasn't me."

Christ almighty! The fuck is wrong with me?

Drew looks between my giant period stain and the waffling countenance I prance about his bedroom. I'm sure he's looking right at my bloody crotch, too. Was that toast in his hand? Because it's on the floor now. A billion crumbs begging to be vacuumed by whomever comes by to do his cleaning. "It wasn't you, huh? Then who did that? *Me?*"

He turns around, as if to look for a giant blood stain on his ass. I sigh, eyes closing and body sagging forward.

Before tears can stream from my eyes, I pick up my things and dive into the bathroom.

Lucky me, Drew has a detachable showerhead. Don't think for two seconds I'm using it to get off, however. Not like last night, when he "surprised" me in the shower and made me fall to my knees from the judicious application of water spray to my fucking pussy. (If I thought that was the last orgasm I was getting from him last night, I was wrong. As soon as I announced I was clean, he showed me he had gotten hard again. Not ashamed to admit I thoroughly enjoyed one last pounding from behind, complete with another need to shower.)

That ain't cum I'm washing off my thighs, though. That's the result of me effectively using birth control and avoiding what cum can do to a poor girl.

"Oh my *Goddd*," I whine, scrubbing my thighs and crotch as if I can single-handedly get rid of all the blood that usually takes four days to leave my system. I'm not sure if those are tears in my eyes or the steam playing tricks on them. I don't care. I'm miserable either way.

Trust me, the last thing I want to do is leave this bathroom. Yet I'm trapped. At some point, Drew is breaking down that door and confronting me about ruining his sheets. Besides, this is a *guy* we're talking about here. How many men have you dated who knew how to handle something like this? We women barely know how to deal! If I were home alone right now, I'd wash the crap out of my sheets and spray down my mattress while cursing myself for all the extra work. But I would suffer in silence, grateful that no one else was around to behold the mess my insides made.

"Heeeeey." That's Drew at the door. I've long since shut off the shower and now hang my head in shame on the toilet. "Got a fresh T-shirt for you here. Want me to make you some toast?"

I peer through my fingers, as if he's standing before me. "Leave me alone," I moan.

"Alrighty."

That's all he says. I can only guess that he's gone. I pick up the T-shirt I had been wearing, but notice it was long enough to be stained as well. Great. This T-shirt doesn't look sentimental in the least, but hot damn, I shouldn't be getting period blood all over the shirt of the guy who was hired to...

No. Wait.

This is brilliant!

What better way to get back at the bastard than by rolling my Aunt Flo all over his expensive bed sheets? Yes, yes, this is perfect. Ha, ha! Suck it, Drew. You'll have to buy a new mattress if you ever want to sleep in your bedroom again. Cher Lieberman was here, and she left behind a biological hazard to change your life.

That's what I think to puff myself up. Naked aside from my underwear, I throw open the bathroom door and march out, nearly tripping over the fresh T-shirt he left in front of the door.

Intoxicated

I snatch it up. Might as well wear something so he doesn't get a free show as I walk around his bedroom.

Drew isn't looking in my direction, though. He's busy ripping the sheets off his bed and leaving them in a pile on the floor. His own T-shirt, that he's put on since I first saw him a hot minute ago, is baggy enough that it flutters with every strenuous movements. He doesn't see me as he whistles some God-awful tune. Nor does he further embarrass me by spraying deodorizer. If I weren't here at all, I doubt he'd be acting any differently.

Suffice to say, I don't know how to take this.

I'm not saying I've never dated a guy who wouldn't act nonchalant about me bleeding all over his bed. For all I know, I have. My most long-term boyfriends didn't get to know a damn thing about my monthly visitor. Because telling your rich boyfriend, *"By the way, sweetie, no touching downstairs because of you know what,"* is a great way to remind him that you're some kind of human. You're talking to a woman who has made a living pretending to *not* be human. I'm a manic pixie dream girl. I'm the girl-next-door you first jacked off to when you realized boners could be great. I'm the seductive porn star who will get in any position and always tell you that your cock is "too big" for little ol' me. I'm a caricature. Whatever one you need in the moment.

I'm not sure what I am around Drew. Now that I'm no longer working him, I'm... me.

I may have a T-shirt and underwear on now, but this is the most naked I've ever felt in front of a guy.

"Hey." He politely avoids eye contact as he kicks aside his dirty linens. "Everything okay? I've got some ibuprofen if you need any. There's also a Rite-Aid on the corner. Need me to grab anything?"

My jaw wants to drop. Instead, I decide to test these unknown waters. "What if I told you I need a very specific kind of tampon? You're gonna go get that for me?"

"I need to get some laundry stuff anyway. You should probably write down what you want so I don't forget and have to text you. By the way," he motions to the T-shirt gracing my torso, "your tits look great in that."

Unbelievable. One moment he's acting like the best boyfriend in the world, and the next? A chauvinist pig. Am I really surprised?

"I don't need anything," I say, turning away. "I've got medicine and tampons." I say that word a little louder, gauging his reaction. Drew doesn't flinch.

"Cool. I can hold off the trip, then. I still haven't had breakfast yet. You want anything?"

I gaze at the faded splotch of my blood left behind on the mattress. Fighting back the ingrained shame, guilt, and embarrassment I've carried since puberty, I say, "I'm sorry."

"It's cool. Really. Not a big deal."

"I... I should've known. It's three days early, but..."

"Hey." He holds a hand up to me. "It's cool. You don't have to explain. Shit happens. Now, are you hungry?"

My arms cross, as if to keep him away. "I guess. Can't say I have much of an appetite right now."

"I hear ya."

That's all he says. He turns to head back to the kitchen. I keep my eyes bored into the back of his head, waiting for a gotcha.

There isn't one.

As nice as it is to have a guy who isn't freaking out about perfectly normal biological issues, I'm not in the mood to stick around and find out about how tender and understanding he is. I'm getting the hell out of here before I'm so weirded out I look at him as if he's grown a second head and a tail.

While he's in the other room, I squeeze into my dress, now one size too small thanks to the period bloat wrecking my body. Yet I hold my head up high as I step into the other room and make my intentions to leave clear.

"So soon?" Toast pops out of the toaster. Drew leans against his island counter, checking out my cleavage.

"I need to go take care of some things, if you haven't noticed. If I leave now, I can catch the next streetcar heading home."

He sucks in his cheeks. "Hey, I'm not weirded out or anything about..."

"Let me know how much it costs to fix up everything, and I'll pay you back." I approach the door, hand extended to dramatically open it like I'm about to leap off a cliff. "See you around, I guess."

"Cher."

I stop halfway out the door. The cool blast of the AC in the hallway makes my bare shoulders shudder. Or, perhaps, that's his soft voice caressing me in ways he never did last night. Do you know how discombobulating it is to have a guy go from *wham-bam-right-in-depths-of-your-cunt* to *I-would-love-to-play-some-Barry-Manilow-for-you?* Because I do. I'm experiencing it right now.

"I've gotta go to Seattle later today," he says, "but I'd like to see you again next time in town. Or maybe you could come see me up in SeaTac."

I turn my head. "You think I want to see you again?"

Finally, I behold a smirk that is much more like the man I'm used to hanging around in this God-awful-misery of a city. A man who wants to slap my ass and plunder my holes like he's bought full-access to them.

Great. That's definitely a shudder from my memories of the night before. Great. *Great.*

"You can't get enough of me." Drew bites his lower lip, as if the mere thought of doing me again has him suppressing his innermost desires – namely, a desire to get hard and ram his cock into any orifice I offer. "Like I'm kinda sure I can't get enough of you."

Is this a joke? This man only went after me because he was paid to. His job was to fuck me like he does and make me feel *bad* about it. Is it the fact that I refuse to feel any guilt about rough sex? That I don't care how hard he stuffs my throat with his cock? That he could ram me in the ass and I'll scream how it was my idea all along? Am I a *challenge?*

Do I have a problem with that?

You see, I have no guarantee that he's not still playing. I keep telling myself that he's not. That would be silly, since he's been made and I'm onto him. Surely, he knows how clever I am. I'm a chameleon, for God's sake. I can easily keep playing him, too!

A part of me wonders what it would be like to keep seeing him. Casually, of course. See how far we can take a simple relationship that revolves around sex and nothing much more.

But the other part of me doesn't listen to my pussy. It listens to my heart. My gut. The two things that keep me on my path of greatest independence.

They tell me to stay clear of this man. That he's nothing but trouble. Nothing but heartache I never signed up for.

I've never fallen for any of the men I've dated and fleeced. That's not my style. My heart is as hard as the floor beneath my feet. Why should I let someone like him inside of my heart? He should be grateful he's been inside my body. That's no great feat, though. Many men have been inside my body. You can call me a whore and I'll barely shrug. In reality, I haven't been with half as many guys as some of the other women I know who live this kind of life, but I've been in more loveless relationships for the pure profit I receive. I'm basically a whore.

Looking at him definitely makes me feel like one. I can't say I asked for that.

"Goodbye, Drew." I don't thank him for anything, least of all for being cool about what happened this morning. I'm not going to pat a guy on the head for doing the bare minimum. I don't believe in positive reinforcement. That would imply he's an animal. Most animals are better than most people.

I close the door behind me. I don't know if I should admit how hard it is to not look back.

CHAPTER 15

DREW

"Sucks to hear that it didn't work out." My assistant carries my overnight bag into the office. The Seattle skyline is right outside the windows, and I stop to take it in before turning to the man who runs the place in my absence. "You were getting pretty good money for her, right? Now you've gotta refund it all."

I snort. "Rothchild isn't getting his deposit back. It's in his terms." Deposits are only refunded if I don't get anywhere with the girl at all. In Cher's case, I got somewhere with her. *Really* somewhere. Not that I've told Brent. Until now. It's heavily implied in what I said.

"Dang, dude." He's impressed, but not surprised. This is me we're talking about. I don't exactly struggle to seduce women. Not when I flash my wallet or my name around, anyway. "You're a rock star, man."

"I know." I say that with a cheesy grin. Before long, I'm back at my desk, one I rarely sit at if I can help it. When I'm between gigs or playing a long game with my current mark, I'll come back here and do some paperwork and fish for new clients, but it's not something I look forward to doing. Brent mans the place. That's all I really need. "She made me by the end of last weekend. She must have hired a private investigator who really knew what they were doing. Oh, well. I still got to tap that crazy ass." Twice.

"Before or after she made you?"

Oh, this is the part I've been looking forward to telling Brent. "After."

"No way." He laughs before grabbing us some coffee. "You're that good, man!"

"Yeah." Why am I not reveling in this as much as I wish? The whole drive up here, I was thinking about how great it would be to brag about my sexual prowess to Brent, a man who totally gets it. Yet after a restless night's sleep in my Seattle apartment, I concluded that what I have with Cher goes beyond her hotness and me wanting to make her come as some way to prove my masculinity. "Although there's a reason it still happened, even after she figured out who I was and what I was doing. Shit, she figured out it was Rothchild who hired me! She's way more clever than anyone gives her credit for." I mean that, too.

"Why's that?"

Brent places a cup of coffee on my desk. I steeple my fingers and swing one leg over the other. Although our equipment and furniture makes us feel like fancy rich bastards, we're both in T-shirts and jeans. I've got my green forest ranger trucker hat on, and he's got a gauge five miles wide in his left earlobe. We're far from the usual professionals you would expect in a high-rise office. Especially when we're not expecting anyone.

"Hmm." I tap my fingers together. "There's something about her. Some *je ne sais quoi* that makes her hotter than your usual pretty girl. You feel me?"

"I mean, I've seen her pic, dude. She's hot."

If you're wondering what a man with a husband is doing saying that, don't. Brent is the first guy to tell you his door swings both ways. Before he met his husband, he wasn't much better than me when it came to getting women to spend a night with him. Well, I have more finesse. And higher standards, but that's not a knock against my assistant, who has been happily monogamous – as far as I know – since his marriage.

"Yeah. She's hot." I'm not above sharing details of my conquests with Brent, and I don't doubt he's waiting for some hot memories. I could tell him about how hard Cher's cunt grabs my cock when she comes. Or I could share that her tits bounce like they've got somewhere to be. Does he want to know about her gorgeous snarls of depravity? Or how she sucks cock like a champ? I want to pull her hair and fuck her ass until she's screaming in untold pleasure. I'd *love* to get her caught in a compromising position out in a fancy restaurant. She seems like the type to get off on a little humiliation. At the very least, she'd pretend that wasn't happening. Like it was her fucking idea to get caught with dick in her mouth or elsewhere.

Her insistence on acting like everything is exactly according to her plan, although I damn well know it's not, is amusing. And hot. It makes me want to up the ante every time I take her for another spin.

Intoxicated

"Dude, don't tell me you're already catching feelings for an established playgirl."

"That would be as absurd as her falling for me."

"Especially since her ex-boyfriend paid you to fuck her up. How *were* you going to do that, anyway?"

"I wasn't sure yet. You know I usually take my time figuring that part out." It's true. Every woman is different. You may look at her file and guess she would be most devastated in this fashion or another, but after you get to know them and their little quirks, another, deeper truth usually comes out. I was about to approach Cher in the same manner. Go out on a few dates with her. Fuck her. Figure out what motivated her the most and use that to my advantage. So far I've fucked her and gone out on two dates with her - if you call margaritas a date - but not much else.

"Don't tell me you've met your match."

I consider that for a moment. Met my match, huh? I know what he means. I've come up against a woman who can dish it as well as I give it to her. We're two of a kind. Two sides of the same fucked-up coin. Two peas in a cozy little pod made of despair and madness. We're sad. Depraved. Assholes.

We're the same exact brand of toxic.

In reality, I'm thinking something totally different form Brent. I've met my match. The woman who might be *the one.* Absurd, isn't it? Cher isn't looking for a boyfriend. She's made that clear. She wants hot, rough sex and then nothing for days. She doesn't care if she bleeds all over a guy's bed and he goes out of his way to make her feel okay. (Yes, I noticed.) This is a woman who envisions a world of her, herself, and she. There's no room for me. Maybe for my money, and my cock for a short period of time, but not *me.*

She's using me. All I can hope for in return is getting to use her, too.

"Earth to Drew." Brent is sitting on the edge of my desk, coffee in his hand. He doesn't seem to be drinking much of it, though. "You thinking about that hottie, huh?"

"Thinking about a lot of things, honestly."

"You better think about what you're going to tell Rothchild. He's not going to be happy that the deal has fallen through."

Considering this doesn't happen hardly *ever,* I'm not happy, either. I'm a professional businessman. I'll be upfront and honest when I can't come through on a deal. Rothchild isn't getting his deposit refunded, but I also won't be charging him for more of my services. With any luck, he'll keep the yelling to a minimum and not bad mouth me to every Tom, Dick, and Larry David in Seattle.

Maybe I deserve it, though.

What is this? Some kind of epiphany? Am I realizing that it's wrong to treat women like disposable trash, even if the exes they've wronged pay me for the pleasure? Do I feel some regret for what I've done to women over the past few years? Am I *growing?*

Jesus. When did I become the hero of a fucked up romance novel?

Brent goes back to his desk. I study my all-in-one for a few moments before grabbing my work phone and looking up Rothchild's number.

Now's my chance to call him and tell him the deal's off. I'll tell him the truth, in that Cher has made me. He should be pleased, really. It means he was taken in by a woman who is *that good.* So good that she got me, too. He shouldn't feel bad. If anything, this will give him a chance to move on! Get a new girlfriend! Someone a little closer to his age and not only after him for his money...

I dial his area code. The phone is in my hand. The receiver leaning against my shoulder.

My finger hovers over the last number.

CHAPTER 16

CHER

My cramps felled me for two days. Two days of lying on my couch and watching reruns while the sun blazed outside. People jogged by, walked by, and drove by with the tops of their convertibles down. Another prime night for going out and finding a real boyfriend blew by. I tortured myself with my financials, looking at both how much money I have in the bank and how my investments are doing. I'm far from my goal of being a multimillionaire by thirty. My plans include at least three more rich bastards fawning over me before that can become a reality.

I'm almost a millionaire. Granted, I don't get to touch most of that money if I don't want to prematurely lose out on better gains in ten years. (Assuming the American economy hasn't completely collapsed by 2030. You honestly never know.) If I

Intoxicated

cashed in some of the smaller investments, I could buy a nice little place somewhere around here. I'll have to go closer to Slabtown, though. I can't say I'm a big fan of Slabtown.

Call me greedy, but I want one of the old Victorians. A Victorian like my ex owns only a ten minute walk away from here.

I don't seem around that much, honestly. We have different haunts. He hates the stuck-up, high-society lounges that I frequent, but there's always that chance that we'll be in the same place at the same time.

Like the first day I come out of my apartment, feeling better now that the worst of my period is over. I put on a flowy sundress and don a straw hat on my head. I deserve some wine after everything I've been through lately, yes?

Of course I torture myself by going back to the wine bar where I had my first "date" with Drew. Not the first guy I've taken there, but he's become the most memorable. Damn him.

"We currently don't have any tables available," the server tells me at the door. "It will be about a fifteen minute wait, but you can sign in here."

I survey the room. It's impossible to tell who might be leaving in this wine bar, but I see a lot of empty dishes and people looking antsy. I probably wouldn't have to wait more than five minutes. If that couple in the corner is really speedy, I could have my favorite spot...

I take a closer look. Two blondes. One in nice shirt and slacks, and the other wearing a fashionable dress like mine.

Don't blame me for not recognizing my ex and his new woman right away. Preston Bradley looks like so many basic guys from the back of the head, and his girlfriend is painfully... Portland. Not in the ear gauges, dyed hair, and anarchy-themed

- 179 -

shirts kind of way. I mean the *hippie* kind of Portland. Long, flowing skirts, wavy blond hair, and entire wardrobes purchased from thrift stores. Yet she looks like a million dollars, because Preston wouldn't be with someone who looks any less.

"That's okay." I turn around before either of them see me. "Thanks for letting me know."

In the end, I'm saved by a full wine bar. Otherwise, I might be seated next to Preston and What's-Her-Name. (What *is* her name, again? Penny? Penelope? Feeble-Minded? Wait.)

Phoebe. That's it.

Preston and Phoebe. What a pair.

I step out onto the warm street and decide to go to a nearby Mediterranean brunch spot that has good wine. It has to be better than nursing my anxiety as it flairs up in the middle of a crowd. It's not usually the kind of place I go to by myself. I've taken a hundred dates there, of course, but when you go alone, you tend to get a few *looks*. Never mind the woman reading the paper while her dog sleeps at her feet. Or the young lady on her Kindle, guzzling every word she sees like it's the wine in her hand. The only men you see here flying solo are over the age of seventy and have nowhere else to go at this time of day.

Dutifully, I fill those ranks. As soon as I'm seated in a small booth, I order the wine of my desires and a cheese plate to go with it. My fingers drum on the table. Usually, I'd crack open a paperback I carry in my bag, or at least browse my phone, but...

Something's in the air.

No, I swear it has nothing to do with Preston and his woman yucking it up like it's their first date. I'm so over him that it's amazing I remember his *name*. Although I can't say I'm proud of how things ended with him. So what if I had been using him for

Intoxicated

his money? So what if he was technically my first "mark," one I picked when I saw how good my coworker got it when she started dating Preston's business partner? My backup plan had always been to breakup with him and sue him for sexual harassment should it come to it. Sure, the whole world paints me as a terrible bitch for it, but the man was so *gullible* that I had no doubts he harassed half the women on our staff. Once I gave him an opening, he took it. No dawdling. No moral hem-hawing. I barely cocked my hip and licked my lip in his direction. I can only imagine what happens when he *misreads* a woman's intentions.

Does it matter? I was younger then. Far dumber. I've apologized to him and moved on with my life. He's certainly moved on with his. The money he paid me as settlement lasted me more than a few months. Long enough for me to find my next so-called boyfriend and establish my mid-twenties career of being a serial sugar-baby to Portland and Seattle's wealthy men. To think, some of them *have* asked me to marry them.

Suppose those facts go to a woman's head. When you're always getting guys, getting attention, and getting money, you know you don't have to work hard at a mediocre date. I go on Tinder and have five men asking me out by the end of the hour. Actually, one of them accuses me of "not being as hot in real life as I am in my photos," but I take it as a compliment. Because, you know, I actually am that hot.

So, maybe my weird feelings right now have more to do with self-reflection cringe than anything else. Nobody likes to be reminded of how they acted before their brains fully developed. Just because I was good at using my body to lure in whoever I wanted into my bed *doesn't* mean I had the finesse I now do. Then again, who knows? Maybe I'll be looking back on this moment ten years from now and cringing so hard people think I'm having a seizure.

I'm content to chalk up my strange feelings to such things. Then, I hear the conversation going on in the booth behind mine.

"My son really is an idiot," an older woman bemoans. I can't see her face, but I imagine the type who always has a martini in one hand and a little yippy dog in the other. She sounds too refined to go with the fake spray tan and hot deals from TJ Maxx. No, this is a woman who goes to the nicest, most secret salon in some high rise on the waterfront and dons herself in simple designer dresses she picks up in LA, New York, London, and Hong Kong. She's the "effortless" rich woman. She's who I aspire to be when I am fifty-five. "He spends all his time up in Seattle. When he does come home, it's usually to go out with women I'm never allowed to see. Take this last time he was finally back in Beaverton. I told him, *just once,* I'd like you to bring by a girl you're seeing. I'll pretend that I don't care she's utter gutter garbage with no pedigree or her own decent career to speak of. Well, I leave that part out. You know how sensitive my son can be when I bring up how poor people are in this town."

"To be fair," a woman with a whinier voice says, "the property taxes in this area have been going *nuts.* How much more can they tax us before the guillotines are brought out?"

"Uh, do you know who they're going to behead after they're done with the politicians?" She was met with another snort. "Anyway, my son tells me that he's not actually seeing anyone. Except I see the stupid look on his face. When he thinks *I'm* not looking, he's got the goofiest grin of a dumb man in love. Can you believe it? Thirty years old and getting all slack-jawed about a woman he won't let me meet."

Intoxicated

"Is that unusual?" asks the whiny woman.

"Hmm. I suppose. The boy gets around to the point that if I didn't already know he had a vasectomy... well, never mind. Point is, I think *he* may think he's in love."

This is the part where we acknowledge what we're all thinking. This woman I overhear? She's obviously talking about Drew. Or, if she's not, then the guy I'm boning has some doppelganger out there who is also thirty and spends most of his time in Seattle. Oh, and he has *this* kind of woman for a mother. We don't have to debate that, however. I know exactly who this woman is after scanning my memories and recalling meeting her once before when I dated a so-and-so who ran in her social circle.

Cindy Benton. *The* Cindy Benton, current matriarch of all things Beaverton Benton.

Maybe you can't tell from listening to her for two seconds, but she's not actually some tactless rube from the sticks. Nor is she a native of Portland (if you also could not tell that.) Cindy is as east coast as the blood flowing through her veins. Her Virginian origins aren't well known around here, but I like to think it adds to her sophisticated smarm that straddles the line between Southern Hospitality and Yankee Abominations. No wonder she fits in so well around here – and hates it.

I could also tell you how Cindy became a Benton, because that's how well I've immersed myself into that world. I've heard every version of the story, of course, but the real truth is boring if you're a gossip-monger. Alexander Benton met his future wife through a mutual acquaintance while they were both attending college in Southern California. One thing led to another, and before you knew it. Drew's older sister was cooking in the oven and Cindy had to decide between becoming an early Mrs. Benton or aborting that kid so fast she would forget all about it after one night of partying.

We see what she chose, hm?

Oh, it was plenty gossip back then, I'm sure. I wouldn't know. That was about ten years before I was born, depending on who you ask. Drew was their Band-Aid baby meant to save their marriage, and it worked, but only because he was a boy. Joke was on the Bentons, I suppose, because their daughter is still the one due to take over the company one day. Meanwhile, spoiled, bastard Drew is out there cavorting with whores like me.

Whores Mrs. Benton is apparently talking about right now.

"You need to hire someone and figure out what's got him grinning like a fool," the whiny woman, someone I don't immediately recognize, says. "It's only a matter of time before he starts telling you about her, and before you can get excited about grandbabies, you need to know what you're dealing with."

"On one hand, I'm simply excited he might be serious about *anyone*," Cindy says. "Especially if it keeps him here in Portland. You know how much I miss my baby boy. Our housekeeper Opal also remarks on his absence. You ask me, he used to have a crush on her." Cindy chuckles. "Typical. Boys falling for their pretty housekeepers and nannies. No wonder they're always trying to marry them, let alone *actually* marry them."

"Watch out for boys in love," the other woman says. "If I had a dollar for every boy who ends up with someone taking him for a ride, I could make my yearly donation to the WHO."

"Why are you donating your hard-earned cash to a band that has enough money?"

"No, no, Cindy. The World Health Organization. Number three on Carol Cruz's list of Charities to Watch Out For?"

Intoxicated

"I can't say I've received this quarter's newsletter yet."

I thank the server for bringing me my cheese plate and wine. While Cindy and her friend switch topics to some inane shit I can hardly stand to follow, I mull over what she has said about Drew. *He's in love with someone from around here, huh? Recently, you say?* I don't believe for two seconds that it's me. Oh, they might be *talking* about me, but Drew is absolutely not in love with me. Maybe he's enamored with my pussy and how my mouth looks bobbing on his dick, but he's not in love with me. Not Cher Lieberman, a human being with her own thoughts and personality. He might be in love with sex with me, though. I have to admit, it's been on my mind much more than the sex I usually have, even for *fun,* whatever that means anymore. I'm not about to think I have some magical pussy that's roped in a guy like Drew, though. I don't *want* to rope in a guy like that anymore. He's not worth the drama. He's barely worth the occasional date and screw.

I'm still in the middle of my snack when Cindy and her friend pay their bill and step out. A baby blue dress swishes against my arm as Cindy absentmindedly bumps against me with absolutely no regard for my personal space. No sorries. No apologies of any kind. Her friend merely tugs on her arm as Cindy turns around and barely acknowledges my presence.

Wine is on my lips as we briefly see one another. In her eyes, I see a middle-aged woman who has given up on many things. Not because she has spent most of her life struggling against an impossible system built to keep her down, but because she's had everything handed to her so easily she has no idea what to work for anymore. She doesn't see me because she thinks I'm so far beneath her. She doesn't see me because she sees nothing but her inane existence.

Well, there's a small flicker of a spark in her eyes *now*. I tend to have that effect on people. They see me and instantly feel alive.

I better mind myself, though. I'm not working Drew's mother like I might work some of my sugar daddies' mommies. I have nothing to gain by making myself memorable to this woman.

I do, however, have a lot to lose if Drew decides he's in love with me. For one thing, I might lose my damn sanity trying to shake him off my leg.

CHAPTER 17

CHER

Surprised to see me again so soon? Aw. Sometimes I do that. Completely bust expectations because I have nothing better to do.

Like when I surprised Drew by texting him and asking him to buy me a train ticket up to Seattle so he could spoil me. He offered to buy me my own chauffer for the ride, for the sole purpose of avoiding the chaos that is the meth-fueled mess outside of Union Station (Portland or Seattle? Pick one.) I declined, however. Told him that the locals don't bother me. I can hold my own, even when I'm wearing flowy sundresses and wedge sandals that hobble half of my steps. Union Station is nothing. Amtrak is nothing. I don't need him to pick me up at the train station. Tell me where to go and I'll hail my own Uber to get me there in no time. He acts like I haven't done this a hundred times before for other men.

He acts like I haven't done *so* many things for other men. I don't believe he thinks I'm as naïve as I sometimes portray myself. For God's sake, this guy knows how I screw.

So why would he be surprised by how I deep-throat?

"*Holy...*" That's right, Drew, look me in the eye as I draw my teeth all the way up your shaft and suck your salty tip like my favorite lollipop. I live for you looking me in the eye as I make you come undone. Because you're the kind of guy who likes to pretend he's got it *all* figured out. We know the truth though, don't we? You and I... ah, I tickle your balls, you rub my clit, together we have this grand ol' time that nobody else compares to, because why not?

The only question I bother myself with is... do you act like this with every woman you're with? Or only the big slutty sluts you thought you were wrecking with this cock I could bite off at any moment?

Maybe that's what gets him off. The uncertainty of whether I'll end his reproductive viability with one bite. I've met my share of women who wouldn't touch their mouth to a guy's dick for a million. (Trust me, they're out there. Easiest million I could make, assuming they're good for the money.) You ask me? It's one of the only times I feel like I'm truly on top of the world. I'm not witless enough to call it *empowering*, though. That's silly. Sucking cock is more like reminding the guy I'm with that I could either be his greatest source of pleasure, or his worst fucking nightmare.

Honestly, tonight could have gone either way. It depended on whether he said anything about what happened last Wednesday morning, when I lost half my body's blood to his mattress.

He didn't say a damn thing. What a considerate guy. Maybe there's hope in this world.

He better hope so. Because when he gazes into my eyes, my mouth working him until all I can taste is his skin and precum, he knows he's looking into the eyes of a woman who has had a *lot* of practice.

I have to admit... he has a very satisfying *girth,* doesn't he? Not so big I feel my mouth splitting open. Not quite like I'm going to choke to death if I forget how to breathe like a woman who can fucking deep throat. Definitely not so big that I look at it and heave the heartiest guffaw you've ever heard coming from a woman about to throw down on a dude's dick. (Seriously, I've seen some massive cocks in my day. I once went out with a guy who was so big I legit asked him how he kept that thing tucked into his trousers without alerting security everywhere he went. He didn't think it funny. Nor did I think it funny he wanted to stick that in one of my orifices.) But I also appreciate a guy who is the right size for me. Maybe that's why it feels so good to fuck him. It's not only emotional catharsis of getting the guy who thought he could *get me.* It's the physical might of a guy who fits into your relaxed, wet pussy so well that you also can't wait to get this thing down your throat.

Honestly, he could take it a little further, if he tried.

"Is that all you got?" I cajole, my mouth totally off his dick but my grip wound tightly around the base of his shaft. I lift my head far enough for him to entice me with a kiss. I don't let him have one, though. Kisses are for men who give me what I want. And I *want* a different experience. The more I put my mouth on this guy, the more my body craves the kind of "loving" I'm not going to get with merely anyone. I'm craving sex like it's going out of style. You could tell me this is my last chance to get laid, and I'd believe you. Or, at least, my body will definitely believe you. It's throbbing for his thumbs to press into my shoulder blades and hold me down while he rams me. I don't care from what direction. I don't care if he comes all over my ass because he got too excited, as long as I get to come first. "Come on, Drew. You got this obnoxious bitch to come up to see you alllll the way from Portland." I languidly stroke him as I tease his chin with my lips. My hair falls against his open shirt. He continues to grip the edge of his bed, where he's been clinging ever since we came in here and I sat him down. He thought he was slowly undressing me and taking me every which way to Sunday? Ha! I'm the conductress of this night's performance. He merely has to play the instrument I hand him.

How about my throat, Drew? Do you know how to play that like a fiddle?

"I know how you look at me." With one hand still on his dick, the fingers of my other hand lightly brush against his stubble. A man who was *in love* with me, as his mother loves to put it, would lean into my hand and try to kiss my palm. (Been there. I know what it looks like.) A guy who wants to put me in my place and use me for his own lascivious ends? He's doing what Drew soon does.

He's keeping his face pointed toward me, throat growling and knuckles turning white.

"How do I look at you, Princess?" he asks, as if he doesn't know. "Like I want to fuck you until you scream? Because that's what I'm thinking."

"Why scream when I make a multitude of other fun sounds?" Both of my hands land on his legs. I didn't wear a bra on my trip

Intoxicated

today. Makes it easier for me to pull down the bust of my dress and entice him with my naked breasts. Not to touch with his hands, oh, no. These things exist for one purpose right now, and that's to tease his cock with their cleavage. The guy doesn't have to work for a titty fuck. I hand it to him on a silver platter, and I do all the work.

For five whole seconds. What? Did you think I was putting *more* effort into that? Ha! I'm merely planting seeds in his imagination. I want to see how good he is at reading my signs. Let's see what kind of lover I really have in my hands here.

I don't travel to Seattle for just *anyone* after all. I want to know that the guy is worth it in the bedroom department.

"I dare you to do it." I drop my tits and flick my tongue against his tip again. Drew hisses through his teeth, as if I'm the sexiest gal he's ever beheld. He better think so. When I take him into my mouth again, it's for the sole purpose of getting what I want.

"What exactly are you daring me to do, Princess?" he continues to hiss.

He wants me to talk with his dick in my mouth? Fine!

"Fuck me," I purr.

That purr is two-fold. He gets to hear my scintillating response, *and* Drew gets to feel my throat vibrating on his cock. I do give a great hummer, don't I? Except hummers are for men who take their time to appreciate my skill.

It's kind of hard to give a guy a hummer when he's fucking you right in the throat.

My hair snaps against my scalp. My nice dress sleeves fall down my arms. I don't have time to think about anything else. My throat now belongs to Drew, and if I don't want to completely choke and ruin the moment, I better concentrate on what I'm doing.

This isn't one-sided fucking. Drew doesn't *just* get to pull my hair, still my head, and fuck my mouth like it's my willing cunt. My muffled cries of surprise and pleasure aren't reserved for his future spank-bank and nothing else. You think *I* don't get something out of this? Please! It was all I could think about the whole train ride up here. "*I'm going to blow him so hard he won't be able to think about anything else for the rest of the night. Blow him so hard he can't get it up again.*" Yes, I thought that to myself with quite the smirk on my face. I daresay everyone on the train knew I was thinking satisfyingly dirty thoughts. You see, it's the last day of my period, and I have a very firm *no below the belt sex when I'm on my period* rule. I don't care if it's day six and there's hardly anything left from my uterus. It's not happening, and once it *is* officially done, I'm taking the longest shower to start a new month. I don't care about a man's opinion on it. It's my body. I fuck when and how I want.

Also, I'm not stupid. Drew was going to want sex. It's his whole reason for agreeing to bring me up here for a couple of days. When he's not taking me to eat in some of Seattle's nicest places, I'm treating myself to a little shopping spree. There are boutiques here in Seattle you can't get in Portland. Shit, sometimes I come up here by myself, using my own money, but I won't say no to a man wanting to spoil me.

Even now, Drew is totally spoiling me.

My mouth, jaw, and throat are completely compliant as he fucks me. Maybe I brace myself against his legs a little harder than necessary, but we'll consider those bruises my love marks for him to remember this moment by. I'm not afraid of what he'll do to me. He should be afraid *of me!*

Intoxicated

He should be afraid of any woman who continues to look right into his eyes as he fucks her throat.

Every time I lose a little of my concentration, I thank God Drew hasn't noticed. I don't want him to stop until he comes. This may shock you, but I actually *want* his seed shooting into the depths of my throat. I consider it a triumph. The harder he comes, the more I win.

Go on, Drew. Do it.

I fucking dare you.

He gleans as much from my intense stare. I am unwavering in my stance as he tears me apart, trying to make some chauvinistic point about using my throat for his own ends. He's unrelenting with his thrusts, the power of his hips always two centimeters away from my face. My own depths are hot with arousal and pleading me to get off his dick and hop on it somehow else. But I'll deny myself for today. Tomorrow, though. Tomorrow, he's getting the full Cher Lieberman experience.

Right now? I'm his ultimate cool girl fantasy. The one who loves it when he fucks her mouth, slaps her on the face with his wet cock, and works her throat until the first hot wave of seed hits the back of her tongue.

Does she take it a champ, or what?

The struggle was apparent in his eyes. Drew knew that if he came, that was it. He'd be spent, with nothing leftover for other parts. He's young enough for a shorter refractory period, but we're at least one hour before he's ready to go again. I don't doubt he'd step up and eat me out or finger me wherever I wanted, but I can't say I see the appeal tonight. Let him have his little fantasy.

Drew collapses back onto his bed. I take my time easing off him, letting both spit and seed linger on his softening cock. He can look at if he likes. I merely prefer to leave a little bit of his own mess behind for him to clean up. (What? I'm not his maid.)

"Did you come all the way up here to do that?" He has one arm flung over his face. I slowly round the corner of his bed, helping myself to the tissues he keeps on the nightstand. "I mean, I'm not complaining, but you've decimated the poor guy."

"Did I?" My one sleeve is still down my arm. Although my tits aren't popping out of my dress, Drew doesn't mind staring at my chest. "Weird. I could've sworn that was you using up all my energy."

"You dared me. As we've established, I'll almost always do some sexy thing you've dared me to do."

"Tell me." I ignore the rest of his statement. Since when am I interested in hearing his excuses? "Do you usually fuck like that? Or am I special, because I'm such a bitch for you to hate-fuck?"

"Are we still calling it hate-fucking? Because I was fondly thinking of your visit today. Could barely keep it in my pants as I thought of all the tender ways I was about to fuck you."

The sarcasm in his voice isn't lost on me. I sit next to him, not bothering to lie down. Drew's hand lazily plays with the base of my zipper. If he had any sliver of strength left in him, he'd pull down my zipper and undress me with the intent of giving me that *tender* shit. Hmph. "I'm not your girlfriend," I remind him. "I'm your current fucktoy."

"If you insist on such wording, I'd hope you at least acknowledge the toying goes in both directions."

"You think I lie in bed at night fucking myself in the face with my dildos? Hardly."

"Sounds painful."

"What do you think that was?"

Intoxicated

"Wait a minute..." Drew finds the excuse to sit up. "Wasn't that what you wanted?"

"Sometimes, the kind of sex a girl likes skirts the edge of... well, pain." I give him one sultry wink to take his mind off thoughts of accidentally hurting me. I'd be pleased that a guy cares so much, but for one thing, I don't believe him... and for another, I don't have the wherewithal to deal with this right now.

He bites his lower lip. It's not strong enough to get him hard again, no matter how much he thinks we're gonna keep going. "Give me like... an hour... sorry, Princess. You were more of a Succubus again. When you get that way, I'm drained for..."

"There's no need." I turn away from him as if he's utterly nothing to me. His hand instantly drops to the bed. "Consider it my thanks for letting me come up here on your dime."

"Huh?"

I pick up my skirt and grab some toiletries from my overnight bag. "Is it all right if I leave these on your sink?" My travel kit is ready for his sink and shower. Mostly stuff I'll throw away before I go back to Portland. I prefer to not bring mementos back with me. "I'm going to take a quick shower. Get the travel grime off me. Maybe think about what I want for dinner. Is there any decent curry around here?"

"Uh... I don't need... *payment*... for..."

I don't let him finish. It's more than enough for me to shut the bathroom door behind me and flick on the fan. As I prepare to brush my teeth at his bathroom sink, I face my reflection. Flushed cheeks. Tousled hair. Wrinkled dress. I definitely look like I was up to no good.

"Got him," I mouth to my sultry reflection. Fucking with men shouldn't feel this good.

Hey, if I'm not milking him for his financial potential, then what am I doing? Let's not pretend I'm suddenly having changes of heart because a guy *might* have caught feelings for me. Let alone a man like Drew Benton, who makes his living ruining women like me.

We'll see who breaks whose heart first.

CHAPTER 18

DREW

Every time I'm around this woman, I'm completely thrown for another loop. It's like Cher grabs me by the hand, pulls me in a hundred little circles, and releases me to throw up in the wind. Centripetal force is a bitch like that. Always getting chunks on your face.

I had no idea what to expect when she messaged me a few days ago, asking me to buy her a ticket to Seattle. I offered her more than that. Why not a personal chauffer, so she can avoid Union Station and the stress of traveling by train? No? At least let me buy you a plane ticket, sweetheart. I know a guy - personally - who has a charter service that runs twice a day between PDX and Sea-Tac. It would be easy to get her a seat, but nooo, she insists on traveling her tried and true way. Which tells me she has reasons beyond seeing *me* on her mind.

I only become more suspicious when she pushes me onto my bed and goes to town on my dick. This is a woman who knows what the *hell* she's doing. We guys always joke about getting a girl who used to be a porn star. Gals who can deep throat you until you're coming so hard you no longer know which way is up – nor can you hear their squeals of protest as you choke them with your cock. I mean, that can't be helped. I'm sorry, ladies. When you're *that good,* your man will only be found on another plane of existence, and nowhere else.

It takes a lot to unnerve me, you know. Especially when you've given me the gift of *holy shit that's called coming.* So when Cher implies she blew me and asked for nothing in return because, in her words, "*Consider it my thanks for letting me come up here on your dime,*" I'm going to feel a certain way.

Not exactly bad. Definitely not good. Dunno. Can't put much better words to it. Yet if there's one thing Cher knows how to do, it's keep her on my mind.

I half expect her to be gone that first morning in my Seattle apartment. Yet there she is when I wake up, sleeping on her side, wearing nothing but a silky negligee she packed in an overnight bag. When she's not conked out from sex, she wears her hair in a loose twist to sleep. I suppose when you're someone who can't sleep on your back, a good way to take care of your long hair is to wear it like that. I can't say I'm used to it, though. This woman always wears her hair down. Down and free, flowing on the breeze as it blows against her face. Her straight and silky locks are like Heaven to touch. They're more fun to pull when you're fucking the life out of her. I mean, I'll take 'em either way.

Intoxicated

All right. It's time for a mulligan. Cher is peacefully asleep, albeit so far on the edge of my bed that it's liable she's disgusted with my presence. Probably dreaming about the real reason she's here. (Let me guess... searching for some poor Seattle sod to screw over? I'm saving her travel money. I bet if she comes up empty, she'll "let me" fuck her. Great. Can't wait.) Last time we did this, I had to have my sheets dry cleaned and the blood scrubbed out of my mattress. Not my finest moment. Not *her* finest moment, but I think I'm a gentleman. You know, when *I'm not screwing over people instead of her.*

We really do deserve each other, don't we?

Maybe it was the toast that was unlucky. I'll make some oatmeal, instead. Steel cut oats cooked with cinnamon and a dash of milk. I have fresh berries out my wazoo, thanks to Brent's husband's affinity for all things natural produce. (You know I pay Brent too much money when his house-husband can grow his own black, blue, and strawberries in their tiny yard. Couple that with some freshly squeezed orange juice, I might be doing this pseudo-boyfriend things all right.

Oh my God, I have no idea what she likes. Does she like orange juice? Why the fuck do I care!

"Hey."

She half-startles me as I survey my kitchen. Yet Cher's voice carries that well from my bedroom doorway. She's leaning against it, one strap of her pink negligee falling down her arm. Her makeup-less face isn't *that* much different from when she has it applied. Sure, the cat eyes are gone. The lips aren't as full and colored. She has a couple acne scars that you only see because she hides them so well. Yet if she thinks she's frightening me with her hideousness, she can think again. She's as different like this, with her hair piled in tangles on her head and her body spilling out of her negligee. That's all I see. Not an imperfect face. Just... a regular, beautiful woman rubbing sleep out of her eyes and licking her dried-out lips.

"Hey." I turn to her, one hand clutching my island counter. "You like oatmeal? 'Cause I'm thinking oatmeal."

"Don't wanna keep you from whatever you're doing. I'm sure you've got places to be and women to ruin."

I don't let her words affect me. Doing so would be to give her exactly what she wants. "Taking a little time off, actually. I figure you're the one who has places to be."

"I mean, I would love to go shopping. With the added bonus of I don't expect you to buy me anything."

"Ooh, brought your own money, did you?"

"That, and it's a little weird having a guy you're not really going out with buy you Chanel. Maybe it's me. Some women are absolutely shameless."

"Especially the women who don't have the funds you've amassed for yourself?"

"Hey, I'm not a millionaire." She turns toward my bathroom door. "Well, I don't get to access that million. Not for another few decades when I'm retirement age and a million barely means anything anymore."

"Tell me about it," I drolly say.

Cher disappears into my bathroom. At least there are no firecrackers lit beneath her. Dare I believe the bleeding times are over? When I asked her for the millionth time, "*Are you sure you don't want anything, Princess?*" I got a spiel about how she doesn't let anyone touch her down there when she's courting the crimson queen. Color me surprised to know women can go for that long. I then got a *lengthy* description about heavy flows, light flows, "brown stuff," and mucus, mucus, *vagina discharge mucus*. I am now the most educated man you know when it comes to the biological functions of the human vagina.

Yet I would still love to get to intimately know a few of those other functions...

I almost dare to intrude upon her morning ritual to ask her to shower with me. At the very least, I'd like to see that naked body getting wet in my steamy shower. Yowza. You know, I got rid of my morning wood, yet here I am acting like a caveman again. Few women get this reaction out of me. I can't help but wonder if part of the reason I'm attracted to her is because of how unobtainable she really is.

I'm not supposed to want her. She's a mark. A tigress who plays with her prey before snapping their necks. Every inch of her is a trap. She lures me in with promises of mind-blowing sex, but I know that deep, deep down she either resents it or... worse... she doesn't feel anything at all. I'm another guy she has to fuck to get what she wants. Cher Lieberman no longer knows the difference between orgasming for pleasure and climaxing for her own health.

So I oscillate between wanting sex with her, since we know it doesn't matter – and wanting to shake her by the shoulders and demand she tell me the secret to her fucked-up unhappiness.

There has to be something. Something that triggered this behavior and turned her into the black widow who leaves men sobbing in front of their families and chucking their grandmothers' engagement rings into the Puget Sound.

That something will probably be the death of me. We'll find out if I die with my dick somewhere inside of her. That's the only way I want to go.

***

"A rich guy broke your heart when you were barely out of high school." I mix a generous helping of paneer with my biryani rice. The spice level at this Indian buffet isn't as high as I might like, but I get it. When you're dealing with Pacific Northwestern palates, you keep heat levels... low.

Cher doesn't seem to mind. When she said she wanted Indian cuisine after a long morning and early afternoon of shopping, I knew the place to take her. There's this well-known Indian buffet right here in Seattle's heart, Belltown. For a reasonable rate, you can get all-you-can-eat Indian staples that fill your stomach to the point of popping an antacid. The place is quaint enough, even if it doesn't "pop" like so many of the trendy restaurants around here.

Right. We were having a heated discussion about what turned her into a bitch.

"Nope." Her nan dips into the bowl of paneer we share. "Never had my heart broken, actually. Isn't it funny that you thought you'd be the first one to do it?"

"I've got it." My fingers snap as I ignore what she said. "Your mother trained you in the fine arts of sugar-babying. She was a professional sugar baby herself back in the... let me guess... late eighties. Is your father really a CEO somewhere? Ooh, a rich dentist?"

"One of those things is somewhat right, but only because you got lucky with that ludicrous guess." Cher takes a bite of her nan. Her aviator sunglasses perch atop her head, hair now back down and loose around her shoulders. She's wearing a baggy pink T-shirt that tucks into the same black skirt she was wearing when I rammed it in her the first time. (Ah, such sweet and spicy memories.) Big plastic bracelets jangle against her wrist. Teardrop earrings brush against her long throat. She isn't wearing as much makeup today. This is a woman who wanted to dress comfortably for her big day out with *me,* the man who insisted on tagging along with her modest shopping spree. The only thing missing is a necklace around that lovely neck. Do you think she'll let me leave a trail of hickies there? How about a pearl necklace? She seems the type. "My dad's a podiatrist. A successful one, at that."

"Buuuut..."

"My mom's never been a sugar baby, as far as I know. Shit, I'm pretty sure she was a virgin before she met my dad. I would bet money on him being the only man she's ever slept with. How's them apples?"

"Drat." I drum my fingers against the table. "You're a sociopath who gets her jollies fucking over men. Since you're incapable of understanding empathy or most social cues you haven't forced yourself to learn, it's easy for you to use your perceived beauty to..."

"Nope." Cher continues to chow down on her nan. "I've had therapists. A lot of them thought I was fucked up, but never once did they bring up the possibility of sociopathy. Probably because I *am* capable of empathy. For people who, you know, deserve it. Like refugees, abuse victims, and survivors of animal cruelty."

I sit back in my seat. "Because you matured early, you quickly learned the value of your appearance. Girls didn't want to be your friend in school, but you always got boyfriends easily."

She cocks one wary eyebrow at me. "What's that got to do with anything?"

"So I'm right?"

Cher snorts. "I never wanted for a boyfriend, no, but I had friends growing up. Guy friends, girl friends... they come and go with life, as is usual. I'm sort of transitioning between friend groups right now. Trying to decide if I want one bestie, or a whole *squad*."

I honestly can't tell if she's joking. Is she joking? Somebody please tell me.

"Honestly, why are we talking about me so much?" Her red lips purse around her glass of water. She puts it back down with a small pop of her jaw. Ice? Between her teeth? Thanks, oral fixation, now I'm thinking about how well she swallows cock. And other things. Right here in front of my paneer and biryani rice. In this public place. In front of these nice strangers.

Ahem.

"I'd much rather crack the code behind Drew Benton." Cher leans over her plate, elbow on the table and fingers playing with the fine strands of her hair. "What makes this rich playboy so eager to ruin a woman's life? A woman he doesn't know. Because, for all he knows, it's a bastard of an abusive ex behind the will to destroy someone's life. At least I'm not intentionally hurting people. My exes willingly gave me money, paid my rent, and offered me gifts. What do you do? Go out of your way to extract revenge on behalf of other men."

Who whittled her such a sharp spear? She's plunged it right into my gut. There goes my blood and entrails, pooling on the floor of this nice establishment. You know, I eat here about once a month. Sometimes by myself! What is the nice Indian family going to think when they walk out here and see me white and blue on the floor, my dried blood congealed beneath my body?

Intoxicated

Will they take a picture for posterity? A picture of Cher stepping on my body so she can reclaim her deadly spear?

"It's a long story," I say.

"Try me."

"I mean..." I clear my throat. I suddenly don't have the appetite for my Indian food. "Guess it started while I was in college. I had a buddy who got massively fucked up by an evil chick who thought it would be funny to make her fall in love with her only to dump him. She never intended to marry him after school, which was what she originally told him she wanted to do after she lured him into her web of lies." My words make Cher roll her eyes. She may be unimpressed, but what I say is the truth. My best friend, dear old Hank - yes, that was his real name, because he hated Henry with the fire of a burning sun - fell in with the wrong girl. We all knew she was trouble, but he wouldn't listen to us. The girl was so spoiled that it meant nothing to her that the only way she could amuse herself was by playing with others' feelings. "When she dumped him on his graduation day, I decided to get back at her on his behalf. You have to understand..." I hold up my hand before Cher can protest what it was like being twenty-one and watching my friend slowly waste away from depression. "Hank was in a *bad* way, and this girl was seriously bad news. Luckily, I knew she had the hots for me. She tried multiple times to hook up with me while she was with Hank. So, while Hank stayed in bed for a whole month, I invited her to a party I threw at my family's summer house."

"Where you fucked and dumped her in front of everyone, I'm assuming."

"I fucked her, yes." I don't go into the details. Like how I fucked her as if she were a worthless woman not worth the label *human being*. It wasn't my proudest moment. Everything I did with her was fueled by anger for my friend, who refused to answer my texts and calls. His mom was always blowing up my phone, though, telling me how worried she was about her only child. The man had just graduated college and couldn't be assed to go to the job he had lined up. He lost that job, you know. He was bound to become one of Portland's hottest architects, and he was too depressed to remember he had his whole life ahead of him. "Long story short, I made sure she was good and smitten with my looks, dick, and body before humiliating her in front of everyone we knew. It was our senior year, you see, and I wanted to ensure she would be mortified until the day she either graduated or dropped out."

"Dare I ask what you did?"

I glance around us and lower my voice. Cher leans in closer. "I got us nice and toasted the night before the first day of classes. The campus was crawling with froshies at their orientation and seniors getting ahead of the game. I may have had her so blazed I convinced her to engage in some late-night hanky-panky in the great outdoors."

Cher continues to methodically chew her food.

"And we were *nasty*. Ahem."

She swallows, still unperturbed.

"After she was passed out, I left her there. By then the sun was coming up, so I barely had enough time to drag my naked ass back to my on-campus apartment. Half an hour later, she wakes up to everyone laughing at her lying naked and hungover in the middle of campus. Never saw her again after that."

Finally, Cher shakes her head, but it's hardly in admonishment. "Stone cold. Was your friend vindicated?"

Intoxicated

I wait until she's well into her next bite before responding. "He killed himself the next day. He never heard about it."

She stops chewing. That's the only response I get, until, "I'm sorry to hear that."

"Yeah, well... so am I. He was a good guy who didn't deserve any of that."

"Unlike that nasty bitch, right?"

"Figured you'd be on her side." I barely think about the food I'm consuming. Thinking about Hank and how he slid into that darkness. What was he thinking? How he would never love again? How all women were only out to use and abuse him? That he would rather die than take another breath? Obviously, I'll never really know. I'll never know if there was anything I could do to save him, to drag him out of that hell. I didn't find out about his death until a week later, when I contacted his mother and found out the funeral already happened. Best I can do now is visit his grave down in Silverton once in a while.

"I'm not on anybody's side," Cher says. "I don't know either of these people. She sounds like a bitch, yeah, but your friend probably had other shit going on in his life. She might have pushed him over the edge, but..." She stops, aware that I'm not finding this amusing. "Sorry. Your friend didn't deserve to die. I'm not convinced that girl deserved what you did to her, either. She's not responsible for his death."

"Yeah, well... you wanted to know what got me into my line of work? That was it. Was in a pretty bad spot for a while after his death. Had another buddy ask me to get back at his ex like the way I got back at her, and... one thing led to another..."

"Now you have a successful business humiliating and ruining women who had the nerve to break up with men."

"It's a lot more complicated than that."

"Sure." Still unimpressed, Cher sniffs up whatever's clogging her nose and pulls more paneer onto her plate. "Thanks for being honest with me."

"Unlike you?" When she gives me *the eye,* I explain, "you still won't tell me what led *you* down your path of unrighteousness."

"Maybe I don't have a reason." Cher shrugs, as if that's all there is to it. "Maybe this is how I came to survive this crazy world. Maybe you can't understand what it's like being a woman."

There are a million testy things I want to say. She doesn't have a right to put this all on her gender. Not when it comes to the pain I've seen in the faces of some of these guys who come to me for some sliver of justice. You can't arrest a woman for treating you like crap. I mean, you can if she technically broke the law, but most of them don't. Most of them get away with being stone-cold bitches who don't care what happens to you or your money.

Yes, I know... the more I sit here trying to explain myself, the crazier I sound. Suppose it is crazy. Yet after my grief for Hank faded and I realized that this may not be the best course of action for my life, I had stopped caring. This was what I was good at. Not whatever it was my family wanted to do. In my twenties, it was my way of getting back at the world. Striking my own path. Doing what I wanted and going about as I cared. For every woman I was paid to sleep with, there was one who was in my bed for fun.

Now I look in these blissfully brown eyes and wonder what the hell I'm supposed to do. Cher has become both. I've been paid to break her. I was committed to splitting her apart, body and soul.

Now, I'm not sure what the hell is going on.

Intoxicated

Cher pulls out her phone and scrolls through something on her screen. Yup. Right in the middle of our conversation.

"Whatever," I mutter, going back to my food.

"Hang on a sec." She glances up at me, then back at her phone. "Says here I can get some of the weed I like two blocks over. Now I know what I want for dessert."

"Weed," I repeat. "If that's what you really want, I've got some in my..."

"Yes, I saw what you have. I don't care for that, though. You smoke what you want, but I'm getting what *I* like."

Can I help it if I'm surprised by this change in topic? One minute we're talking about my dead friend, and the next? Marijuana. Will wonders never cease with this woman? "Far be it from me to stop you from getting what *you* want."

Her sly grin punches me right in the chest. "Good," Cher says with a tawdry purr. "He's finally starting to learn."

It being the Pacific Northwest, I already smell pot in the air before we step into a dispensary.

CHAPTER 19

CHER

Go ahead and guess what I'm like when I'm high.

Go ahead! Guess!

If you think I'm the chillest girl in the room, biding my time until I get my next handful of tortilla chips then... ahaha, oh, my God, is that *SpongeBob on TV?*

It's a haze of smoke in Drew's apartment. Half the windows are open, the fan is spinning, and he was probably dumb enough to turn on the AC as well, but we still exist in a foggy cloud of poisons. Drew raided his personal stash as soon as we got home. Me, with my little bag of what I prefer. Ah, yes, this is how you spend an afternoon and evening with the guy who gets paid to humiliate women to the point they drop out of school their senior year of college.

Intoxicated

I wasn't in the market of walking down terrible memory lanes. I came here to hang out. To chill. To get high, apparently.

No, no, *no.* I don't smoke as often as you think I do. If anything, I keep my consumption of pot down to the bare minimum. It's something I indulge when I'm overly anxious, okay? Or when I'm so bored I need a little pick me up. My boyfriends range from teetotalers who rage against any kind of fun (minus their cognac, of course) to tech bros who toke up every night. It's easy enough for me to swing between the type of woman who never, ever indulges, and one who takes a hit of whatever my sugar daddy is offering me that day. (Trust me, tech bros have the worst taste in strains. There's nothing worse than a bro who spends half his money on shit pot that stinks up the place and makes you more irritable than it's ever worth.)

Drew, though... his stuff is all right. At least its scent blends well with mine.

Right. We were talking about what I'm like when I'm high? Have you guessed yet?

"Stop!" I lurch forward on the couch, my hand slapping the remote out of Drew's hand. "SpongeBob!"

He looks between me and the TV. Nickelodeon has reruns on, and I'm not about to pass up my favorite childhood show. As soon as the jingle begins, I'm singing along.

"Man..." Drew slumps back down into his seat, fly half open and hand tenuously down his pants. "Can you imagine what it would be like to live in a pineapple? I don't like pineapple. I'd rather live in a... hallowed out watermelon. Yeah. Fuck. I want watermelon. You think GrubHub is still going?"

I pull my feet up onto the couch and perch my elbows atop my knees. My joints are so loosey-goosey that I don't cringe at the pressure this puts on my hips. Although now my mouth is so dry that I need more Fanta. Yes. I'm drinking Orange Fanta, because this trip to Nostalgia Valley isn't complete without it. "Don't you have grapes or something in your fridge?" I ask. "I saw them in there earlier."

"Riiiight. Man, I don't wanna get up. I wanna sit here and stare at this ugly squid."

"Dude! Have you seen that creepy pasta about Squidward?"

Drew flinches at the volume of my voice. "No, can't say I have."

"His eyes fall out. Or something."

"Of course they do. Wouldn't be a creepy pasta without it."

"I want pasta."

"Me, too. Did you know Olive Garden delivers?"

I grab my bag of puffy Cheetos and wipe cheese dust on my T-shirt. "I want pasta. And breadsticks. Fuck me up with the carbs, Benton."

He picks up the last of his blunt and exhales the sweet-smelling smoke that will make up the remainder of his high. After furiously blinking, Drew puts a hand on my leg and asks, "What time is it?"

"I dunno. What time is SpongeBob usually on these... holy shit, I love this episode. I wanna have a rave in a pineapple under the sea."

Drew unearths his phone from the coffee table in front of us. "How is it seven already? We got home an hour ago!"

"Did we? I thought we got home at four?" Home! Listen to me, acting like this is *my* home, when I've only been here for a day! "When did we start smoking? Hey, wanna make some brownies?"

Intoxicated

Good thing Drew is done with his pot. I think he's entering the paranoid phase of his high. See, I *told* you guys he didn't have the really good stuff. I had an ex who used the same strain for his depression. Every time I tried it, I thought someone was about to push me off a train platform. Go figure.

"I'm getting something to drink. Something that's not Fanta." Drew stumbles into the kitchen. After a fit of hacking and a hearty sniff, he opens his cupboard and pulls out a huge bottle of something. He soon takes a swig right from the source.

Oh, good! We're totally doing this! Drunk *and* high!

You'd think we were college kids from how quickly we devolve into a mini-party just for us. One minute we're watching SpongeBob, and the next he's found old music videos on some forgotten channel. Or maybe he's switched to YouTube and playing his old favorites. Some of these videos are so grainy that they might as well have been uploaded in 2008. Is that Pearl Jam?

"Gimme some of that." I grab the wine bottle out of his hand and take a chug. Ugh. Tastes like fermented piss. Am I sure this isn't beer? Whatever.

"You know." Drew hangs over the back of the couch, his peach fuzz practically rubbing against my cheek. Oh. I think it might be. I don't have a great feel for reality at the moment. "I had spent this whole day thinking I was gonna stick it in your brown."

I take another swig of this beer-wine. "You like slamming the D into the A, huh?"

"I hear *some* women like it. Especially if you loo... lube them up real good... first."

"It's an acquired taste." Like this swill in this bottle.

"I was gonna fuck you in the ass and come all up in it."

"Bet you were."

"Does that turn you on?"

I wash the taste of this gunk out of my mouth. With Orange Fanta, yes. "Not really. Can't say I'm super wet from the thought of you going at my butthole."

"Bet most of your boyfriends love doing that. Men are sick, you know. Always sticking it in weird places..."

"Does that make you sick, too?"

"Girl, you fucking know it."

I laugh. Drew is so pleased with himself, that he must think I'm laughing at his joke. Yeah, right. I'm laughing at how pathetic he is when he's drinking *and* toking. This is the kind of shit we can only get away with at this age. I imagine us ten, twenty years from, still behaving like idiots.

Because what else should I be doing in my inebriated state besides thinking about what it would be like to grow old with this asshole?

I wash those thoughts away with whatever swill this is. The more I think about a *future* with Drew Benton, the more I want to die a little. In some alternate universe where we're actually compatible, let alone capable of a healthy relationship, things can only end with me becoming the permanent trophy-wife arm candy of the only Benton boy. I'll have to put up with his mother's inane ranting and his father's preposterous ideas about wifery. His older sister, the true heir of his family's fortunes, will probably have nothing but disdain once she got a look at me and read anything about my personal history.

Sounds like I deserve it, doesn't it? That should be everything I've ever wanted. A rich, handsome husband who jokes about fucking my ass when he's high out of his mind.

Intoxicated

He'd probably be one of the few that makes it feel good...

"You know what we should do?" Drew slams back down onto the couch, his sweaty T-shirt clinging to his muscles in ways that instantly attract my attention. Oh, good. I'm forgetting about that mushy shit that almost made me puke. I'd much rather drunkenly stare at his body and get lost in heavy thoughts of *fuck-fuck-fucking.* "We should go into the matchmaking business together."

Whelp. So much for that."

"Hear me out." Drew steadies himself with his hand on my arm. More sweat. God. He's a *sweater* when he's drunk. My luck. Good thing I don't have any plans to hop on his dick now. He ensured that by bringing up such a cheesy thing. "When you think about it," he continues, although I certainly did not ask him to, "it makes a lot of sense. I know the guys who want to find young, hot wives who will pretend to love them in exchange for money. You know what it takes to be that kind of woman. You know, a professional sugar baby."

He's got me there.

"With our powers combined, we could be the *hottest* million-dollar matchmaking service in the Pacific Northwest. I'll gather up the sorry losers here and in Portland. You help me review the women applying to be future trophy wives. It's perfect! You could like... tutor them! Prep those powerful pussies for a lifetime of sucking dollar bills out of old, hairy balls."

"Drew," I mutter, head hitting the back of the couch. "I'm too fucked up on this shit for you to make imagery like that." We won't discuss how many hairy balls I've seen in my life. Every guy, old and young, is so damn proud of his own pair, too. I don't get it. I don't have to get it. I only have to show up, put out, and get paid.

Drew kicks up his feet and stares at his ceiling. He's completely drunk and toked up, isn't he? Great. How quickly can I catch up with him? "That's what I should switch my business to when I'm over breaking hearts and taking names. I should be at the *beginning* of the toxic relationship, not the end! There are enough guys out there looking for the next big heartbreak of their lives. I could serve it to them on a silver platter. I mean, *we* could."

"What in the world makes you think we could ever go into business together? You realize this is some bullshit we're indulging for a while, right?" Dare I panic that he's suddenly getting serious on me? I can't handle a real relationship right now. Let alone with a loser like Drew. The man fucks women up for a living! What kind of boyfriend would that be? You know, assuming he could ever make a *real* boyfriend. That's absurd.

"Yeah, yeah." Drew briefly closes his eyes. "I'm spoutin' off nonsense. You know, as I am often wont to do."

"Are you?"

"You might not know me very well..." When he opens his eyes again, I get the full, bloodshot view. "But I am a very nonsensical guy around those I like."

"Is this where you open your true self to me, Drew? When you're so intoxicated you don't know any better?"

He grins. A big, goofy, *sloppy* grin that shouldn't endear me as much as it does. "I guess so. I can regret it in the morning. Maybe I'll be hungover, too, but hey, as long as you're in my bed and thinking about going into business with me, it's all good."

"Oh, you think I'm still getting into your bed? After everything we've already done tonight? Because if there's one thing I know about drink and drugs, Drew, it's that most guys can't stand up to it." I don't have to explain myself. He damn well knows what I mean.

"You think I ain't hard as fuck right now? I've spent the past half hour thinking about sticking it in your ass. Of course I'm hard."

I glance at his lap. What's going on down there is a far cry from what Drew usually sports when he's ready to roll. Like that night we met, when he openly dared me to grab his cock in the middle of a busy lounge. I don't have to touch it now to know how pathetic it is. "Tell me more about how whiskey-dick never gets you."

He follows my gaze. "Hmm. This is concerning."

I've been with some eyeroll-worthy guys before. Right up there with totally sober dudes who whip it out beneath the table and encourage me to stroke them off. During charity galas, no less. So many men out there can only get off if there's a risk-factor involved. Since the radio silence from the STD clinic suggests I don't carry *those* risks, they've gotta come up with something else. Handy-Js beneath the table while a bald woman talks about her struggles with chemotherapy are just the ticket!

Yet I'm still not prepared for Drew to unzip his jeans and take out his flaccid prick.

"Aw, poor little guy," I say with an exaggerated wibble. "He's too tired to get up and say hello."

Yup. You guessed it. Drew picks his dick up with his thumb and forefinger and gives it a sad, *sad* wave in my direction. It's rather amazing how much it's shrunken while he's inebriated. If this were my first time seeing it, I'd be running for the hills. I'm not saying I'm Stretched-Out Sally, but I'm thinking about those hot dogs and hallways analogies. If I'm hooking up with a guy for pure sexual satisfaction, I better be getting some*thing* out of it. A sensation! Some fullness! Something! C'mon, send me a dick mulligan!

"Wow," he says. "Nothing. I've. Got. Nothing."

"What was that about my ass again?" He might be able to smack that against a cheek, but we're not going to pound town tonight.

Drew blows air from his cheeks. Between that and the flapping between his legs, he looks like the saddest balloon animal in the world. Send me back to Portland already. I can't take it.

"I think there's hope," he says. "You know. If you took off your clothes or something."

"Do I look like I care enough right now?"

"Nope."

Good. Because I'm one sleepy woman. The pot and alcohol are starting to do their intricate dance in my system. For a woman who was wide awake an hour ago, I can now only think of one thing.

Slowly, I doze off. I wake up at one point long enough to realize Drew has thrown a light blanket over me. Where has he gone? I have no idea. Frankly, I don't care.

CHAPTER 20

CHER

Juuuust like that, I wake up God knows when.

I jerk up with a start. It's dark outside, and this close to summer, I'm inclined to believe it's past ten. Sure enough, after I'm done rubbing the sleep from my eyes, I look at the clock and realize it's a little after midnight. The blanket falls off my body as it adjusts to waking up after a cramped nap. I'm still feeling pretty loosey-goosey from the pot - okay, and probably the alcohol, too - but there's no denying that I would like to have a little more sleep.

Fuck if I'm gonna spend the whole night on Drew's couch, though. Let alone in my day clothes. Not when I brought perfectly fine pajamas. At the very least, I'll sneak into his room, where he's probably passed out, and change into more comfortable clothing before recommencing an early night.

"Hello, hello."

I didn't knock. Why would I, when there was hardly any light coming in from beneath the door and I can only assume Drew is asleep? I felt lucky enough that the door was unlocked. Yet did I think for two seconds he would be awake, sprawled across his bed in nothing but those delicious sweatpants he loves to sleep in?

His eyes aren't bloodshot. There is still sweat gleaming on his skin, but I assume it's from his lack of a shower than him still being high or drunk. It's been a few hours. If he's anything like the other men around his build and age, he's sobered up a bit.

Maybe he's like me, though. Still feeling a little loose. In both body and morals.

"Hi." My hand lingers on the doorknob. Was I opening the door? Closing it? I have no clue anymore. I wasn't expecting to be greeted by a man perusing a magazine before bed. "Sorry. Came in here to grab my pajamas. I'm, uh..." Why am I so flustered? You'd think I had never seen him half naked before. Or had my face in a Drew-Thigh Sandwich. Because I have to slap my cheek to make it stop wanting to press into his warm, sweaty skin.

I bet he smells like man-musk. You know the shit I'm talking about. *You know.*

"Have you had a moment to consider my offer?" He chuckles, one hand popping up to cover his upper lip. "Jesus, what was I thinking? Matchmaking services... this is why I shouldn't mix pot and alcohol."

My overnight bag is on the other side of the room. I hurry to it, my tangled hair getting in my face as I dig through the contents. I have a clean nightshirt here somewhere. I'm fine with sleeping without pants on. Even if it means this guy will probably be feeling me up all night.

Intoxicated

Gulp.

Why am I aroused? My stupid nipples are poking through my clothing, for fuck's sake. Heat builds between my thighs as I wrestle with my clean clothing. I've already kicked off my shoes, but if I were still wearing them, this would end with me digging my heels into his carpet. I'm already biting my lip and trying to stop thinking about that head I gave him yesterday. Or was it two days ago? Since it's dark and I've had a few hours of sleep, it feels like a new day already. Like the sun is about to come up and we're off to get pancakes at the local diner.

God, I want pancakes.

I want *food*. I want something in my mouth. I think an oral fixation is flaring up. Assuming Drew can also get something up...

Hm. What do I want more? Pancakes, or cock? Do I have to get them in a particular order? Maybe I should let the man make the decision for me. Just a cool glance over my shoulder, and...

Aaaaand he's looking right back at me, his goofy grin from before now replaced with a knowing smirk.

"Problems, Princess?"

"No." I clear my throat. "Thinking about pancakes."

His smirk does not falter. "Pancakes?"

"You know. Flapjacks. Crepes. Maple syrup and some marionberries..."

Drew's chuckle does things to my stomach. Crazy things. *Infuriating things.* "You are such an Oregonian he says." The magazine closes. "Marionberries."

"Something wrong with marionberries?" I turn to him. Does he see my nipples? 'Cause I can feel my nipples.

"Only Oregonians care about marionberries."

"Aren't you an Oregonian?"

He shrugs. "Depends who you ask. My birth certificates say I am. My mom says I am. Me? Eh, I can take it or leave it."

"Because it's changed too much from your childhood?"

He hooks his finger at me, as if I'm the reason we're not getting busy right this second. "There's one thing that hasn't changed about Portland, that's for sure."

Slowly, I go to him. Curiosity? Desire? We'll say a bit of both. I'll probably smell hints of wine and pot on him as soon as I'm close, but for now, the only reason he's so interested in me is because of stone-cold sobriety. He sees a woman he wants. A woman he knows he can take. That lascivious look in his eyes has me already taking off my panties. Whoops. There they go. Right on the floor. In case he doesn't know how skirts work, I pull mine up a little ways before pressing my knee against the edge of his bed. "What hasn't changed?" I ask.

"The abundance of interesting women who keep me on my toes."

"I don't see you standing on your toes right now." I keep my hands to myself, but it's a challenge. If you saw the finely chiseled torso that I do right now, you'd be having issues, too. If I weren't so in control of myself right now, I'd be slobbering all over this chest and grabbing those hips like I've never had sex before.

As if to taunt me, Drew leans slightly back, the stretch of his sweats on full display. Ah, yes, he seems to have regained control of his dick. The blood is flowing free again. His brain says *get hard* and the trouser snakes says *well, okay.* My teeth graze my button lip as I imagine teasing him to the point I see a fine little wet spot right where the tip of his cock is. I like those things hard and dripping, if you couldn't tell. Especially if I'm expected to put some kind of orifice on them.

Intoxicated

To hell with expectations, honestly. Especially if I'm *wanting* to fuck one of my holes with those things.

Let's see... how many holes do I have? At least three. Two are self-lubricating and have fantastic little nerve endings that make things a hundred times better. But he was saying something about the third earlier.

Maybe some other time. When I'm in the mood to be a bad, *bad* girl.

"Tell me one thing," Drew says, head propped up on his hand. The way he lays, with one foot kickstanding behind him and his chest open to my line of sight, has me in such a tizzy that I believe he's doing it on purpose. "Are you looking at me like that because you're hungry for more than pancakes? Or because you smoked a fat blunt earlier?"

Only now do I realize I'm chewing the inside of my cheek a little too enthusiastically. That oral fixation, man. It's getting me. The more I look at him, the more I want to repeat yesterday. I want his cock rammed down my throat, the taste of Drew Benton overwhelming me as he fucks me so hard I struggle to breathe. I want him to make me feel like the most depraved woman in the region, as if I don't get more, more, *more* of him, I'll completely combust. I don't usually feel this way about a guy. Usually, the passing fancy ends with me having sated my curiosity and ready to move on to someone else. Rarely does money and pleasure mix in the same man. Yet I keep forgetting who Drew really is. He's such a... *bro*. He may be thirty, he may have his own successful (albeit deplorable) business, and he may have the funds to live off of for the rest of his life, but I look at him and see a regular guy who takes care of himself. There's nothing more to it than that.

Dare I believe I'm falling for him?

"I don't know how I'm looking at you," I lie, "but I can tell you what I'm thinking."

"Go ahead. Tell me. Lie to me, if you want. I don't mind, as long as you make it hot."

I untuck my T-shirt from my skirt. The damn thing was all askew and wrinkled, anyway. "I'm thinking about your sad, pathetic dick from earlier." Ooh, am I doing a little domination tonight? Make him feel insignificant, to the point he fucks me until I'm convinced he's the greatest shit in Seattle? I could get into that. "And wondering whether it's had time to recover."

"Yes, yes, I knew you'd be into what I'm packing soon enough. That's why I was back here sobering up for you."

"Liar. You fell asleep, too."

"Only for a couple of hours. You slept way longer than me."

I ease forward, my nose coming closer to his. "Everything working downstairs?"

"Why?" He asks that, yet Drew's hand doesn't hesitate to reach up my shirt and clasp my breast. I half expect him to *honk* it, considering the playful mood he's in. Yet all I get is an infuriating flick of his finger against my nipple. "You want me to fuck you like I'm taking payment for buying your train ticket?" It takes every drop of effort to not let my eyes roll back.

I don't have enough effort. There they go. Can't see shit now. Can only feel heat rushing to my pussy and tingles exploding in my tits.

"Mm-hmm. That's what I thought." Drew pulls his hand out of my shirt. I nearly fall forward. "You're an easy slut."

He says it with a nonjudgmental click of the tongue. Although everything from his tone to his posturing is facetious, I can't help but take his words to heart. Does he sense that I take

Intoxicated

him seriously? Because Drew changes tune, sitting up to take me by the hands and draw me down into his lap. Soon, my arms are wrapped around him, his hand pushing up my skirt and sinking into the heat of my thigh. I'm so secure in his embrace that I almost forgot what he said.

"I mean," Drew says, "you know what you want. Some people would say that makes you an easy slut."

There's something poetic about the way he says the word *slut*. Most men say it with disdain. They've picked up the cadences from society. From the men in their lives. From the very women they tell are sluts. Of course, a slut can be any woman they sexually disagree with. She could be the purest virgin at the nunnery and *still* be a slut. I fully understand the connotations of that word. My exes have called me a slut, a whore, a floozy. Women call me Jezebel.

I call myself *complicated*.

"You've already said it," I say. "You can't take it back once you've said it."

"I guess it's a good thing it doesn't bother you, then."

"Who says it doesn't?"

"You."

I don't ask for an explanation. It's in his eyes, which are as clear as they were the first night I met him. I can only imagine what he sees in my fucked-up eyes. The truth of who I am? What I *really* am? Deep down, we know what I am. Who I am. What powers me to do the things that I do. He can treat me like some puzzle to be solved, but why put that much thought into it? Anyone can look at how I interact with the world, let alone the men in it, and discern how I function. It's been this way since I hit puberty. Since before, if we really dig into it.

With his hand up my skirt, I slide mine down his pants and clutch his hardening cock.

Ah, yes. We're in business.

Without a single word uttered between us, Drew rips my skirt upward, clutches my ass, and spreads my legs across his lap. I get very little say in the matter. To the point I don't care. This is what I want. Isn't it obvious, from how aroused I already am? Just the thought of him calling me by my real name and throwing me down for sex has the *wet* dripping down my legs. I don't hold back the gasp of surprise – and a little pain – as his half-erect cock burrows into me. The louder my acceptance of this pain, the more we're both turned on. I want every sensation he can give me. Pleasure. Pain. Teasing. Satisfaction. I know that as my cunt gets him fully erect and my neurons fire up with desire, it will feel good. So good, in fact, that I'm nothing but a bouncing doll in his lap.

I really don't deserve the kiss he plants on my lips or the soft inhale he gives my cleavage. My high-neck T-shirt separates his mouth from my skin, but the sheer amount of heat spreading across my chest has me gripping his shoulders and slamming myself onto his cock. Every thrust has him filling me in ways that only gravity can accomplish, whether I'm riding high or he's piledriving into the core of my being. For every part of me that hates Drew Benton for being so good at fucking, there's the other part that wants this to keep going forever. I'm probably never going to meet a lover who gets me on this level again. We'll inevitably split, because we're the toxic, sorry excuses for people that we are, but until then... ah, I'll fuck him as hard as I dare.

"You look a mess." Those accusatory breaths turn me on more. Drew's hands are on my hips, pushing down my pelvis, making me a slave to his cock. Slowly, but surely, his tip is traversing the eager spaces of my cunt and getting ready to strike my elusive G-spot. Say hello to one of three men in my whole life who have ever found it. He may be the first one to find it with his damned cock, though. Go figure. "You always screw guys looking like you rolled right out of bed?"

My smile of triumph only grows as he talks dirty. "That's right. Tell me how nasty I am."

I slam down in such a way that his response is nothing but a garbled mess of masculine words. My shirt quickly ascends my torso, but doesn't go over my head. Drew only raises it high enough to give him unfettered access to my breasts. As he sucks my nipples and slips his tongue beneath my tits, I arch my back and roar like a lioness from the overstimulation crashing down upon me. A thick cock in my cunt and a big, nimble tongue on my breasts? Heaven, here I come.

Or Hell, I suppose. I could be going to either.

"Didn't even shower for you," I say into the top of his head. Hair covers my face. Could be mine. Could be his. Either way, there is no trace of shampoo in this rendezvous. We're only a pair of dirty lovers getting dirtier. "You have no idea what I'm covered in. I could be covered in another man for all you know."

We both know that's not true. Yet the fierce look I encounter when Drew lifts his head again tells me I've unlocked a beastlier part of him.

Oh, good. I had no idea my pussy could get tighter. Bet he didn't, either.

I'm soon on my back. Abandoned. That's how I feel when Drew pulls away from me, my legs left spread open and my pussy missing his presence already. My eyes instantly go to his glistening cock. Before I can take pride in how hard and wet I've made it, however, Drew pulls my skirt off and tosses it onto the floor like it doesn't matter. Like I might not plan on wearing it ever again.

"You're in trouble now." His growl is both reassuring and menacing, or maybe I mistake it for attraction. I do not fight him off when his hand lightly encloses my throat. I never struggle to breathe. Not as long as I stay perfectly still. Except those panic-driven parts of my brain are now alive with adrenaline. Will we stay like this while he fucks me? Am I supposed to feel like his prisoner? His sex slave? God knows how many boyfriends have gotten off on that scenario, especially those that never admit it. They go for the throat and the one-two pumps.

Not Drew. Every movement, look, *breath* is part of a moment. He's getting himself off. Getting *me* off. I don't want to stop. It can't end. Not when my legs are spreading so wide for him that he *has* to call me a slut again. That's all I want. Just tell me what a big ol' whore I am, Drew. Call me *your* whore. Take a little dominance and possessiveness into your hands. I may be a sullied, dirty whore, but by God, I can be all yours for a few nights.

Yes, I know I sound insane. No, I don't care. Not when I'm so aroused that I can't stop thinking about his cock consuming me.

His hand lowers from my throat. The look in his eyes does not fade, however.

I expect him to flip me over, bury my face in his bed, and fuck me until he can't manage another thrust. Every inch of my body is ready for it. I'm prepared to hold my breath and *take it*. Honestly, it can't come soon enough.

Instead, Drew sits back and pulls me back into his lap. Except this time I'm facing forward, his hands securing me to his chest while his cock slams against the brunt of my pussy.

Intoxicated

"I want you to look in the mirror while I fuck you." Sure enough, I open my eyes to discover we're looking right into the vanity on the other side of the room. My vision may be obscured, but I can make out *us*. He's got his pants on. I've got my shirt on. That's the only clothing between us. My hair is a mess as he tosses it out of the way so he can suck on the side of my neck and the top of my shoulder. My hands have nowhere to go except the arm wrapped around my chest. My pussy doesn't have to think about where it's going. It's on his cock again within two seconds, my cries of desire echoing in this high-rise bedroom. "I want you to know what you look like when you fuck a man dry."

I'm not vain enough to film sex tapes and watch them later, but I understand the thrill of watching myself have sex, especially when I'm meant to get off from the latent shame infusing my body. Isn't it amazing how easily my body accommodates him? He's so much bigger than me. His cock stretches me wide open in this position. If this were porn, the camera would be making a beeline for my pussy milking his shaft like I needed his cum yesterday. It's not just him bouncing my ass with his thighs. I'm 100% throwing myself into it, completely abandoning any and all propriety so I can get off on the moment.

"Yes," I say, as he hooks my hands beneath my thighs and spreads my legs so wide that I now rely on him to do all the fucking. My arms wrap behind him. My fingers can almost touch. I don't want them to touch and ruin the sensation of him completely owning me. "*Yes!*"

Yes to what? To this feeling? To him getting everything he wants? Yes to who I am? Yes to the orgasm forcing me to close my eyes so I can appreciate every damn moment? Definitely *yes* to the growl perpetually sounding in my ear.

"Call me a slut again." My orgasm wans, but another is hot on its heels. This time, he better come with me. "I fucking love it when you call me a slut."

One finger touches my clit. I'm almost off like a rocket, but it was only a tease.

"Why tell you?" That's all Drew says before he thrusts up into me so deep that I'm split wide open.

Do I see my face the moment it happens?

You tell me. I've only come so hard again that I see nothing but stars before my face.

I feel more than that, though. I feel the natural guilt embedded into me from birth. Guilt that arouses and excites me. The feeling that I shouldn't be doing this. Not with a man like this. Not when I have so many *smarts* and so much *sophistication* built inside of me that it's a waste to fuck like this all night. I could be doing so much more with my life, right? More than squeezing a cock so hard that the man attached to it completely loses control and comes in two firm, satisfying bursts.

I fall down to the bed. Drew isn't too far behind me, but he's no longer touching my hot skin. It doesn't matter. He's still inside of me. I feel him dripping out, sticking to my thighs, and promising me that I'm all I want to be and more.

This intoxicating feeling is mutual, I'm sure.

"*What a waste,*" I can hear someone say in the deepest corners of my mind. "*What a waste to take so much of a man when you have an IUD. You can't trap him with a baby. You like it, don't you? You're just a slut.*"

I push myself up and look right into Drew's mirror. My lover may have his arm flung over his face as he recuperates, but I'm instantly renewed by the view of my countenance.

That's a woman who isn't afraid of the truth. That's a woman who will always shamelessly get what she wants, no guilt to get in her way.

That's me. *I'm* that woman.

CHAPTER 21

DREW

My father was never big on teaching me important life lessons. By the time I was born, he was absorbed in his work and completely checked out from the family. My sister was old enough for him to take under his wing and show the ropes from the time she could recite her ABCs. (Which was obnoxiously early, of course.) That left me to flounder my way through life as a trust fund kid, always looking for a little meaning in a life set-up to fail in the most fantastical of ways.

So I got few "talks." Those fell upon his step-mother, who took it upon herself to teach me the birds and the bees and how to prevent syphilis when I inevitably ran out there and started sticking it in any girl who would have me. I can't tell you if that was a boon or not. I mean, what man wants to hear about sex from his *grandmother?* In retrospect, she also left out a lot of crucial things. Including facts that could have only come from a man, like my father.

Like, oh, say... the difference between infatuation and love.

I'm well acquainted with infatuation. Desire. *Need.* For a woman, specifically. I know all about seeing a beautiful woman and instantly wanting to get to know her, both intimately and carnally. She can tell me her childhood dreams while I rub my stiff cock up and down her body. Hum her favorite Sunday school song while she blows me. Help me study for my chemistry exam as she sensually strips for our entertainment. Go ahead, girl! Knock yourself out!

Yes. I know all about that. My whole life has been an endless stream of women who infatuate me, both those I genuinely pursue and those who I'm paid to woo.

Love? Real, passionate, *romantic* love? I'm not sure I know what that looks like. Nobody's ever been around to show me. My own parents are a mess of ignoring each other's cheating. My father has always had a mistress of some sort, and my mother? Occasionally I hear her flirting with a man more around my age than my father's, but for the most part, she sequesters herself in sexless bubbles. My sister is the only one who has had "real" relationships, but considering how quickly she goes through them? Meh.

If you've lasted this long listening to me whine about this crap, then you know what I'm thinking. Who am I kidding? You've been snickering in my direction from the moment I encountered that vixen in a downtown Portland lounge. You probably would've laughed had you been around for my first meeting with Jason Rothchild, the man who hired me to completely destroy Cher Lieberman in all the ways she destroyed him.

Uh huh. We're all yucking it up now.

Do you think I don't know that woman is poison? Every time I kiss her, I drink a little bit more. Merely brushing my hand against her cheek or her damned ass brings me closer to death. People don't call her black widow for nothing. I'm quickly en-route to become the next man caught in her dastardly web. Why? Because she sucks cock like a goddess and screams like a lustful siren when we fuck?

No. That's infatuation. Let's be real. While love can certainly encompass all the blissful ways two people come together in their bed, *only* sex is attributed to infatuation. Isn't that one of the core differences between lust and love? Damnit, why hasn't anyone ever been around to teach me these things? I'm thirty-years-old. I shouldn't be figuring this out on my own! Although, to be fair, I always assumed I would know by now.

Wouldn't I know if I'm in love?

What does it mean when I can't stop thinking about her? For every memory of the curve of her body, the gasps of her orgasms, and the clench of her cunt around my cock, there's a glimpse into her sultry smirks and the honest way she cackles when I've amused her. If she's using me for my money and bed, then she's doing an admirable job of making it look like she fancies me. Even if we both acknowledge that this is a casual thing that will come to an eventual end - probably sooner rather than later - that doesn't mean we can't be friends. With benefits.

That only works if we're on the same page, though. If she truly is playing me for a convenient fool, or as a way to get back at me for what I do, then I'm fucked. In more ways than one.

Intoxicated

    This is something I've been suspecting for a while. Since the morning I saw her humanity displayed on my bed. No, I'm not talking about *that*. Whatever you're thinking. That's not it. I don't need to see a woman bleed to know she's human, for fuck's sake. I did, however, see fear and anxiety on that morning. Two very human things that I'm sure most people never see in the likes of Cher. She guards her heart like I guard my reputation. Yet that wasn't enough for me to assume I might be in love with her. That didn't come until she was in my Seattle abode, commanding my bed like she might command an entire army.

    If she's Helen of Troy, sending thousands of men off to their deaths, then that makes me some poor Grecian sap about to spend the next twenty years bumbling about on the waves. Didn't that poor fucker also have to deal with sirens? I apparently live in a hell where one woman has taken the mantle of every female in Greco-Roman lore.

    We didn't just make love that one night, when a little high and drunk enough to think it a fantastic idea to go all night. We went on into the morning. The afternoon called us to get something to eat, but then we were at it again, two people who one moment pretended to not know a single thing about each other, only to follow it up with accusations of seduction and delusions of grandeur.

    Cher is a woman you take every which way to Sunday and then want to go on for another week. She leaves you both completely satisfied and hungry for more. It's not enough to make such sensual love to her that she's biting her lip and squeezing her eyes shut in crowning ecstasy. You have to fuck her so hard she's screaming your name and begging you to completely ruin her in ways you were not paid to make happen. "*It's our little* secret," she whispers in your ear, her naked body pressed up against yours as her hand slowly encases your hip. "*I won't walk right ever again. Because that's how hard you go. Bruises up and down my thighs from the impact of yours. Now, flip me over and do it again.*"

Right when you think you can't go anymore, she says something or moves in such a way that you're hard all over again. And it's not the *fun* kind of hard. You keep banging away at her, yet none of the sweat, the curse words, or the ejaculations sate you. You're not halfway to finished until she finally falls down to your bed, breathless, her legs slowly closing as self-satisfied giggles fall from her lips. Only then do you collapse into a heap of exhaustion, your whole body angry at you for pushing it so damn hard.

You struggle to think of ways to show her your appreciation – ways that *don't* include more sex. You buy her dinner. You treat her to the movies. You buy her train and airplane tickets to wherever she wants to go, although you better be going with her. Wouldn't she look beautiful in a summery sarong? How about those jewels you see in the store window every time you go to your favorite pub?

Then you realize... it's only been two full days together, and you're already acting like this! You're acting like she's your girlfriend! Your fiancée! Your soon-to-be-wife! You're in deep, man. Deep like your cock in that trap of a pussy. Or that ass, when she cheekily reminds you of what you said when you were high off your rocker. You live for the way she growls at you to keep going, to satisfy her needs before you think about yours. You want to subvert her expectations, to take complete control of the situation and tell *her* when to come, but one perfectly timed look later? You're filling her on *her* command. She's the queen of your body. You thought you owned it. You thought bodily autonomy was a done-deal from the day you were born. You were wrong. Cher has arrived, and she's going to ride you until your eyes roll back and you tell her she can have whatever she wants.

So, yeah... I'm fucked.

It's probably infatuation. When you're having this kind of crazy good sex with a hot woman, you get infatuated. It's not love. How could it be love? You know she's not capable of that. Although she turns down your gifts and immediately calls you when she discovers her rent paid for the next month, you know it's not love she feels for you. You're her victim. Her mark. You're wrapped up in the long con. You'll do whatever she wants from three hundred miles away. She texts you at two in the afternoon asking for a dick pick? You whip that fucker out and later wonder what the shit you were thinking. Then you consider it *worth it,* because she sends you back a picture of her cleavage in a pushup bra. You're in the bathroom taking care of business, and all because of a five-minute interaction that didn't happen in real life.

She asks you when you're coming back to Portland. You want to tell her you'll be there one hour ago, if that's what she wants. Instead, you play it cool. Tell her you can come down in a few days, because work has you tied up. Oh, but you probably shouldn't remind her what you do for a living.

Then again, you're seriously thinking about some life changes.

I'm not happy. Sure, I always knew I couldn't stay in this business forever, but I don't have a backup plan yet. I'm not about to close up shop and tell Brent he no longer has a job in an expensive city. Although it's a huge waste of money for me to keep this place open. Between office space, Brent's wages... fuck, I might as well be flushing money down the drain. I already break even as it is. If I'm not working, I'm not being paid. And if I'm not making taxable income in my business, the IRS comes tsking at me.

Gee, maybe my father taught me *one* lesson after all.

I was drunk when I told Cher we should go into matchmaking together. While that was obviously a joke at the time, it's something I've been thinking about ever since. I run the idea by Brent. Not doing it with *Cher*, duh, but figuring out a matchmaking service that would work from my unique perspective in this crowded industry.

"That would be a serious switch, man." He scratches his head as he sits at his desk. Another overcast Seattle day displays behind him. The only sounds in this office are the hum of Brent's desk fan and the White Stripes music playing on my phone. Yet I swear I hear Brent's adrenaline pump when I tell him I'm thinking of changing career directions. Like I said, it's an expensive city, and the man has a house-husband. "You'd have to completely change your image among your clientele. You'll go from being the guy who gets them some twisted sense of vengeance, to the guy who hooks them up with their next relationship."

"Could be a fun way to give back to the community in a new way." Why, no, I'm *not* repenting. Not yet. Give me a few more months of this elastic love I feel around Cher. "Can you hear my pitch now? '*Remember the guy who helped you feel better? Now he's back and ready to help you fall in love with someone new, someone better!*' My target audience would be rich guys who are terrible at picking out girlfriends for themselves. Really, they go together." I leave out the part about Cher recruiting the sugar babies that would make up a bulk of the matches. Of course, for a job like this to work, we'd have to pick hot women who *want* to marry, and not only suck the money out of wallets. Would Cher understand a point of view like that, though? She's made it clear her only interest is independence. This is a woman who happily barks orders at you when you're balls deep inside of her, but you never feel a real emotional connection. Only the deep, dark sadness of realizing she'll never really love you.

At least I know it, unlike the poor saps she's left in her wake.

"It's definitely a neat idea. You should develop it," Brent says.

"You think?" I admit, I wasn't expecting him to say something like that.

"Why not? Maybe you're onto something. Now, did I tell you that you had an appointment for your *old* job today?"

I turn back toward him before I can disappear back to my desk. "Come again?"

"Rothchild's in town and wants a follow up with you."

Bile is in my throat. Didn't take long for that to happen. All Brent had to say was *Rothchild* and I'm hissing through my teeth. No, I haven't forgotten about him. *No,* I haven't been in contact with him since the last time you saw me call the bastard. Did you think I was calling him to say our deal was off? That may have been my original intention. Then I decided on something different.

I still wasn't sure how things would go with Cher. Now I know.

"I don't recall signing off on any appointments today," I say to Brent.

He shrugs. "You're currently working with him. You've never turned clients away unless it was an emergency. What's the problem? You took all those 'days off' to work Cher, right?"

Yeah. *Working.* That's totally what I was doing as I followed her every whim. You know, it was *my* idea to give her a pearl necklace. Just because she turned down the actual jewels and suggested something kinkier, doesn't mean it still wasn't my idea. Although she looked me right in the eye and purred with her legs spread wide open as I came all over her breasts. (Yes, yes, I may have missed my target a bit.) It was all part of her plan to ensnare me, anyway. Do you actually think she likes having cum on her tits? I doubt most women do, yet we guys have to keep hoping we'll get to do it once in a while.

"Earth to Drew, yo." Brent waves his hand in front of my face. "I said he'll be here in fifteen minutes. Come on, man, read your schedule I give you sometimes. I work hard on those!"

"Sorry. I appreciate it, really." I clap him on the shoulder and turn away in the hopes he doesn't see me take a harried breath. Jason Rothchild is on his way right now. I'm gonna have to come up with *something* to tie him over. Either that, or he's here to collect his deposit.

Fifteen minutes isn't enough time to adequately plan.

"Mr. Benton." The man sitting in front of my desk dresses better than my father. We're talking three piece suits in varying colors. Pocket squares. High-end watches that are *actually* checked. Rothchild isn't old enough for a cane yet, but when he is, you can bet your ass it will be polished myrtlewood with a gold cap and tip. He smells better than most of my clients, too. That's because Rothchild is old money. He's taken his family's money - that was already impressive, mind you - and expanded it in ways they never dreamed. For him to call me means he truly felt so wronged by Cher that there was nothing else in the world his money could buy to soothe his gaping wounds. "I hope you don't mind that I

Intoxicated

dropped by while I was in town. I'm *most* interested to know how things go with... the woman."

He won't call Cher by name. He won't call her *my ex*. The way he dances around her identity only seals how much she hurt him. Usually, I'd feel for the guy, but my judgment is so clouded that I struggle to think of something diplomatic to say.

"I have good news and bad news." I've left my door slightly ajar. Brent glances in when I say that. I'm compelled to get up and close the only thing separating me from my assistant's curiosity. "The good news is that she's become quite attached to me already. I suspect she's playing me like she plays most of her victims. I've been... generous, to say the least." You know what the nuttiest thing is? I write most of my dates off my taxes! Cost of doing business, indeed.

Rothchild grunts, but does not look at me. "I am not surprised. At the first whiff of money, she's on you like a fly on honey. The fact that you're..." Ah, yes, now he's looking at me. With mild derision. "Sufficiently attractive helps. I can only assume that a mosquito like her enjoys her games more when she's attracted to the man in question."

Rothchild isn't awful to look at. Honestly, he's everything most people think of when they conjure up the image of *old money sophistication.* He's fit for his age. Tall and lean. Salt and pepper hair, not to mention *still* having his hair. His dapper dress and vintage mannerisms undoubtedly make him friends, both male and female, wherever he goes. What I know about Cher tells me that she would be attracted to this debonair man, at the very least. I'm not convinced she needs six-pack abs, a giant dick, and a head of pure-colored hair to keep her happy. Those are a bonus.

"What's the bad news?" he then asks.

I sit back down in my seat. Hands fold on my desk. Now, I must be careful to not look like a reproachful teacher about to scold his (much older, I must remind myself) student. But I have things to say. Things that could end my career before I ever intended.

"I'm not sure I can seal our deal," I say.

Rothchild studies me, as if searching for the truth beneath my words. He already has the truth, though. I *don't* think I can seal the deal. Not with Cher. Maybe not with any other woman in the future, if I dare believe my own worries.

"What exactly do you mean by that?" he asks. "You've said so yourself, she's taken in with you, Mr. Benton. Now, do what I'm paying you to do." Great. He's got *that* look in his eye. The one that acknowledges I'm banging the woman he was so in love with. I'm not dumb. I know Cher was sleeping with this man. I can almost imagine them doing it. Can he imagine me on top of her. Behind her? Does he know how hard she bit my sheets a few days ago, as I roared like a mighty beast and came so hard that I had to immediately go at her again?

If he couldn't see it before, he does now. Some of my clients go into minor fits of rages when they realize they're paying me to seduce their exes. It's part of the deal. Adding sex to the mix always makes it sweeter when the women realize what I've done.

Except, in this case...

"Cher is unlike anyone I've encountered in my few years of doing this, Mr. Rothchild." Jesus, isn't that the truth? No woman has killed me the way she has started to, and I'm about to smash my face into my desk to make the memories *go away*. "She's quite possibly a sociopath. The only way I could do what you're asking me to... well, I'd probably have to find a way for her to commit a crime and go to prison. I'm sure you can understand how difficult that would be. My usual tactics aren't going to work. I can't ask her to marry me, obviously. Nor can I make her fall madly in love with me without dedicating a few more months, *at least*, to this endeavor. Even then, it wouldn't be a sure thing. Usually, at this point in my process, I've all but put the final nail in their coffins." Then again, most women aren't Cher Lieberman, professional sugar baby from hell.

"You're right in that she's probably incapable of feeling the usual assortment of feelings a human being is expected to harbor." Rothchild leans his elbows against the arms of his chair and steeples his fingers before his face. I feel like I'm in *his* office, not the other way around! "But I've seen some of your work for myself. That's why I felt so confident in hiring you, Mr. Benton. If there's anyone in this sorry world who can give her a taste of her own medicine, it's you. I don't care how you go about it." He leans forward, the madness in his eyes now clearer. "I don't care how long it takes, or how much it costs me. That woman's crimes go beyond my own... unfortunate moments. Do it on behalf of all the men out there who can be spared her cruelty. Do it for the young women who might want to emulate her."

Whelp, now I'm thinking of that business idea I pitched to her. "*Hey, Cher, how about you train me some sugar babies to pair off with some rich bastards? We'll get rich on our own!*"

"That requires manipulating emotions we're not sure are there, Mr. Rothchild."

He leans back again, his knowing smirk unnerving me. "Tell me, Mr. Benton. How much does the woman fancy you? Don't worry about offending me or making me jealous. I'm past such petty things. Spare no details of how you've ensnared her, if you must."

Before I struggle to think of anything to say, my phone buzzes beside me. Normally, I'd turn it over or tuck it into my drawer while I'm in a meeting, but I instantly see Cher's name on the header of a photo attachment.

While Rothchild watches on in mild amusement, I hold my phone up to my face so only I can see what my supposed girlfriend has sent me.

It takes a few seconds to register what it is.

"Tell me..." The only thing I can do is swallow my pride and act like the scuzzy asshole I usually am when talking to a client. That's who they want to see. A guy who isn't afraid to stick it in the crazy, to pump and dump them on his way out the door. Maybe make them think they're in love. Humiliate them in public. Ruin their reputations, drain their funds, and break their hearts until they no longer know who they are. That's who I am, after all. A professional heartbreaker. "What does this look like to you?"

I show him the intimate photo Cher has sent me. While she's savvy enough to know anything she texts or emails could end up in a cloud dump somewhere, she still assumes that I won't *maaaaybe* share it with others. Let alone her ex-boyfriend.

That's why she had the confidence to send me a candid photo of her in her apartment. She's fresh from the shower, her makeup-less face glowing. The bathrobe barely clings to her body, but it's not supposed to. The eye may be drawn to her cut-off face, but you're soon staring at her supple cleavage and the water droplets left behind. While it's an artistic, *very* aesthetic shot, we're all thinking the same thing while looking at it. *Sex. With her.*

Now, what if I also told you that there's a little something inked on her right breast? In elegant script font, the French *je t'aime* bursts from her skin.

Rothchild glances away. Whatever he's thinking – personally, anyway – is lost to the moment. Because what he soon says is, "Do your worst, Mr. Benton. Destroy her while she's in your clutches."

I do not let my gaze waver.

CHAPTER 22

CHER

"Are you sure about this?" I lower my voice to a hush. I don't need any of the people around me hearing what has me so upset. "Are you sure that's him?"

"Oh, that's him."

I ease my grip on the wicker chair I'm sitting in, as if that's enough to save my palms now. Across from me, Stella the PI tucks away her photographical evidence of Jason Rothchild leaving Drew's office. That isn't the look of a guy who has been told he's getting his money back. That's *smug smug smuggity smug* all over my ex-boyfriend's visage, and it's taking a healthy dose of reality to keep from slapping a photograph.

"I didn't ask you to do this," I remind Stella. Indeed, I haven't. She did all the work I needed from her when she looked into Drew's identity. To say that I wasn't expecting a phone call from her this morning, urgently asking me to meet her at a café around the corner from her office, is an understatement. I could only imagine what she had to present to me. Obviously, it was about Drew, but could I anticipate that he was still working for Jason?

Yes, I could, actually.

I've had a hunch this whole time. Do you think I keep jumping into bed with Drew while assuming he's pure of intention? Hardly! There may be a mutual sexual attraction between us, but it ends in the bedroom. Actually, it's more accurate to say it ends with his cum all over me (and all up in me) but I'm trying not to think about that right now.

According to the time stamps on these photos, Jason left Drew's office shortly after I sent my *boyfriend* those photos. Very art school, I know, but part of my amusement comes from making him think about me so much that he shortly loses his damned mind. There's something erotic about knowing you control a man's orgasm from hundreds of miles away. Plus... it's fun to take tasteful nude photos sometimes. What?

Now I know he's probably sharing them with Jason. God only knows who else. It's not like I didn't already have seeds of doubt planted in my head, but those seeds are growing at a pace I can't keep up with, and my skull is about to fracture. Nice to know that all those hot moments we shared really *were* empty. Jesus. All that grunting, sweating, and daring one another to push themselves a little bit farther in the bedroom was nothing but a toxic game. Like I didn't know. I always went to bed with Drew knowing that it probably wasn't good for me. But it *felt* so good. Physically, I mean. It's a rare guy who can fuck you like that without making you legit fear for your life. I was taking all I could get while I'm still young and elastic. Call me again in ten years when the soreness has settled in and I can barely ride cowgirl, let alone get piledriven in the ass for ten minutes.

Stella closes the folder from whence the photos came. "No, you didn't ask me to go checking up on him, but I was in Seattle on other business yesterday and decided to drop by. I know you've still been seeing him, so thought it might be good to do a quick follow up. I apparently showed up at the right time."

Apparently! "Do I have to pay you for this? How do you know I'm still seeing him?"

She shrugs. "I see and hear a lot of things around this town. It's sort of my job. Yet if it wasn't the private investigating, it would be some other part of my past. When you've done undercover work as long as I have, some things are instinct."

"I suppose." I'm still not paying her for this.

"I thought you should know." Stella gets up, leaving behind her iced coffee. "Sorry to be the bearer of bad news. Let me know if you need anything."

I'm left alone at this blasted café, where happy couples, families, and BFFs are out on dates and having the fucking time of their lives. There are a million dogs tied to table legs and hiding beneath chairs. It's one of the first really warm days of the season, and I'm on the brink of a meltdown.

"*We need to talk,*" I text Drew. "*About Jason Rothchild.*"

He's not going to respond. Or, if he does, he'll quickly change the subject to my tits.

No good will come from this.

***

Intoxicated

It's eight at night and I've barely heard from Drew. We had a little spat over text, I left him a nasty voice mail, and now I'm back to hating his guts. Suppose you could say I'm stewing in my self-governed misery once more.

At least I have some old vinyl to soothe my soul.

"*What do you do when a man ain't worth it?*" an old jazz singer croons. "*What do you do when you've gotta kick him to the curb, but your heart ain't in it? Oh, girl, you gone and done it now.*"

I'm not a smoker, but here I am, vaping a little pot so I don't go completely bonkers. This is what *my* stash is for. Drew may use his for extracurricular fun, but I need pot to keep my head on straight when I'm mad at some fucker for being a total douchebag.

Someone buzzes my door. I'm not inclined to answer it. Probably some of the neighborhood kids playing pranks again. There's a group of them that like to stop by my small apartment building and buzz everyone's doors. While I don't live in a converted Victorian, I *do* enjoy an older yet updated building that has certain amenities. Like old buzzers that sound through my whole one-bedroom while I'm trying to enjoy the sunset.

It buzzes again.

Then again.

Then my phone buzzes.

"*Come on,*" Drew texts me. "*I didn't drive three and a half hours through I5 traffic for you to turn me away. I see your light on.*"

Let's get one thing sorted here, shall we? Drew has never been to my place before. The closest he's come is where we've had a few dates over on 21st and 23rd. I don't doubt that he knows where I live. It's not like it's difficult to find out if you're savvy enough, and like I looked into his background, I'm sure he looked into mine! (I mean, the man was working me, after all. Hell, he still is!) So here I am, sitting here in my reading nook, staring at the sleepy residential street beneath me, expected to entertain an idiot out to ruin my life.

"Fine. I'll be at my place on the South Waterfront if you decide you want to be an adult about this."

I stare at his final text for two seconds before tossing my phone into a plush chair on the other side of the room. My vape is finished with a giant blow of air that can only compare to the relief you feel when a giant weight has been lifted from your shoulders.

It's while lying on my bed, staring at my ceilings, wondering what it's like to be a frog - blame the pot, please - when I entertain the notion of going to see Drew one last time. Except I wouldn't have as much rage this time. That was reserved for when I found out who he really was. Can I actually be that angry right now, when I knew this about him the whole time? Doubtful. That would be silly. I have no honor to protect. I'm really no better than him. Ah, now there's a thought I continuously come back to these past few weeks.

I don't bother to change out of my old T-shirt and lounge leggings when I order a Lyft. Sheesh. Doesn't this feel awfully familiar? Seems like yesterday I rushed to this apartment to blow a hole in his dick, only to start begging for it inside of me.

Maybe the pot will relax me enough to keep the blow-up at bay. My goal isn't to fuck him anymore. I know who the hell he is. I know what he's capable of doing. To sleep with him now only makes me more culpable in my own demise. I suppose I deserve it, don't I?

Intoxicated

Is he surprised when I show up at his door? Or is he more surprised that I look like *this?* Dressed like I'm not expecting to leave my house, let alone have anyone recognize me on the street. Let's not mention the little bit of buzz in my eyes. Bloodshot, huh? Is that it? I don't think I had *that* much.

Yet Drew merely walks away from his open door, silently inviting me inside.

"All right," I huff. "I'm here. You wanna be adults? I guess I can entertain you. Since you made so much effort to rush down here."

"Don't make it sound like you're doing me a favor." Arms crossed, he leans against his island counter. That isn't a look of lust in his eyes. Nor is that bite of his lip for my pussy. The man is thinking. Mulling over words? Deciding the best way to throw me out on my ass? I wouldn't blame him for either, although I should be the one beating his ass with the little purse hooked over my shoulder. "So, you found out I'm still talking to your ex? How many eyes and ears do you have around here? Let alone up in Seattle?"

"Don't change the subject." I meant to snap that. Instead, it came out in a pathetic whisper. I need to sit down. So I pull out one of the stools by the island and help myself, elbows sagging against the marble countertops and face falling in latent disbelief. "You led me to believe that you dropped Jason and were seeing me purely because it tickled your fancy." I don't go beyond that. Like how he was clearly getting off on fucking a demonic princess such as myself. I was still the cool girl, after all.

Drew sighs. "I don't recall telling you that at all. I had thought about it, yes. I honestly hadn't thought much about him since he fell off the radar for a couple of weeks. He showed up at my office unannounced yesterday. My plan this whole time has been to drop him and give him back his money. I don't need it. I don't want to do this job anymore."

Now there's a lie if I've ever heard one. Not even a good one. Does he really think I'm going to fall for that? "I thought it was your moral mission to rid the world of heartbreaking bitches?"

"Very funny. You know it wasn't really like that."

"Come on, Drew. Don't insult my intelligence. We both know what was in it for you. Hot, crazy pussy in return for some cold, hard cash. You were basically a man-ho for hire."

"I still am, according to you."

"Not to you?"

He shakes his head. "I'm not lying to you, Cher. I'm not playing you. I'm not taking his money. He continues to believe I am, though. He's very determined to see you come off your pedestal. You really did a number on him. I'd think most of my clients would give up by now, if I told them I thought it was hopeless."

"Hopeless? What's hopeless?"

We make solid eye contact for the first time since I walked through the door. "You've already made me, Cher. Even if you never did, *somehow,* you would still be too tough of a nut to crack. I'm good, but I'm not that good. I can't break a heart that's unwilling to fall in love."

"Is that what you think?" My mouth is dry. That also must be the pot. I'm not the type to wake up in the middle of the night suffering from cotton mouth. Yet why would I waste such precious saliva on him? He's had enough of it in his mouth and on his dick already. "That I'm unwilling to fall in love? With anyone?"

"You've said as much yourself. You're too independent for the coupled life. This whole time I've assumed we've been fooling around." His arms lower from his chest, yet his hands are soon in the air. "Having some great sex before we go our separate ways. Probably when we've had enough of each other's bullshit. Or you find your next mark."

"If you really think I'm such a terrible person..." I almost slip off my stool. My sandal catches me before my fall – or before Drew can leap forward and catch me. "Then what makes you think I still wouldn't fool around with you on the side? Like you said, I'm great in bed."

"Excuse me. It takes two to have great sex. Give me some credit."

Is that a little smile on his face? How can he not be angry at me? Totally sober me would be in here chopping his balls off. Again. (Yes, yes, and we know how that ends. The more balls I filet, the more I gotta fuck, fuck, fuck.)

"You've got your goals," Drew says. "I've got mine. At some point, they'll diverge. Sex won't keep us together forever."

Why am I slumping so badly against this countertop? It's as if the weight of his words press down upon my back, threatening to cut off my air supply. Only this is worse than when I put his hand around my throat when he's already deep inside of me. It's one thing to get off on a little erotic asphyxiation in the heat of the moment. It's quite another to look this monster in the eye and realize he has the power to destroy me. He only has to try hard enough.

"Maybe not," I say. "Like you said, though, I don't give a fuck about the men I date. Just because I'm using the next one for money and status, doesn't mean I don't want some real sex on the side. I mean, you have to know by now that one of the reasons I'm all over your dick is because you actually know how to use it. Most of the duds in this town don't know their balls from their ass. They..." I sigh. "Never mind. You don't want to hear this."

"I mean, I'm into you stroking my ego. But you're right. I kinda know that about you. Like you must know by now that I'm infatuated with you."

"Infatuated," I repeat. "You're infatuated with me."

"What? You want me to lie and say that it's love?"

"No. God, please, no. Anything but that."

"Excuse me." He chuckles. How could he still not be offended? I'm over here trashing his heart. Next, I'll be trashing his mind. Maybe his body. He really isn't as good as he thinks he is. Nope. Not at all. "Come on, Cher. I have nothing to gain by playing you any longer. I haven't been for weeks. Anything that's been between us since we first had sex has been purely organic. I fool around with you because you're fun and, like I said, I'm kinda infatuated with you. Don't worry, though. I'm sure that infatuation will die soon."

I have no idea what to say. Drew's words hit my ears, but do they mean a damn thing? What does he *mean* when he says he's infatuated with me? That I'm some anomaly that's pinged his radar? That I'm good in bed? That I make him reevaluate his life and what he wants from it? Or is that his lighthearted way of saying he's in love with me? Love. God knows he can't actually be in romantic love with me. In love with my pussy, maybe, but me? I thought he was smarter than that. You don't fall in love with a mark. That's not how it *works*. No matter how hot, how witty, or how great their genitals are, you don't fall in love! That's like cutting off your nose to spite your face! You're better off going to your rich daddy and saying, *"Pound sand, Dad. Donate my inheritance to charity for all I care."* Drew has been doing his disgusting thing long enough that he knows what the repercussions are.

So does that mean it's *real?* He knows better. He should know better, anyway. Like I don't fall in love with the men I'm using, he's not falling in love with the women he's destroying.

Actually, maybe it's not real. Maybe he really is simply "infatuated" with me and waiting for the fancy to pass. Yet that also means he's no longer working me. If he's allowing himself to fall into a flight of fancy with my pussy at the helm, then that means he has nothing to lose. No money. No reputation. His only end game with me is to survive our encounters. Whether I'm sucking him dry or going crazy on his ass.

"I'm not working you," Drew repeats, as if he can read my mind. "I don't know what it is you and I have, if anything, but I'm not receiving money in exchange for it. I don't have nefarious plans to break your heart or dump you in the middle of nowhere. We're only hanging out and having sex. Now, what you're planning to do to *me...*"

It may sound overly defensive of me, but I can't help but say, "I'm not using you, either. Honestly rather put out that you paid my rent without asking me."

He grins. "Would you have 'let' me?"

"Absolutely not. Because that implies this is..." I puff out my cheeks, hands meeting my hips. "A means to an end. I don't think of it that way."

His approach doesn't go unnoticed, yet my senses have dissociated enough that I barely recognize the moment his breath meets my cheek and his hand takes mine. "So neither of us are playing the other or going through with meeting up for the sake of money or gifts. Strange. It's almost like..." My senses return to my body his lips lightly graze my cheek. Here comes the tingles. The shudders. The sensations of physical touch as they light up my fucking life. "We're a casual couple having a bit of fun until something happens."

"Something?" I duck out of his grasp, my heart aflutter and my mind struggling to make sense of what I'm feeling. Drew Benton is not my boyfriend. We're not on track to get married. Even if his family would approve of me, he's too much of a younger playboy, and I'm too independent. I don't give a fuck if he's richer than half the men I've dated. I don't care if he has a body from God and the stamina to go for twelve hours straight. Drew can be the funniest man on Earth. We're not *together*. This is casual. A fling. When it's over, I'll look back on it and wonder if the good dick was worth it. That's it. Please, God, let that be it.

I'm not ready for more. I'm not *meant* for more.

"Either we'll go our separate ways for one reason or another... or things continue down a course that looks like those love stories you see on TV."

Is that supposed to be funny? Supposed to make me feel better? I bet he thinks he's soooo cheeky, implying that either he or I will be in this for the long haul.

"I thought that's what we were cool with." Drew shrugs. He's close enough that I feel the brush of his arm against mine. Why are there so many *shivers* in me right now? Why do I want to scream in sexual frustration? This guy's hot, but he's not so hot that I would set aside my fucking dignity for another lay. I don't want him panting on top of me and spanking my ass a little. I want to talk. I want to remember why I hate him so much and why we would never work out, not in my girlish dreams. The

Intoxicated

more I'm around him, the more I forget. I forget my independence and my goals for the rest of my life. None of them include a guy like Drew. They don't include any guys at all! I barely include visions of my dad at Christmastime in these dreams for my life!

Drew is still waiting for a response. I take refuge against his island counter. I may be trapped, but at least for a few seconds... I'm away from *him*.

Although I expected him to follow me, he stays a few feet away, where I had been standing only a second before. "Or is this it?" he asks. "You're mad again, because you won't listen for two damn minutes? I've already told you my piece. Jason Rothchild is tenacious, but I have the authority to turn down clients if I think it's hopeless and a waste of their money."

"Only because I figured out what you were doing before you had a chance to do your worst." That implies he would've had a chance at all. I don't think so.

"Nah. That's not the only reason." Drew turns toward me again. It's like he's laid everything out on the counter behind me. Or across that broad chest – that broad, *muscular* chest infuriatingly strapped within that tight T-shirt. See? Even when I'm mad at him, I can't stop thinking about humping his bones. The man is a nuisance. A public nuisance. "I know when I've met my match."

There are about five different interpretations for that blasted line. His match? The spark that will light him on fire? The only woman on this planet who could foil his nefarious plans?

The girl who has finally stolen his heart?

I need to get my mind off that thinking. I am *not* his match. Not in that way. Maybe I'm smart or clever enough to destroy his business, but I'm not in this game to make him fall in love with me. When I first met him, before I knew what he was really about, I would've played at love to get what I needed out of him. That's my real MO. Now, though? That's too dangerous. Having him genuinely in love with me could prove to be my own downfall.

Why? I don't know. I'm not interested in finding out.

"Think what you want about me," Drew says, "but I thought I should say something. I'm already putting plans into motion to change my line of work. Rothchild is gonna be the last guy I talk to. Technically, you were my last job." He's only three inches away now. "Not sure what I'm going to do next. I was half-serious about that idea to go into a matchmaking service. Maybe I'll look into that. Hey, I'm privileged enough to not be too worried, but if there's anything I've learned these past few weeks, it's that I don't need to be in the revenge business anymore. I'm too old for that shit. Time to move onto something else. Something that uses my time more productively."

Whatever this spiel is supposed to accomplish, my reaction is to say, "I still don't quite believe you."

"That's fine. As long as you're not angry. Being so angry all the time isn't good for you."

I snort. "It's not my favorite thing to feel."

"So, are we good?"

There's still one thing weighing on my mind. Might as well get it out of the way now. "Did you really drive down here when you found out I knew about your meeting with Jason?"

"Only when you weren't answering your phone. What? Did you think I'd let you stew in your rage long enough to come up with a diabolical plan against me? I value my life way too much. Shit, I value the time we've spent together a little too much."

'What does that mean, exactly?"

Our gazes lock. Although his is unwavering, I fight the urge to look away again. "It means I like you, Cher. Does it have to mean anything more than that?"

He doesn't love me. He *likes* me.

Do you realize no guy has ever said that to me before? They always jump from "you're interesting" or "you're fun" to "*I fucking love you, Cher. Marry me, baby.*" The men I date have no damn chill. Including the ones not looking for a Missus soon fall into the trap of pledging their hearts to me, assuming I've strung them along enough. (Some of them fall faster than others, though. The longest I worked a guy to get him to love me was about four months. Most only take half that time of constant dates.) But like? A guy realizing that we might have something, but it's not going to happen overnight... that's as rare as a potential mother-in-law fawning over me. I have no idea how to react. Like. Love. Those two are so fundamentally different, yet one has the power to transform into the other. Like blossoming into love is a tale as old as time. Love into like? That's a death knell. Once you hit love, there's no going back. Watching men bend over to hit that like their gas pedals hit sixty in three seconds means I know their *real* infatuations are being misconstrued as love. That's when I leave. That's when I pack it in and get the hell out while I still can.

Like. Drew Benton *likes* me. That's like saying, "*Let's take this slow, hon.*" Our sex life may be anything but slow, but emotions have the chance to catch up if we let them.

"Do you mean that?" I ask. "You *like* me?"

"Is that so hard to believe? I like you enough that I don't want you to get the wrong idea. I value the fun we have together. I'm not gonna give you credit for changing my life or anything, but I admit that since I've met you, I've had a good, hard think about what kind of man I want to be. Maybe we won't be talking to each other six months from now, but I think there's potential here for us to not regret a thing."

"What in the world do you like about me?" Whispers claim my voice. Is it because I need to swallow more? To wet my tongue? To lick my lips? "I'm not likeable. Even I know that." I'm that bitch. That harpy. That *siren* who steals your husband to get into his pocketbook. I don't have real friends for a reason. My own family doesn't like me. I'm charming until I've got what I need from you. In my ideal world, I float through life with only myself to rely on. Only me to be my own friend. "You must be crazy."

Why is Drew laughing? Is this so funny? "You're hilarious, for one. Even when you're being a cynical bitch, I can't help but laugh. I appreciate that viewpoint of the world. Also, uh... you've got a great body?"

I roll my eyes. I should have guessed.

When my vision settles on his face again, I witness a curious, analytical look that has me holding my arms to my chest, fingers tapping against my chin as I anticipate his final advance. "What?" I ask. "You need something, Benton?"

"Yes, Lieberman." He lowers his face toward mine, although he doesn't go for the kill quite yet. "I need to kiss you. If you'll let me."

Of course he's put that ball in my court! Drew insists on being an infuriating bastard like that. One that I can't help but lean in to kiss, because damn my body, and *damn my heart.*

I didn't realize I had one until my lips meet his tonight.

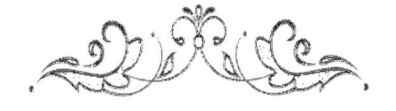

CHAPTER 23

CHER

Gone are the urges to do nothing but throw each other down on the bed and slam bodies like jackhammers. Although my skin is on fire to touch, caress, and be stimulated in return, I'm not thinking about the *hottest* sex. I don't care that Drew is packing a dick made for me. Nor do I consider how good he feels when we're on the same diabolical wavelength. Our whole so-called relationship has been nothing but rough and passionate sex. Now it might simply be passionate.

Slow, but passionate.

I haven't willingly *made love* to someone in so long that I barely remember what it's like. Oh, I've done the whole slow and methodical sex thing with my exes. Because that's what *they* wanted. Me... well, you know what I'm like. I want to slip into an effortless fantasy full of hard fucking and a slight sentiment of danger. I want bruises on my hips from where my man has held me down to do the dirtiest of deeds. I want hickies on my throat and cum all over and all up in me. I want to be so sore in the morning that I forget how to walk, let alone in flats or heels. *That's* what I fantasize about. Big, hungry dick and impossible positions that make me feel both possessed and utterly possessive. Slow lovemaking? Things called *lovemaking?* That's reserved for people who are earning my heart. You have to be one special bastard for me to take my time kissing your lips while you slowly undress me and get between my legs.

I don't know how I've fallen so easily for this. Drew said the right words, that's all. I'm emotionally vulnerable. I'm probably ovulating. Some women get mad PMS. I get my most emotional when my ovaries are craving some fertilization. This is the time of the month when I watch Hallmark movies and dive into romance novels that are more than wall-to-wall kinky sex. (Yes, I own a whole two of those books.) So is it really a surprise that a man like Drew could turn on the romantic charm and cajole me into bed for *lovemaking?*

Honestly, saying the word makes me want to shudder.

We don't say a single word as we make our way into Drew's bedroom and start the undressing. He pulls my T-shirt over my head, mouth diving for my throat while my hands fight for a place to go. I should feel self-conscious in nothing but a pair of unflattering leggings and an old sports bra that takes much more effort than usual to get off. Yet Drew's attentive motions keep lulling me into a false sense of security. I sway in his arms, ready to fall onto the bed at any moment. Even when he takes off his shirt and tosses it on top of mine, all I can think about is turning off the lights and exploring his body. It's no longer about getting hard, getting wet, or getting off all night. It's about indulging my stupid heart as it navigates these unknown and treacherous waters.

Would it be too boring to describe such simple sex? While I'm not the one to gab to my girlfriends about raucous cowgirling or leg shaking doggying, I do feel that I should have something *interesting* to say about the sex I'm having. Yet it's so simple, isn't it? Drew takes off the rest of my clothes. He slides between my legs, kissing every inch of my skin that stretches from forehead to shoulders. The intentional hicky he leaves on my neck isn't the side effect of giving into forbidden pleasures. It's his way of marking me as his for at least one night. Every time I look in the mirror for the next few days, I'll see that unflattering mark. Then I'll smile to see it, remembering this tender moment when Drew Benton slipped his tongue into my mouth and his cock into my body.

There's never any hurry to get off between us. Never has been. Definitely not tonight, as he takes his slow time to undulate against me. Sometimes he lies still, the only sensations of sex existing in the hardness inside of me. I accommodate him as easily as ever, yet without the constant thrusting and groaning, I have more time to appreciate the softer moments that occur between two people having sex. The way he caresses my breast before wrapping his lips around my nipple will haunt my memory for at least a few years. That sweet demeanor I see every time I open my eyes almost makes me feel like a kid again. Back in those days when people didn't seem to play so many games with each other. You took people for how they presented themselves. That girl in second grade was awful to you, but at least you knew it from the moment you met her. It wasn't until later you realized that manipulation and machinations make up a bulk of the human experience. Everything was tainted after that. Cynicism settled in.

Don't I know what it's like.

Allowing myself to be raw in front of anyone is deceptively freeing. I almost fall for it. This idea that there is one person out there I can bare myself to, heart and soul. Maybe there are people out there suited for that. Me? I don't know.

Maybe I don't want to know.

"You are so gorgeous." Drew distracts me from my worries to tell me something that almost means nothing. This man has called me all sorts of things in the bedroom. We easily go from *"damn, you're beautiful,"* to *"who's a big ol' nasty slut, huh?"* I call him hot. That's about it. Oh, and bastard. Asshole. Total shithead. But it's not that kind of night, is it?

My hands curl around his shoulders. I urge him to continue his slow and deep thrusts before I regret what we're doing. Yet he's too focused on my face, looking me in the cloudy eyes as I fight to regain any clarity in my brain. "You like stating the obvious, huh?" I ask, my husky voice unintentional. I'll take it if it means he starts going again.

"Sorry. I can't stop looking at this mesmerizing face of yours."

I encase his cheeks, bringing him down for a kiss. Drew resists me.

"You don't understand," he says. "You look like an angel every time you're into it."

"You're trying to tell me that you'd rather talk about my O face than keep fucking me?"

"I can take a little break. Why, can't you?"

"Maybe taking a break means I lose all concentration."

"I'd love to see what you look like when you're really concentrating."

"There are ways to facilitate that, you know."

We figure out the best way in another five seconds. I may have been beneath him a moment before, but now I'm top, my legs easily spreading across his pelvis as my own drops into his lap. Drew pierces me right in my core. The ache for him remains, long after he's filled me like he always does. It's not enough, though. Neither is bracing my hands against his sturdy chest or letting my hair fall between us. Drew draws his hands up from my hips and down my arms, hands momentarily encasing mine before raising them back up to stroke my face.

No more words, all right? I don't want to say anything. He better not say anything. I'm conflicted enough as it is, since I barely know how to have sex without the fury of need and desire fueling my every motion. All I want to do is finish this. I don't care how it feels. I only know that, to enjoy it a little, I need to throw my whole consciousness into it. I've gotta ride this man until the saddle gives out and I land with my face up to the grand, blue sky.

There's only one way to go. I don't know which way that is. Does it matter? Let fate take the reins and drag my horse wherever it needs to go. I'd rather follow the current of this moment than get bogged down in the fears that constantly plague my heart. Yeah. My heart. That stupid thing I had completely forgotten about until today. Who knew that thing could still feel shit? Not me. I've been too busy bringing feeling back to the rest of my body. Stimulating my brain and my clit. I hear they're related.

Drew can do whatever he wants, as long as he doesn't speak. Grab my tits, hold my hips, or throw his hands down to his sides and maul the sheets. I don't want to look at *his* handsomeness or whatever, either. I want to... *be*.

I want to float on the breeze coming through his opened window. I want to remember what it's like to not give a shit about inconsequential – or consequential – things. Let's not consider what it means for a man to say he likes me. Let alone a man like Drew Benton. Even without his job, or the circumstances through which we met, there's the fact that he's his father's son. He's a *Benton.* He's good looking, charming, and knows how to trick you into thinking he's an everyday guy. Even when there's no pretense with him, there's a ton of *pretense.* He'll always have that family history and experience backing everything he says or does in your presence.

I'm not supposed to be thinking about that. I'm supposed to flying through the air, thinking of nothing but how good this feels. Right here. This moment.

Do I come? Does he come? I don't know. It doesn't matter now, does it? Our lot in life is to lie next to one another, our chests gently rising and falling as our breaths sync. Drew folds his hands behind his head and considers the ceiling. I slowly close my eyes and try to remember what had me so angry earlier. It couldn't have been so bad if I ended up in bed with him again.

"Hey..." Drew breaks the silence, although he doesn't break the unspoken vow between us to no longer touch. We're both on our respective sides of his bed, never minding our nudity or thinking about going to the bathroom. Not yet. I'm too weirded out by what's happened to get to that. "Why not be my girlfriend? Why not make it official?"

I don't turn my head. Such a question doesn't deserve so much attention from me. "Come again?" I mutter.

"I guess it's a nice way to say we should make this exclusive. Not that I think you're running around with a bunch of other guys. I mean, I haven't been with…"

"That's not what I'm talking about."

He takes in an audibly deep breath. "Are you trying to say you don't feel like there's something more between us than sex? I mean, if that's all there is, would it be so bad if we explored a possibility of more? At least then we'd know."

I want to say, "*You mean* you'll *know.*" I don't. That's asking for an argument, and I don't have the energy. "I don't think it's that deep between us. We have sex. That's it."

"Things don't really have to change," he argues. "We meet up when we feel like it…"

"No. That's not how it would work." I sit up. "A casual thing is meeting up when we feel like it. Calling each other something more than a fuck buddy is trying to meet up whenever we *can.*" That's the distinction I must drive into his head. "There's pressure. I don't want pressure."

"What pressure? You're not feeling pressured right now, are you?"

"I'm not talking about that kind of pressure…" If he conflates what I said for failing to secure consent, then I don't know what to tell him. Here's hoping it was the sex that addled his poor, dumb brain.

"What are you talking about, then? Do you really not care that I like you? Does this truly mean nothing to you?"

Who is this man and where did he come from? Why the fuck is he asking me these stupid questions? You know, I keep thinking stuff like that, yet all I really get out of this is… fatigue. I flop back down onto the bed, tears forming in the corners of my eyes.

Not to cry, no. I'm not upset enough over *nothing* to cry. The water in my eyes is more about frustration. Why do I have to be dealing with this right now? Drew isn't someone who should be on my radar. I shouldn't be considering his prospect that we meet up every weekend to giggle over drinks and swing in hammocks by the sea. If I agree to be his girlfriend, this ends. No more hooking up. No more playing fun little games to see who can outdo who. I can ask the man paid to ruin me to go ahead and fuck me like the town bitch everyone despises. I can't ask my *boyfriend* that. He'll want more of what we did tonight. Even if he gets so horny he can't help from pounding me like a drum, he'll always be holding something back. I'll have to meet his insufferable family. We'll start showing up in the society pages. Jason, my blasted ex, will make Drew's life hell. Every ex of mine will come up to Drew and ask him what the hell he's doing throwing his precious life away on me.

You see, I know how this goes. And I'm not sure I have the energy – or the fortitude – to play that long con with Drew Benton, no matter how much I like hanging out with him or how much money he's got in his bank account. He can give up his business today and start doing something much more respectable tomorrow, and it would only be another sign that he's changing... *because of me.*

That's when it goes south. That's when I start planning my escape. Things will change. I will change. He's already changing.

Fuck me.

I get up and grab my clothes. It takes me a while to find my T-shirt, since I forgot it disappeared underneath his. Funny. What a lovely example of where we're heading. A metaphor for how we have sex when it's most convenient. Him. Smothering me.

Intoxicated

"Cher." Drew is up in his bed, one arm tentatively reaching toward me. The man is naked and waiting for me to come to him. Yet here I am, getting dressed, putting up my shields of plain, inconsiderate fabric. "Talk to me. I don't mean to put pressure on you. It was something I was thinking about." He flings back against his headboard. "Damn me for mentioning it."

"I shouldn't have come here." That's what I say as I pull my shirt over my stomach. My hair is a mess, but I need to get out of here. There's no time to stand in front of his mirror and primp. I'll be taking a Lyft home, anyway. I don't need to look nice for a Lyft driver, who will probably smell the sex on me.

"Don't say that," Drew says. "I wanted you to come so I could explain. Why do you think I drove down here from Seattle?"

"I didn't ask you to."

Drew snaps his mouth closed. He's utterly silent as I finish getting dressed, grab my bag, and head out.

He doesn't follow me. He doesn't text me as I head to the lobby of his building and ignore the concierge in favor of hailing a Lyft. The way the guy looks at me insinuates he knows why I was there. To get laid. Probably with Drew, a hot guy with a lot of money and one of the more expensive apartments overlooking the Willamette.

It's not like I want Drew to follow me, to blow up my phone, or otherwise intrude upon my life tonight. His silence speaks the volumes he couldn't upstairs.

I get in the back of a white Subaru. My driver makes very little small talk as he takes the fastest route to Northwest Portland. The only sound I hear is the hum of the jazz station and the gentle rumbles of the car on the road.

And my heart. It thunders in my head.

CHAPTER 24

DREW

What do you do when the girl you like runs out after making love?

I was hoping you could tell me, because I'm honestly at my wit's end here.

I think it's safe to say that Cher and I are at the pivotal crunch point of our so-called relationship. I've broken the fundamental rule of casual, friends-with-benefits arrangements. I've gone and caught a few feelings. Against the advice of *everyone* I know, by the way, including her. Somewhere in Seattle, Brent is clicking his tongue and wondering if this means the end of his job. It's certainly the end of my sanity.

You know what the worst thing about her walking out was? How beautiful she was in her self-doubt and confusion. The humanity was on her face. Even from across the room, with my whole body aching from the love we had made, I could see those lines of uncertainty and the clouded look in her eyes. Cher was caught off-guard. Unawares. Wondering how the hell she would face me again should our paths ever cross. This isn't a woman who is used to falling in love. Neither am I, for that matter. This is uncharted ground for the both of us. That is, if I dare to admit I'm falling in love with the worst woman on Earth.

Is she, really?

Logic says that I should watch myself around her. She could still be playing me for a fool. Tonight, she looks over her shoulder and has the face of a woman battling with her heart. Tomorrow, she's laughing about me to her gal-pals, if she has them. *"You won't believe it. I totally have him wrapped around my finger. Drew! Drew Benton! The guy my ex hired to fuck me over! Now he's the one eating out of my hand, waiting for me to slap him silly. How long do you think it will take until he asks me to marry him? Tomorrow? A week from now?"*

No, I'm nowhere close to asking her to marry me. I may be foolish at times, but I know better than to propose to a woman I barely know. Let alone one who has a history of running out on guys the moment they pop the question. We've established that my father is top-tier trash at doling out advice, but if there's one thing he told me, it's that you *don't* propose to a woman you can't foresee yourself growing old with. Good advice, isn't it? Some guys jump to the altar with the first hot girl who says she loves him, but she's awful wife material and only gets worse with age. Granted, the guys aren't much better themselves. I've gone to many of these weddings. I've also gone to the *congrats, you're divorced!* bashes that usually follow two or three years later.

The next day, I get a call from Brent asking when I'll be back. I don't know. Cher won't respond to the single text I've sent her. I should head back to Seattle sooner rather than later, but a part of me stays here in Portland, wondering if she'll show up again by the evening.

She doesn't.

Finally, I drive to her place late Friday morning. My overnight bag is packed and ready for the drive back up to Seattle, but I'm willing to hang out here if that's what Cher wants. She could ask me to crawl into her bed and stay there until I waste away, and I might do it.

Infatuation. Is that what this really is? How badly do I want to behold my raven-haired beauty as she goes about her business, however dirty it may be?

I buzz her apartment. Like last time, she doesn't answer. I'm pretty good at guessing which unit might be hears. She's the type to cling to a reading nook in a bay window overlooking the street below. Ivory pillows with gold stitching adorn one of the nooks on the second floor. A feminine wind-chime hangs in front of the glass. Every time it catches a bit of the sunlight, I imagine Cher sitting beneath it, gazing out at the Northwest Portland goings-on as she either reads a book or holds her phone to her head.

There are no lights on. No signs of life. She's not home.

At least that tells me what I need to know. Go back to Seattle. Figure out what I want to do with my life. If Cher contacts me, great. She can meet me up there again. I'll pay for her ticket. Maybe we'll talk things over like mature adults. I'll lay out what I'm feeling at the ripe old age of thirty, and she can rebut with what a loner she is. It'll be perfect. A perfect way to reach an impasse that will only end when one of us needs to bail.

Intoxicated

You know, there was something kinda strange about her behavior when I last saw her. While Cher is never forthright about her emotions, she never hesitates to tell me - actually, that's *demand*, if we're being honest - what she wants. It's one of the hottest things about hooking up with her. How many women will look you in the eye and tell you to call them a filthy slut? I mean, you're sitting there with your dick hard in your hand like a total jackass, wondering how far you can push the dirty talk. When you're in the heat of the moment, things get... *crazy*.

Crazy enough that you're making connections that you never thought possible.

Cher was mute the other night. Although she followed my lead and appeared to enjoy herself, I can't say she was *into it*. The more I attempted to engage her with my words or kisses, the more she pulled away from me. Am I really surprised that she ran off when it was over? This was a woman I had asked to be my girlfriend. My declarations for something more concrete between us only made her skittish. Whatever went through her head wasn't good news for me.

I think it's best if I don't hunt her down. Nor should I be quick to get back to Seattle, where I'll only stew in everything that upsets me. That's not how I want to live my life. I'm better off with more distractions.

Who better to give me something productive to do than my own grandmother? I had promised her I'd stop by soon, anyway. Not sure if she actually wants me there, but I'm not big on leaving her alone for weeks at a time. This is a woman who is getting a bit up there in age. Irene Benton may be perfectly capable of taking care of herself when she's sound of mind and able in body, but who knows how long that will last? Besides, knowing my luck, she's lost another chicken and hasn't bothered to tell me. Probably thinks my work was so shoddy that it's my fault she's lost one of her feathered daughters.

I veer off I5 when I reach Centralia. I'm already alleviated to get the hell away from both Portland and Seattle. This time of year, Eastern Washington is a sight to behold. The mountains are crisp with the very last remnants of snow, assuming it hasn't all melted yet. The trees are full and green, with wildflowers blooming on the sides of the highway and deer and elk crossing signs giving you a taste of what you might encounter around another curve. The buildings are old, but functional. Occasionally, you see an old, dilapidated barn, but there's usually a more recent one another mile down the road. Pastures of cows, sheep, and horses are the norm in this part of the country. Your cell reception comes in and out. More in than out. If you don't get gas now, you're looking at a 47 mile wait, and the prices will make you laugh until you realize how serious they are.

This part of the world gets grief. While it's true you meet some characters on your travels, most of the people out here are all talk and little real interest to ram their hunting rifles up your ass. Or, at least, I've never gotten the feeling they'll make good on their anti-trespassing promises. Sure, that trailer may be cooking meth, and that barn is home to a breed of raccoons you don't *want* to ever see, but people are honest. Not like in the city. What you see is what you get. Nobody's going to pretend to be anyone other than who they are. It's pretty great, especially if you're not naturally the most trusting person.

Liiiike my grandma.

I still think it's nuts she's moved out here all by herself. I don't care how spry, whip smart, or capable she is. This isn't the kind of place you come to be an old lady by yourself. I'm going to get a phone call from a nice Eastern Washington sheriff one day who says my grandmother was found in her yard, torn apart by a pack of mountain lions and grizzly bears. Mark my words.

Until then, I'll do what I can to prevent that.

The sun glares through my windshield as I turn off the highway and into her driveway. The little white house at the end of a straight, gravel road doesn't take form until I'm practically there. It's a good thing I was finally allowed the gift of sight. I'm not used to there being a car in the spot where I usually park.

I don't recognize the black sedan. The plates are Oregonian. A rental? Who the hell is renting a car in Oregon to come visit my grandmother? Why do I smell her award-winning smoked ribs as soon as I step out of my truck and slam the door in announcement of my arrival?

"Hey, Gram." I slowly approach the porch, where my grandmother appears in an old pair of jeans and a baggy sweatshirt that says she didn't go out today. She leans against one of the posts and cocks a wrinkled hand on her hip. Am I in trouble? Because she's looking at me like I'm about to have my allowance taken away. Which only happened *twice* in my youth, thank you. I never made a habit out of smoking after she caught me with a cigarette at fifteen. Nor did I ever again sneak out to see a 21+ concert when I was only seventeen. When your allowance is the size of some parents' paychecks, you learn how to hold onto them. "What's going on? Did I drop in at a bad time?" I gesture to the unknown car in the driveway.

"Actually, you're right on time for dinner. Got ribs a'cooking, and we're in here shelling peas. You better get in here and join us so it goes faster. Earn your dinner, while you're at it."

"Us?"

"Oh, yes." My grandmother opens her screen door. The front door is already open. "*Us.*"

I don't know how to take this. Am I in trouble? If I am, is it with my grandmother or the unknown guest? I look back at the car again, searching for any identifiable marks. Nothing. No vanity plates. Nothing hanging from the rearview mirror. No dashboard ornaments. Not even a ding in the door that tells me they're a shitty driver. Is it a man? A woman? If it's a man, I might be in trouble. But if it's one of my clients, like Jason Rothchild, then what are they doing driving such a lackluster car? It's a Honda sedan, not a Mercedes!

I'm over thinking this. Time to get my ass inside and see what the fuss is about.

My grandmother leads the way back to her kitchen, where the smell of ribs is the strongest. There, in the center of her round table, is a huge bowl of peas recently taken off the vine. What survived the deer, anyway. I have a faint memory of Gram expecting me to help reinforce the garden fence against deer.

It's not the peas we're shocked by, now is it?

Because if you're seeing what I'm seeing, then somebody has a lot of explaining to do. Mostly Cher, who is sitting on the far end of the table, shelling peas like it's second nature.

What. The. *Fuck*.

CHAPTER 25

CHER

You're probably wondering what the hell I'm doing here. Surprised, are you? Sure, once you saw the look on Drew's face, you probably started putting two and two together. Congratulations! You can do basic, first-grade math. I bet you also read simple sentences and can tell me what an adjective is.

How about this adjective? *Shocked.* A great way to describe Drew Benton as he stands in his grandmother's kitchen, staring at me like I've come back from the dead.

"Hey." That's all I say. I'm busy. Shelling peas, or whatever you call what I'm doing. It's been an hour of me popping open these little green shells and watching peas plop out of them. While I wouldn't call Drew's grandma a *little old lady,* she's little, old, and definitely a lady. She may wear old clothes, live in this grody house, and cook like she's afraid of spending money at the supermarket, but my God, you can still smell the Benton on her. She's wearing Chanel No. 5. The classic, especially if you're of an older generation.

By the way, can we address the elephant in the room? No, no, I'm not calling Irene Benton an *elephant*. Do not take me the wrong way, thanks. (Seriously. Step away from Reddit. Or Tumblr. Or Facebook, I don't care. I'm not in the mood to be in your daily list of *These Bitches Who Seriously Said Shit*. I used to have such a list, so I know what I'm talking about. Back. Away.) I expected all sorts of women when I rolled up to her door for an introduction for reasons I'm *still* attempting to explain. I was prepared for either a scruffy woman in farmer's clothing, or a well-to-do former socialite who plays at homesteading. Well, I definitely got the scruffy farmer.

I thought, you know... she would be white?

Look! I'm in Eastern Washington, not exactly known for its racial diversity. And the Bentons are well, shall we say, *old-fashioned*. Things may change over the generations, but I didn't peg Drew's grandfather as someone "progressive" enough to openly marry a black woman instead of keeping her as a secret lover. Then again, having hung around Irene for about three hours now, I get the feeling she's not someone's dirty little secret. She would never in a million years let things stay that way. Either Drew's grandfather married her, or they separated.

I get her appeal. She speaks her mind and is handy around the house. If I were Drew's grandfather and looking for a new wife, I might be inclined to tell my country club friends to kindly withdraw the sticks from their asses and then promptly beat them with said sticks. They would kind of deserve it, yes?

"Uh..." Drew still has his keys in his hand. He looks between his grandmother and me. I go back to shelling peas. Irene hops into the kitchen and checks on her ribs. Oh, you can still smell them? My olfactory fatigue settled in an hour ago. All I smell is the regret simmering deep in my heart. And the lust I'm probably building from looking at Drew Benton in his tight flannel and tighter jeans. Should I tell him off for wearing such *compressing* pants? Or should I let his grandmother have the honors? I bet we're similar in the ways we love to verbally beat up the men in our lives. "Someone wanna tell me what's going on here?" he continues to ask.

Since Irene is busy in the kitchen, I'm left to do the honors.

Hm. What should I tell him?

I guess I can tell *you* the truth. Or what there is of it. There really isn't much to say, if I'm being 100% honest. I spent most of yesterday feeling like a fool for going as far as I have with Drew. My mind remains a cloud of unrest, every drop of precipitation threatening to fall from it only compounded by the lightning stirring in my gut. Lest you think that's a statement about the food I eat, let me assure you - I listen to my gut a lot. When it starts stirring, let alone inviting electrical storms into my life, I take heed. Usually you run for cover in a crazy electrical storm, right? It's the same in this situation. Pardon me if I'm a bit frank when I say I'd rather shit lightning than get struck by it.

Guess that's a convoluted way to say I couldn't help but look into what kind of man Drew is. I mean, anyone can hire a private investigator to dig up the dirty stuff. I could find some of his friends and get their biased opinions. Yet I remembered an off-handed comment he made more than once. One about his own grandmother who currently resides in this town (technically) in

Eastern Washington. If the silence in our conversations were too much, Drew would change subjects to his grandmother, the little-known Irene Benton. She was only married to Drew's grandfather for a few years. Very few pictures, or at least I didn't see *any* when I went looking. I was able to dig up her address based on the info he leaked, however.

What possessed me to rent a car and come here, however? Not sure. Too much to drink, maybe. The need to get out of Portland. To drive for the first time in months. To put as much distance between myself and Drew as I feasibly could at such short notice.

I had to know, I guess. I wanted to know what kind of grandmother had him coming around to take care of her all the time. I needed to see who had temporarily raised him when he was a boy. I wanted her damning opinions of his worst traits and to hear what she thought was a decent case for his character.

You can imagine her reaction when I showed up at her door. When I told this stranger that I was dating her grandson and needed some advice, she didn't ask any questions. Just opened her doors and motioned for me to come inside, like she had expected me all along. Maybe she has. Maybe she's been waiting for Drew to set aside his playboy ways long enough for a woman like me to appear and change his life.

Yeah, no. I'm not mantling that moniker anytime soon. But I can't lie. These past few hours have been *interesting*. While I didn't tell Irene the whole details about how we met, I *did* tell her that he and I had the kind of volatile dating histories that made it difficult to trust one another. He thinks I'm a sugar-baby sponging off his money. When I said that, Irene nodded over her bowl of peas, as if she agreed that's what I looked like. Yet when I followed that up with, "*I have no reason to believe he's not a total dick*

Intoxicated

working me too," she continued to nod. She agreed that we both suck.

Now here we are. I've been telling her a little about myself, mostly some of my dating history and what I like to do, while she throws in the random comment about herself or relates it back to her grandson. Drew showed up not too far into a story about Jason Rothchild and how I turned down his proposal last Christmas. Irene was halfway through saying, *"Typical, putting you on the spot like that,"* when she heard Drew's truck coming down the driveway. I've been steeling myself since.

"Thought I'd meet your grandma." That's all I say as I finish this small stack of peas. Irene comes back to fetch the bowl, rinse the peas, and add them to whatever she's cooking as a side dish. I don't have the heart to tell her I'm not really into peas. "You told me such interesting things about her."

His mouth drops. "I didn't tell you *anything* about her!"

"No kidding." Irene has her back to me. I raise my eyebrows at her grandson, and he knows exactly what I'm thinking.

"What does that have to do with anything?" he mouths.

I shrug. Can he blame me for being surprised? This is the Pacific Northwest. People don't expect rich white boys to have black homesteading grandmas. Least of all me. I can't think of a single ex of mine who did except, you know, the ones who were black themselves.

"She's surprised I'm black, Drew!"

I almost spit out the pea I've snuck into my mouth. Drew puts his hands on his hips, exasperated. "What has she been telling you about me, huh?" he shouts into the kitchen. "She tell you I'm trouble?"

"Oh, nothing but! I hear she's trouble, too!"

"You really have no idea," he mouths in my direction.

We eat dinner half an hour later. Although I offer to get up and help Irene serve the ribs and peas, she insists that I am her guest and I should stay seated. Drew, however, is recruited to help before he has the chance to sit down. Grandma and grandson bicker about what a lazy ass he probably is (although he isn't, says the subtext.) I brush pea remnants off the table. By the time I'm served dinner, I'm hungry enough to eat my hand.

Drew sits next to me. He shoots me a glance as I help myself to the iced tea with lemon.

"You know," Irene shakes a spoon full of peas in our direction, "you two ain't so bad looking together. Almost as nice to look at as my ex-husband and me."

"Do you mean Mr. Benton?" I say.

"Mr. Benton! Ain't nobody calling him that around here. I called him Charlie. So that's all I know him as." She takes a bite of her ribs. Sauce dribbles from her fingers as she nods and *hums* at how grand of a cook she is. "Anyway, no. I had another husband before him. Now *that* was a nice looking fella. Married him for his looks, though. Turns out that's a terrible reason to marry somebody. Looks fade, kids."

"Marrying my granddad for his money worked out great?" Drew dryly asks.

"Who said I married for money? I was in it for the big dick."

Drew spews his iced tea across the table. As I fall into a fit laughter, Irene says, ignoring her grandson's mess in favor of her own cooking, "The money was a bonus, especially in that divorce. At some point, a woman realizes the dick ain't worth it."

I'm still laughing, although Irene says that while looking in my direction. Oh, come on. She can't know this about us. Was the quip about marrying for looks directed at Drew? Is that why we're together? This whole time, I thought it was about his money. And his dick. Guess I'm not better than Irene, although she clearly wanted the respectability of marriage to go along with her pursuits. I think I'd be better off jumping into the Willamette like my ex-boyfriend Preston's current woman, but whatever.

We all have our reasons for doing what we do. Some are less glamorous than others. Some make our grandsons spew tea onto the dinner table and exclaim, "Oh, come on!"

"Never underestimate the power of good dick," Irene says before another chomp of ribs. "By the way, do you think these need a little more salt? You know what, I'll go get it."

Drew has completely lost his appetite by the time his grandmother leaves. I'm still snickering in my seat when he turns to me and says, "Glad you think it's so funny. That's my grandpa she's talking about."

"What? I don't know your grandpa." My chuckles finally die down as he continues to glare at me. "At least I know where you get it from, though."

"Get *what?*"

He instantly regrets asking that. For good reason. "Your big dick," I mouth at him.

"Come the *fuck* on." That's what greets Irene when she returns to the table. Things don't get much better for Drew after that.

You know what? Irene's fun. I like her. Think she likes me, too, because we spend most of dinner and the dish cleanup afterward making light fun of Drew and his "tragic" taste in women. Irene regales me with tails of his high school and college girlfriends, one "floozy" after another who were either too stupid to realize they never stood a chance in his family or were only *too* familiar with who he was. When she asks me which one I take myself for, I honestly tell her, "Not sure why I can't be both. I'm a pretty big floozy, but I'm smart at it." For a moment, Irene looks like she's about to kick me out of her house. Then she erupts into uproarious laughter, like there's nothing else so funny.

"Woo, Drew, I think this one might be a keeper!" That's what Irene says as she heads upstairs. "Although that doesn't mean I condone you two having premaritals in my guest room. Drew, you take the couch tonight. Guest gets the guest room."

Drew is already half passed out on the couch in the living room. He drags the afghan down and acts like he's about to fall asleep. I know better, of course. He's simply avoiding me.

"So, uh..." I lean over the back, strands of my hair falling down and tickling his cheek. He doesn't move. "Your grandma's fun. Best kept secret in Washington."

"Best kept secret of the Bentons, you mean?" he shoots back.

"Hmph. I wouldn't know about that."

His gaze lingers on mine. "Why are you *really* here, Cher?"

While I understand his doubt, I can't help but be mildly offended by his tone. "I told you the truth. I wanted to know more about you. Meet this mysterious grandmother of yours you like to talk about. Does she know what you do for a living?"

"No, and I'd appreciate it if you didn't tell her."

"Wasn't gonna, but what does she think you do?"

"I have a 'consulting' firm in Seattle."

"Consulting *what?*"

"She doesn't ask, so I don't make up shit to tell her."

My elbows dig into the back of the couch. Fingertips touch my chin as I entertain contemplative thoughts. "You think she was telling the truth about your grandfather's dick?"

"Don't you think you should be going to bed?"

Messing with him has never been so much fun! Now, if you could guarantee that we'd be feeling like this for the rest of our lives? I might believe that I have finally found my true match.

Too bad we both know exactly where this is going after this. I really am better off going to bed and pretending none of this has happened. Otherwise, I risk liking Irene a little too much and missing her when I inevitably leave Drew's life. And I might end up liking Drew a little too much, too.

CHAPTER 26

DREW

Can we fall back and address what happened yesterday?

Even if I expected to see Cher at my grandmother's place - which I didn't, by the way - there was no way to anticipate the absolute shit show that was my dinner. So glad they could yuck it up like they had known each other for a hundred years. I don't get it. Cher should have offended my grandmother no fewer than five times during dinner *alone*. Yet everything she said only made my grandma laugh or chide her for being a little *too* blunt. Let me assure you, though, that wasn't her truly scolding Cher. She was encouraging her. I dunno. I have no idea what kind of conspiracy blossomed between them, but I don't like it.

You'd think I would, though. The feelings I'm developing for Cher lend themselves to wanting her to get along with my grandmother. She's hated every girl I've dated since high school. Then again, she's never met the ones I was working for a client. If my grandma really knew what I did for a living... I'd never hear the end of it. Hell, she'd probably never talk to me again. My grandmother can be sensitive like that. I don't blame her. She's had a lot in life to be sensitive about.

Cher leaves early in the morning. She doesn't hang around for one of my grandma's stellar breakfasts of sausage and eggs. Yet she lingers for a few minutes outside of her rental car, allowing me a chance to ask her what's going on between us.

"What are you talking about?" she snorts, arm looping over the top of the car door. "Thought we were dating. Let's keep it simple, Drew."

"So you still want to meet up soon?"

"When will you be back in Portland?"

Is she really asking me that? With that cheeky smile and those sexy, *grabbable* legs poking out of her cotton shorts? "What day do you want me to back there, huh?"

"I'd say today, but I overheard your grandmother giving you a honey-do list."

"I can be back tomorrow afternoon. Early." I hold back the door so she can't yet close it and be on her way. "I'm taking you out for a date. Whatever you want."

She glances at my jeans and bites her lip. "You know what I want, Benton."

Really? We've gotta bring that up *again?* I haven't had my breakfast yet.

Cher pulls out onto the highway. I stay outside long enough to watch her car disappear in the distance. Upon my return to the house, my grandma hands me a list and makes it clear I'm not going anywhere until the garden fence is reinforced and her downstairs toilet unclogged.

Sometimes, I wonder about the power some women have over me.

***

"But do you know the unipiper?"

The air conditioner keeps the mall seventy degrees, although I hear tales that it's eighty-five outside. A draft blankets my arms as I whirr down the empty aisles. Well, near-empty. We all know how America's malls are doing these days. It takes savvy marketing and an iron will to get lazy online shoppers into a giant box full of people. It takes more to get them to spend *money*. My tender heart remembers the days of stuffed stores and departments galore. Those were the days when my mother bothered to shop at the mall. She'd grab me, my sister, and her BFF of the moment for a day of shopping in a busy mall. Now? I can swerve my giant animal scooter around a kiosk selling customizable baseball caps – yes, please – without worrying about a soul.

Even if it means spinning a full lap and almost knocking the head of my bull into the ass of Cher's tiger.

She glances over her shoulder. Giant, round sunglasses adorn her scalp, but it's the dangly jade earrings and the sleeves of her green and yellow kimono that have me wagging my eyebrows. Okay, so maybe it's the sultry look, too. She's painted some fantastic makeup onto her face. Yes, I notice these things. I die for a pair of eyes lined in black.

"The unipiper," she repeats. Her fingers remain wrapped around the handles of her mighty plush tiger. Way down at the other end of the walkway is a four-year-old riding on an elephant. You know, the target audience for these things? "Do I know him?"

"That's what I asked, yes." I scoot my bull forward, its butt tapping her tiger's butt. Cher jerks in her seat, cheeks puffing and foot sliding off its rest. Yeah, that was a serious impact. Whoops. "Do you know the unpiper?"

She looks like I've put the spotlight on her. Naturally, she doesn't know that I'm really the police and this whole mall is our interrogation chamber. I want to know her affiliations. Her hobbies. Her haunts. Who has she bribed, and for how much?

This all started because we had a friendly "who is more Oregonian?" fight that began at the frozen yogurt shop and ended by the ice rink, where I spotted these beautiful specimens of the animal kingdom. Speaking of bribes, I basically had to bribe the guy selling the rides to let our adult-asses go for a ride. "*You see that babe there, my dude?*" I asked the young man who had been eyeing Cher ever since she walked over exactly one step behind me. "*I'm trying to show her a nice time today. If you know what I mean.*" My hearty wink came with a very nice untaxable tip for him. He definitely spoke my language after that.

Cher and I have gone from talking about who used to call potato wedges at the deli "jojos" to who remembers when the Pearl was a shady, *shady* place. I've definitely been here longer than she has, but I continue to be surprised by her knowledge of the area and her memories of going to school not too far away from me. Color me surprised that she went to a private, all-girls' school downtown. I spent ten minutes listening to her talk about the MAX's Green Line construction back in the day. Since that line doesn't run anywhere near my stomping grounds, new or old, I learned a few things from *her*.

Now we're discussing some of the human staples that Keep Portland Weird. She started with the guy who styles herself in blue from head to toe and hangs around Pioneer Square. I countered with the "guru" who sold stolen shoes down by the waterfront. Would you believe me if I said he used to be my dad's classmate in his private school in Beaverton? 'Cauuuuse he totally was.

The conversation has come back to the unipiper. That's when you know I'm getting desperate.

"Do you mean *personally* know him?" Cher is nothing but knowing smirks as she turns her tiger in slow, tight circles. "Because I definitely know *of* him. Saw him up in Northwest only a few days ago. Spooked quite a few people out having their cocktails on the sidewalk."

"Duh, I mean personally. Why would I be asking if I didn't mean personally? You're not real Portland unless you know the unipiper by his first name and occasionally get brewskies together. Could tell you his favorite IPA."

I begin a sloooow pursuit of her tiger past two boarded up windows. Geez, more stores are gone now? This place is turning into a veritable ghost town. Pretty soon, it will be nothing but ice skaters, janitors, and security guards.

"So what's his name?" Cher sweetly asks.

My eyes are transfixed on her ass. Is it inappropriate to think about fucking while riding around on a child's toy? I mean, I'm pretty much an overgrown child, so it pans out, but I don't think most of the children feeling like bosses on a bull three times their own size are thinking about what I'm contemplating right now. Mm-*mmm*. Cher has a great ass.

"Are you alive back there?" she asks. "Or is that hat on your head the only thing keeping you from keeling over?"

Intoxicated

Just for this ride, I've turned my cap backward. More aerodynamic that way. "D... Drew. His name is Drew."

She cocks one finely trimmed eyebrow. "Are you saying that you're the unipiper?"

"I *do* own a Darth Vader mask." We come to a stop in front of Hot Topic. I sit up straight in my bully seat, while Cher continues to lean against the tiger's head. "Although, you've caught me. I don't have a set of bagpipes. Or a unicycle, for that matter."

Her little bouts of laughter make me grin like an idiot. "That's silly." She pulls away on her tiger. "You're silly."

"Not as silly as Darth Vader riding around on a unicycle and playing the bagpipes!" As I said before, though, at least he keeps Portland the fun kind of weird.

We play this whole date by ear, never knowing what's coming next or where we might go. Us coming to this mall nowhere near where either of us lives was the first of many surprises. I took Cher out for brunch at what I consider to be *the* place to get authentic crepes. She told me she wanted to stroll the nearby mall, so that's what we did, until we ended up in our pissing contest that lasted our allotted time on the animals. As sad as I am to say goodbye to my new favorite bull in the world, I'm more excited to take Cher's hand and let the whole mall, from the teenagers hanging out to the fifty-somethings likewise passing the time, that she's my gal from now until she decides she's done with me.

I'm not going to press her to give me an answer about our status. The fact she showed up at my grandmother's house - let alone that my grandmother *liked* her - says enough. For now. It may be a matter of time before she completely breaks up with me. Until then, I'll appreciate these halcyon days full of flirting, hand-holding, and pretending that we're actually compatible.

Doesn't she have the best smile? You know you're doing good when she turns to you and smiles like that. It's not her fake *fall-into-my-web* smile that so many guys see before they lose their minds or wallets. It's a smile that tells me she's having a good time, and that I'm this much closer to having her love me.

If that's what I want. I might not get a choice.

We stare at window displays, discuss what kind of style I would have if I were a woman, and promptly decide that I would either be a massive tomboy or the girliest girl to every outgirly Cher. "You'd look great in a romper." Cher points to the outfit hanging on a mannequin. All I can think about is that mannequin having to pee. Seriously, how do you go to the bathroom in those things? What really *is* the price of fashion? Because my bladder isn't one I'm willing to pay. "Maybe a little denim one with daisies stitched on the front pocket. Get you a cute straw hat or a cross-body bag for you to hold your tampons."

"I like how this hypothetical female version of myself is already on her period."

"There's nothing sacred left between us, Drew. You've already seen my blood. It's only right that I'd see yours."

"On your sheets, I should hope."

She nudges me. I deserve that.

We can't stay at the mall forever. Since it's later in the afternoon, I'm thinking cocktails downtown. I convince her to come with me to one of the top-floor lounges that give us a fantastic view of both rivers dividing Portland into its traditional five "quadrants." Cher quips that she can see her quadrant of Northwest from where we're sitting. I point out that I can *literally* see my building down at the South Waterfront. Our server is a guy who also happens to be named Drew. The moment we see his

Intoxicated

nametag and I out myself as a fellow Drew, we're already having laughs and asking each other if Nancy is our favorite Drew. From the way we both laugh like it's the funniest joke we've heard, you'd think we've never told it to anyone else before. Cher merely rolls her eyes and says she'd love to meet "the" Cher for once.

"Which one?" I ask, as our waiter goes to get our drinks. "The queen of retirement, or the queen of plaid?"

"I'll have you know that Cher Horowitz is a fashion icon," she informs me. "Also, she got to have a really weird relationship with Paul Rudd, so we can't fault her for that. Actual queen and living legend."

"Right. Wasn't he like her stepbrother in that?"

"And in college, while she was sixteen."

"How badly has that movie aged, again?"

Cher props her head up on her hand and wistfully stares out the window. The early evening sun glistens against the glass. It's enough to keep my eyes averted, but Cher continues to stare. I'm not convinced she's actually looking at anything. Probably a forgotten memory.

Sometimes I wish I could pick her brain. Other times, I'm content to swim in my blissful ignorance.

"What do you *really* want to do with your life?" she asks me.

My man Drew picks a helluva time to return with our drinks. I don't engage in any jokes this time. Just a simple *"Thank you"* that turns into me wishing he'd get the hell on with it already. Come on, man. I have to plot out my future here!

"That's a loaded question," I say. "I could easily ask you that."

"I've been pretty open about what I want to do. Travel the world, read every book that's ever interested me, drink tea in the most interesting nooks and crannies around Portland."

"Is that really a whole life, though?"

She shrugs. "Fine. I want crazy-good sex, too."

"There you go. That's what I want for my life. Let's build an existence around it."

"Says the guy wearing a trucker hat in a high-class lounge?"

"This is high-class?" I look around. I'm far from the only guy in here wearing a hat or jeans. Hell, there are guys in open-toe sandals. Women in short-shorts and tank tops. For every person dressed at least business casual, there's another treating this place like the local taqueria. I didn't think anything of it until Cher said something. When you're as loaded as I am, you don't question dress codes. Not when you go out to eat. Not unless you're trying to impress somebody. Say, like a date. "Huh. The more you know."

She levels a rueful gaze on me. "You know what I meant. For the average person, this *is* classy. Maybe it's not the place where we met, but..."

"I think that might be one of my favorite places." I pick up my glass and wink at her. "'Cause I met you there, baby."

I set out to make her groan, and I have succeeded. Score one, Drew.

It's only a matter of time before she reminds me of her question. Maybe I'll score some extra points if I go ahead and *try* to answer it now. "Anyway, I've actually been thinking a lot about what I want to do with the rest of my life. The era of Drew Benton, Professional Avenger, is over. I'm only keeping my business open and my assistant employed because I'll eventually turn them both into something else. Start over. Maybe I'll go into real consulting like my grandmother thinks I do." The sooner I do it, the better. If dementia doesn't get my grandma, she'll figure out the truth, and I'll be in *so much hot water* I'll boil alive. "But I'm also thinking about my drunk-high idea to do a matchmaking service. Of course, that would be a serious rebrand. Do you think my old, happy clients would go for it?"

Cher tilts her head. I can't tell if that look is intrigued or pure disbelief. She has yet to touch her drink; meanwhile, I'm over here already half-finished with mine.

"You mean, can you go from being that angry guy who gives them that vengeance... to the guy who tells them, '*Yeah, bro,*" she adopts a stance, mannerism, and tone of voice that is *nothing* like me at all, "*I totally got the right hot chick for you. She's got a Master's in Physics with a Minor in Blowjobs. When can I hook you guys up?*"

"Come on, it wouldn't be like *that.*"

"I seem to recall me helping you find hot women willing to learn the sugar baby life."

"I mean, I'm not guaranteeing they'll find the life partner of their hearts and loins. Just the loins of the moment. I would do my best to match compatible people, all right?"

"Right." Cher sips her drink. Is that sour face from the taste, or what I said? "You can't fix stupid, though. Or people with impossible standards. Or men who don't realize they need to be marrying a woman they see as a human being first, hot piece of ass second."

"And the women? I'm doubting most of my female clients will be hot young heiresses looking for rich old daddies." I might get a few, though. There is always that occasional gal with serious daddy issues. Can't be helped. Well, *I* can't help it. Society isn't my problem. "What do they need to realize?"

Cher shrugs. "That they're disposable, unless they play it safe the whole way through. Even then? Disposable."

If I needed anything to completely kill my enthusiasm, that would do it. *Disposable.* She's not saying that she thinks women are disposable. No, what she's implying is that it doesn't matter how much a woman thinks highly of herself, lowly of herself, or anything in between. The rich man she's with isn't going to see her as anything more than a convenient toy to move on from the moment she gets a little too old or opinionated.

I wish I could say that's ridiculous, but I've known my fair share of guys, both my age and older, who have fallen into the trap of always needing younger and prettier girlfriends. Once their first wives start to show their age, let alone have children they don't immediately bounce back from, guys are already thinking about the next honey to catch their attention. I grew up in a house where youth and beauty fade, but smarts don't always improve. My sister seems to be an exception to both rules, but she's still not yet thirty-five. Give her a few more years, and we'll be grateful she turned out to be the smart one.

"I love men," Cher says, "but they can be so dumb."

"Doesn't really help if the women they're seeing are playing them for fools."

She snorts into the back of her hand. "It's a chicken and an egg conundrum, Mr. Benton." That husky tone she adopts is awfully familiar. I heard it the first night we met. Combined with *Mr. Benton,* it's clear she's pretending to play me. Or this is her default state when she begins to dissociate. I probably know her better than most of the guys she's dated in the past few years, but there are still aspects of her brain I cannot fully comprehend. I doubt I ever will. "What came first? Women playing men to the point the men no longer took us seriously? Or the men disposing of us to the point we picked up these games for our survival?"

Intoxicated

"Is that what it is, Ms. Lieberman?" I lower my face across the table. "All the odds are stacked against you, so you either go for the financial gold while you can or go completely independent?"

"No money." Her drowsy eyes lull me into their web. If I'm not careful, I'll never untangle myself again. "You grow up without any money and find out you've got two choices in life. Do you work your ass off in the capitalistic grind to *maybe* retire in relative luxury one day? Or do you use what God gave you to make the most of your youth?"

"Sounds like either way you lose that spark that made you so attractive to begin with."

"You mean like you did?"

Ouch. *Ouch.* I could pretend that I don't know what she means by that, but I do. It hits me so hard that I'm almost awestruck at her gall. So, what can I do? I'm the one who willingly told her what happened to my friend and how it affected me. She knows what I do - did - as a way to bide my time until I figured out what I really wanted to do with my life. Now here we are. She's calling me out for being no better than her. I'm acknowledging that, yes, she truly is the closest thing to a perfect match I have ever met.

I have no idea what to say. To admit defeat? To challenge her?

Or maybe I should take her hand on this table as a reassurance that I get her.

We exchange no words as I finish my cocktail with my other hand and Cher gazes at the view. Conversations continue around us. My namesake shows another couple to some seats a few tables away. My eyes glaze over as I focus on the touch of Cher's fingers – and the fact she hasn't yanked them out of mine. She has such delicate, ladylike fingers. Nicely buffed and painted. Does she do her own nails? Or does she go to one of the many salons in her neighborhood? Like most young women who haven't worked outside of an office or a schoolroom, her skin is soft and her knuckles softer. I could get lost in the way her skin stretches across her bones. Shit, is that weird to say? It made more sense in my head. Because if you could stare at her hands like I am right now, you'd get what I'm saying. Beautiful. Perfection. Like her, if she would damn well admit it.

Yup. I'm that fool who has stumbled into her web. Am I going to deny it any longer? I'm falling in love with her. I may already *be* in love with her, but I fear regrets. This isn't a woman you knowingly give your heart to, not if you know who she is and what she can do. Look at that expression on her face. Can you call it that? Or should you admit that she's an unfeeling wraith who bides her time until she has you in her snare? For all I know, she's thinking about what to have for dinner. With or without me.

Has she learned that she's so disposable, that she's now made *me* the disposable one?

Whether you know you're getting into shit with her or not, you can't help but embrace the chance that you're disposable. I get it now. That phrase, "*It's better to have loved and lost, than never to have loved at all.*" I've never really been in love before. Not like this.

Something startles Cher so her hand falls out of mine and she whips her head toward a man coming up to our table. It's not the other Drew. It's a man who looks a bit older, and with blond hair and a black shirt that goes with his tan trousers. He has the air of respectability while retaining a hint of playboy charms. I know this type well. Aside from the retirement aged men who hire me, this guy is in my key business demographic.

God help us all. These two obviously know each other.

Intoxicated

"Preston," Cher says with an indifferent façade. "Funny running into you again."

The man glances at me before giving his full attention to Cher. "Thought I'd pop over and say hello so we didn't have to pretend to awkwardly ignore one another. Phoebe's here, too, but I waited until she went to the little girls' room to say hello."

"I'll be sure to hold it in a while longer so I don't bump into her there." Cher glimpses in my direction, a diabolical smile tugging at her mouth. "By the way, do you know Drew Benton? I'm sure you've noticed we're seeing each other." Yeah, we hadn't exactly been hiding the hand holding. Now I'm roped into this. "Do you know Preston Bradley, Drew? He's one of my many, *many* ex-boyfriends."

"I believe we've been acquainted a time or two over the years." I offer to shake Preston's hand. I'm always impressed when a guy has a good handshake, and today is no different. I mean, if I have to imagine Cher having sex with this guy, he might as well have a strong handshake. "Although I don't believe I've had the pleasure of a conversation."

"Preston's a venture capitalist, from Bradley & Marcus," Cher continues, in that silky, haughty tone she adopts when impressing rich guys like us. "He's dating a yoga instructor."

"My Phoebe is also quite the accomplished romance author."

"Slide that in there, why don't you, Preston?" Oh, here it comes. Cher's unable to let him get away with humbragging like that. "Drew owns his own business up in Seattle, but he's from *those* Bentons. The Beaverton ones." Why, I wasn't aware there were other Bentons. I learn something new about my own family every day.

"I'm well acquainted with your father, Drew," Preston says to me. "We've done business together."

"I don't doubt it, if you really are an investor. My father loves asking for money."

"As long as he does good things with it."

"Doesn't he always?" I reply.

A lean blond woman in a floor-length sundress cautiously approaches us. From the way she looks at Preston – and the way she frowns at Cher – I surmise she is the new girlfriend, Phoebe, bestselling romance author and yoga instructor. "Hello," she coolly greets Cher. Instantly, I feel like I'm in the middle of an awkward divorce battle. It doesn't help that Phoebe then looks at me, nothing but pity in her bright, observant eyes.

I wince. Not my smoothest move in front of affluent strangers, but I can't help it. They might as well have shone a spotlight on my naivete.

"Take care. Enjoy your drinks." Preston turns to Phoebe, arm encircling her waist, and escorts her back to their table. Drew the server looks on at us like we're about to start a blood bath.

Nah. *Nah.*

I don't order another drink. As soon as Cher's finished with hers, I think it's a good idea to get out of here. Her demeanor has suffered to the point that I'm not sure I can salvage it. Not even with my cock.

Guess there's only one way to find out. Wish me luck.

CHAPTER 27

DREW

Much to my pleasant surprise, Cher transforms into a hearty little minx once we're back in my Camaro. The valet has barely tossed me the keys when Cher hops in, the slit in her kimono showing off an enticing thigh. I only notice because her knuckles gently rap against it. As soon as I'm in my seat and putting on my safety belt, that flirtatious hand reaches over and grabs the inside of *my* thigh.

"Hel*lo!*" She has taken me by such surprise that my seatbelt instantly snaps back into place. The valet looks over his shoulder. There's no doubt he's caught my girl making a lunge for my cock. He's probably jealous. I'm more concerned about getting out of the parking lot before I rear-end the parked car a few yards ahead of me. My foot turns more into lead the harder I get in my pants. "*Get home, motherfucker!*" both scream at me. "*You've got pussy to plow! Pussy! Plowing! Lots of coming! Ready to burst already! Get us in there, buddy!*" I have to inhale a deep breath and pull her hand off me to regather my bearings. Hell, to even *think* about my lost bearings.

"Do me a huge favor, would you?" Cher coos into my ear. "Stop playing your cute little games and take me somewhere. I don't care where. Fuck me wherever we go."

We're stuck behind a car waiting to pull onto Broadway. My brain attempts to calculate how long it will take me to drive us back to my place. It might be faster to drive up to *her* place, but mine offers more discretion. As much as I'd like to announce to her neighbors in Northwest that I'm fucking her brains out, sober me in the morning would appreciate the privacy. Come on, how long until we get there?

"You want me to fuck you here?" I growl.

Cher's fingers tip-toe across my thigh, ready to plunge beyond it again. "Bend me over these seats and make the valet watch."

Ten minutes. It takes *ten minutes too long* to get to my parking garage.

Let me tell you, the amount of restraint I practice getting her ass up to my apartment before I rip her clothes off is unprecedented. I've always wanted her, of course, but not so *badly*. Not when we're this far from my bedroom. That wanton gleam in her eye tells me she's up for anything. All I have to do is ask for it, and she'll probably do it. Right here in my fucking car.

I lift the hood on the Camaro. Cher is already out, pulling back her hair and making sure I get a great view of her cleavage. Should I go ahead and stick my dick in there, or is that where I'm finishing? I really wish she'd tell me. I can't tell if she'll only get off if we do it in public, or if I'm looking at a long, *nice* night of sticking it in every hole I can find.

Should I ask which one to start with? Because I've got enough virility in me to go multiple rounds. We can take a break in the shower. If we must.

"Seventeen floors," I mutter, hitting the elevator button. "Then your cunt is all mine."

The doors haven't closed before she pushes me against the wall and kisses me.

Actually, I'm not sure it's a *kiss*. More like an oral hit to the face. Cher grabs my T-shirt and almost yanks my flannel down my arms. Her kimono falls open as my mouth follows suit, and I can't tell if I'm less of a man for letting her lead this moment or stronger for it.

All I know is that I'm so turned on that I don't think twice about her getting on her knees and unzipping my jeans.

"What the *hell*…" My voice trails off into breathy nothingness as I close my eyes and knock my head against the wall. The elevator continues to lurch upward, and her hand continues to stroke my cock until it's too hard to turn back. Every drop of blood in my body has gone down there. If she stops now, I'll have the *worst* case of blue balls. You know what? I wouldn't put it past her. "You're fucking crazy." I say that as she sucks my tip like a damned lollipop. Oh, shit, I should *not* have looked down. Her gaze is set to destroy, and I'm the blasted warship sitting like a duck on open waters. Cher means business. She's going to swallow me *whole*. "Somebody could try to catch this elevator at any moment."

I don't know how I got those words out. Took a damn miracle, because my chest is tight and my erection is hot. Cher only takes her mouth off long enough to say, "Let them watch, then.

Or join in. I don't care."

I might care. I don't say that, though. Because no guy I know is going to pull his dick out of a hot girl's mouth when she's going at him like *that* with promises for so much more. I'll simply pray that this elevator stops to pick up another hot chick on my way up to my apartment. Cher seems down for a threesome with another woman.

Actually, how about the elevator doesn't stop at all? I needed to come five minutes ago, and the closer we get to my floor, the more likely that's about to happen.

"Fucking crazy," I repeat under my breath. I'm lulled into heady bliss as the sounds of her sucking my cock echo. "You wanna get caught, don't you? That shit turns you on."

A purr erupts around my cock. Fuck me, I'm getting a hummer, and I'm about to explode in her throat. Too bad Cher pulls off two floors shy of mine. "I get turned on by lots of shit, Benton. Like when you call me your slut."

"You sure are acting like it right now."

I don't think about what I say, and her reaction proves it. Yet instead of taking offense to it, her cheeks flush a deep pink, like a flower that could poison me if I come too close. "Am I your slut?" she sweetly asks. "Or am I just *a* slut?"

Shit, shit, I'm confused. Which is the right answer? Should I deny either? How can she ask me these trick questions when my brain has shut down to send blood to my fucking dick?

"You're not a slut," I whisper.

"Oh, no? Would some blushing virgin know how to do this?" Before I can tell her there's much more between *slut* and *virgin,* she deep throats me. Takes me straight to the hilt, her voice gagging in her throat. Her eyes flutter shut as she takes a deep breath. The elevator doors open. There's nobody there, and I can barely reach the *hold* button.

A satisfied gasp tickles my senses as I push her off me and jerk her up by the arm. Her bag smacks against her ass. She trips in her heels. Cackles follow me out of the elevator, my damned dick hanging out of my jeans as I haul her to my apartment a blasted forty feet away.

Can I make it to my bedroom? Do I throw her over my shoulder like I sometimes love to do? Me Drew, she Cher? It's always fun to watch her tits bounce when she lands on my bed. I'm already enjoying the sounds of her shoes falling off her feet and clacking to my hardwood floors.

"That's right, Benton," she says with another devilish laugh. "Own this slut."

Her skin is hot in my hand. Every inch of her is alive with excitement and sex. Fuck it, so am I. All I have to do is look down to see what I'm doing. I bet if I put my hand between her legs, my fingers would be covered in her cum before I had the chance to stick one in.

Nope. We're not making it. I need her now. I need her cunt like she needs my length. We're not taking off any clothes unless absolutely necessary, because that's the kind of hurry we're in.

She lands on her feet. I waste no time pushing Cher against my couch. Neither do I bother with shutting the blinds or turning on the lights. My apartment is fairly dark at this time of day. Maybe it adds to the ambiance. I don't give a fuck. I only have fucks to give to the dripping wet pussy I uncover beneath her clothes. Bless her for always wearing such accessible fashion.

I also hope she doesn't need these panties again. They're ruined, and not just from how hard I yank them aside, a rip exciting her senses. She's so wet I almost miss her with my cock. I slip right out the moment I let go, intent on plunging into her and riding her until I'm empty.

"Fuck me," she whines, braced against the couch, hand fisting her own hair. "I need it, baby." The desperation mounts her body before I have the chance. It's precision. That's what slamming my cock into her takes, and I'm so excited I forget what precision *means*. "Make me your dirty little bitch."

Before I go completely nuts, let me point out that this kind of language is not unique tonight. When Cher is hornier than hell, she screams about sluts, bitches, and fucking. Some combination, anyway. Far be it from me to tell her what she can and can't find hot. That ain't my place. *My* place is giving her what she needs. Sometimes that means falling into the moment and letting loose the dirty talk she clearly craves. Other times, I'm a silent fucker. Literally. Just silently fucking her as she screams a bunch and coaches me like these are the Fuck Games and we have a shot at the gold medal.

Finally, I hit a home run instead of so many foul balls. I slam into her, forcing her to take my whole length in one stroke. Every part of her tenses, both against me and the couch. Her voice is caught in her throat. When she eventually makes another sound, it's a strangled cry that tells me I've found her G-spot on the first try.

Cher matches every one of my thrusts, daring me to go deeper, harder, and more brazen with my need for her. My grunts are no match for her dirty words and naughtier claims. She calls herself the most sordid names in the book. Sometimes she begs

Intoxicated

me to call her this insult or some other phrase that would raise my grandma from the grave – you know, if she were dead. Instead, she's climbing into her truck to come slap me for such filth.

She demands I pull her hair. I yank. She begs for a spank. I smack her flesh. She spreads her legs wider and combusts into a pile of sporadic movements. It's no orgasm. It's like the opening move that preps her for climax. The hedonistic sounds of my flesh slapping into her wet body and the garbled cries of slobbery passion she screams into my couch means I'm about to completely lose it. Dare I waste energy on announcing it?

"Give me your hands," I snap, taking both of her wrists into my grasp. Cher is so amiable that I worry she's passed out. Oh, no. I should know better than that.

"Come in me," she begs. "Come inside this nasty slut."

I go in balls deep, holding myself there as I pull her up by the hair. A small cry of painful pleasure greets me when my lips hit her ear. "You're no slut," I say. "You're my girlfriend. That's better than some town bicycle I get to pound from here to across town."

She drops back down to the couch. I brace my hand against her hip and wail on her cunt, my cock so hungry for her that I don't feel my orgasm until I realize my cum is spilling out with every crazy thrust.

Cher screams into the couch the whole time. Her knuckles are whiter than the camisole beneath her kimono. I don't know how she's still alive, let alone has all her teeth. The woman doesn't lift her head until I finally slow down, taking the time to empty my balls with a long, hearty groan.

I'm not satisfied. Neither is she. I can see it in her eyes when she slowly turns her head and gives me that come-hither look that always undoes me.

"Fuck." My clothes are left in a pile as I pull Cher up by the wrist and drag her - quite willingly, I might add - to my room. The only reason she can't keep up with me is because of how hard I fucked her in that position. My legs are sore, too, but I'm gonna persevere and fuck her some more.

As soon as I tear these clothes off her, anyway.

Is she upset about it? Not right now. Even if she is later, I'll buy her new whatevers. The kimono is fabric, for fuck's sake. Her underwear is worthless. I pull down the front of her camisole so hard that we both hear something tear inside the stitches. Her now-useless bra shelf spills out her breasts. They're so swollen and her nipples so hard that I immediately grab them. Whatever softness had come to my cock is gone again. I need her. She needs me. Look at that face. That's the visage of a famished woman who never gets enough hard cock. If I'm gonna be with her, I need to work on my stamina.

"Fuck me," she continues to chant. Cher is on her side, one leg hoisted in the air. My cum mingles with hers and covers the gape I've left behind. She's so ready for me that this time it takes absolutely no precision to enter her. My whole body hovers over hers, that leg swung over my shoulder as I hold onto her breast and fuck her for my life. Cher's forced to hold herself up on one arm, lest we both collapse and have to start over again.

Her need to scream herself hoarse is as great now as it was before. It doesn't matter how hard I pull her hair or pinch her nipples. I don't touch her clit, yet she's shuddering in one endless orgasm, the depths of her cunt squeezing the whole length of my cock. Yet after that climax from earlier, I'll last much longer. There's no mercy for her this time.

Intoxicated

I've seen this look on her face before. It's the face of a woman surfing through Heaven. I've probably shown her nirvana, and she hasn't asked me to choke her yet. Not something I make a habit of doing, but when a woman whines for it, you give it to her, damnit.

This is who she is, after all. Maybe the reason she gets bored of her other boyfriends and dumps them when shit gets serious is because they can't give her the sex she craves. Cher hates lovemaking, doesn't she? She wants to be called a slut and fucked like a toy. Even if another guy can give her that now and again, it's never quite right, huh?

I'm not sure I could do this every damn day. I'm exhausted. The only thing keeping me going is the promise of pleasing her.

"Look at me." Her labored words are because of her restricted airway. I lessen my grip, momentarily afraid of hurting her. Yet that only gets me a bigger grin of defiance. "I'm your slut, Drew Benton. Make me feel like it."

Maybe it's what she's said. Maybe I've been fucking for so long that I can't go any more. Or maybe I'm such a sad sack of shit that there's no hope for either of us.

As Cher's eyes roll back in her head, I pull my cock out of her and jerk the very last of my cum wherever the hell it will go. Some of it lands on her face. More of it lands on her tits. Cher collapses into a panting lump of cum-covered glee.

While I finally succumb to the end of my bed, she throws her head back in laughter.

Those aren't euphoric giggles. That's her embracing who she really is.

And that other sound you hear? The one knocking you unconscious from how powerful it is?

That's my heart plummeting into my empty loins. I get it. I finally understand. The puzzle that so many men have tried to solve. The secret to destroying Cher Lieberman.

Who she is. Why *she* is the way she is.

How had I never seen it before? It's right there in the glistening seed sliding down her breast.

"You get off on it." I back away, my cock still not quite soft after all of that. Yet I feel it. I'm about to collapse. The nightmare has only begun. "You fucking get off on it."

Her laughter comes to a slow. Cher pushes herself up, unperturbed by everything slipping down her skin. Seed. Sweat. Her own dignity. "What the fuck are you talking about?"

My sigh isn't for me. Nor is it for her. It's the only way I can think clearly, now that my need to *fuck fuck fuck* has been temporarily sated. "You get off on feeling like a slut. That's why you can't stand being in a 'real' relationship. That's the honest reason you want to be alone. So you can fuck anyone you want and keep that dream alive."

After everything she's begged me to call her, you'd think that would please her.

Instead, Cher slowly stands up, facing the truth I've flung in her face.

I know she's going to slap me and leave. I don't expect it to sting so much.

CHAPTER 28

CHER

You know when things seem to be too good to be true? When the guy you're seeing magically forgives all of your terrible personality quirks with unfounded grace? Or when you think that maybe, maybe you've found your magical match and things might actually be changing in your life?

That's when you bail, girl.

It's one thing for a guy to get too clingy too quickly. Or to declare his undying love for you after only a few weeks. There are some seriously desperate men out there, so it's never surprising when it happens. (Assuming you're hot. I have it on good authority that makes a difference. Bonus points if you've tailored your grift to match their ideal type.)

It's quite another thing for that man to *insult the hell out of you*.

Thought we had a good thing going, Drew. Thought you knew our relationship was founded on sex, even if I allowed you to call me your girlfriend. Not just any sex, either. Angry, fucked-up sex. You may have been one of the first men I've ever been with who didn't make me feel like a total freak for what I like, but that doesn't give you the right to say what you did.

It's been almost a week, and I'm still pissed the hell off.

Naturally, Drew tried to contact me. I blocked him. I made a point of being away from my apartment from morning until night, even if it meant camping out at new-to-me cafés so I could avoid seeing his mug. He had come to my door once before already. I wouldn't put it past him to try it again. Whether he has or not, I have no idea. I've found no notes or heard whispers from the neighbors, If he's sneaking around my door, he's not hanging around.

Good.

I'm not a crier. I don't cry over men. The only way I could cry over a guy leaving my life was if my dad died tomorrow. That's it. If I got that dreaded phone call, I'd cry. For a few minutes.

Drew won't make me cry.

Not his absence, anyway. There may be an ache deep within me, but it's not a hollowed heart. It's my stupid pussy missing his dick. If Drew Benton could do one positive thing, it was fuck like a damned jackhammer. Doubt I'll ever find a guy like that again. Hot, great dick, *and* knew how to screw a girl? That's the holy trinity, friends. The money only makes it so much better. Most hot dudes with nice dicks are absolute snores in bed. Great lovers with nice dicks tend to be way below my level in the looks department. Don't get me started on hot and good in bed. At some point, the little winky drives me out the door again.

Yes. That's the only heartbreak here. My pussy is doing most of the crying, but my logic will win out.

I spared ten minutes the night my anger subdued. A few tears fell down my face. This was after my nose wrinkled and something burned behind my eyes. I had been at my desk, attempting to use my laptop, when the tears began to flow. What happened? No, I don't give a fuck about Drew Benton. He can take his gorgeous body and shove himself up his own ass. I can pay for my own five-star dinners. Camaros are so damned overrated, the only reason I was caught in one was because I like free rides. I'll treat myself to a brand-new vibrator that gets the job done as well as he ever did. Maybe I'll hop on Tinder and get myself a mediocre rebound to totally prove I don't give a fuck.

I think we both know what made me cry for the first time since rewatching *Pay it Forward*.

"You get off on feeling like a slut. That's why you can't stand being in a 'real' relationship. That's the honest reason you want to be alone. So you can fuck anyone you want and keep that dream alive."

Thinking about it makes me want to knock the pencil holder off my desk.

How dare he? How *dare he*? Who the fuck is he to tell me who I am or what I'm about? I get off on feeling like a slut? He's being way too literal about the sex we had. I bet he thinks women who like the missionary position and getting tender pecks to the lips are pious princesses. If I'm Mary Magdalene over here, then they must be the Virgin Mothers! That's how it works, right, Drew? You either like getting your ass smacked and your throat choked or your little rosebud flicked with the tip of a tongue. There can never be anything in between. There are never emotions behind it. People are sooooo one-note, am I right?

Fuck him. Fuck him in his Camaro. Fuck him so hard his whole family going back four generations can feel that shit jam into his ass.

Maybe I don't know why I'm crying. We can agree that I'm upset about what he said to me. You'd think I'd be over it after stewing in it for a couple of days, though. Yet for some blasted reason, his insinuation has hit me right in the diaphragm. He left me speechless. There I had been, reveling from some of the best orgasms of my fucking life, and suddenly he tells me I'm a bitch and a half because I like to feel like a slut?

Go to hell, Drew.

He's not the first guy, you know. I've had a few exes tell me in their breakup spiels what they really think of me, and more than one insinuated I was a "fucking whore" who only cared about money. This is different, I guess? Drew wasn't lashing out at me with the most misogynistic shit he could pull out of his codebook. He thought he was making a genuine observation! Hope he chokes on his next beer. Nicest thing that could happen to a lovely chap like him.

I don't get off on feeling like a *slut*. Not outside of the bedroom.

Let's be real, that's what he meant.

You can't tell me I'm the first lover he's had like that. He's too natural at taking complete control, even when I'm growling and daring him to be *badder*. Drew's that guy who is a total cuddly teddy bear when you need him to be, and a ruthless porn star when the hormones are high. So, he gets the difference, doesn't he? He knows the separation of bedroom personas and real life monikers. Just because I like it hard and rough doesn't mean I prance through society going, "*Look at what a slutty slut slut I am! Tee hee! Bet you've never seen a cunt gape and be filled with so much cum before!"* Ugh. I want to barf thinking about it.

I want to do a lot of things. Like wring his neck.

One day, I shall write my memoir. (Maybe I'll call it *A Slut's Life*, huh, Drew?) In it I'll pontificate about why I never married. *"A hundred men fell in love with me, but none of them were good enough. There was always one or two major flaws that completely outshone the good things. Maybe he had a tender heart, but he was terrible in bed. Or maybe he treated his daughters like human beings but thought I should be held to a higher standard. This guy donated millions of dollars to charities every year, but his job was running low-income people out of their homes. This guy was perfect in every way, except he expected me to a baby-making factory. Even one baby would make me feel like a factory. Piss off, Frank."*

There's no such thing as the perfect lover, but does that mean I have to *settle*? Does it make me a slut if I'd rather be serially monogamous than be in an OK relationship? It's not always about getting my payday. Sometimes it's as simple as realizing it's time to move on.

It's time to move on from Drew. I'm done with him. For good.

Of course, an idle Cher is the worst possible scenario. If I'm coming out of a breakup as gross as that one, I need something lined up. A new guy. A new life. Something.

I need to get back into the game. I need to get back to what I was doing before Drew attempted to ruin my life. Because nothing would get back at him *and* Jason Rothchild more than being up to my old tricks again.

It's too soon to make an appearance at the lounges and country clubs. Usually, I alternate lounges with the golf clubs in Lake Oswego and Hillsboro. Lots of big tech and athletic wear guys in those places, but I'm afraid Drew might go looking for me there. I'm still vulnerable enough (God, I hate admitting that) that I should check out my Seeking Arrangement profile.

Although fruitless, I update my bio and some of my pictures. It's the perfect time of year to snap some selfies and set up shots of me drinking tea or enjoying the sun. Flirty dresses, audacious kimonos, and slinky tank tops always attract attention. Better if I throw on some sunglasses and keep my hair freshly washed.

It's while taking gratuitous shots of myself on a café balcony when my thumb accidentally opens my address book. There, toward the top of the list, is a man named Brian.

Brian... *Brian*... hmm.

The guy I had been working before Drew showed up in the lounge that night. Mediocre Brian. New money Brian. Brian, the guy with enough money to get an after-hours drink in a lounge like that. Mr. I Have A One-Bedroom In the Pearl Brian. The guy looking for the flirty girl-next-door of his adolescent dreams.

My lips curve into a smile. Sure, it's been a couple of months since I met the guy, but how much do you wanna bet he wouldn't mind hearing from little ol' me right now? Never mind he didn't try to contact me. Nor did he cross my path again, but... you never know.

"Hi, Brian! I don't know if you remember me. It's Cher, from the lounge a couple of months ago? I'm SO sorry that I never contacted you until now. I ended up breaking my phone two days after we met, and I'm only now getting things back in technological order. Hey, don't you work in software? I bet you know all about this!"

Oh, you want to gag reading that? You want to tell me that no man is dumb enough to fall for a woman messaging him two months later, acting like he'd still remember her?

Bold of you to assume he doesn't remember me. I'm a hard woman to forget, especially after the impression I left.

Hmph. It's always possible he doesn't remember or care anymore. Maybe he's met someone better since then. Maybe he's come to his senses. Maybe he's moved away and no longer has time for little ol'...

"*Hi. Of course I remember you. Sorry to hear about your phone problems. I actually work with computer software so don't know much about apps and such. That's a different department in my company, haha :)*"

See? Cher Lieberman is back in business. Bet you a hundred bucks I'm attending a public function with him by this time next month.

Seriously. I'll bet you a hundred. Prepare to pay up, and never mention Drew again.

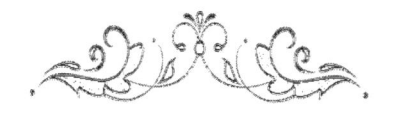

CHAPTER 29

DREW

You know what sucks the most?

I was fucking in love with her.

Sure, laugh. Point at me and tell me what a lousy fucker I am. I probably deserve it. After the number of hearts I've broken, it was bound to happen to me. Karma, or some such.

Fuck me. Fuck her. Fuck us. I hate everything.

This isn't mere post break-up emo bullshit I'm suffering. This is... *depression*. God, maybe I am man enough to admit it. Cher not only fucked with my heart, but my head as well. She drove a stake right into one and fried the other. What did it, though? Was it those crazy good looks, the suave smile she laid on me every time I beheld her... or that perfect pussy that grabbed me by the balls every time I fell for her trap?

Intoxicated

I believe all three of them. When a man falls in love, even for the first time, he's liable to make some seriously bad decisions.

It's so clear for me to see now. I loved that hot mess of a woman. She worked me as well as she worked any man, but I saw a side of her not many got to witness, I bet. While I never saw her heart on her sleeve or the empathetic tears of someone who isn't a raging narcissist, there was information that *I* was privy to, but nobody else ever heard. She was human in her own way around me. A confident gal who didn't care if I heard her body's natural functions or saw the blood of her womanhood. (Okay, so she definitely cared about that, but we got over it, huh?) This was a woman I met again at a freakin' STD clinic. Nothing was sacred between us. I told her about my friend in college, for fuck's sake.

She changed me. Cher is the reason I'm getting out of this stupid line of work and doing something better with my life.

She's the reason I'm lying in the dark, drinking myself half to death.

All right, so I'm not drunk 24/7, but I'm not in a hurry to get out of here, either. There's nothing for me beyond my Seattle apartment. I used the last of my pride to drive up here, if only to get the hell away from the woman who refuses to admit what she is.

I don't... care about that. Maybe I did the wrong thing by telling her - let alone when my cum was dripping out of her - but it had been such a clear-headed thought that it was like every filter on my mouth came flying off and smacked her face.

Cher isn't your average woman. Not the one who likes it a little rough every once in a while. I'm convinced it's the only real way she gets off. Maybe not balls-to-the-wall flesh-slapping sex full of naughty words and hair-pulling, but she definitely needs *something* naughty to keep her interested in the bedroom. I thought her detachment from slower lovemaking had more to do with neglecting room for dirty things like *feelings* and less to do with boredom. I've never met a woman who hated slow and sensual things so much. Did she realize it? Is the reason she dumped me because she didn't want to hear those truths?

I see now how it could be taken the wrong way. Women aren't supposed to be like that, huh? That's a message yours truly got loud and clear growing up. Women aren't supposed to enjoy sex. Are we crazy? Only "fallen" women, as my biological grandmother would put it, like it in any capacity outside of martial relations. Because they're Jezebels, or something.

Let's face it. Jezebel is an amazing name, and one that perfectly suits Cher.

Do I have regrets? God, yes. I shouldn't have said what I did, let alone *when* I did. You'd think I was the guy who got off on hurting women's feelings. Hey, just because I did it for a semi-living doesn't mean I *enjoyed* it. Maybe there was a hint of satisfaction on behalf of the friend I lost, but... fuck it, I'm over that now. Harry is somewhere in Heaven shaking his head over my whole damn life since he left this earth.

I kinda get it now, though. Why it hurts so much when the worst woman in the world dumps your ass. Especially if you loved her.

Especially if you loved her.

What hurts more? The fact that I have loved and lost, or the fact that the woman I love is probably out there right now working on her next target?

I'm no fool. She doesn't love me back. Clearly, I hurt her feelings, but any guy with the right dick and arsenal of words could hurt her feelings. She might be plotting her revenge against me right now. That's part of the reason I came back to Seattle. Get away from the more emotional memories. Get away from her reach.

Am I going to be one of those guys who sees her around and feels the sting? Or am I special enough that I will fall over in a wave of my own vomit because it hurts so damn much? I'm convinced that most of the other men who think they loved her didn't *really*. They didn't see the parts of her that I did. How could they love her if they didn't hear her most annoying laugh or see her blood all over their beds? The woman suggested that I'm a disease-riddled assbutt by going to an STD clinic. Do you think your average Joe would still be enamored with her after that? What Cher and I had was... special. Yeah. That's the word. Special.

I kinda want to die.

Okay, okay, back off. I'm not *actually* suicidal. Please, ignore the empty bottles of whatever I scrounged from my cupboards. Don't look at the dirty dishes left on my nightstand. Have I showered yet today? I don't think so. Don't care. I'm not going anywhere. I did, however, forget to cancel the cleaning lady for the week. She walked in on me feeling sorry for myself and was unable to look me in the eye for the rest of her visit. At least she did my dishes for me. God knows I wasn't about to.

I will get over this. I have to.

I simply don't know what this actually means for my future.

Of course, I want to change my profession. Have a few ideas of how to go about that, but how do I dissolve my current business? What do I tell Rothchild? *"So, I really pissed her off and made her feel like a disgusting bitch, but I'm not charging for that. I'm closing shop after this one. Thanks for being my last, you prick!"* Sigh. I still haven't told Brent that I plan on perhaps, *maybe* switching to a matchmaking service for the rich and terribly infamous. It will mean dealing with a bunch of wannabe Chers looking for payday. Maybe that's the hard part.

Maybe it's setting up men for love. You know, when I'm not really feeling it for myself.

On the fifth day, I finally rise from my bed, bedraggled and slightly hungover. I take a shower for the first time in two days. I throw my dirty clothes into the washing machine. I make myself a vegan smoothie in the hopes it will perk up my mood. The only thing I'm allowed to watch on TV is old cartoons. Stuff that I loved when I was a kid. Stuff I had long-loved before I knew someone named Cher.

SpongeBob is on. Damnit. Didn't I watch that with her when we were high?

I turn off the TV and pack a bag. There's a voicemail from Brent telling me I have a new client. I don't respond.

Instead, I get in my truck and head up I5 toward Centralia.

The sun is bright, the pollen thick, and the trees so green that it's almost possible to forget Cher for two seconds as I stare at the wonders of nature. My truck glides around turns. My elbow leans against the opened window, one hand on the wheel and the other enjoying the breeze. Horses graze behind fences along the highway. The wildflowers are in full bloom, perhaps their last hoorah before summer heat comes to claim their dried-out souls. They occasionally get fires up here around August and September. I hope it can be spared this year.

I need these wonders to exist. They're the only ones that can somewhat clear my mind when I'm desperate to see the most toxic woman on Earth.

Might as well see another one.

My grandmother acts as if she's expected me all along. With a silent wave, I'm invited into her house, where she's already baked an apple pie and has leftover fried chicken from two nights ago, when she entertained a pair of neighbors for dinner. I slather my grandmother's special sauce on the chicken and eat it on her back porch, where I gaze at the green hills, purple mountains, and thick, dense woods full of bears, hawks, and deer.

This is the good shit. Realizing that you're a small speck of dust in the cosmic stratosphere. Who needs romance and petty heartbreak when there's a whole universe out there? Blue skies, white, fluffy clouds... some chicken is screaming bloody murder because another chicken got too close and ruffled some feathers, but that's nature for you.

I feel you, screaming chicken. I want to scream, too.

"You gonna tell me what's wrong?" My grandmother steps onto the porch, her old and worn boots scraping against wood. The screen slams shut behind her. A few birds take off from the nearest tree. Sure, the chicken wasn't enough to scare them off, but a little old lady marching onto her porch is. What kind of relationship does my grandmother have with wildlife, anyway?

Right. I'm deflecting.

"You look like your dog's died." Grandma snorts, right side bumped up against the post. She doesn't smoke anymore, but if she still did, there would be a cigarette in her hand right now. "What the hell happened? You lose a big client or something? That was the only thing that brought the humanity out of your grandfather. That and a pair of perky tits."

I shake my head. "Worse than that. Cher broke up with me."

"'Bout damn time!"

My grandmother certainly knows how to make me turn my head. "Thanks."

"Girl like that has better ways to spend her time than with the likes of you. That's a woman who doesn't need playboys. If there's anything I know, it's that you're a cad."

"Again, thanks."

"I'm only joshing you, boy." The porch creaks as she sits down beside me. "Didn't think you felt so strongly about her."

"She came to meet *you*, didn't she?"

"First time something like that ever happened! So, what did you do to piss her off enough to dump you? Don't tell me you didn't fuck up."

Her faith in me is awe-inspiring, isn't it? "I insulted her. Accidentally, but..."

"There ain't no accidentally when it comes to insulting people. I don't know what you said, but you probably meant it."

Our pause in conversation grants the neighborly quail to run across the yard. Mama quail, papa quail, and five little quailettes sprint in a zigzag pattern from the underbrush to the vegetable garden. Somewhere, my grandma's chickens know there are trespassers, and they raise hell about it.

"Would you lot shut the hell up!"

Grandma's barely regained her bearings when she looks at me again. Magically, the girls in their pen have stopped screaming. My grandmother has that effect on living creatures. "You don't want to know what I said to her. But one moment everything's hunky-dory, and the next... she slaps me and runs off. Blocked me on every device and won't answer her door." I only tried once, but I tried. "We've had some ups and downs since we met. I think it's for real this time."

Intoxicated

She looks askance at me. "Real what? Real breakup, or real love?"

I hesitantly meet her gaze.

"I always knew that the only woman who could steal your heart was one who saw straight through your bullcrap. How many girls have you been with? No, don't tell me. All I need to know is their caliber of character. Ain't great, I bet."

"If you want to go that route, I can easily say that Cher has the worst character of them all." I'm not lying, depending on your parameters.

"Bad enough character that you felt the need to insult her?"

"It wasn't like that."

"Then what the hell was it?"

For being the easiest person for me to talk to about this, my grandmother is also the roughest. She's a lot like Cher. See's straight through my shit and clocks me for who I really am. We can say the same thing about me toward her, though. I see through her shit. I see enough, yet somehow it only makes me love her more.

But just because she knows you so well, doesn't mean you can easily subject yourself to her hard truths and harsh criticisms.

Gradually, as we watch the sun hide behind a few fluffy white clouds, I open up what I dare to my grandma.

I still don't tell her about my line of work, but I do tell her that I met Cher under false pretenses. Actually, the same went for her toward me. We were playing games with one another. We built a shaky foundation on a bed of lies. She tried to grift me, and I tried to use her. Somehow, we came to a mutual understanding of what we were doing and how we felt about it. We still had chemistry, though. Crazy enough chemistry that turned into a toxic adhesive. The more I inhaled her, though, the move I fell in love. I guess it didn't go the other way around.

"If I hadn't insulted her then, it would've been something else," I say. "Something would have made us implode. Guess it's for the best that it happened as early as it did."

My grandmother shakes her head. "You're giving up that easily? You really are your father's line. Bunch of cowards, you Bentons."

"I know when it's hopeless. Why would I subject myself to more misery?"

"Sometimes you have to know true misery before you know true happiness."

I mull over those words. Still not convinced she's right.

"Maybe you do go after her again. Not right now, though," Grandma continues. "You've gotta prove to her that you're not the man she thinks you are. You have to be better than the best she's seen in you yet. You have to make amends for what you said to her, and you've gotta keep groveling, if you want her back."

That's the thing, isn't it? I'm not sure I want Cher *back*. I tell my grandmother as much, and she laughs like she's seen the future already.

"You want her back," she says. "You wouldn't be here moping on my back porch for the first time ever if you didn't want her back."

She's right, huh? I wouldn't have come running to my grandmother if I didn't know she'd say exactly what I needed to hear. It's probably not the best time to decide what I'm going to do. Cher was hurt enough she'll need a little time to cool off. In the meantime, I'll figure out what I'm doing. With my life. With *ours*.

No, I won't back down. Not from the only woman who is my true match. At the very least, I won't die wondering *what if.* Perhaps that will finally be the thing to break me from my old, toxic habits.

That's a lot of pressure to put on one woman. Or myself.

But I'll do it.

CHAPTER 30

CHER

High above my head flutters colorful flags. The stereo plays luau music that I've heard a hundred times before. Tiki torches are alit, and every other bastard in this place is wearing a loud Hawaiian shirt they took out of their closet for this occasion.

This is where Brian has decided to take me for our sixth date.

Oh, yes, I've been counting. Six dates. Our first date was at one of the mid-scale chain Italian restaurants. Hey, I got oysters in my pasta and *didn't* have to pay for it, but the wine left much to be desired. For new money men, though, that's a safe first date bet. Most women find Italian restaurants utterly romantic. They're also impressed when a tech guy is willing to spend fifty bucks on their booze and meals. I dressed up in my most summery sundress and wedges, and he dressed in jeans and a T-shirt. Brian paid for my Lyft home, and didn't so much as kiss me on the cheek. He kissed me on the hand, instead.

Since then, every date has been a "trip around the world." Our second date was at a Mexican taqueria near his place in the Pearl. Our third was dim sum near my place. Ethiopian. Vietnamese. Now we're sampling Hawaiian barbecue with rum filling our glasses.

Did you guess whether Brian's wearing a Hawaiian shirt? My goodness, that's *much* too easy. We're going to step it up a notch and make you figure out which color it is. Go on. You can peek through your fingers now. Ignore me in my black jumper and heavy sunglasses that blot out the July sunlight. I'm nowhere near as garish as the man sitting across from me.

What color did you guess? Are you surprised that it's bright baby blue with white and green parrots? Me neither! Let's toast to our observant genius.

"Are you going to eat that?" he asks, gesturing to the rest of the food on my plate. I don't have much taste for barbecue, but we're still early enough in this relationship that I try not to rock the boat. You see, I've pinned down this man's exact type. Oh, I already figured it out before. He likes the girl-next-door. The flirty, happy chica who is the definition of feminine and isn't afraid to flaunt it. I played that hand right from the beginning, because the most important thing was roping Brian into thinking I'll be his perfect match.

Now I know who he *really* likes.

Brian's perfect woman isn't only flirty. She's a bit naïve, so her flirtations don't always land, or she acts a bit more demure than anyone anticipates. She's inexperienced. She may not be a virgin, but whatever guys she's been with before meant a *lot* to her.

She doesn't jump right into bed with anyone, you see. She takes her time, and in a culture obsessed with one-night stands, that says something about her character. (Gag.) So, on one hand, it's been nice to not have the demand for sex shoved down my throat right away. Brian's an okay-looking guy, but I can already tell he's "all right" in bed. He won't give me anything I really need, but considering what happened with That Other Guy, it's probably for the best that I rebound with a boring tech dude who squeaks when he comes and can't go for more than fifteen minutes, *tops*.

Not that I would know for sure yet. Since Brian is all about the demure, naïve maiden, we haven't slept together. I go to Orgasmtopia with the new vibrator I bought myself in the wake of You-Like-Being-A-Slut-Apocalypse, but those are solo trips. Usually with me stopping halfway through because I thought of *him* and can't do it anymore.

What a great fucking feeling.

"I'm full, thanks." My elbow touches the table, and my chin rests in my hand. Ukulele continues to shred above me. Brian helps himself to my leftovers, and I look away before he chows down like a dog at dinnertime. "You know I don't have the biggest appetite."

"That's the thing about you skinny girls," Brian says with a mouthful of food. "You eat like birds. Bet you don't know how pretty you really are..."

I feign a bashful smile and twirl my hair around my finger. I'm so used to pulling this off that I don't think about it. Yay.

Ugh. Send help. I'm utterly dead inside.

You see, it doesn't matter how used to this I am. Years of playing the dream girlfriend is starting to take its toll, I guess. I dunno what caused it. Was it my brief relationship with Drew?

Intoxicated

Realizing that I could probably be as happy on my own than with someone perfectly made for me? Having that taste of the shit I *really* like for a short time? Dealing with men has me in such a tizzy lately that I'm this close to calling things off with Brian. Mostly because I can't stand him.

Look at him. He's got food in his teeth. I can tell, because he's chewing with his mouth open. It's only a matter of time before he wipes his mouth with his napkin and slams the cloth down on the table. I'll get to see that big barbecue stain for the rest of our dinner in this kitschy place that makes me want to scream.

Oh, I'm sorry, it *entrances me,* because I'm enthralled with every place he takes me. Doesn't help that every restaurant we've visited has brought with it questions about my travel experience. With a guy like this, I don't know if I should be truthful and tell him I've been to Hawaii, Italy, and Mexico. (Preston *really loved* Mexico. It got him the most bang for his buck. In so many ways.) If I tell him I'm well-traveled, he may chip away who I am and figure out how many men I've been with. I've already told him that my parents aren't that rich, so it's not like we traveled everywhere and then some when I was a kid. On the flipside, he may get excited to have a potential travel companion who doesn't need his constant handholding. Then *again,* this guy loves his mansplaining and handholding. He's already explained my own phone to me three times. I thought he told me he wasn't an app guy!

"So, about Hawaii..." Brian winks at me as soon as he swallows. Here comes the napkin. Ah, yes, on his mouth. Boom. Back on the table with a giant smudge of no discernible color. "Everyone goes to Maui because of the great marketing campaign, but if you ask me, Big Island is where it's at. Been there a couple of times. Got this great deal on a resort room through a..."

Yay. A spiel about timeshares. Specifically, how they're *not* all that bad! (Meanwhile, every old-money man of wealth I've dated made sure I knew what a raw deal timeshares are. You should've heard Preston go on about his parents getting sucked into an Alaskan one when he was a kid. An Alaskan cruise timeshare. How does that work? He couldn't tell me, so I'm genuinely asking.)

"I've been to Maui, yeah," I offer. "But not to Big Island."

"Oh?" His disappointment is palpable. This is better than admitting I've been to *Italy,* although I suppose that's easier to pass off as studying abroad or a class trip than the whirlwind weekend I spent with a guy who drilled way better than this guy probably can. I admit, I didn't see much of the Tuscan countryside. I was too busy. Inside. "Like I said, Big Island is much more interesting. It's like being in a completely different place." He haughtily sniffs, in case I missed the derision from before. "I'm planning a trip for Labor Day weekend in a couple of months."

I smile and nod, but offer no opinion on that. No *real* opinion. The words coming out of my mouth is a wistful, "Sounds lovely," as if deep down I'm hoping he'll take me with him. Which is what he's starting to plan now, because look at him. He wants to take me. He simply doesn't know if I'm the *right one* to take to his precious Big Island yet.

If I play my cards right, I will be, but I'll have to decide if I think it's worth it.

There's something I'm expecting Brian to ask me sooner. You see, it's been six damn dates. This guy has a growing social circle that goes above his means. The guy is ambitious. I've already fed him a steady stream of experience in other areas beyond

Intoxicated

relationships and sex. Namely, he thinks I work remotely as a market and network influencer. I've namedropped more than a few people who made him double-take. I may or may not have included the Bentons the last time I did this. He *really* liked hearing that name. I'm not surprised. Drew's dad has a big software company in the area. Big as in money, not staff. Getting to work for him would be one of the big times for a software developer like Brian.

Trips around the world and dinners in tiki bars mean nothing to me if we're not hobnobbing with the social elite. I don't care where it is. Portland, Seattle, Honolulu, Rome... give me some glitz and glamor. Give me women in vintage stoles and carrying $5,000 clutches. I want to dress up in a flashy new outfit and look like I have a million dollars.

Is that too much to ask, Brian? I know you're invited to the occasional shindig around town. How much do you want to put your networking dreams to work?

"I've been thinking. About something that happens a little before Labor Day." Brian motions for me to take his hand. His sweaty hand, I may tell you. Yet I pretend it's the sweetest gesture as I take his sweat between my fingers and bite my bottom lip in excitement. (Yeah, right. I'm suppressing gas from that barbecue. I might as well look cute while doing it.) "I don't know how you feel about parties, but..." He leaves me hanging. I pretend to look like I think he's talking about some friend's cookout up in Raleigh Hills. "There's this soiree a colleague of mine has invited me to. Downtown. *Really* ritzy. You might have to get a new dress, but I think you might like to go. As my date, of course."

How do I properly convey my excitement? How do I *contain* my excitement? I can't decide if it's better to act super excited about something my character shouldn't know much about, or to feign indifference in the hopes Brian would explain it to me.

Might as well go with the old tried and true.

"A ritzy soiree? Wow..." I let my voice trail off as if I've never considered such a wild fantasy. "*Like the ones on TV, ma!*" That's probably what I look like. It's probably what Brian wanted. "That sounds magical. I didn't know they had stuff like that in Portland."

"They're not as common as they used to be, but there are a lot of old families in the area that like to throw parties. It's a black tie event, but... well, I do hate going to them by myself, and this next one is in two weeks. I'll admit, baby, it's a great chance for me to do some networking. I hear Alexander Benton is gonna be there, and I don't have to tell you he's like the holy grail of software design when it comes to benefits and promotions." He chuckles. "One of the best tricks is having a pretty gal on your arm. So, what do you say? Are you available two weekends from now?"

Of *course* I am!

I let him feed me some of the details while he finishes his supper. After this, it's either drinks at a club or going straight home. Apparently, I'm going to my apartment."

"How about we meet at my place next time?" That's what Brian says as his Audi idles in front of my building. My door is halfway open. I was prepared to step out and blow him a kiss before going inside. Instead, he's caught me unawares in the passenger seat. "I've been trying my hand at Italian cooking. It'll be like our first date."

I giggle. "Here I was going to suggest we go to Thailand next time." Seriously. There's a nice Thai place around the corner from here, and I'm lazy.

Intoxicated

"I'm serious, Cher. If you don't think it's too fast, I'd love to have you over to enjoy my view. I've been eating on the balcony. It's not huge, but it gets a lovely view of the sunset."

"*It's not huge, but it's lovely,*" is what I expect to hear when we finally sleep together. "That could be nice," I say, looking away as if a virgin bride. "No funny business, Brian. Not yet, anyway." I can wink too. Quite good at it, actually. My other eye *never* closes.

"Wouldn't dream of asking you to go farther than you might like, baby." He takes my hand to give it his customary kiss. I'm not surprised when he leans in for a kiss on the cheek. I've always let him kiss me on the cheek.

It's when he goes for my lips that I'm surprised.

You see, Brian has not yet made this kind of move. He plays the consummate gentleman, and I have considered it a boon given my recent breakup with Drew. I *need* a little distance from sex right now. I may be dating men who give me different ends than just great sex, but it's not far from my imagination that I may like it sometimes. Only sometimes, though.

I had been a little too lucky until now. At some point, Brian would ditch whatever FWB's he's undoubtedly been seeing on the side and make me his main, monogamous squeeze. He wouldn't be the first with this pattern. I'm so used to it now that I hardly find it offensive. Guys sleep around. Big whoop. Even if I were looking for a real relationship, I wouldn't have it in me to get mad about him ditching his previous dates because he's decided *it's time* to have me as his bedmate. He's thinking that he'll teach me everything he knows. You know, the stuff he likes!

A kiss out of nowhere wasn't on my radar. This is something I expect him to do when I willingly enter his apartment with the lovely views.

"Ah... sorry." He pulls back, hands on the wheel. "Don't know what got into me."

I bite my lips. Let's say I'm protecting them from another oral attack. "No worries, Bri. I know you're a good guy." Yeah, right. Real smooth move, fucker. You're lucky I'm working you like you probably hope I'll work your dick soon. Only question is, what gets you off more? Coming in my face, or on my tits?

"Good night, Bri. Thanks for the Hawaiian food. I'll see you soon, 'kay?" I'm Miss Perky Big-Tits as I blow him a kiss. Deep down, though, I feel like I need a shower.

I take one as soon as I'm back in my apartment. I also brush my teeth, not that Brian tongued me or anything. God, *why* do I feel this incessant need to scrub every inch of my body and to wash my mouth out with Listerine? He barely touched me. Everything is going exactly to plan, and absolutely nothing has surprised me.

Except that peck to my lips. For some reason, that feels like a step too far.

I haven't kissed a guy since I last saw Drew a few weeks ago. When it's a kiss like *that,* well... I don't know what my deal is. You'd think I was still hung up on the bastard.

Just because I can't touch myself without thinking about him...

Just because I'm rebounding with a guy I met that night...

Just because fucking Brian Samuels or whatever his last name is has got to be the polar opposite to Drew "Bang-You-Against-The-Wall-On-the-First-Date" Benton...

Why is he still haunting me?

Why are *you* still haunting me? I never met you before this happened. You were silent for my whole life until that night I met

Intoxicated

Drew. And Brian. As if you're somehow related to them. Well, it's over with Drew. I never want to see him again, not after what he said. So why are *you* still around? Is this some sign that things aren't over with Drew?

Tell me, damnit!

I towel off and collapse onto my bed, naked. What's the point of covering myself up if it's you and me? You've seen me at my lowest already. I practically invited you to partake in my mad love life. The biggest fling of my twenties. The closest thing I've had to a real, genuine relationship since high school. God, I was so dumb and innocent back then. If I knew this would be my life, I would have...

I don't know what I would have done. Avoid some of the crazier marks.

Why are you looking at me like that? What do you know that I don't?

Have you been talking to Drew again? Has he said something about me? Is he still thinking about me? Does he feel bad? Is he doubling-down on his...

You know what? Don't tell me. I don't want to know.

(Yes, I do.)

I curl up on my bed, wet hair strangling my throat. I don't care. I don't care if it reminds me of Drew's hot and heavy caresses. Both the gentle and crazy ones. He's the first man I've ever met who can combine my kind of hard loving with absolute tenderness.

If only he hadn't blown it by calling me a...

What other man is going to do that for me? Brian? I'll get off on stringing him along for a while. If I play my part right, our first few nights together will give me enough of a thrill to help me orgasm, even if his ineptness can't. After that, it will be my gradual descent into boredom and madness. I'll lose interest. All the soirees and trips to Hawaii won't be enough. I may no longer be looking for a payday via litigation, but our breakup still won't be pretty. He'll accuse me of being a bitch. I'll tell him he's finally showing me his true colors. Then I'll be a whore. I'll say at least whores get to have fun.

My face presses into my comforter. My skin grows cold, but I don't care. I'd rather lie here naked than strangle in clothing. It's my right as a human being to go out the way I want.

Maybe I'd rather go out with Drew's lips upon mine. That would be better than most things I've experienced.

Oh, my God.

I know why you're still here. I know what *you* are.

You're my fucking subconscious. My conscience? I don't know the difference, but you're that voice in my head who pops up when I have a moral crisis. An ethical dilemma. A *holy shit what am I doing* moment. That little voice I'm supposed to listen to like it's been there my whole life. But it hasn't.

You haven't been there.

You didn't come into my life until I met Drew Benton. The guy who is seemingly perfect for me because he's as terrible as me. My other toxic half. The bitter side to my sour coin. The man who is probably out there right now wrestling with his own newfound conscience.

No wonder I feel like shit with Brian. I know what I'm doing is wrong, and that it won't make me happy. I'm using him. He may not know it, but he's using me, and this is the same song and dance I've employed since I couldn't think of any other way to live. Does this mean this phase of my life is ending? That I'm ready to move on with a real career, or at least some direction in my life that will steer me toward a long-lasting, fulfilling relationship?

God, is this what full brain development feels like? I'm barely in the latter half of my twenties. How do I handle this? What do I *do?*

Is it time to admit that I can't stop thinking about Drew and what he said? That I get off on being seen as a slut?

You didn't arrive until he did. I'm not going to say this man brought me my conscience, but the irony is too good to be true, isn't it?

What if what he said is true? What if the reason you're *still* here is because my story with Drew isn't yet finished?

If there's anything I've learned about you, though, it's that you come and go when it's most convenient. When you get the juiciest details. I suppose you don't want to sit here and watch me fuss with my emotions for the next several hours. So how about you skedaddle for a few days or weeks? We'll reconvene when I have something new and interesting to report. Even if I don't know yet what that will be.

I have a feeling that Drew Benton will be involved, though.

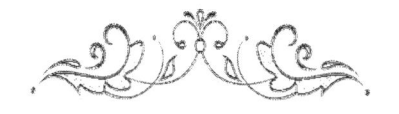

CHAPTER 31

DREW

"You really should wear a tuxedo more often," my mother says, hands primly in her lap and ankles crossed in that insufferably ladylike fashion. She's wearing a gaudy silver dress covered in sequins, like this is the '80s or something. Her hair is only big, though, because she has it up in a giant twist that shows off her dangling diamond earrings, but not the birthmark on the back of her neck. That's been covered up with concealer. According to family legend, my mother hid her birthmark from my father until their fifth wedding anniversary. He claims to have barely noticed it, and she was so mad that she had covered it up from him for so long that she chewed him out for another two years. "You look fetching, darling."

"Thank you." Yes, I look great in a tux, although I hate the things. Dreadfully itchy, even when they're bespoke. Plus, it's early August, and although it's been a relatively tame summer here in

Portland, it's still humid as shit. If it weren't for the air conditioning in the back of our limo, I'd be dying. "Where did you get those earrings?" I ask my mother. "Or were they a gift?"

She looks longingly at my father, currently scrolling through his phone. "They were a present for my birthday. Two weeks ago. You might have remembered that I invited you to my little garden party? The one you missed because you refused to come home for half the summer? I'm still a pillar of salt about that, Drew. There were some lovely young women I wanted you to meet. A few families of generous means have moved to the area this year, and every one of them has a lovely young woman of college age."

"Bit young for me, really."

"Nonsense," both of my parents say, because that's what gets my father to look up from his phone. "You're barely in your thirties. That's still plenty appropriate for a relationship with a young woman, as long as you keep it civil for the press," my father continues. "It's only when you reach forty that it starts to look a bit untoward. Then you have to wait until you're sixty for it to be en vogue for you again."

How do I keep from rolling my eyes at my own father? I wish I could say he comes from a different time, but he's hardly twice my age. You know, that magical time when it's suddenly okay for him to date twenty-year-olds again?

"Still, it's nice of you to come since your sister couldn't," my mother says. "Even if your motive is to butter those men up for your business." She sighs. "Changing careers can't be good for you. Why you couldn't stick with consulting, I'll never know."

"I'm more weirded out that he's going into matchmaking." Father shakes his head. "No offense, my dear, but that's women's work."

My mother shrugs. "I suppose that gives him an advantage, though. Who would you rather get matchmaking services from? A woman you barely know, or a young man who was raised the way we raised him? He knows what men like you are looking for in women like us."

"He'll have his work cut out for him, that's for sure. There are so few good women out there these days. Young women are such floozies."

Instead of getting offended, my mother sniffs and agrees. "Even if you were a hussy in my day, you still kept it to yourself. Your husband was none-the-wiser, and everyone was happier for it. These days, women are advertising their number of boyfriends on social media. Can you believe it?

My father pockets his phone before anyone could see what he was looking at on Instagram. (Let me guess... sexy bikini-clad "influencers?" I would be disappointed, otherwise. Also, not cheating on my mom my *ass*. He's probably sliding into some DMs where he sits.)

"Dating is rather a chore, yes," I say, and leave it at that.

They're right, though. The only reason I've decided to attend this soiree with them is because it's one of the biggest in downtown Portland all year. It's a great opportunity for me to shake hands, remind colleagues of who I am, and namedrop my new business venture I plan on launching later this fall. Brent nearly fell out of his chair when I told him, but said he'd be down for anything I had in mind. My old business is closed. We're turning away prospective new clients and will soon rebrand with a new office and a new name. I'm still kicking a few around. Benton Matchmaking sounds hokey, but it's my placeholder for now. I'll probably consult with an old buddy of mine who is killing it in marketing. Granted, he does toothpaste and paper mills, but I'm sure he'll spare some time for his old frat buddy who has some money to throw at him.

This is simply me testing the waters, anyway. I plan to expand my business to here in Portland as well as Seattle, because I'm familiar with the men (and women) in both. I'm sure I'll bump into some of my old clients who are agog that I'm going into matchmaking when I just broke them up with their old bloodsucking honey.

I really don't want to go, though. It's Portland. Fancy rich people will be there. You know who else will probably be there because of that?

If you said *Cher Lieberman,* than you really are paying attention!

I know she'll be there, unless she gets food poisoning at the last minute. The question is... does she know I will be there? Second question: what will I say when I ultimately see her walking around with some new guy?

Let's assume I don't actually see her. How disappointed will I be? Will I go home and wonder what I'm doing with my life? Why I'm still hung up on a woman who slapped me in the face on her way out the door?

We've established that I was in love with her. I still am, I guess. I haven't done a damn thing about getting her back, though. That's not my style. She wouldn't respond to it, either. That would reek of desperation, and any chance I had of getting her back would blow away.

No. Getting her back includes a long game. Some distance between us. Giving her time to calm down and become open to talking to me again. Don't think I've been sitting on my ass, though. I've been rehearsing an apology speech. Will I say it to her tonight? Probably not. It will be enough to make a quick appearance in her line of sight. Maybe coolly sip my champagne as we lock gazes. I'll turn around first. Make her think I'm not interested in her anymore. If anything, I'd like to find out who she is dating now, because I don't believe for two seconds she's stayed single. In fact, I'd be disappointed. That wouldn't be the Cher I know.

And love.

We reach the venue twenty minutes later. You know Portland has changed in my lifetime when we step out of our limo and meet an empty city street. Not entirely empty, I suppose. There are valets and security present, but the only through traffic are the buses. The sidewalk is closed to pedestrians and scooters, something your average man couldn't score without greasing some serious wheels at city hall. For all I know, the mayor is here tonight. We are certainly serenaded by the voices of those put out because they have to cross the street to get around the building. But the hearts of the people attending this party tonight are too "soft" to put up with what Portland really looks like on a daily basis. It honestly doesn't feel the same without someone screaming at me to give them money or simply screaming at themselves. At least we still get that faint whiff of pee.

Nothing makes a man feel fancier.

"Stay close." My father wraps his arm around my mother's and escorts her into the building. I stay a bit behind to chat up the doorman because he looks familiar. Turns out he used to hang out with a buddy of mine and we've met at a party before.

My parents know I can take care of myself, so they go ahead. This party's fancy, but it doesn't require us to be announced

Intoxicated

together. I'll saunter in once I'm done saying hello to everyone who looks half-familiar. By the time I enter the ballroom, I've had my fill of heady perfume and overpowering cologne. One of my father's golfing buddies runs up to shake my hand. Did I say golfing buddies? Actually, I know him best as a former client of mine. Seems he has a new squeeze in his life, or else I'm misremembering the lovely young lady clinging to his arm. This guy is in trouble. How do I know? Because she looks like the same woman I humiliated for him a year ago. *Not* the same, though. He simply has a type, and that type will be his downfall one day.

Many of these men are with women who will clean them out, either in a divorce or when the men aren't looking. I don't only mean the younger ones who are clearly hanging on for the money, either. I mean the First Wives Club, some of whom are currently none the wiser about their husbands' wanderings. Or he'll come home one day with a brand-new Porsche and she'll realize he's cleared out the retirement fund to fuel his mid-life crisis.

Sometimes the women are at fault, of course, but after you've seen a number of these breakups, you notice that the most common denominator is the clueless guy who doesn't realize he needs to change himself before he finds lasting love. Why do that when his money always ensures the next hottie is around the corner?

Here's my first ethical quandary about my new business. Should I attempt to get my future clients to understand their own relationship failings? Am I selling a lasting relationship? Or do I merely give them what they want at *this* moment? Which is almost always going to be young, nubile pussy...

Tonight would be an excellent chance to test those theories. There are many single men here, as well as those that seem happy in their long-term relationships (for now, anyway.) Even some who are with their young sweethearts continue to look at them with hearts in their eyes. Some of those young women look at them with the same hearts. Almost makes me believe in love, you know?

Fuck. Of course I believe in love. I've felt it, haven't I?

I don't get a chance to test any hypotheses. I've barely bumped into my father over by the open bar when he quickly grabs me by the arm and turns me to the man he's been talking to since I wandered away.

"Drew! Let me introduce you to my new friend, Brian Samuels. Been playing a bit of golf with him. He has a handicap of negative six down at the country club! Can you believe it?"

I flash a smile at the man who can't be that much older than me. Brown hair and a brand-new tux clings to his body as if he's wearing it for the first time. Outside of somebody's wedding a few weeks ago, it probably is. You can always tell who is used to wearing a tuxedo and who is pretending to be used to them. How often they tug their jacket down is the number one indicator.

"Pleasure to meet you, Brian. I'm Drew." I withdraw my hand after our firm shake. No, I have no idea who this guy is. Should I? I can't be assed to remember every single acquaintance my father introduces me to. I can barely remember what I had for breakfast sometime. Unless I liked you at some other party or you're one of my former clients, I'm probably not going to remember your face or name. You know, unless you're a woman. "Don't listen to whatever my father tells you about his handicap. I know for a fact that his golf game is much better than his story-telling skills."

My father claps me on the back before wagging a finger in my face. "How can you know when you're never down at the links anymore? Do you know how long it's been since he last went golfing with his old man?" he asks Brian. "Three damn years! We're lucky he ever comes down from Seattle these days."

I chuckle. "Never was into the game, if you can believe."

Brian's smile is as fake as his laughter. What a kiss-ass. Like I can't tell what's going on here. Before I know it, my father will tell me that Brian is in software development. Everyone knows that Benton Basics is one of the biggest software creation and deployment firms in Portland, and that's with a smaller crew than some of the others around here. My father was always a believer in spending extra money for the right talent. "*You buy Italian loafers that will last you ten years, don't you?*" he once explained to me. "*Why wouldn't you entice the best in their field to come work with you, even if you spend a little more on their salary and benefits? They'll make you back double what someone cheaper ever could.*" Sound advice, Dad. Now, hire more people to ensure that great, bright talent you've hired doesn't die of exhaustion before they retire with your generous 401k.

For all I know, that's what he's doing with Brian here.

"I'm not as good as he says I am, anyway," Brian says. "I'm always getting distracted on the course."

"Damn straight he is!" My father claps Brian on the shoulder like he's the golden son. Fine by me. I can only get beaten up my dad so many times before my doctor questions the clap-marks on my own shoulder. "Last time we met, he couldn't shut the hell up about this girl."

Blushing, Brian replies, "Are you complaining, sir? Gives you an edge."

"No edge is worth it if not honorably earned. Then again, from the way you tell it, you've got an edge over all of us in the romance department! Drew recently broke up with a girl."

I shrug. "Not all of us can be so lucky in love."

"Ah! Here comes the lovely young lady." My dad flags down someone. I don't bother turning my head, although the splash of color in my peripheral vision piques my interest. "Why don't you introduce your lovely girlfriend to my son. Careful, though, he might steal her."

My father jams his elbow into Brian's side. Brian, who is still all laughter as he coddles his bruised rib looks at me as if it might be true. I'm compelled to wink at him. "I am a bit of a ladies' man," I say. "I make no promises."

Brian's face falls. My father roars in laughter.

"That would certainly match everything I've heard about you, Mr. Benton."

Such a familiar voice was expected tonight, but not now. Not like this, on the arm of a guy who barely looks like he's out of college and making his own way in the world.

Yet there she is. The radiant queen who has graced us with our presence. A woman so above us with her lofty ambitions that she makes my father's businesses look positively quaint.

I'm statue-still as Cher places a gentle arm on Brian's arm. He turns to her with that knowing look of lust in his eyes. Right here, in front of God and me, he kisses Cher on the cheek and turns to me in a dare for me to steal her.

I just might.

CHAPTER 32

DREW

She's wearing a cherry red off the shoulder dress that brings the eye straight to her bare clavicle. The sultry slit running across one of her thighs reminds me of the night we met, when she wore that gorgeous black number that still makes my head spin. Her makeup is different from that night, though. Bright red lipstick complements the dress, and the generous use of pink mascara reminds me of a girl I used to know in high school. Only because she wore pink eyeshadow every damn day. Cher looks much more sophisticated with it, though.

So sophisticated that I already feel about five leagues beneath her. That must mean Brian's ten leagues lower.

"This is, uh..." Has Brian forgotten the words now that he's in her presence? I suppose kissing her cheek so brazenly would do that to a man. "Cher. Cher Lieberman."

My father waggles his eyebrows before sending me a somewhat dour glare. No, that's not a reprimand toward me. That's a look that says, *"I've heard about this woman."* Gee, Dad, so have I. How about that?

Imagine if I ever brought Cher home for the family. I'd never hear the end of it once my dad figured out who she really was. *"My buddy Ross Jenkins – you remember Ross, right? Come on, you remember! – used to date that Jezebel. She cleaned him right out before heading straight to his business partner's bed! Stay away, Son. For your own good."*

"Cher, this is..."

"We've met," she softly says, gaze never leaving mine. "We actually travel in many of the same circles." Her white and red smile is unlike anything I've ever seen. Probably because this is her fake, put-on smile meant to bedazzle and charm, to help her keep her emotional distance, and to make men like me fall in love with her. Wouldn't this be the moment where I realize she always had a genuine smile around me? Or am I thinking else?

Like how much I'd love to rip that red dress off her body and relive the old times?

I clear my throat and address the men before me. "Indeed. Cher and I have met a few times before, but it's always nice to see a familiar face around these parts."

"Indeed," Cher concurs.

Does my father pick up on our energy? Does Brian get that we've slept together? Do I give a rat's ass?

Not really.

"Excuse me," I say to everyone. "I was actually on my way to say hello to an old college buddy of mine." I nod to Brian. He nods back. To my father, I say, "Thank you for the introduction. I'll be around."

"Now, Drew..."

I've firmly put my back toward them and have no intention of looking back. Instead, I shall head straight to the open bar and attempt to figure out my life.

You see, I thought I had things figured out before I got here. I thought that a few weeks was enough distance between me and her. That I would face her, look into her devilish eyes, and be stronger than I am.

I was a fool.

What is this asinine feeling taking me over right now? I ask for a gin and tonic to get me through these next few minutes. This feeling... I can't tell if it's jealousy or sadness. Is it possible for both to roll into one? Can I be so jealous that it makes me sad? Because looking at that nobody kiss her cheek sent me into a tiny tizzy. A little one. I swear.

He doesn't deserve her. She definitely deserves someone better than *Brian,* whoever the hell he is. Sounds like the kind of guy she'd pick up in the lounge where we met. Oh, God, was he that guy who had to leave before I swooped in and charmed the panties off her? Oh, my God. That's almost worse. She went straight to him to feed when she was done with my shit.

That guy is fucked. She really wants nothing to do with him, does she?

Why do I care? Shouldn't I be relieved to know she's not in love with him? Why does this make it worse? That she's probably sleeping with him, although she doesn't love him? Would it really be better for her to go to bed with a loser who golfs with my dad if they are in love? Does that make it easier *for me?*

Is this what it's really like to be in love? Because I fucking hate it.

I down my drink in about two gulps. Although the alcohol burns like a bitch, I tell myself it's for the best. Maybe I deserve some burning for the dumb shit I said to her a few weeks ago. You know, when I had her in my grasp? When I was learning everything about her, in the most wonderfully hellish way? God, I blew it. I really blew it. Cher may play by her own ethics, but she still has some integrity. It told her to get the hell away from me, and I don't blame it. I would've ran for the hills when I said something as stupid as *you get off on feeling like a slut and that's why you sleep with so many guys and bail on any relationship that get serious.*

What was I thinking? I wasn't, was I?

I look over my shoulder. Through the crowd passing me by, I barely make out my father's salt-and-pepper hair as he speaks to Brian and the vixen in the red dress. Seeing Cher stand so closely to that pecker pisses me off in ways I can't explain. It's like I'm a kid and someone has taken my favorite toy. For himself.

She glances in my direction. For a moment, our eyes meet. Something stabs me in the gut.

So much for coolly winking and pretending I don't really care about her.

The next half hour doesn't go much more smoothly. I find someone to talk to, but he immediately senses that there's something "off" about me. I tell him I'm getting over a summer cold that knocked me on my ass. "Gotta watch out for those wildfires out there," he tells me, as if I don't know. "Just because you can't see the smoke in the air, doesn't mean there isn't any there." Thanks, buddy. I'll keep that in mind.

Like I'll keep Cher's presence in mind.

I don't see her much more after I leave the bar, but I feel her presence everywhere I stand. Rose-scented candles on the tables remind me of the red of her dress and the crimson of her lips. The peal of a woman's laughter makes me remember when we got so high we barely knew where we were. The knowing chuckles of men about to get lucky tonight make me think of every time we shared a kiss that didn't necessarily lead to sex.

Of course, I also think of the damned sex. I don't need a specific trigger for that.

I have to decide, tonight, what I want to do. Should I march up to her and demand a moment to explain myself? To ask her to take me back? How much should I prostrate myself at the shrine of Cher, Professional Succubus? Or should I end it for good? Say my piece and kiss what we had goodbye, but on my terms?

Am I seeking a second chance, or closure?

Let's be real. I already knew she'd be here tonight. She wouldn't pass up the opportunity to hobnob, with or without a guy. Even without someone's invitation, she would have found a way to get in, even if it meant bribing the doorman. Cher lives for this shit. The dresses. The tuxedos. The champagne.

The drama.

I haven't seen her for fifteen minutes. Even now, as I look around the ballroom, I see no sign of Cher or Brian. Maybe this is my chance to simply leave. I'll hire a ride back to my South Waterfront apartment. Be done with this. Be done with *her*. Who needs closure when...

When...

She's standing in the foyer, where I have gone to decide whether I should leave. I was not expecting to see her here. Not sure what I expected, hanging out in one of the smallest areas of the whole venue. You know, that's *not* the men's room. Suppose I shouldn't be shocked to see her there, too.

Her back is to me. What is she doing? Reapplying makeup? Waiting for someone? Checking her phone? Do I say something now? Or do I walk by, hoping she'll say something? How much of a man should I really be?

Ugh. *Fine.*

It's now or never. It's my chance to get closure. I owe myself - and her - that much.

"Cher."

A compact snaps shut. Shoulder blades tighten. The fringe of the red dress grow taut across her back. A deep breath is inhaled and, slowly, Cher turns one critical eye toward me.

It's like cutting yourself on glass but continuing to dig through the shrapnel. That's what it's like to willingly enter these moments with Cher Lieberman.

Although she says nothing in acknowledgment, she continues to gaze at me with one eye cast over her shoulder. It's the same damned look she gave me whenever she dared me to go harder, faster, or *more, more, more.*

I hate her for it. Damn it, I love her.

"I'm sorry for interrupting your evening." Where the hell did *calm and polite* Drew Benton come from? Because inside I'm a total wreck. Everything is shaking. My mouth and throat are dry. I swear to God, I wore too much cologne. Either that, or I've picked up the fragrances of every rich asshole in this venue. I don't smell anything radiating off Ms. Chanel No. 5, though. No Victoria's Secret body spray. No Ralph Lauren. No Britney Spears. None of the other scents she enticed me with earlier this year. I would know. I had my nose buried deep in those scents so many times that I can tell you what *Britney Spears perfume* smells like. It actually smells good! Like really high quality!

Intoxicated

It smells like Cher.

"Wanted to say I'm sorry, that's all." My hands hang in my trouser pockets. It's either that or twiddle my fingers like the nervous wreck I am. Cher's demeanor hasn't softened or otherwise changed since I started talking to her. For all I know, she's plotting my demise. Or she'll go stone-cold and completely ignore me after two more seconds. "I'm sorry for what I said the last time we saw each other." We're attracting a little attention. Probably because most of the people here know who I am, and if they don't know who she is, they at least know she came here with another guy. That in itself is noteworthy. "That was wrong of me to say. I shouldn't have thought it. Besides, there's nothing wrong with who you are."

She looks away again. A few eyes are on us. I'm not sure they know what they're witnessing.

"Just wanted to say that. I'm sorry if I hurt your feelings or made you angry. I'm not asking for your forgiveness or anything."

Slowly, she turns her whole body, eyes widening as if I have utterly offended her with my presence. "Then why are you telling me this?"

She's not merely hurt, is she? She's wounded. *I* wounded her. Maybe not now, but I've at least opened the fresh mark I left inside of her a few weeks ago. That glistening in her eyes is the remnant of the tears she cried when I offended her. That clench of her hand around her compact is her withholding the urge to slap me again. Although I've tried to avoid angering her here, I've done it anyway.

"Because I had to," I say, with a bit of a frog in my voice. "Maybe it's selfish of me to corner you like this and say something, but I would've felt worse if I never apologized."

"You think this is an apology? Or about your feelings?"

I clear my throat. This is *very much* not going how I played it out in my head.

"I don't think it's about my feelings at all." Where has my confidence gone? Oh, it's right here in my pocket. Next to some lint and my dick. Yay. "It's about yours."

"Come again?" she snaps.

"Your feelings. I know that you have them."

Ah, shit, that was a little too snarky.

"Look," I continue, "I'm sorry. I mean that, too. I'm sorry for a lot of things. Not only what I said the last time we... yeah." I try to be a gentleman in public. Really. "I'm sorry that I treated you like I did the whole time we were together. You're not some anthropological specimen for me to dissect. Nor did you deserve the aggression I took out on you. You were always pretty open with me about who you were. I thought I was with you, too, but I guess... ah, never mind. You know what?" Here it comes. Words I had rehearsed, but they're not coming out the way I rehearsed them. There's some desperation deep down in my gut, ready to be unleashed upon the world. Upon *her.* "You deserve to be happy. You deserve a life that will make you content and fulfill you in every way possible. Maybe that's with a guy who is your best match. Maybe that's by yourself, doing your own thing and living life the way you see fit. I don't know. How can anyone know? You deserve happiness. I'd be a bigger asshole than anyone originally thought if I begrudged you that."

A shadow moves behind me. Here comes Brian, sensing the confusion on his date's face as she talks to me. Or takes my weird words, I suppose. Either way, he's here, and he's wrapping an arm around her like they've been lovers for an age. "Everything okay, hon?" he asks her, both eyes always on me. I offer a reassuring smile. He is not reassured.

"Yeah..." Cher washes the bemusement from her visage and softens her gaze in my direction. "Was having a chat with someone I used to know."

Ouch. Guess I deserve that one, though.

"Sorry for the interruption." That one's for Brian, who has gone from wanting to impress me in front of my father, to wondering how the hell I know his hot girlfriend. "I'm heading out. You two enjoy your night." I stop beside Brian before I have a real chance to pass him. I can't help myself. I've inherited something from my father, and it's called *pat the bloke on the shoulder*. "Good luck, man. She's a feisty one."

I show myself out and grab an Uber at the end of the block. My mother messages me to ask where I'm at. I tell her I'm going back to my apartment because I'm nauseated.

She doesn't ask any questions. Yet the car ride back to my place has all sorts of things swimming in my head.

CHAPTER 33

CHER

Can we talk about what just happened?

Did Drew Benton come up and *apologize* to me?

Then walked out like he owns the place and can do as he pleases?

Of course he did. Because he's Drew Benton, and it's in his damn blood. Ask me. I've learned much about his father since Brian finally got cozy with him. Fucking golf. *Nonstop golf.* I already knew what shit like "birdie" and "handicap" meant before, but now I'm learning lingo and buying golfing gear for the first time in seven years because Brian's convinced this is gonna be our "thing." Never mind this wasn't *his* thing until he finally got that precious introduction at the country club.

The things I do, I swear.

Intoxicated

Brian is flummoxed that I know Drew, although I've led him to think I'm not so worldly. At some point the truth would come out, though. How did I expect to hide how many people I really know in this small city? We would bump into one of my exes sooner rather than later. I simply didn't expect Drew to be the first one.

He *apologized* to me!

He didn't ask for my forgiveness. Didn't ask me to get back with him. Didn't even undress me with his eyes, the fucker. While he's standing there looking like a billion dollars in his bespoke tuxedo, something I had never seen on him before. Mr. Trucker Hat and Flannel never wore a tux around me. Why would he? That wasn't him.

It looked damn good on him, though. I hate him for it, because now all I can think about is the so-called whirlwind romance we experienced. The kisses that felt like atomic punches to the heart. The caresses that ingrained themselves into my carnal memory. The damned *fucking* that gave me pleasure I had never seized before. Not like that.

I almost forget what he had said to me the last time we saw each other, but I don't forget. It's always right there, taunting me. It replays in my head over and over, like a movie burned into my TV. I can still see the dawning realization on his face when he came up with the preposterous idea that I might be a... a...

Maybe he didn't mean it maliciously. Is that what I'm missing here? Was I so offended because I was used to men who *would* mean it maliciously? Because that's the definition of most of the guys I've dated. Brian over here would definitely say the S word in the most derogatory way possible.

What if Drew was just dumb as *hell?*

Because if there's one thing I've realized in turn, it's that he's right. I can't deny it any longer. The biggest sexual thrill I get in life is doing what I'm not supposed to do. I'm a carnal contrarian. A woman who completely owns her body and doesn't want any man laying claim to it. Or woman, for that matter. Who are they to say I belong to them? They don't belong to me. Humans don't work like that. The moment you think you own me, I'm out. This isn't about being possessive, really. It's about that most misunderstood aspect of monogamy.

That, *"This is it. No more sexy fun, ever again. I see you in a new light, my love. We can only make sweet, sensual love from here on out. It makes the best babies, I hear."*

I work with what the world has given me, and we live in a world that says I'm a slut. So be it. Maybe I am a slut! Maybe I look at guys like Brian and think about all the ways I'm going to dump him when this is over. Do I do it to intentionally hurt them? Of course not. That's an unfortunate side effect, but I can't deny who I am or what I need from my life.

Drew was different. He was the first man to completely get me. He understood what made me tick, even if he didn't *know* he understood me. He showed me a possible future in which I was in a happy, long-term relationship with one man who gave me the kind of love and attention I fucking want.

And he didn't judge me for it. I only thought he did, because that same society that calls me a slut says I should be deeply ashamed by it.

What if I left too soon? What if I now regret how things ended between us?

"Hey, Cher." Brian sits me down on a satin couch along the wall. He's brought me water and gently taps my cheek to get my

Intoxicated

attention. I take the cup of water without much thought. What is there to think about? "You all right? What did that guy do to you, huh?"

It's kinda cute, really. Although Brian is in the business of kissing Drew's dad's ass, he's still willing to hear me out. Maybe he's not so bad, too. I mean, is Brian my type? Hell, no, but he might make some other woman very happy soon. A woman who isn't lying to him from the moment they meet.

Someone who isn't me.

"I'm sorry." Eventually, my bearings return to me. I look up and realize that it's Brian sitting before me, and not someone else. Someone I desperately want to see right now. "I... I think I'm with the wrong person."

Brian sits back. "Excuse me?"

I hand back the cup of water. "That guy. Drew. He's the one who got away."

"What?"

I stand. Do I go after him? Do I sit here like a complacent idiot, doomed to make the same mistake over and over? Dare I go after the life that might make me happier than what I'm doing now ever could?

"Ch... Cher!" Brian leaps up, but I'm too fast. I pick up the skirt of my dress and fly out of the venue. I don't head to the coat check to pick up my jacket. Oh, my God, I don't need it! *"Cher!"* Brian's voice continues to echo behind me, but who cares? I have my clutch. I have my wallet and my keys. I don't need anything else. I'd argue I don't really need those, either.

I need Drew.

I don't bother calling a Lyft. Brian might catch up to me, and I need to hurry before I lose my nerve. No, I catch a damn taxi for the first time in years. When the driver asks me where to go, I tell him the intersection of Drew's building.

All I remember is how I felt every time I entered it.

Angry. Hot and bothered. Expectant. Humiliated. Desirous.

The car turns toward the South Waterfront. I look down at my phone, wishing I hadn't deleted Drew's number. I do, however, have a voice mail from Brian. A few messages, too.

I delete them all and hold my phone to my chest.

The cost to get here is way too high, reaffirming why I always take a rideshare, but who has time to fret over money when I'm standing outside Drew's apartment... and he might not *be* here tonight! I'm lucky the concierge recognizes me and Drew has apparently not told them to turn me away. I head straight up to his door and knock before I lose my nerve.

He answers.

Time stills. My breath is frozen in my lungs, like ice cubes clinking around with every breath.

He isn't completely undressed. He's taken off the tuxedo jacket and undone the bowtie, but everything else, from the shirt to the cummerbund, remains on his person. If I didn't want him before, I do now. I want him like the earth wants the sun to rise every day.

Drew leans against the doorway and looks me up and down. Is he nervous? Surprised? Can he hear the erratic beating of my heart or how much it sings for him? He calls me a siren, but does he know what that means? Does he know that I've spent my whole life singing to him, hoping he'll come to me?

"Damn," he says with that low, husky voice that has probably ripped off a thousand panties in its day. "That red is absolutely vivacious."

Intoxicated

I try to speak, but my words won't come out. Instead, I fist handfuls of my red dress, memorizing this moment so I'll remember exactly what it was like fifty years from now.

"By the way," he continues. "I fucking love you."

Fifty men have told me that they love me, some in the most grandiose of ways. Tears have been shed. Songs have been sung. Violins played and choirs came together in unison. But not until now, when a half-dressed man leaning in his apartment doorway said a vulgarity, have I believed it.

Nor have I ever wanted to hear it so badly.

"I love you too." The first words I've managed since I got in the taxi. Those are them. The truth. "*I love you, Drew Benton.*" I've said the L word a thousand times in my life. I've told a hundred men that I love them. When's the last time I meant it, though? Must have been high school. Young, foolish, and naïve. I thought love was when a boy puts his face between your legs and doesn't declare "*Ew!*" because you're not porn-star hairless. Now I know.

I think I know what real, adult love is.

It's when a man wishes you the best in your life and encourages you to go out there and find out what makes you happy. When he whispers sweet nothings in your ear one moment and gives you everything else you want the next. Waking up with blood all over his bed and finding out it's not the end of the world. Never feeling like you're defective because you're "the fairer sex" and carry yourself a certain way. Realizing that you don't have to pretend or put on a show to keep him interested.

It's when he looks you in the eye, and all you see is the universe you create together.

"Whoa, whoa." Drew sits up, arm lowering from his doorway. "Come inside, hon."

Was I on the verge of tears? That explains the burning behind my eyes. Yet it doesn't explain why I so easily wrap myself in his arms and press my cheek against his chest. The door shuts behind me. My nose meets one of the buttons of his shirt. Suppose I was crying a little. There's this wet spot on the fabric that wasn't there before.

Drew encircling his arms around me only makes me want to cry more.

We stand in silence, as the thump of his heart and the hum of the air conditioner lull me into tranquility. Is this the moment when I memorize every rise and fall of his chest? Or am I doomed to be haunted by that caress against my cheek for the rest of my miserable life? He can't want me that badly. That's not what's happening here. He's not really in *love* with me. You heard what he said about me. How can a man love a woman like me? Hell, how can I love a bastard like him? Even if he changes his ways a hundred times over, it will never erase the pain he's caused others over the years.

Nor will any changes I make in my life eradicate the men – and women – I've hurt.

Maybe we are perfect for one another. Two twisted souls who have left a lot of broken hearts behind us. Here we are. Looking at our reflections and deciding if we like what we see.

This only works if we're on the same page, though.

"What about that other guy?" Drew softly asks. There's a slight edge of jealousy in his voice. Enough to placate my battered soul, but not so much that I become afraid. "He was pretty smitten with you. Then again, so am I."

I'm almost lulled into a stupor from the way his knuckles graze my skin. Every part of me is waking up for the first time since we were last together. That fire spreading from my loins, to my heart, to my skin has got to be that most familiar sensation now that I'm with Drew. I know that it's all me, but he's the one who brings it *out* of me. He awakens my deepest instincts and inspires me to be nothing more than a beast that devours his love.

This could be perfect, but I have to eschew perfection. I can't wallow in the what-ifs of our relationship. I can only live in this moment and hope to God that we're both strong enough to enter the next phase of our life together.

"There is no other guy," I say. "There never was, not even before I met you."

All those men I dated and dumped meant nothing. They weren't learning experiences. What do I need to learn when all of my answers are right here? Because of Drew, I know who I really am. I know my true potential, both for greatness and destruction. I see the diverging road before me. One way takes me to transformation. The other leads me to ruin.

I expect Drew to counter me. Instead, he tilts my head and smothers my mouth with his.

This is it. The moment I completely surrender.

To him? To my life? The universe? I don't care. All that exists is him and me. This is the kiss that reignites the engine. The one I'll remember for the rest of my life. That first kiss we shared in this space a few months ago? It doesn't mean anything anymore. *This* is the one that matters. For the first time in my life, I'm kissing a man that loves me for who I really am.

And I love him. Why is that so frightening?

Drew isn't the kind of guy to let me wallow in my fears, however. He'll distract me with such powerful kisses that I have no choice but to give him every ounce of attention spared in my conscious. My hands cup his face, speckled with a five-o'-clock shadow that sends chills down my arms. My chest presses into his, awake and in need of his touch. I had to go and wear a bra tonight, didn't I? Could've totally gotten away without one, but noooo. I had to go and prevent my precious nipples from getting any closer to this man about to eat me whole.

I want him. Is it terrible how much I need him? I've always prided my independence. My inability to rely on anyone, unless there's a financial gain in it. Even then, I'm stashing away that money for the inevitable end of our relationship. I have a certain lifestyle I want to maintain, but I also, apparently, want *love.*

Go figure.

The only time I allow his mouth away from mine is when I speak. "Make love to me," I whisper. "I dare you."

Drew reacts to me jumping up as if he anticipated it all along. My legs snatch around his hips. My hands latch behind his shoulder blades. He holds me by the thighs as we slowly move from the entryway of his riverside apartment to the bedroom where this all began.

The anticipation kills me. I hate that we aren't having intercourse yet. I hate that it will soon be over, even if it goes on all night.

You only get to make love for the first time once.

CHAPTER 34

CHER

He doesn't drop me on his bed like he did the first time we boned like filthy animals. We're still filthy, at least. We may be dressed in some of our finest clothes and smelling like thousands of dollars, but we're lousy, dirty people. It doesn't matter that Drew slowly lowers me to the end of his bed like I'm made of antique porcelain. The intent in his eye is as clear as our reflection in the mirror. He may be gentle, but it's *our* kind of gentle. Because I'm a doll, all right. Just nobody's baby doll.

I'm more like a fuck doll. A fuck doll that completely consumes you. The best one you've ever had.

Here in the bedroom, at least.

"Is it trite to call you beautiful?" Our eyes remain locked together, but Drew makes a compelling argument for me to look away as he pulls his belt out of his trousers and tosses it to the floor. "Because holy shit you are fucking gorgeous. It honestly hurts to look at you."

Is this where I tell him that I ache to look at him as well? Right between my legs? "Is that your poetic way of saying I make your dick too hard to deal with?"

His smirk comes with a sadistic chuckle. "You're not the type for poetry."

"Anything you have to say can be said without words."

Drew cups my chin and moves his thumb across my bottom lip. Both have parted, my tongue lightly tasting the tip of his thumb. My eyes flutter shut. I breathe so deeply that my chest raises and my head falls back. My chest never falls back down. My head never comes back up.

But my legs spread open. Because I'm a slut for this man.

Drew's sleight of hand somehow drops the bust of my bust around my waist. The off-the-shoulder sleeves strain against my elbows, my strapless bra the only thing separating his tongue from my nipples. I'm teased by that tongue. It dips into my cleavage, Drew's hand gliding against my thigh, coming unbearably close to my cunt.

He doesn't stroke it. He taps it with the back of his hand.

I jerk up, eyes snapping open and moan teasing out of my mouth. I search for his, hoping for a kiss to distract my poor tongue. Instead, I get another tap on my pussy, harder than the one before. Drew's hand slips beneath my thong and squeezes my nether lips. The taut sensation spreading through my loins has me bracing against the bed and my knees shaking in the air.

"Tell me who you are." That husky voice nearly obliterates me. It doesn't help that my need to fuck has risen so greatly that it's a miracle I'm not humping his hand. Or the air, for that matter.

"Tell me the truth. I want to know who it is I'm madly in love with."

He's got me by the theoretical balls. My only recourse is to cover his fingers in my immediate arousal. That little smirk of achievement prompts me to smile back at him and say, "I'm a temptress." He may growl, but I purr. A kitty-cat to match his dog. Or maybe I'm the bitch to his tom cat. "I'm that gorgeous siren that lures you to your inevitable death."

"Might not be so bad if that death is in a few decades." He lightens the grip on my nether lips, but does not release me. I'm tortured with a finger to the swelling clit. Breath hisses through my teeth. I break eye contact for the sole purpose of looking at his crotch. I want to make sure he's hard for me. As soon as he pulls that hand away, I better be on the other end of his dick.

"Still inevitable," I whisper.

"You gonna be around for that, huh?" He looms over me, easing me down onto my back. My legs fall open. Kisses cover my chest and bury beneath my bra. One nipple is summoned from the depths, quickly swallowed by a pair of lips that won't let it go. Not until Drew insists on saying, "You gonna watch this guy grow old and lose some of his stamina?"

"I hear hormones are hell on women, too," I say. "You gonna be around for *that*."

"Watching you succumb to aging?" That ruthless grin sucks me right into another kiss. "I wouldn't miss it for the world."

"I'm not old yet."

"Hell, no, you aren't. Neither am I. We can go all night."

This isn't helping my incessant need to screw. "Careful, Benton," I say. "Go all night with a succubus, and you might lose your life."

"Worth it."

"Even going all night with a woman who loves to feel like a *slut?*"

Yes, I'm insane. Choosing now to throw that in his face. Ah, see? He flinched? How terrible of me. Making him *flinch*. "As long as she's my slut, I don't see what the problem is."

"You don't get to own me. Nobody does."

"It's not owning you if you willingly stay with me."

I was prepared to continue the banter. After all, that amazing cock is coming out of his trousers, hard and happy to see me again. I should be thinking of all the hot ways I want to play with it. Where I want to put it and how hard I want to fuck it and suck it. Instead, I'm mulling over those words that hit me right in the horny gut.

"I'll stay for as long as you give me what I need."

We both know I'm not talking about money.

I don't have to tell him twice to make love to me. Once his mouth is on mine, my back is on the bed and my fingers back on his cheeks. We're so wrapped up in what our lips can do that I almost don't notice the gentle glide of his cock inside of me. In true, ridiculous fashion, the tip barely penetrates me before it falls right back out again. Drew sighs against my chin and takes the matter into his own hand. It's such a common occurrence when you're having sex. Yet for the first time ever, the moment is not a hindrance to my having fun. It's a part of the larger portrait that shapes our relationship. Him acting like a mere mortal who has to manually steer his dick inside of me is more humanizing than anything he can whisper in my ear.

Likewise, I hope he enjoys that garbled groan I just choked against his arm.

Intoxicated

Oh my *God* I missed him. I missed *this*. How often do you meet a man who can fill you with such precision that it takes your breath away? When you open your eyes and look up into his, you're overwhelmed by how beautiful he is. The tousled hair. The grizzly look coming to claim his face. Those big, blue eyes that stare right back into your soul. The wrinkled collar falling away from his neck. The little red mark on his skin that *you* left behind with nothing but your mouth.

It's unreal. If I could bottle up any moment as my treasured keepsake, it's this one right here. The moment when it all begins again.

Unironically, I'm the first one to move, because I can't stand it anymore. The love of my life is inside of me. He's looking at me like I'm the light in the darkness. Everything is boiling over, begging me to either clamp it with a lid or let it spill from one end of my soul to the other.

I let it spill.

A famished eruption occurs when he kisses me. I've gone from being his lovely doll to the woman who is about to make him come so hard that he sees every star in the universe. My legs are wrapped around him like a vise. His fingers dig into the flesh of my thigh, the heady growls in his throat coaxing me to arch my back and take him in deeper. How can he be so perfectly shaped? I meld right into his hold and take him in so deep that my nether lips meet the hairs of his thighs. They call this the hilt and my pussy the sheath for a reason. That thick sword of his will cut deep if we're not careful.

"Make love to me," I mutter on his lips. The sensation sends one of his hands onto the bed, where he grasps his own bed covers like they're the only thing separating him from death.

We're not joking when we say I'm a succubus. I really am, aren't I?

I'm destined to take every drop of his manhood and breath from his body. I'll bend him over backward, giving him the most mind-blowing sex of his life. All I want is every piece of him, body and soul. That's how I earn my keep while he earns his. The bedroom is our hunting grounds. Our *feeding* grounds. I'll greedily eat every bit of him. I'll take my spoils as he launches his hips against me, spearing me so hard and so deep that I cry out in both relief and pain. Except I like the pain. I love the reminder that we're not perfect. I need the reminder that we're human.

This is how we make love.

He rips my sleeves down past my hands and yanks down my bra. He pops the buttons off his shirt and kicks his trousers down his legs. He growls into the crook of my neck and angles so I feel every agonizing inch of his cock as it plunges in and out of me. He taunts my core and challenges me to hold up my end of our lovemaking. If I want to come good and hard, I have to meet his thrusts and follow the rhythm of his hips with my own. But he will be happy to fuck me in any way I need. Any way *he* needs, lest I think this is all about me and my insatiable desires.

My fists ball against his chest, pushing up my breasts and giving him something to suck as he ups his speed. I feel it. Down there. It's almost frightening how easily he makes me come. Let alone this hard. It's like every piece of my soul is pulled from my extremities. The magnet in the core wants my soul all in the same place. Right here, in my loins, my soul goes to get fucked.

It's all I can think about.

"I'm coming..." My uncharacteristic whine is only met by the clench of my cunt and the rush of heat freeing from spirit.

"I know." That's the last thing Drew says before slamming his hands onto the bed and slamming his cock into me.

The edge isn't something to trip over. You're either thrown off it or completely collapse. In this case, Drew hauls me to the edge of climax and tosses me into the ether. My screams of surrender echo in the room where he first made me his willing slave. This place where he showed me the kind of love I need is right at my fingertips. I have no words for him. No visions for myself. Nothing beyond the thigh quivering, leg shaking pleasure that wracks my whole body as he relentlessly pounds my depths.

I both want him to come inside me right now and to hold back. I want the instant satisfaction of that intimacy while also wanting to hold out for more.

This is Drew we're talking about. He probably decided when he saw me at his door that he'd take every one of my holes before giving himself over to orgasm. I wouldn't expect any less.

"Don't stop!" I say that as soon as my first orgasm wanes. He's got me by the arms, pining them to my sides. My breasts continue to shake in their cups although his thrusts are now slower, more methodical. Drew's teasing the last of that orgasm out of me, making my eyes roll back and my legs slack around his hips. The only moment of peace I'm allowed is when he slowly pulls out the whole length of his erection, the tip glistening in my cum. Drew licks his hand and tugs on his cock. I think he's about to come on me when I meet that monstrous look in his eye.

You think I don't recognize it? Honey, it's what I'm here for.

"Don't stop," I repeat, fisting the skirt of my dress in case he can't see what he's already done to me. To *us,* honestly.

He doesn't say anything. Why would he have to, when he can do all his talking with those glistening eyes and the little smirk on the corner of his lips? The man is fueled by that hard-on, and I'm the only one he wants to fuck.

That's a pretty powerful feeling, honestly.

In the future, I'll probably need a safe word. One I'll never use, but *he'll* feel better knowing that I have a way to shut down that hungry cock with one word. Hmph. Like I'd ever want that.

Why would I want this any other way?

My yelp of excitement is the other fuel to his internal fire. What else did he think he'd get, though, when he flipped me over? Now here I am, my face pressing into the covers as my ass is pulled into the air and my dress yanked off. My shoes fall to the floor. My soaked thong stays behind. Drew needs something to grab as he pulls my left leg up and slams back inside of me.

What's the only thing hotter than wild, passionate sex that dominates every position you can concoct in your dirty imagination? Sex infused with raw, romantic love, I suppose. This isn't our first time his thumb encircles my ass as he fucks me, but it *is* the first time I allow myself to be washed in love. The man must really love me if he's using this golden opportunity to create treasured memories that are nothing but rough and ready. I'm a fucking goner when he pulls my hair and forces me up on my hands. The only way I can stay upright is if I dig my knees into the bed and become a landing pad for his hard cock. The sounds of our crazy lovemaking drips out of me and covers that cock that occasionally slips out and rubs against my ass. Drew still doesn't say a word. I told him he didn't have to. I'd much rather feel how much he loves me. I want to feel that I'm his.

I want reasons to willingly stay by his side.

My bra finally falls off my body. I collapse again, this time with him following. His teeth nip the top of my ear as I struggle to breath beneath his muscles and sweaty skin. I'm sweating, too, but how can I care when every bead of sweat is more proof that that I'm living in this moment? For all I know, my thighs are covered in cum, anyway. I hope they are.

"Tell me again that you love me." That heady sound sends shivers straight into my ear and down my shuddering spine. If Drew's goal was to spread my legs wider, he's succeeded. I feel so open to him that it's only a matter of time before I trap him in my body forever. "Do you love me, Cher?"

"Yes." I crane my head around, swallowing much-needed breaths. "I love you. Do you love me?"

"I love you so much that I'm going to give you the hardest fuck of your life."

"Promises."

He flips me back over again. I don't have time to miss his touch. Drew is down on his bed, pulling me into his lap. But not to ride him. Oh, *no*. My hair is in his hand again, my nose soon filled with the scent of his manhood. My mouth immediately goes to his cock. My tongue, lips, and hands are soon covered in our sex as I work his base and suck his shaft. I'm given advance warning of his next move – a hand to the back of my head, traveling down to my neck. I take in a careful breath through my nose and forego my chance to protest. You think I'm passing up the opportunity to swallow his man's cock? I can only hope he chokes me with his cum.

"I'm gonna keep giving you what you want for the rest of my life." That's his verbal promise to me as I'm made completely nonverbal. His cock is so thick and hard that I struggle to take every inch into my mouth. It's a point of pride to do it, though. Like hell I'll let myself drown tonight! "You think I'm afraid to put in the work? The only thing I'm afraid of is you walking out again."

My wincing isn't because I hate what he says. What can I say? Sometimes a dick punches you right in the throat and knocks the breath out of you. I've got my bearings back by the time he starts fucking my throat, though. So, this isn't a mere cleanup job, huh? He's getting off, and I'm the lucky lady to deep throat him.

"I'll give you sweet and gentle love if that's what you want, my spoiled, selfish princess." Drew both pulls on my hair and pushes my head down. It's a steady rhythm that matches the thrusts of his hips and gives me ample opportunity to reorient myself with the breaths I need to keep going. "Or I'll fuck your ass against the window if that's what keeps you with me."

I grab his thigh and moan. It throws me off rhythm just enough that I legit begin to choke. Drew is quick to pull me off his lap and to get on top of me again, his kisses on my throat as if to say he's sorry.

It's my fault. I got caught up in the moment and forgot that deep-throating is kinda hard.

"Make me come and then fill me with yours," I say when I have my voice back. One leg is already thrown against his hip again. Soon, he rolls me over and pulls me back against him. Fingers plunge into my cunt. A moan completely obliterates what I was about to say before he so rudely interrupted me. "That's all it takes to keep this slut around."

Yeah, I wasn't gonna continue until I got the chance to say that.

Drew's hand gently encircles my throat, a finger entering my mouth as my leg lifts and his cock drives back into me. He wraps his other arm around my torso and squeezes my breast. He fucks me so hard that I hear his balls spanking my ass. I have no chance to feel it, though. Only my spoiled cunt getting more of that good shit.

I've almost forgotten everything leading to this moment. I forgot the insults, the histories, and the man I left behind at some stupid party to come here. I've forgotten the exes and the embarrassing shit I did in the name of advancing my life. I've forgotten the stories he's told me about his own life. Why do I care about any of that when we're doing *this?*

Of course I'll stay. If I get this whenever I want for the rest of my life, why the hell would I leave? Don't tell me he's making some great sacrifice by fucking me like the woman he both wants to sully *and* marry. Most men only get one woman like that in their lives. I better damn well be his spoiled slut.

I'm sorry. His spoiled *princess.* That's what we're calling it now.

It doesn't take me long to come again. My body clenches so hard while I'm screaming and writhing that my cunt's almost too tight for him to get back in again. But where there's a fucking will, there's a fucking way, and Drew moans like I'm about to milk him dry.

I wish.

He's got plans for me, see. I have to ride his lap while he spanks my ass. I have to hang over the edge of the bed and feel my G-spot take more of his tender caresses. I'm thrown from one end of the bed to the other, only to end up against the wall above his headboard, where my head nearly knocks down a picture of some stupid bridge. I'm *busy,* okay. Too busy having an orgasm as he sucks my throat and squeezes my thighs.

I'm sore from head to toe, but it's the kind of soreness that keeps you going. If you stop, you can't start again. So we go, go, go, our insatiable lust only matched by how often I come once the third orgasm comes and goes. Does it actually stop? Or am I in some rich, orgasmic haze that makes me pliable and convinced that I'm already married to this man?

I don't know what surprises me more. That he intends to finish in the missionary position, or that I love it?

"*Look into my eyes when I come inside you,*" isn't the kind of thing I used to find romantic, let alone hot, but it's all I can think about as he settles between my legs and makes long, hard love to me. It's not as frantic and determined as it was for the past half hour, but his stamina does not waver, nor does he slow to catch his breath. Or maybe I don't really notice, because I'm so enraptured by his flushed complexion that everything both slows and speeds up like we're traveling through every timeline to ever exist.

"You finally ready for me?" Drew pushes himself up on his hands and stares right into my eyes. "Because I've been ready for you for like twenty minutes now."

"Do it," I dare him. Even in the most romantic of moments, I have to dare him. It's in my blood.

He smothers me with one last kiss before I hear the relieving gasp in his throat and feel the surge of heat filling me up inside.

Drew never hesitates, like he never relents.

Is it weird that I don't really notice the actual moment he comes? When everything slows down so much, I'm busy staring at the ripples in his muscles, the sweat dripping down his skin, and the crease in his face that displays his vulnerability to someone he loves. I'm only aware of how *sore* I am because he finally slows down, taking a moment to rest inside of me as one last breath heaves from his lips.

Intoxicated

The ache inside of me is temporarily sated. A kiss seals my intentions.

"I love coming inside you," he mutters against my mouth. "It's the best damn feeling in the world."

"Physically?"

"I should hope emotionally, too."

"Sorry, I'm stuck on the physical right now. Remember, I'm one-track-minded."

Drew pulls out. I had hoped to spend a little more time together like that, but I also don't mind letting my legs fall limp and sticking my fingers in the fluids spilling out of me. Drew is such an overachiever, but I'm pretty sure it's mostly me down there. I was so wet when he first entered me, and now I'm like a dam that's burst open after a torrential storm.

My fingers travel down my swollen clit. Drew is still stroking himself.

"Come again," I purr, toes curling into the blankets. "Come on me and make me your slut once and for all."

"I'd rather do one better."

"You want me to suck you off?" Dare I dream about that fantasy coming true again? "Come all over my face or give me a pearl necklace?"

"I'd rather come inside you again."

My legs are permanently stuck open, so... "What's stopping you? I'm open for business all night, and you're my only customer."

"You know what I want."

It takes me a moment. I'll blame my orgasm-riddled brain. That and my body is so pussy-centric right now that I forget I told him I wanted all my holes possessed tonight.

My fingers continue to massage my sensitive pussy. I poke one finger inside and lick it before circling my clit again. Under Drew's attentive gaze, half the shit inside of me slowly slides down my ass.

Eventually, I flip over, my wet ass in the air.

Pretty funny, isn't it? He's fucked my ass before, and we had the usual to-do over lube and careful, deliberate strokes to make sure it felt good on both sides. Oooh, not tonight. For some blessed reason, we're so damn wet that he barely has to test me before the entire length of his cock is back inside of me.

It's so fucking tight and satisfying that I have to hold back an instant orgasm. Not Drew, though. He just went nuts inside of my pussy. He's going to take his time working his way back up to climax. In the meantime, I get what I wanted.

I don't have the words – or the breath – to express it.

Not to you, anyway. Trust me when I say I use the last of my energy to tell Drew how hard to fuck because I know he's afraid of hurting me. I ain't afraid. I've got an arsenal of colorful language to make sure he finishes the job right. You're not going to fuck my ass after everything we've been through and *not* make me feel like I've been through the wringer. The man I love knows how to fuck me good and hard. He doesn't hold back. He can't hold back. He's so into me that he knows my cries are of pleasure and not pain. My languid moans are because my hand is on my clit and the last of the cum I'm holding inside of me runs down my leg and squirts on the bed. He's right, I guess. I wanted to feel like his slut, and we *both* made that happen.

He throws the language right back at me. Drew both tells me he loves me and calls me the dirtiest shit as he erupts one more time. In my ass, of all places.

We crumple on the bed together. I think I've finally tuckered him out. I know that if he tries to go at me again I might finally have to put one of my feet down.

"I only wish I weren't such a stupid mortal," he says with a labored breath. "I'd keep fucking you like you deserve."

"It's my own fault. I drained it all out of you."

"I let you."

Do we bicker? Do we cuddle? Do we gaze longingly into each other's eyes and imagine some twisted future together? Or do we wait for some strength to return to our legs so we can take this to the shower?

If you know me, I love a good challenge. I elect we do it all. Again. And again.

Every damn day until we die of intoxication.

EPILOGUE

DREW

"Of course, there are no guarantees when it comes to love." I show my client the six-sided dice I keep on hand for these brilliant explanations. "Are you familiar with Dungeons & Dragons?"

This man, Mr. Jeffrey Klein, has to be at least fifty-five. Yet he's that self-assured and rather sophisticated fifty-five. You know, three-piece suit, groomed hair and nails, and the right scent on his person that doesn't completely overwhelm everyone around him. He's as likely to drive himself in his Bentley as he is to hire a driver for the day. When he walks, it's with those careful steps that turn every lady's head.

You'd think he doesn't need dating help. If anything, he'd usually be coming to me for help with an *ex,* but here Mr. Klein is, having heard about my new, unique dating services.

Intoxicated

And I'm over here dropping nerd shit on his head.

"I may be familiar with it," he diplomatically says, as if that tells me anything. Was he part of the satanic panic in the '80s? Because that won't help me. "Role-playing in your sunroom while the dungeon master rolls a twenty for charisma?"

"Right. Sunroom." All right, I admit, I wasn't expecting him to know that much. Let alone... sunroom? At least he didn't say basement. I wasn't ready for those flashbacks to high school. "Then you're familiar with the roll of the dice, so to speak. Every time you interact with a woman you have your eye on, there's a chance that things will go really well..." I tip the six-side up. "Or really poorly." The one appears. A discerning gentleman will imagine snake eyes, of course, but we're talking nerd magic here. "Of course, there are ways to up your chances of success. Like you wouldn't invest in a company that can't prove itself, a woman looking for the right husband won't go for someone who doesn't prove his worth. You have to create your character, so to speak."

He taps his chin. There are only a few white hairs there. Enough that a woman would be inclined to drape her fingers against them and giggle. But I get a feeling that our older friend here isn't looking for a sugar baby. Based on what Mr. Klein has said to me so far, he's completely over women who are only into his money. He's been burned a few times. Not ungrateful enough to hire a professional heartbreaker, but jaded toward the dating scene. He doesn't want to hide his wealth, but he also doesn't want to advertise a big target on his back. These waters can be tricky to navigate if you're a man like him.

That's where I come in.

"You seem to know much about this, considering your age." He sits back in his chair. A waiter in a tie and tails comes forward to offer us refills of refreshing cucumber water. Mr. Klein flashes him a genial smile before the man is on his way again. All around us is the refracting sunlight of a Seattle's autumn day. Probably the last one we'll get for the rest of the year. Then again, when you're this high up in a well-to-do restaurant that offers you a whole room to yourself – and your client – the sun is always within your reach. "Forgive me. I'm not used to younger men such as yourself having this all figured out."

"To be fair, Mr. Klein," I say with one of my characteristic, devil-may-care shrugs, "sometimes it's easier to take care of other people's lives than your own. A healthy distance, you know?"

"Too true. It's why I'm so good at investing in other people's businesses, but often lack the mind to start my own. Besides, I hear you're not doing too badly for yourself these days. Am I correct in saying that you're dating a certain Ms. Lieberman?"

I should let my little smirk do all the talking. Instead, I open my big mouth and say, "She's practically my wife, sir."

I don't know his history with Cher. He could be one of her exes. Or he knows one of her exes. Either way, he definitely knows her name well enough to remember that I was dating her. That's probably a mark against me. Openly dating Cher hasn't exactly been... easy. Only because her reputation fiercely precedes her. When you're with a woman who has a history of breaking hearts and pilfering the heavy wallets around the region, men either look at you with great envy or *great* pity.

"I've known a few men who have said that before," Mr. Klein says, "but you're certainly different from them."

"Let me guess. I'm a bit younger?"

He laughs. "The proof will be in your relationship's pudding, it seems. Well, I won't say no to help from a young couple who know a thing or two about dating in this age. You know my parameters. You know that, even with my money, the men in my family tend to age early and leave this world earlier. Perhaps genetics will be kinder to me, but I don't desire to spend the last couple of decades of my life utterly alone, if I can help it. Nor do I want them to be flittered away on someone who is only biding her time until I'm gone. I want a proper family, Mr. Benton. I would like a partner who understands that concept well."

"I understand. I think you'll find you're hardly alone in that sentiment, Mr. Klein."

"Ah, well, the company I keep there isn't the kind that can help me. Unfortunately, I don't swing that way."

It takes me a moment to realize that's a joke. When I finally laugh, it's with an unfortunate snort that echoes in our little room. He must be pleased with my reaction, though, for he reaches his hand across the table for a shake.

Mr. Klein becomes the first official client of Benton & Co. Matchmaking Services. Naturally, it's been a hard sell, since many of my would-be clients are aware of what I used to do. Those who didn't know are not expecting to see a thirty-year-old man sitting behind the desk. If they catch me unawares, it's in a trucker hat, flannel, and jeans. But if there's anything I've learned in this gig, it's that sometimes being the last thing a client expects works for you. They've already worked with the people they're expecting. Maybe it's the wild card who will finally get some results.

Since he's the first client, however, he's paying me a comparably small retainer fee. For the low cost of five grand a month, I'll be on the lookout for potential matches. You see, part of this gig is networking with men *and* women who are looking for their forever soulmates. (Or forever enough to get me a good review.) In theory, we will eventually have enough women in our roster of "potential mates" that we can start referring from the moment a male client makes his first payment. Which will be much higher than what Mr. Klein is paying now.

It will be exhausting, to be sure, tapping my networks like this. Most men my age have no interest in a matchmaking service, and the women I know tend to be of the... women you get away from *type*. Yet that's why I have a secret weapon to draw in female matches that will make my clients happy. Because Mr. Klein may *say* he simply wants a family-minded woman who knows how to budget and not take things for granted, but he totally wants her to be pretty, too. Oh, yeah. She better be *pretty*.

We finish our meeting with another handshake and promises to meet up again in two weeks, assuming I don't have anything lined up before then. Mr. Klein is from the area, which gives me time to head back to Portland and interview people there as well.

Until then, I have someone else to meet.

***

CHER

If there's one thing I hate, it's *smacking gum between one's teeth*.

Thank God I never did that. I'd punch myself in the face before I ever did something as socially heinous as smack gum during a meeting! Seriously, who raised this girl? Was it in a barn? A dress barn? Look, I've met some very lovely women who came from a dress barn. I've also met some real winners who make me want to denounce my entire gender.

Liiiiike this dumbass right here.

"I gotta be taken care of, you know?" Fried blond hair twirls around Missy's finger. That's right. Her name is *Missy*. Missy! Did I believe for two seconds that was her real name? No! Yet she insists it is, so I guess it must be. She definitely sounds like a woman who has been called Missy her whole life. "*Listen here, Missy,*" I can imagine her mother saying, "*you don't get to huff your tits and make a damn scene in this here Nordstrom. Stop it or we're going home!*"

I write down "Taken care of" in my list of things about Missy and what she wants from a potential partner. "Uh huh," I say. "What do you plan to bring to your future partner's table?" I make sure to enunciate the word *partner*. Missy needs to realize that relationships are not one-sided affairs. She doesn't get to make a slew of demands and expect nothing in return.

"Look at me," she says with a snooty shrug. "I've got a rockin' bod. What guy wouldn't wanna spoil this?"

Yes. Indeed. Ms. Missy has a *rockin'* bod. Probably bought and paid for with college money she never spent for its intended use. Those breasts are definitely not real. Now, I don't begrudge a woman for playing a loser's game in this world, but those tits aren't even done well! They're so disproportioned to her body that I can't stop staring at the plastic shine taking over my retinas. At least her skin is naturally tanned and not the fake stuff. Her hair, though... so fried that I want to dunk her in a bath full of shampoo.

"While we undoubtedly have male clients who are looking for a partner who prefers not to work," I lie, as if we have anyone like that yet, "I have to remind you that this is not a short-term dating or escort agency. We are a matchmaking service, which means our matches have the intention for marriage down the line."

She shrugs again. "I'm fine with getting married. As long as he's rich."

God, is this what I used to sound like? No, no. I sounded nothing like this. I may have been after wallets above all else, but I didn't *act* like that's all I wanted. I'm an actress, damnit. I compose characters. I read minds. I know you better than you know yourself. Now, I'm not saying that's what I want to teach our female clients. All it means is I can smell the same - or worse - shit from a mile away.

Missy has professional sugar baby written all over her. There isn't a part of her that's authentic, and I don't mean her body. I'm not sure she knows how to read.

This isn't what Drew and I had in mind when we put out feelers for women who fit a certain... criteria. You see, the women we keep on standby for dates and matchmaking with our male clients don't have to pay a retainer. Not yet, anyway. They do, however, have to maintain a certain look and personality to be kept for consideration. Drew may not really get this yet, but our male clients have standards they don't think they need to broadcast to us. Yet I bet when I meet Mr. Jeffrey Klein for the first time, I'll know his ultimate type by the end of the meeting. It's my job to make sure we have a roster of women who might be his forever.

Missy ain't gonna be it.

"Siri, take a note," I say into my phone after I bid farewell to the biggest dud I've met all week. "Adjust parameters to ensure candidates aren't made of tits and ass and nothing else."

I'm not going to hold some young rube's hand to make sure she doesn't flip her shit when she sees her first diamond ring. Nor am I going to take time out of my day to teach them how to dress appropriately to their bodies and the men they want to marry. Ideally, our female clients will either be older and already sophisticated, or they'll be the younger breed who have been doing this a while and want to find a husband who is serious about settling down. What that man will never tell us is that she must be conventionally attractive (and if plus-sized, have curves in "all the right places.") And she'll never tell us that he better have a big wallet to make up for his faults. Hot women in need of our help are either hard up for money or old enough that their biological clocks are ticking. Since Drew is a slobbering man, though, it's up to me to cultivate the roster and coach the women who are almost there but not quite meeting perfect expectations.

Help. I've somehow stumbled into a full-time job.

You know I'm in love when I agree to go into business with someone. Let alone someone I'm fucking. You hear that, Drew? There isn't a man I've dated before you who could convince me to do this with them, let alone after only a few months. Yet here I am, splitting my time between Portland and Seattle so I can both be with Drew and help him turn his business around. *"From breaking to making,"* he keeps saying, usually right before he climbs my Mt. Pusseverest. I swear, if he keeps up the corny shit, I'll have to break up with him. Or at least withhold deep-throating privileges. Do you want me to choke from one of your stupid jokes, Drew? Do you?

Fuck it. I'd probably like it.

I wrap a sweater around me to combat the autumn breeze. It may be seventy degrees and sunny, but I'm not falling for it, Seattle. You're going to get cold, quickly. It's time to adjust to my favorite sweaters, even if Drew complains it means he can't see my "awesome rack."

It's a short walk to Occidental Square, but my bag full of work crap weighs me down. By the time I reach the bistro tables and food carts, my arm is falling asleep and my head hurts.

Good thing my boyfriend already has food and bubble tea waiting for me.

"There she is." He leans back in his seat, that hat on his head the only thing telling me that it's really, *really* him. I should know. I gave him that hat for his birthday. That and the most amazing hummer of his life, thank you very much. I intend to collect on my birthday. "The belle of the ball and the joy of my heart."

I don't need my sunglasses to blot out the sun any longer. Not when I roll them so hard I might go blind. Yet the scent of my favorite food truck fare lures me to sit down at the bistro table with my dumbass beloved. He's lucky he looks so good in that shirt and those jeans. Every time I feel like snapping at him, I simply remember the joys of riding that lap and I'm back to Placation Vacation.

What? You think that's not *healthy?* Honey, where have you been for the last 200 pages? Little Drew and I do is healthy. That's why we're in therapy together. Therapy! Together! Fuck me with a razor-sharp saw, I'm actually in couple's counseling with a guy who intends to hang around for a good long while. I make no promises about forever. Things are set up that we can cleanly breakup. I'm not financially invested in his business, and I haven't given up my cute Portland apartment. I may have clothes and toothbrushes at both of *his* apartments, but I value my independence, you know. Maybe there's a night I'd rather be by myself, singing along to Nina Simone while cleaning out my closet. Maybe I need a break. Maybe *he* needs a break.

Our therapist agrees that it's good for us, so there.

Intoxicated

"Please tell me you got us some ladies." Drew slides a drink in my direction. I don't sniff it before having a generous sip. Good. There's alcohol in it. Barely, but it's enough to take the edge off. "Because I just nabbed Klein as our first official client."

I suck some sauce off my thumb and tip my head back in my seat. "We need to adjust our PR. Everyone I interviewed today thinks we're an escort agency."

Drew sighs. "To be fair, a lot of them call themselves *matchmaking* agencies these days."

"Don't I know it."

He flips back the lid of his lunch and stabs a pile of noodles with wooden chopsticks. I rest my chin on my hand and *bask* in the mundane reality we now occupy. Me. This man. Our humble business of hooking up rich people with the poors of their dreams. I'm in freakin' Seattle instead of Portland. This time next week we'll be in a different Pioneer Square.

What if I told you this is a calm before a storm? Tonight we're hobnobbing at a gala. Drew will dress in his little tux while I cram into a golden cocktail dress I bought two days ago. When I wasn't bloating. I am *definitely* bloating now, so this will be fun.

It's been about two months since Drew officially pranced me around as his girlfriend. His father was stone-cold silent when I first came to visit, probably because he recognized me from the soiree where I was some other guy's girl. And, you know, he's heard about me from his buddies. Yet his mother merely looked me up and down and said, "At least it's not the maid."

Drew and I had a nice, long chat after that. Especially when I found out the maid *still worked for the Bentons*.

He hasn't met my family yet, but it won't be long. We're having Thanksgiving dinner with my parents, who still can't quite believe I'm actually bringing someone home. Irene, the grandmother nobody in the Benton family wants to talk about, figured out how to text on her phone to send me daily reminders to "keep the boy in line." Drew says that's a sign she'll ruin his life should we ever break up. It's cute that Irene makes a million mistakes when she texts me. It's like deciphering ancient code when she says, "*if he talks back to u, tell him u know he used to pee his pants until he was 7.*"

Is this what love feels like? When we're not being too passionate for our body parts' own good, we're sitting quietly at lunch, looking through our phones and occasionally laughing loudly enough to garner the other's attention. We hold hands when we walk around town. We talk about trips we're inevitably going to take, starting with a romp in Hawaii in two weeks. Trust me, we're not planning a wedding *anytime* soon. I don't think Drew is ready for that kind of talk yet. We're still young in this relationship. Just because you're pretty sure that *this is the one,* doesn't mean you rush into things, right? We're taking our time, making sure this is what we really want, and examining our long-term options. Maybe we'll get married five years from now after a nice, long engagement. Maybe we'll never get engaged and simply cohabitate for thirty years. Maybe we'll never officially live together, but sleep together every night. Hell, maybe I'll have five of his kids over the next decade.

Haha! Kidding about that last one! He'll be lucky if I agree to cat. Definitely no dogs.

I will, however, most certainly agree to him taking my hand and giving me the kind of look that suggests he wouldn't mind eating me alive right here. Drew Benton knows how to press my buttons in all the right ways.

"So I hear the gala will be full of your exes," he says with a gleam in his eyes. "I'm thinking you dress nice and sexy so I can parade you around with my hand up your ass all night."

"What am I? Your puppet?"

"Nooo, you're my girlfriend, and that's what I need to make sure everyone at the gala knows. That I'm the lucky bastard who actually won your heart."

I look at him as if he's lost his mind. Because he probably has. "Who said anything about my heart? This whole time I thought you were owning my pussy."

"Same diff." He snaps two fingers before pointing them in my direction. "Because this is you we're talking about."

"Uh *huh*."

"Come on now, babe, I save the fun words for the bedroom."

"You sure do." Wooo boy, does he. Drew has nailed more than me in the past few weeks. He is now a master dirty-wordsmith who knows how to get me going in about two seconds flat. All he has to do is give me a virile look, call me one of the magic words, and I'm hopping in bed faster than a kid who found out it's a snow day. Our therapist thinks we're nuts, but hey, if it helps us *bond* or whatever, so be it. I'd much rather have a boyfriend who calls me a slut because he loves me and not because I'm breaking up with him.

What? I don't care how twisted that sounds! I'm happy! Fuck off!

I'm happy...

Who knew that this would be my life earlier this year? Drew Benton wasn't on my radar. Yet there he was, sweeping into my lounge and seducing me like it was his job. (Turns out, it was.) If I had known we would go on the whirlwind of sex and emotions we've experienced this year, I may have turned around and invested in time traveling machinations. Go back to high school, when things were much simpler and I thought it possible to be happy the old-fashioned way. Whatever that meant.

Embracing who I really am and not taking any shit from those who would deride me for it has made me such a happier, stronger person. I don't how many times I've looked at myself in the mirror and thought, *Yup, that's confidence.* Or how many times Drew's reflection approached me in the mirror and said, "*Yup, that's my sexy woman.*"

One step at a time.

Do I still have doubts? Absolutely. Do I wish I was a little different, or that *he* was a little different? I suppose that's natural. But I'm a realist. I work with what I've got, and to do that, you have to admit what you have.

We've got two toxic fuckwads who may be in love with each other. Hm. Sounds kinda messed up when I put it that way.

"You know," Drew says, with that tone that declares he's got a hard-on happening in his pants, "we have a little time before the gala tonight. I'm thinking we'll be really tired when we got home later, so maybe we should..."

"At this rate," I interrupt him, staring at my lunch of grease and sodium. It's the perfect PMS concoction. One I will soon regret when I'm too bloated to fit into my new dress tonight. "I'll be spending all our time before we leave getting into my dress. I might have to hit the gym as soon as we get home."

"Whaaat?" He looks me up and down like he's never seen my body before. "There's no way you've gained a size since Tuesday."

"You say that, but I don't think you understand the wrath of hormones."

Intoxicated

"Tell you what." Although his hand doesn't touch me, his foot moves beneath this table. "How about I help you get into that hot dress you bought? Let's say... every time you struggle a little, you struggle a... uh..." He cocks his head and ruefully grins at me. "A different way."

I look right into his perverted eyes as I eat my French fries. Ah, there it is. Images of me halfway into my dress and with a dick in my ass. I'm sure I'm grabbing the edge of the bed, the back of the couch, the kitchen counter... uh huh. Poor Cher. With her contorted O-face and little cries of pleasurable defiance as her big, bad boyfriend rams her for not fitting into her dress. Life is so hard.

There are other hard things around here, too. That's what's setting this off.

I take my time eating my food. Drew goes back to his phone like we haven't said anything at all. We still need to go over work stuff, but I'm sure that will happen on the ride to the gala tonight.

First, we have to get home.

We hold hands while I punish myself with what I just ate. Already I feel my waistline expanding and my face bloating. Hell, I tell you. That dress will be my personal *hell*.

"You know what everyone is going to be thinking when they see you in that dress tonight, right?" Drew whispers in my ear as we pass a nice old lady out walking her dog.

"That I've really let myself go?"

He chuckles. "That I must only see you for your body and nothing else. You're probably sucking me dry, and I'm too stupid to realize it."

"Are you? Too stupid to realize it, that is."

"Oh, I'm well aware." I'm pulled to his side, his arm stiff around me. Slowly, my arm encircles him as well. "Like you're aware I'm only with you for your hot body."

"I want your money. You want my pussy. Sounds about right."

"Natural order of things, right?" He nips my ear. "By the way, I've got a *really* big dick."

I don't know why, but that makes me throw my head back and cackle. That poor old lady nearly has a heart attack. Her little dog barks at me. Neither Drew nor I care as we walk toward his apartment and imagine all the ways we're going to pass the time until we have to get ready for the gala tonight.

Turns out, I really can't fit into my fucking dress. Drew helps me feel better about it, though. Every time I get down on myself, I *really* get down. Right down on my knees.

Always keep my guessing, Drew. That's how you keep a trashy mess of a woman like me around and making your life excellent hell.

Tell him I said that. You know, when you're on your way outta here, and outta our lives.

Cynthia Dane spends most of her time writing in the great Pacific Northwest. And when she's not writing, she's dreaming up her next big plot and meeting all sorts of new characters in her head.

She loves stories that are sexy, fun, and cut right to the chase. You can always count on explosive romances - both in and out of the bedroom - when you read a Cynthia Dane story.

Falling in love. Making love. Love in all shades and shapes and sizes. Cynthia loves it all!

Connect with Cynthia on any of the following:

Website: http://www.cynthiadane.com
Twitter: http://twitter.com/cynthia_dane
Facebook: http://facebook.com/authorcynthiadane

Printed in Great Britain
by Amazon